POISON & LIGHT

GILLIAN POLACK

Poison and Light

Gillian Polack

SHOOTING STAR PRESS

First published in Australia in 2020

by Shooting Star Press

PO Box 6813, Charnwood ACT 2615

info@shootingstar.pub

www.shootingstar.pub

ABN 63 158 506 524

A catalogue record for this book is available from the National Library of Australia.

POLACK, Gillian.

Poison & Light

ISBN: 978-1-925821-47-5 PB

ISBN: 978-1-925821-48-2 ebook

Cover Model by Lewis P Morley

This novel is being released during the strange bushfire season of 2019-2020. So many of us are affected by it. Poison and Light was written after another, lesser bushfire season when my stepfather died and his hospital bed was then used by a burn victim. Grania's slow return to the shared world was my way of handling that summer. This means that this novel is for you. All of you. Friends, to-be friends, people who I will never meet: everyone who has shared this hellish season with me.

1
———

FRED SETS OUT

"New Ceres is our past and it is our future. We do not join wars. We do not take sides. We have created a civilisation of courtesy and beauty through exploring the glorious history of Mother Earth. New Ceres doesn't just talk about enlightenment: it is the Enlightenment."

This is what the tourist brochures say. What do they mean by it? I'm going to help you understand.

New Ceres is the most exciting planet you'll ever visit. One of the most human planets in the Galaxy and one of the most secretive. Important events happen at dinner parties and in coffee houses. Daggers and poisons and plots are everyday politics.

New Ceres claims that it's neutral. It didn't join the war that destroyed Earth. It's officially Not Guilty, and it's proud of this. It's also where the last person to flee Lost Earth took refuge.

I shall discover just how neutral New Ceres really was in the recent war.

I shall meet with the Last Earther.

The food is as poisonous as the people, and the clothes are as glamorous as the culture. Nothing is straightforward on New Ceres.

I've got a visa, I've got eighteenth century clothes: I plan to use them to visit the planet. I'll document my experience, one article at a time. In writing, as befits a planet that wants to live in the past and uses old printing presses to control minds and hearts. Watch for me.

Love you all, your favourite roving correspondent,
Fred Xian

2

**NEITHER WORLD ENOUGH NOR TIME,
PART ONE**

"That's Io."

Grania's eyes discovered they could see through the telescope after all and she made out the craters. She looked closely at the acned sphere, reddish and uncomfortable.

"It's so lonely," she said.

"Familiar, I would have thought," and Alphonse's hands copied his words and started acting familiar, creeping where they didn't belong. She couldn't do anything about it; her position was too parlous. Grania retaliated verbally, hoping she could make Alphonse shy away.

"Io here is nothing like old Io from Earth," she said. "This solar system is entirely strange. In fact, you could hardly see Io from Earth. Not using telescopes like this. It takes more than a name."

Alphonse's hands paused and Grania held her breath, hoping.

Then he said with a touch of impatience, "Io, the Moon, who cares." His hands gently encircled her hips and he leaned in closer. "If you look carefully, you can see fumes."

"Fumes?" Her mind was hazed by them, even without seeing.

"I spent an hour adjusting my telescope. It's precisely targeted. The image is perfect. You'll see faint plumes above several of the peaks."

She had forgotten that these old-style scopes were not automatic. Finally, something useful in this retro society.

Grania had been so grateful at first, because the eighteenth-century revival had given her a place to hide: New Ceres held itself aloof from techno worlds with their techno battles. But the world that took in so many refugees was not perfect, and Grania was just beginning to discover the nature of some of those imperfections. There was the odd sunlight that left her eyes a little glazed, and those scuttling twelve-legged spiders. The water was tinted and the untreated food was slow poison.

And then there was Alphonse.

Grania could do something temporary about Alphonse, even if the rest was beyond her control. She took a small step back onto the hem of her evening dress and stumbled onto the arch of his foot. Her arm took the scope with her.

Alphonse cursed. He reached for his instrument and let her fall.

The quiet man from dinner rescued her from an ignominious (though very useful) tumble. Everyone else was downstairs, drinking port or playing cards. Pretending they lived in the eighteenth century. Pretending that New Ceres held humankind with grace, and not grudgingly.

"It'll take me all the time I have to find Io again and set her up before the eclipse."

"I am so sorry," murmured Grania, "I lost my balance. I'm truly not used to managing long skirts yet."

"You techno types are simply not accustomed to life on a real world," Alphonse's tone cut.

"Would you like me to see her home?" asked the other man.

"You'll miss the eclipse." His voice was an annoyed mutter. Alphonse flitted round his precious telescope with small irritated movements. Restoring it to its position was taking his attention. Even his focus on Grania was diminished.

"There will be other eclipses," her saviour replied, "And it seems to me that Grania stumbled because she was tired."

"It's true," Grania lied.

She hoped that the man who was taking her home was safe. She'd missed his name and hadn't even heard his voice until now. It was a pleasant tenor, not remarkable in any way.

"Go!" Alphonse dismissed them with a wave of his hand.

NEITHER WORLD ENOUGH NOR TIME,
PART TWO

As the two walked out the door, the servants brought their things.

"Thank you," said Grania as her cloak was placed about her shoulders.

"You really haven't been here long," came an amused voice from above her head. The man was tall. "And you're not from an Alliance planet. You still thank servants."

"I'm from Earth," Grania replied, as calmly as she could. "Which was an Alliance planet, in its own way."

"Earth? When you mentioned Earth tonight I thought you meant you had just visited Mother Earth, like the rest of us."

"No, it was home." She felt weary to the bone.

"I am sorry." His voice was surprisingly soothing as he handed her into the carriage.

"I missed your name." Grania owed him that much, at least. It was a rare person who didn't feel the need to expound on the loss of the mother world and how it surely affected all of them. All humans together was the mantra, wasn't it? All humans on Earth dead or in compounds monitored by the aliens and their friends. The thought of it made her mouth taste vile.

That mantra: Grania and her friends and her family crowded into holding areas; vids of the aliens and their allies; vids of millions and millions of deaths. Intercasts connecting them with safer worlds. All humans together. Grania had seen the glory of the coming from the Stars.

Here on New Ceres, everyone was human. But where they thought 'Mother Earth', she thought of frangipanis scenting the night air as she walked up Glebe Point Road to Rozelle Bay. She dreamed of family and friends, and sand in everything at summer picnics. She thought of her first exhibition in Paris, and how she had not understood a thing anyone had said about her holos.

"Dal," he replied. His name was Dal. She was having trouble thinking straight. Her mind had not been itself recently.

He didn't let the silence grow, but chattered gently about inconsequentialities. Deftly he led into personal questions. Grania's mind slipped back into her body and she tried to answer him. A tiny part of her wondered why she was talking to this stranger. This tiny part looked up at his face and was trapped into a smile. Dal kept talking, as if he was scared he might break a spell.

Grania finally processed his questions. "An artist," she said. "I'm an artist."

"It's funny the number of your fellows Alphonse admits to his circle. He's tone deaf and artistically deficient, which makes the whole thing a bit surprising."

"He likes other worlds," Grania said, lamely.

"And he likes to feel big," Dal commented.

Grania was silent at that, remembering the pressure of Alphonse behind her at the telescope. She wondered how she could avoid the inevitable next step. The one Alphonse had been inexorably seeking since the moment they met. Three days and then her rent money was due. At that point she would have to spend the last of her cash on a roof over her head. Or go where Alphonse told her. Do what he demanded.

Alphonse was her sponsor. He was supposed to provide for her until she could earn a living. Patronage and sponsorship were New Ceres' very enlightened answer to social security. Damn Diderot for inspiring the settlers into developing this particular variety of retro society. Where her life depended on how big she made a patron feel.

Alphonse wanted to feel big in far too many ways.

Being a refugee never stopped. There was no safety, only a cessation of immediate danger.

"I know some people you should meet," Dal said suddenly, breaking the silence. "Do you have an hour?"

"Yes, I can spare an hour." 'People' sounded safe, anyhow. Safer than being alone.

The coffee house they went to was perfectly secure. Bristling with bustle and warmth. She settled down to the drink Dal bought her and chatted amiably with Dal's friends. They were charming.

Grania had a moment of gratification. Her name was repeated, accompanied by the smug smile one sees when cognoscenti pronounce Names. She was still a Name. Grania, Famous Artist. Work on show everywhere. Then the truth of the situation returned. Grania, Refugee. On show to lechers.

"I can't practise on New Ceres," she admitted. "I don't know oil or water colour. I can't even use charcoal properly. I was a techno-artist, which means I'm no artist at all in this society."

"Hah!" said a slender woman, as if the restrictions on technology had no influence on anyone's life. "You're still a great artist. And you have that perfect memory for faces. All you need is a bit of training in technique."

"My memory for faces is a parlour trick. I need money for training." Grania was beyond being polite about her position. It was not fair to these nice people, but somewhere, in the course of the evening, she had ceased to care about being fair.

The slender woman - Vlasha - was obviously not a font of tact. "Dal has money," she announced, with a wave of her hand, "And he is a refugee too. Most of us are, if it comes to that. But Dal has money."

There was a momentary pause. Everyone looked at Dal: he looked back, eyes opaque, daring them to betray his secrets. Obviously Vlasha had something against Dal, because she broke the silence.

"Politics, my dear, and power. He has more money than any three of those disgraceful excuses for sponsors put together. All they want is sex."

Grania hoped her face was not as bright red as she feared. The crimson reflected the delicate tightrope she walked. While she walked that rope, she was preyed upon by Alphonse and his ilk. If she fell, she would plummet into New Ceres' devastated underclass. Landing on Alphonse's foot had merely let her remain balanced on that rope a little longer.

A young man across the table proved that tact was in very short supply in Dal's circle. About as short as proper names.

"You know," he said, reflectively, looking over at Grania's warm face, "You have exactly the right background. You could be Dal's mistress and run that salon he wants."

Dal was exquisite in his annoyance. "You value your reputation," he said. "What makes you think that Grania doesn't value hers?"

"But you are attracted to her," was the surprised reply. "If you hadn't been, you would never have brought her here. You don't bring outsiders here."

Grania's curiosity was piqued.

"If you will excuse us just for a moment," Dal said. To Grania's surprise the whole group stood up and left the table. What kind of refugee was Dal? Not her kind, that was for certain.

Grania was given time to think about the way everyone had instantly obeyed him. He gave her that time. He appeared in no hurry, in fact, and he looked at her with a kind of restful contemplation in his gaze.

She looked back at him, amused. She realised that this whole situation should have been immensely uncomfortable, but it wasn't. It was like the moment when she left the dinner party. There was a connection between them.

He kept on looking, his eyes full of questions.

There was a long wait before he said, "I have a dream about running a salon. But my compatriots were wrong; I don't need a mistress, I need a wife."

He lifted her hand from the table and turned it over, then gently kissed her palm. Grania held her breath. When she let it out, clarity crumbled the beauty of the moment. This was not an eighteenth century novel: it was real life.

She forced herself to answer with an uncomfortable truth.

"I'm really, really middle class," she said. "From Sydney. To me, marriages of convenience are something you read about in novels or history books. Maybe I'll get used to the idea one day, because I know they're normal for New Ceres, but right now the whole idea is alien and it scares the hell out of me."

Dal did not let go of her hand. Even when she gently tried to extract it from his grasp, he held on. As he spoke, he started to stroke lightly with his thumb.

"It's easier for me," he said, "Where I come from they are

normal. But I wasn't thinking along those lines. I watched you tonight and I don't believe that it would be entirely a marriage of convenience." The words and the movement of his thumb sent a frisson down her spine.

Still, it was just another trap. It had to be. Escape was the only real hope in her life, and she could see no escape. Sleep with Alphonse. Marry Dal. She didn't want to contemplate the third alternative. She had faced death too often in her last six months at home, before she had joined the select few who had crept away, ashamed at being given passes and transport and their lives. She forced her thoughts away from that period of her life. She would expunge the memory; the pain would cease to exist.

Contemplating her near future, Grania remained honest. Almost brutally honest. She wasn't going to deceive someone like Dal, no matter how tempting his proposal and how simple an answer it would be for everything.

"I'm not sure I can live with that," she said.

Dal asked, "But are you sure you can live without that? I can give you security. I can provide the money for you to retrain. I can give you a haven."

"You would let me practise as an artist?"

"Naturally."

This surprised Grania. She had not thought that a marriage of convenience would allow her that level of independence. She examined his face very closely: he seemed sincere.

While Grania was probing for truth, Dal finished his plea. "All I ask," he said, "is that you give the marriage a try. And that you run my salon."

"Why is the salon so important?" She had to ask. It just didn't make any sense to her.

"We're all refugees," he said. "I'm accepted at the borders

of society because I'm rich and because once I was important. You're accepted at Alphonse's table because he wants to go to bed with you and because even New Ceres has heard about your art."

Grania turned red again; she had hoped Alphonse's interest had not been so transparent. Dal's hand continued to soothe hers, and she continued to listen.

"We're the exceptions, you and I. Everyone else lives from day to day. They support each other financially and lead a life, but it's not a rich life. This coffee house holds all of our higher intellectual selves, and it's not enough."

Dal looked at her so intently that Grania wondered if the force of his gaze would be sufficient to convince her. The longer she sat next to him, the more aware she was. She forced herself to process his comments.

"Even for artists, it is not enough, to be frank." She saw that. God, how she was beginning to see that. "New Ceres saved so many creative souls, and it won't accept the pasts they bring; it wants you all to conform. I want a salon because a salon is acceptable on New Ceres. It suits their New Enlightenment. It means that we don't lose all our culture and all our civilisation."

"Can't you find someone else?" She knew this thought was wistful. Stupid, too. Even considering possibilities made her vulnerable.

His answer took a long, long time to come. It left her alone with her desolation. Alone ... except for her hand in his.

"I'm not sure I want someone else. Besides, I observed you tonight. You can do it. You can still sparkle when you have to."

Grania knew exactly what he was talking about. The sparkle was pretence, but it was there. She didn't want to be a saviour, though. She didn't want to open herself to sharing. Grania couldn't find words to explain.

"I don't know," was all she could say.

He laughed. "I'll take you home now and come for you at noon tomorrow."

They walked straight out the door. No farewells.

It was odd.

What was it about Dal that made her agree to odd things and go along with them? Grania wondered at her trust of this stranger. She wondered at herself. She wondered at her hand in Dal's.

After a moment, she realised that the reason was simple: exhaustion. She had fought and fled and survived, and now she was too tired to do anything. Alphonse's foot had been her last attempt at succour.

Grania wondered at the sort of life Dal had left. In her world one just did not dismiss people as if they were lesser beings. She said so.

He looked across the carriage at her. "I promise that you will always be my equal," he said, and his voice was amused. Amused? As if he had never thought she was dismissible in the same way as his friends.

And that was that. No kiss. No farewell. Only a gentle hand down the carriage step. The carriage waited in the darkness until she had opened her door, then it clattered off down the street. Grania listened to it go, desolated.

Grania admitted to herself that she was intrigued by the mystery that was Dal. She didn't believe he would come for her at noon, but the next day she carted water in from the street pump and washed herself very thoroughly and found her cleanest day dress just in case. She hated a society where the poor lacked running water. If she were rich there would be running water and servants and a semblance of civilisation. If she were rich.

She sighed as she sponged herself down. If she had what

mattered, the last two years would be cast into oblivion and she would be catching the ferry to Manly.

Grania placed the bucket near the empty fireplace, as if the memory of flames could warm it. She missed white tiles and hot running water and dreaming of them didn't make a sponge bath in the living room any more tolerable. She had recalled Earth again, however, and had to live with the memory while she washed.

She took care bathing, trying to avoid noticing the green tinge to the water. It was safe, she knew, and pure enough to drink, but it looked like poison. It left her skin clean and her second set of underclothes cleaner. She was secretly proud of still wearing the lighter undergarments of her home rather than the corsets and hard-to-wash linen of this society.

She immediately regretted her pride when a breeze curled itself around her half-naked body. Grania looked around to see where the breeze had come from. She found Alphonse at the open door, leaning and leering.

"Why didn't you knock?" she asked, to distract him as she pulled on her garments.

"I do not need an invitation," he replied. "I have found three sets of possible rooms for you."

"Rooms?" she asked.

"You think that this is a suitable environment for one of my mistresses?" His gesture took in her living room.

"I am not one of your mistresses." Grania's voice was sand and her throat a desert.

"You can be my mistress or you can be my whore. The choice is yours."

Sleep with him and host dinner parties, or sleep with him and be hidden. Either way, she would be safe only as long as his interest held.

When Grania had stepped off the cargo ship onto New

Ceres, she had been impressed with the urbanity of Alphonse. He had reassured her with his museum-clothing and his courtly bow. Now, she was stymied. Mistress or whore - not a happy choice. Her future was narrowing to a poisoned life or a poisoned body. It said so much that Alphonse was not waiting until the rent was due.

He pretended to have lost interest in the conversation and wandered around her room, insolently fingering her possessions. It was when he handled her underwear as if her private self was his personal shop that she rebelled.

"No! Put that down!" She tried to tug her underpants from him. As she pulled and he held fast, the door opened.

"I heard a scream," Dal said. Grania let go the clothing at once, not knowing where to look. Alphonse chuckled and started to paw again.

"What do you think of a townhouse near the park for Grania?"

Dal answered, "I believe that is up to Grania."

"No," said Grania, "I mean, yes. I mean, I don't want Alphonse's townhouse." The words raced out before she could check them. Her heart speaking.

It was done. The only thing left for her was to find a job as a servant and die slowly from untreated food: she would have come to that anyway, when Alphonse tired of her. Or beg on the streets and die faster from more untreated food. This was justification, though. Her denial of Alphonse had not been reasoned.

Dal looked around at Grania's room, his face noncommittal. He looked at Alphonse, holding Grania's underpants. He looked down at Grania, her buttons half undone and her clothing in disarray.

Dal stooped. He picked up the bucket of sudsy water.

Before Alphonse could say anything else, he was silenced by a slush of liquid.

"I believe you might want to go home and change," suggested Dal. There was no anger in his voice. There was no emotion of any sort.

Alphonse left, abruptly, saying as he went out the door, "Tomorrow, Grania, my men will move you. You have forfeited the townhouse."

Grania held herself perfectly still. Any reaction would give Alphonse credence and he deserved none.

"My man is just outside." Dal turned to Grania and bent until he could look her full in the eyes. "We can pack things up at once," he said. "I didn't realise that you had so many possessions."

"The books are mine," Grania admitted, "And the clothes, and most of the ornaments. Nothing else."

"Nothing else?" A raised eyebrow.

"Everything else I had was high tech. I had to leave it behind."

"Alphonse told you?"

"No, Alphonse met me here. He met all the people on the carrier ship and chose to take me under his wing. It was someone else before then."

"And you slept with them all." He was amused again. Did he think he had saved her from an accustomed whoredom?

"I didn't sleep with any of them. There was an empty ship coming here to load up on that silk stuff and I knew the captain." Grania hesitated a moment and then she blurted, "From the Resistance. I knew the captain from the Resistance. He gave me a lot of space, a lot of food and water, and left me alone in the dark for a long, long time. And I was the lucky one."

"You were at that," he said. She suddenly realised that he

might have money, but that this did not mean he was unscarred. She didn't know how he had got here, but if he comprehended that a forever of darkness in a cargo hold was nothing compared with what had gone before, then maybe he needed understanding also.

"Things were bad before you left?" His voice was studiously neutral.

"Yes." She was abrupt. "It was near the end. I was the last to reach safety." She rubbed her damp hands nervously up and down the day dress.

He nodded and opened the door to his man. The man dragged a big trunk into the centre of the room and filled it quickly, gently and efficiently.

She caught him looking her up and down. She blushed. She would not get used to life on New Ceres, not in a million years.

But she had mistaken the look.

"No scars," he commented.

"She's from Earth," Dal said.

No need to add the rider. Everyone knew the fate of Earth. Humans herded like cattle. No physical disfigurement because that would show on intercasts. The anti-Earth movement proving to the Inner Alliance that helping Earth was impossible and that they should save themselves. The anti-Earth movement proving to the Outer Alliance that Earth was degraded, so that the Outer Alliance and its alien allies would agree that complete cleansing was the only possible solution.

Then Earth became Hell. Then the last bitter fights, and the last sour protests. Grania had seized her chance and fled. And that was all.

Gone, everything gone. A toy broken in the squabble between the two Alliances. Earth and all the goodness thereof. Gone.

She had it wrong again. The death of Earth was her own obsession and was not what the man was thinking. His scarred face smiled across an armful of books.

"No rejuv then, unlike His Lordship here."

Inner Alliance. He was from the Inner Alliance. Someone important. No Lordships anywhere else. Inner Alliance leaders had secrets and did not have to be kept pretty for the intercasts. Oh God, he had been tortured. That was why the rejuv. Torture. She didn't know where to look, which way to turn.

"Excuse me," Dal said, and took her by the elbow to the kitchen.

"We all have scars," he told her in that empty room. "Some of them are more visible than others. We all have scars." He held her gently until she stopped crying. She was crying for everyone. For herself, for her family, for Earth, for Dal.

They went back into the main room, clutching each other's hands.

"Maybe we could wrap the glass ornaments up in my clothes," Grania suggested. Still not sure about marriage. Wondering why she was accepting this. Too tired. Grania sagged again.

Dal went back to the kitchen and Grania followed. He flung open cupboard doors with uncheerful abandon.

"I ate last night at Alphonse's," she said, defensively. "And being slender is very fashionable."

Dal looked across at her and laughed. "Where's the nearest pastry cook? Don't worry. I'll find it." And in a twinkle he was out the door.

The moment he was out the door, Dal's man started talking, and talking, and talking. It was as if he had known Grania forever. About the street, about the refitting Dal's carriage needed, about how close Grania lived to the city centre. Was it the hand-holding, she wondered? Or was there something about her that made men from that planet act strangely? She didn't even know what planet it was, just that it was Inner Alliance.

Her eyes misted again. She forced herself to focus on the chatter, so that she wouldn't think about evil things. Within a very short time she knew about son age eight and daughter age seven and all their activities.

"Quite the gardener she is. Has to be kept away from the raspberries. Doesn't want to wait for them to be treated. Wants to eat them all straightaway."

Grania knew about his wife and her ambitions. "Music. Plays like an angel. A bad-tempered angel."

Dal's man (who was still nameless) was working through the favourite people in his life in a very orderly fashion. Lured into normal conversation, Grania finally asked "Can you tell me about Dal?"

"You know, he gets like this from time to time," Grania heard. "It's always about big things. A special sense. The first time it happened he was ten. He was up all night. We could hear his footsteps from the servant's quarters. The next day we heard his father was dead. Dal has always said that if he had acted it would have been avoidable. He might be right, at that, because it was not an accident. At ten though, I don't know what he could have done, really."

"Does this kind of thing happen often?" Grania felt she was encouraging what should not be encouraged, but she had to know.

"Not too often. But every time it's something critical. Last time he didn't sleep for three days. He used every minute to push and push and push. He saved all his people and most of his money in those three days. Only two of us were tortured, despite everything."

There was a little smug smile on the man's face, and Grania realised that the smugness was earned - so many people had lost so much in the glory days of the war. "I kept some scars to remind us. He said he didn't need the scars to know. But I'm proud of having been a decoy."

Two people. Dal and his man. The confidences clicked into jigsaw sense.

Grania was given a full tour of the scars. She found them reassuring. He was marked externally the way she had been marked internally. And she found herself wondering how Dal had understood this so very quickly. She shouldn't dwell on it. It hurt.

"How do you know it was this special sense of his with me?" she asked.

"He came home and told me 'I've found her' and he walked the whole night round the house. He moved things to make space and to make it look more like Earth. Except the household didn't know it was Earth, they just knew there was someone coming. I knew it was Earth. I visited Earth three times when I was younger. It's a big loss."

"I don't know if we'll suit," Grania said.

"He's never wrong," said the servant, just as Dal came in the door laden with pastries and coffee.

"What am I never wrong about?"

"Is it true you were up all night?" Grania asked.

"I nearly came out here straight away," he admitted. "But you needed time."

"What you have given me is not time. We haven't even known each other for a full day."

Silence.

More silence.

Dal looked at her. For the first time, she saw him scared. She found she could not live with that fear.

She looked up at him.

"I'm only marrying you so I can paint," she heard her voice scolding. She wasn't sure where it was coming from, as her brain was still preparing itself for a descent into the underclasses. "If you want an old-fashioned romantic marriage you are going to have to woo me."

"I am very happy to woo you," he said, "just as long as we are married today. I don't want to have to throw more water over Alphonse. Green is not his colour."

He smiled for the first time, his face alight with mischief, and Grania realised she might be falling in love.

4

———

LIVIA'S LOVE

L ivia had once taken an off-world lover. Long, long ago, when she was learning how to arrange her life suitably. "Recondite and bizarre antiquated social customs," her lover had commented, "That's New Ceres. Everything here is a veil covering nonsense." The comment had come the day before he shamed her in public. The day before she decided that ambition was more interesting than pretty lovers.

She made a moue at the mirror. Her pale face with its white-gold hair was haloed by white light, ready for the inevitable pre-dinner powder. That lover had called her an angel, once.

This was not a moment when she could lose herself in the past. The present was enough of a burden. Her husband was more than anyone should bear.

As if responding to a cue, Frederick dipped his head around the door.

"Dinner bell in five minutes, my dear," he said, chipper as an English country gentleman. Livia tilted her head graciously in his direction then stilled for the maid to powder her. Frederick disappeared.

Livia's lips thinned as she contemplated the options her various problems presented her. In her mind she rearranged seating. She would put Grania next to Josephine's husband. He was looking for a mistress and Josephine was not tolerant of rivals. With any luck the Earthwoman's body would be found in a ditch. That would delay the problem of losing the power she obtained from hosting Alphonse's dinner table. Alphonse would start seeking an official mistress all over again. He would waste vast hours at the spaceport, hunting refugees. Livia smiled at her image, sweetness radiating to the room.

The maid twisted her hair too hard. Livia's hand reached out in a slap. The maid cringed.

"Time?" Livia snapped.

"Almost four, Madame."

"Hurry up, then. I want to be downstairs before the guests arrive."

"Yes, Madame. We're ready."

And she whisked the coverings off, leaving Livia resplendent. The gold was replaced by pure white elegance.

Livia found Frederick at the head of the stairs, waiting. She took his arm.

She tried to maintain flowing and graceful movements, but Frederick was impatient to mingle. Livia's mouth tightened further as her famous floating walk disintegrated into quick bobbing steps. She found herself halfway down the stairs far too soon, her sun-pendant flapping gently against her skin. Despite the annoyance, her mind tripped cogs and wheels and set possibilities in motion.

By the time she reached the base of Alphonse's grand

staircase, the dinner table had been reshaped three times. Now it would be perfect.

She signalled to the major-domo and advised him of the final seating plan and of certain other amendments to the night's plans. Polite-faced, he bowed and said that the rearrangements would be made. Livia gave him a sheaf of paper and sent him away with a flick of her hand. A slight awkwardness in his steps betrayed the level of inconvenience the changes denoted.

Frederick said, "What was that paper for?"

"From Alphonse, dear. For the entertainment."

At that moment they reached Alphonse and Frederick was silenced.

Livia allowed a small smile as she stood with her big cousin to greet guests. Alphonse didn't even look at her. Livia was forced to create the body language that made them look like close friends, and she resented the work. She disliked having to insinuate her hand through the crook of his arm, when he ought to have requisitioned that hand with a charmingly apologetic smile. It particularly annoyed her that he peered arrogantly over her head and that she had to fake confiding looks towards him.

Alphonse, Livia thought, is a fool.

Consanguinity had excused her from marrying him and it also allowed her to hostess for him. "Practical politics should be kept away from the home," her mother had advised. Livia lost her company smile for a split second: she did not miss her mother. This small lapse was the only time her control slipped.

Alphonse thought he was finished with the need for a hostess from the family. He kept his politics too, too close. He was a fool.

Frederick - as always - demonstrated no control of any

sort. He looked red and blustering and old-fashioned and he was just that. Even his waistcoat was old-fashioned and over-embroidered. From the bonhomie he emanated to the way the serving maid skirted his roving hand, he played his role perfectly. Not a hint that he might have passed political secrets off planet. Ever the ideal eighteenth century gentleman. Living all the lies.

Livia stopped watching Frederick as the company sat down to eat. Instead, she observed the party as it sat at table. She memorised behaviour and gossip and, as ever, she used taste and texture as an aide-memoire.

Paté was a useful reference for Dal, new, rich, smooth, unsafe. She would have him one day. Until then, he was dangerous. Too wealthy. Too far beyond the wheels of power. Too aristocratic. Too unknown. Handsome, brown as a nut, and as hard to crack. For now, worth watching. For now.

Mushroom pie and eggplant cooked Alliance style represented tall, slender Josephine precisely.

Livia's information on Josephine was very, very good. Josephine was doing rather well considering she married Old but was herself New. Her family had only arrived three generations ago, and yet she was almost accepted. She wore her wide skirts and tight corset as if she were born to them. Such a good politician, and so in need of Old Ceres friendships. A woman who needed Livia and a woman who used similar methods to Livia. The flaky pastry pleased Livia's palate. The mixed textures and the common ingredients said everything that needed saying.

Less pleasing were the dull roast meats. Dull roast meats for a dull husband. She took only chicken and pheasant.

"What a delightful meal," her millstone commented in her direction. "Chicken and pheasant are my favourite dishes."

Then he continued his bright conversation as before, describing the latest duel to half the table.

What a mistake it had been to marry him. He knew this. Everything she ate, he ate. Dull, but not a fool. He obviously remembered the untreated food her previous husband had sadly ingested. Damn the man's memory.

She knew that Frederick was determined to both beat the alarm clock and to trap her and put her on trial. That very morning she'd found some of his correspondence on the matter and disposed of it. As Frederick enthused about a hunting expedition with Dal, she smiled her sweetest smile in his direction. Her husband dropped his wineglass. A small flurry of serving staff caused it to be replaced, and Livia smiled sweetly again. Frederick's eyes caught hers and narrowed.

She cleansed her palate with the entremets. A trifling dish of truffle. She would cleanse her palate of Frederick as simply. He was too watchful. Trifling, true, but also excruciatingly annoying.

The final remove was flavoured by several people. There was fluttery Constance who had so unwisely entered into an affair with Frederick. The smooth sweet confit sliding down her throat would keep Constance's flutter in mind, should it ever be needed. Sweet, frivolous and easily ignored.

Dal was ignoring Constance, which was an interesting development. Livia had carefully placed them together so that he would be yearning for an intelligent conversation by the end of the evening. Instead, he politely (albeit minimally) addressed Constance during every second course and focussed all his attention on that Earther artist.

It was as spicy as the cinnamon in the peach pie, because Constance was husband-hunting and Dal was appropriate. Dal had been all over her the last time Livia had seen the two together. He had obviously found a more interesting object for his attention.

Livia dismissed her half-assembled plan to bring Dal further into her life. His inconstancy was a problem (and she allowed herself a small smile at her pun, a smile that made three of Alphonse's guests pay more attention) but it wasn't the main issue. No-one from his background could afford to do what he was doing tonight: acting distant with two perfectly eligible females (though Constance was a fribble, she was an eligible fribble) to focus on someone who was destined for the demi-monde.

Dal's biggest flaw, Livia thought, her tongue flick-flicking at the frozen dessert, was that he didn't realise how very easy it was to read his body language. Every head movement, every gesture signalled an increasing obsession with the Earth-woman. Who was attractive, but a dead end - and so stupid. Grania was unaware of her own body and of the small signals that men and women give each other. She didn't see that her whole dinner was flavoured by Dal's awareness of her. Very amusing.

What was even more amusing was that while Grania's body was reacting to Dal, her eyes were trying to avoid any sort of contact with Alphonse. Delicious. The longer it was before Alphonse took an official mistress, the more time Livia had at the head of his table, keeping her politics away from the home. She patted down a ripple in her grass-green skirt.

Cowardly Alphonse, seeking mistresses from the scum of the spaceport.

Shame about Grania: on another planet she might have been someone.

Shame about Dal too. Foreign titles, of course, but rich. Livia heard her inner voice and winced at her own wittering.

This course was taking far too long, and her mind was repeating itself.

Frederick said, "And we shot him - the brute - right between the eyes." Livia noted that his hand was now fumbling under the table. As was Alphonse's.

Best to move things along. She signalled for plates to be taken up, causing Alphonse to grumble at her. He liked his food and his flirtations equally.

It was only a token grumble because when the company rose Alphonse excused himself to align his telescope. Livia wondered what he was up to, but dismissed the thought. He would be rejoining the party soon, so there was really only one thing besides the telescope that he could be concerned with.

His interest in Grania wouldn't affect her own politics, so when Alphonse left the men to their alcohol and cigars and ribaldry, Livia led the ladies to their chocolate and tea. She told one of the lads serving to make sure that Josephine was served black coffee with a shot of liquor. She nodded her head to Josephine when her new friend looked up in pleased surprise.

Livia tallied the ladies and moved to arrange them to her satisfaction. Josephine, for instance, did not need to spend even a moment with Constance, but Benjamin was a new physician who needed a patron and who had skills that Josephine would appreciate. He had left the table when the women did: she could take advantage of his social ineptitude.

Once everyone had drinks and wafers and was quietly chatting, Livia noticed Grania was missing. It was not unexpected. It was, however, for the good. If she remained absent for the rest of the evening, it would be easier to manage the important elements.

The eclipse was not an important element. To be sure, it

was the reason they were all assembled, but it was - in Livia's mind - simply an excuse. She spent the time circulating among the women and later the men and the women, arranging and rearranging their groups in social patterns that served her needs. 'Practical politics,' her mother said. 'Every act done for you by someone who thinks they're running their own lives is risk halved.' Practical politics made almost anything achievable, when combined astutely with politics of the impractical variety.

Every now and again Livia slipped in a word to enliven a dull discourse. The war was an excellent topic for this, for her own husband could carry any conversation pertaining to the military. Frederick was a conversationalist second to none. So the hour before the eclipse echoed with talk of battles won and lost and with the heroic last stand at the salt lakes.

Frederick's valour had carried the day at Dead Water and he let others carry the conversation when talking about the victory. He sat correctly quiet, accepting the tributes. He radiated humility. It made Livia want to hiss like a serpent. It made her want to spit. Instead she quietly explained how modest he was. Practical politics.

Frederick looked up and charmingly smiled and even more charmingly caught the eyes of each and every person present, in turn. "It doesn't do to boast," he said. "But I am proud to serve New Ceres."

Finally the eclipse came. Alphonse had insisted on organising this part of the night's entertainment himself. It was dreadful. Only one telescope and far too many people. Hoi polloi come for the floorshow. Alphonse's male friends and their low-class amours. Inside, Livia writhed and spat poison. She hated uncontrollable crowds. Outside, she disciplined her features.

Someone tripped on her skirt.

"Sorry," the woman said, her eyes unreadable in the night. "I'm Lizzie," she said boldly. Lizzie the Floozy, if the cut of her dress were any indication. Deep bosom, no corset and the skirt just a trifle short. The very thought made Livia uncomfortable. Livia gathered her dress more closely and turned her head away.

Eventually it was over.

Livia's moment. She had asked Alphonse to make the announcements "Since it is your house and your hospitality". Not even her husband knew that it was she who had designed the entertainment and provided certain key elements of it. Frederick might guess. She'd given enough indications to make guessing possible.

"If you'll follow Livia downstairs," Alphonse proclaimed in his gravelly voice, "There will be a small entertainment followed by a light repast." The assembled throng - including its more dubious components - flocked after her, like obedient goslings.

The group poured down and down and down the stairs. Livia didn't stop at the entrance foyer, but led her charges, shockingly, through the service section of the house. The staff was fully assembled to welcome the visitors into its quarters.

Livia knew that at this moment each and every staff member hated her. She was the one who led the invasion into their domain, no matter that Alphonse was ultimately responsible.

But what could they do? Nothing. More than anyone else present, house staff understood how powerless they were. A servant's word was worth less in court than an off-worlder's, and it was heard less by the people who mattered. Livia mattered. They would realise precisely how much she mattered by the end of the night: she would always receive full attention at Alphonse's house. Practical politics of a different kind, but still practical politics.

Livia allowed herself a tiny smile as she led the crowd out of the major-domo's private quarters and through a small door into Alphonse's secret garden. She might not pay for stepping over the line, but Alphonse surely would, since he was the one who had ordered the door. Every time the servants' privacy was invaded, they would feel it. Cold food and cold baths would most certainly feature in Alphonse's future. He was stupid. Livia's tongue flicked in and out like a snake's as she sampled the night air. Air was an appropriate taste for Alphonse's intelligence.

The garden was an echoing series of green bowers. Lanterns created grottos of leaf and bark. The ring-ins were stupid enough to think that this was the special treat. How foolish. She allowed them to swell among the candles and lanterns until the twittering stopped.

"Alphonse," Livia asked, her voice carrying on the quiet air, "Would you like to lead from here?"

"It would be my great honour," and she heard smugness.

This little excursion would sort the fribble from the cognoscenti, Livia reflected. Fribble would be impressed by Alphonse's new construction. The cognoscenti would see more.

At the end of Alphonse's private pleasure garden were stairs leading down. Deep, deep into carved rock, the group descended into the darkness, clutching limestone rails for safety. Chatter silenced into hard breathing as the light diminished, step by step.

It was a clever idea, Livia had to admit as she felt the tomb-like air with her tongue. To carve right down into the caves. Most households used their caves to store wine. There was no wine in this lair, however. Only cold stone and a thin and whispering stream of air.

At the bottom of the steps even Livia found she had to stop and blink. She wished she had come earlier and seen the fake neo-Gothic tombs without this push of people. In front of one tomb was a lady in full Earth mourning. Black from soft slippers to dark veil. Perfect eighteenth century dress. Every detail was correct, just as Livia's dinner dress was correct.

Kneeling beside a tomb, the lady was silent, and did not look up. The tomb was swathed in silver-grey carved cloth and it was impossible to see beneath it. Impossible to read the inscription and impossible to see the face of the mourner. Livia nodded at Alphonse to acknowledge the clever touch. They waited beside the exit to this cave until the crowd was ready to follow.

Next came a long corridor. It was a feast of light and shade and movement. Light gauze and white cotton and sheer silk were draped in a thousand clever ways. Sometimes the party walked through a tunnel of light, and sometimes through a shadow haunted by ghostly shapes and faded figures of monks. It was shocking and impressive. Even though she knew how it was done, Livia could not help but react to the blaze of beauty that was a silk tunnel lit from behind.

As she helped lead the way into the penultimate chamber she realised that Alphonse was using illegal technology to create effects. So clever, though, to make artificial light look like lanterns. Silk and gauze and cotton hiding the source of light. And not like Alphonse at all. There was something wrong and she couldn't put her finger on it.

Livia knew what the next chamber contained. Alphonse had consulted her.

It was a very large space, and was low enough for the half

dozen steps leading into it to need careful negotiation. It was wider than the long tunnel, but with low walls. They had been left natural. Black rugs covered the floor to swallow the noise and eat up stray light. From the steps Livia could see wells of luminescence in the room. Light shining off man-size mirrors and being swallowed by the black robes of the monks who held the lamps.

A murmur spread through the party as more and more of them descended the steps and saw the monks. Monks indicated many things. A Gothic entertainment. Old religion. Informers and secret police. Even the word 'monkish' denoted secretive and dangerous activity. So the buzz increased as the crowd descended into the chamber.

Guide ropes led the party in a trail through the room, passing by each mirror.

Livia smiled.

The first monk held up the lantern, the light flickering oddly back at the party.

"Is Constance among you?" he asked, sonorously.

"I'm here," and Constance walked forward.

"I have a gift for you," and the monk held out a small hand mirror.

Constance opened the mirror and admired herself in it. Then she turned it up and down and around, trying to make out the carvings. When she did, she dropped it. It landed with a thud on the carpet. Livia gently knelt down and picked it up.

"Don't look," said Constance.

"I won't," said Livia. She had been with Alphonse when he had ordered the mirror, proffering a picture of Constance to be carved into the mirror's backing. Constance curling in hellfire. Livia had not been displeased, but she had wondered at the time. There was a story between Alphonse and Constance, one that needed exploring.

"Look," Frederick said, "There is a note on the mirror."

"A warning," it said. "And a guide."

"Ugh," said Constance. "And to think some people used to believe in those things." She said this with a huff in her voice. It was she who led the group to the next giant mirror, presumably to divert their attention.

Alas, the next offering was not as dramatic. Livia smiled again. This had been one of hers. The monk handed a dainty lantern to Josephine, saying, "You give light unto this world," and the paper on the mirror was a piece of puffery that had been doing the rounds recently. It described a star on the rise and the joy it gave to all who supported the Lady Governor and this brave New Enlightenment.

"Dammit," Livia heard from behind her. "Why can't we have some hot gossip?" Just wait, she thought. There will be enough to talk about.

The following mirror was a complete waste. The monk followed his rules too closely and refused to hand over the gift to anyone but the right person. The right person was Dal, who was unaccountably absent.

"He and Grania left before the eclipse," muttered Alphonse in her ear, grumpy still. Or was that grumpy again?

"I wish you had told me earlier - we had alternate gifts in case someone was not here." This comment was not what had upset Alphonse. Livia wondered what had caused their departure and why it had upset Alphonse, and her tongue went flick-flick, tasting the crowd of people and their curiosity.

The monk refused to let anyone read Dal's paper. "Move on, move on," he said. "Nothing to be seen here." His off-world accent emerged in the way he slurred 'move on' into one word and Livia grimaced. Who would have thought that Dal's honour would be defended in this place?

The next monk was more forthcoming. Livia found herself hailed. Alphonse had assured her the week before that he wanted a graceful way of thanking her for helping him. Without her as hostess, he would not have been able to invite Josephine or any other respectable woman to his table. He knew it and she knew it, and she accepted her tribute gracefully.

"What is it?" a woman's voice called out. One of the fribble.

Livia unwrapped it carefully. She felt secure in her pool of light, the green of her dress sinuous and shining. The silence around her spread as she slowly uncovered her gift from Alphonse.

Everyone stared. Constance looked at the paper on the mirror. "Grania's last work," she read. "There will be no more."

And nor would there be. For this was techno-art and it was strictly forbidden on New Ceres. Livia would have to declare it. Now though, her eyes were trapped in it as were the eyes of everyone else. Grania was a genius with light and colour: the shimmer and movement on the small statue Livia held made even the snake-green of Livia's dress look artificial and false.

The statue was an insult. Alphonse knew it and Livia knew it. It was illegal to give and even more illegal to accept. Nothing would be the same between them. But even as her mouth tightened in recognition of this, her eyes were filled with joy at the statue's beauty.

Later, she told herself.

There was just one more mirror. Livia closed her eyes to drown out the feeling of joy from the statuette. No moment of this last mirror should be wasted.

Instead of calling out a name, the monk silently gave papers to all who were assembled. The other monks stood in a semi-circle round the group, allowing everyone light to read by. A sun-brooch glinted near the throat of the last monk. Livia caught his eye and fingered her own sun.

"Oh my God," came Constance's voice. "Frederick, tell me this is a lie."

Frederick was a slow reader. In fact, Frederick read as little as possible. How would he handle it, Livia wondered idly?

"Tell me what it says, Connie," he cajoled.

Connie? The man was disgusting.

Constance read aloud a piece of doggerel. One of the ballads so popular with the city printers right now. It was not about highwaymen or young love. It was about war.

When it came to the last stanza, Constance's voice faltered. Josephine took up the reading with glee.

"And so our hero fled the field.

We were victors, though he did yield.

Should we call our Fred a coward, pray,

Who fled the field but claimed the day?"

Frederick didn't say a word.

His copy of the verse drifted to the carpet, the paper a piece of light in darkness. He walked through to the last chamber. No-one followed him.

Once he was gone, a hum began. It continued through the last chamber and out the door. Livia found herself alone with the monks. Not finished yet, she reminded herself. But close. So close.

She walked through the final chamber. It was a replica of the first. Tombs and monuments. A lady in black. Maybe even the same lady in black. Who cared? Livia suddenly wanted to go home and see outcomes. This was the time she hated most, when a task was complete but not quite finished.

The tomb the lady-mourner kneeled at was now uncovered and her eyes flicked over it in vague curiosity. It bore the name 'Livia', written in Livia's own proud copperplate. She scarcely broke her stride, but her mind was suddenly filled with anger. How dare he? How dare Alphonse bury her in effigy?

Livia was not scared to see her own tomb. She was angry. Alphonse had not the brains for this scheme. When this night was fully over, someone would be in trouble. And they would regret having threatened her. Her tongue flick-flicked and she tasted her anger. Metallic and red-hot. It would do the job.

She ordered her carriage immediately and left Frederick to his own devices. She left the statuette at a justice's house before she reached home. "It's beautiful," she explained, "And it was a lovely thought of my friends, but it's contraband and I can't keep it."

"Very wise," said her new friend Justice Harber, his dressing gown slipping away around his rather large stomach. "It is doubly contraband in two senses, being stolen goods as well as high-tech. We've been looking for it. It will be off planet as soon as I finish the paperwork. I'll have to reprimand the friend who gave it to you, I'm afraid."

And that was Alphonse taken care of. His accomplice could wait.

Finally, she came home. Frederick's body was where she expected it to be. He had blown his brains out in the study. She thoughtfully put a copy of the poem on his desk so that everyone would know that his honour had been besmirched and that Frederick had no choice.

Her evening was finished.

The next day brought the beginning of public mourning. It also brought her a small package sealed with an image of Helios. In the package was a certificate signed by the Lady Governor permitting her to own the other item in the package: Grania's statuette.

5

A QUIET INTERLUDE AT THE COFFEE HOUSE

There was no-one suitable at this coffee house.

If it were up to Livia, she would never have entered its too dark, too crowded rooms, bustling with pedestrian people. It was, however, important to put in a public appearance with her daughter. Esther and she had to show the world their perfect relationship. Keeping her gawkish daughter from humiliation was another matter entirely.

Livia let her eyes slowly traverse the room. If there were no table where they could be seen without having to make boring chit-chat to the dull and tedious, then maybe she could find useful company: practical politics always nullified boredom.

There were very few faces she recognised and several eyes she chose to avoid. One of those she chose to avoid was an overweight Earth-origin doctor who always looked clammy and who appeared far too often in her vicinity. He was someone Alphonse knew. Livia tasted the air, laden with coffee and baking and the sweat of the coffee house patrons and contemplated her choices. Esther was always an impediment. An error of fashion.

Finally, Livia's eyes lit on Mr F, alone in a corner. 'Mr F, Printer to the Nobility' – an affectation, but a clever one, and despite his aping of fashionable foolishness by being known by an initial, his manners would suffice inside a coffee house.

As ever, he was reading. As ever, he was perfectly neutral. He supported the Lady Governor, eschewed factions, kept elegant dress and society hours and fully admitted he could not aspire. Mr F was the least impossible company in this place.

She caught his eye and his head bowed, very slightly, in acquiescence.

Just before she and Esther sat down, the plump doctor excused himself and wove through a dozen tables to join them. It was a terrible breach of manners. For an instant Livia was almost irritated, then she blinked slowly as she realised he must be actively seeking patronage.

Mr F welcomed them all with a slight bow, then sat down again to fold his paper.

Dr Benjamin had been on New Ceres long enough to accept the lengthy introductions and pleasantries. Livia noticed he shifted his white and wormlike self on his wicker chair. Long enough but had still not developed the requisite level of patience. Surely he had been less uncouth at Alphonse's dinner? She tasted the coffee house air again and used it to send herself a reminder that she needed to find out more about this doctor. Why should he be so intent on cajoling favour now, when just a few weeks ago he had dealt with her so very casually?

It amused Livia to allow Esther to explain things. Esther was entertaining to watch. There was something about her that was always the merest smidgeon away from correct: her hat was pinned askew, or her reticule drooped. When Livia watched her daughter closely, Esther knew and her manner took on a faint tone of desperation as she worked her way through everything that could possibly be awry, trying to perfect herself.

"We're just doing some shopping," Esther said, then flicked her reticule properly out of sight.

"For any particular reason?" Mr F was always polite and his face was always guarded. Almost a gentleman.

Esther blushed red. "I'm going to school."

"Aren't you a little old?" asked the doctor. Esther looked down at her gloves and then started to pull the right one off, very slowly, in order to straighten it.

"She's a slow maturer," said Livia, with a motherly nod that indicated that she was tolerant of the impossibility of her offspring and was quite aware that Esther was adjusting the wrong glove.

Esther was about to say something to her mother, and it was obvious that the something was going to break the charming image of a happy family. Esther always knew when she was being toyed with. Just as her father had.

Mr F stepped in tactfully and asked about the actual school.

"It's in Hightown," said Esther, curtly. Before Livia could undertake any suitable reprimand, Josephine asked if she could join the table. Unfortunately for Esther, she had over-heard the mention of Hightown and brought the conversation right back to where it started.

"My son George will soon be joining you at Hightown, you know."

"I don't expect he will spend much time with you," Livia said to her daughter. "Boys have different interests, you know."

She was not happy with Josephine. She hoped Josephine would take note before Livia had to disengage from the friendship. Private arrangements with off-world contractors were worrying. They had the potential to destabilise the delicate social structure. Arrangements to buy an off-world present for a little boy endangered that structure (to no good purpose) and might allow the small boy to develop an impossibly high self-regard. Wasteful and trivial. If Josephine wanted a particular book, she could order it printed on New Ceres, using a proper printing press.

"Their interests are particularly different when one is eleven and the other is eighteen," Esther said. She spoke so quietly and so courteously that everyone took her comment literally, even her ever-suspicious mother. Everyone except Mr F, who had so neatly intervened earlier. He threw an uneasy look in her direction, but remained silent.

The uneasy look was wasted. Better distractions were afoot: Benjamin had decided to careen towards self-immolation. He started to pontificate about schooling on New Ceres. Livia tapped the base of her fan three times against the table and then turned to him.

"Don't you find it interesting," she asked, "how very much like an outsider a person sounds when he speaks about subjects he is really quite unfamiliar with?"

Josephine smiled and Benjamin sank his broad white self a little more under the table. If it were any warmer, Livia thought, the lard that is his skin and bone will melt through the cane weave and there will be nothing left of him except his signet ring. It is a rather nice signet ring.

She asked him about the ring, her body still tilted towards Josephine and Mr F. They would understand her body language. Benjamin would have to work harder at ingratiation. As it was, he twisted his ring and stammered.

In short order, Mr F took pity on them all and opened his paper. He showed the society page around and everyone (except Esther) began an animated conversation about the latest on-dits. Gossip was safe. It occurred in a strangely punctuated form, this place having the smallest coffee dishes in the district and the waitstaff being notorious chatterboxes. Livia was being seen by them and with her daughter: that was half her morning's work already accomplished.

After a while, Livia noticed that her daughter was becoming bored. Esther had forgotten her mother's gaze and had started to squirm her body around to see the goings on elsewhere in the establishment. Then she did the unthinkable and pulled at her mother's sleeve.

"Look," she said, and tilted her head very slightly towards the door.

A big masked man stood there, his back to the light, surveying the interior.

His head tilted down to look more closely at their table: he moved towards them swiftly.

His hand came out from under his cape. In it was a pistol. As he came towards them, he levelled the gun and pointed it at Livia. Esther stood up and moved in front of her mother. Josephine also moved. She slid her chair quickly backwards and fell into the gunman. His arm flew ceilingward and a bullet sped towards the ceiling, very noisily.

After the noise there was a silence. Heads were turned. Breath was held. The whole coffee house focussed on Livia and her circle. Livia herself was an elegant statue at table. Her pallor was not exceptional. In the stillness, she took a sip of coffee.

A second later the stillness broke. It was replaced by hullabaloo. Chairs moved and knocked. People called for the owner, for the law, for anyone who could help. Some left, one screamed. The owner of the coffee house was in their midst, adding to the noise. The gunman used the racket to absent himself. Livia took another sip of her coffee. It was too close to dregs, so she signalled for more.

Esther was still as white as a sheet and Benjamin offered to escort her home. A very gracious lump of lard, thought Livia. Or a very desperate one. I shall inquire concerning his finances.

"That doctor has decided you will become his patron, I think," Josephine commented.

Josephine missed the obvious over and over again. Livia shrugged her shoulder and mauled a mushroom pastry. It was the closest she could come to a social disconnect from someone who had proven she still had use in her. She needed to ponder on more dramatic matters.

What worried her a little more than the gun itself (although still not unduly) was that she couldn't place the attempted murderer. She noted it with the decimated pastry and put his rough garb and less rough manner aside for later consideration. She was certain the man did sports and dancing: he knew how to move.

One thing she was sure about. No, two. The first was that he had definitely been after her. And the second was that he was not an off-worlder.

This bore thinking about. It also made the coffee shop a very interesting place to be. Livia ordered more coffee and settled down for the long haul. She wanted to see who arrived next. Livia was determined to make something out of the incident. She could deal with nightmares alone, after dark, where they touched no-one but her.

Esther soon took herself home, after first indulging in an

ill-advised faint. Livia gently re-positioned herself to keep an eye on the entrance. It took two more dishes of coffee and some very tedious conversation before life became interesting again. Eventually, however, another big man filled that opening. This time his size was fat rather than muscle and the black was worn to disguise flab, rather than to hide identity. He moved, however, like a gentleman.

Harber stood in the doorway, surveying the scene. Livia tasted the nervousness of the other diners, as they all pretended nonchalance at Harber's dark shadow. She allowed her conversation to pause for a moment and gave a slight smile. Josephine and Mr F swivelled in perfect harmony to eye the door.

Livia wasn't at all surprised by Harber's advent. Poised between a civilised district and a very bad one, this coffee house was somewhat of a personal domain for him. It was unthinkable that his new friend should be threatened within his tomcat territory.

Once Harber had everyone's attention, he loomed over their table briefly, and asked if he could join them. Livia inclined her head graciously, while the others were more verbose in their acceptance. Josephine was a little nervous, Livia noted, with only slight interest, while Mr F had entirely regained his urbanity. In a logical world, it would have been the other way around. I need to find out more about this printer, Livia decided.

Conversation was strained until Harber took pity on the group.

"I heard that gunman was after you," he said, bluntly, to Livia.

"It looked that way," said Livia, unflinchingly. "Although I cannot think why." She noted that Mr F slightly bowed his head to hide something. A smile, perhaps?

"I hope you don't want to lay charges."

"I can't see how I could do such a thing," Livia replied, "Given that the man escaped."

"I can't be sorry for that. You are unscathed and I would very much like to keep the matter quiet."

"Why?" asked Josephine, with great emotion. "My friend could have been killed!"

"Her cousin's reputation would be greatly damaged if this should come to the law, and I could not wish that."

"Nor could I," said Livia. "Besides, I cannot see the logic in chasing a phantom."

"Surely he can be traced." Who would have thought Josephine would be the one to be hot on the trail of justice?

"With respect," said Mr F, "Madame Livia is probably more able to identify this gunman than a half-informed lawman."

"That's true," said Justice Harber, "But how do you know?"

"I'm always watching for news," replied Mr F, "And in the pursuit of such fare I am often well-informed about the characteristics of prominent citizens." Livia allowed her eyes to narrow minutely. "My feelings on this matter are that it is not in the interest of New Ceres to have it reported or made to seem large."

"But it was an attempt on the life of someone important to all of us, how can you not report it? And how can you," Josephine turned to Harber, "not want to investigate."

Livia tapped her fan to suggest that the subject should end before she became bored. Something Harber had said. She was missing it because of this stupid talk.

"I do not care to pursue the matter," she said.

Harber looked inordinately relieved. Livia realised what was happening and wanted to curse herself for being so slow. Her fan made a series of noises swish/click, swish/click, swish/click reflecting her annoyance. Harber didn't want

Alphonse to look bad. Why? The answer was obvious. Justice Harber was in Alphonse's pocket. Livia gave a little smile and noted that Josephine and Mr F both reacted to it. I should get out more often, she thought.

Livia didn't need to destroy Alphonse: he still had his uses. She needed to shift Harber and make him loyal to her. That had already begun. She hadn't missed the tomcat look, and wondered just how far she could push herself within his personal territory without compromising either of them. She gave her particular smile once again and Mr F suddenly verbalised how shocked and horrified he found himself by the incident, and how much he was now in need of quiet contemplation.

"I trust it will not appear in your newspaper," Josephine commanded. Just how stupid was the woman, Livia wondered.

"Mr F is the soul of discretion," said Livia. Mr F bowed to her, then a little less deeply to the rest of the company and then to Livia again, and then took his leave.

As if obeying some sort of cue from the Higher Powers, that doxy, Lizzie, walked in the coffee house door the moment Mr F was gone. Lizzie the Floozy, Livia reminded herself and carefully sent her body language so far towards Josephine and Justice Harber that Lizzy would entirely avoid her. One thing about doxies – they tended to read body language. Livia watched Lizzie's own body language as she directed her conversation towards the people at her table. She's guilty of something, Livia realised. Interesting. I need to send some feelers out.

Suddenly, Livia found she had had a surfeit of coffee and company. She wanted time alone, to process and to think. Just one more small thing and she could leave.

"Josephine," she said, "I've been thinking about that dilemma of yours. I rather feel you should consult with Justice Harber about your cousin's situation."

Josephine gave a visible start, then smiled bravely.

Harber nodded that he was willing to listen and tipped Livia the wink that he would oblige. It was quite obvious (as Livia expected) that Harber already knew Josephine's situation. She rather suspected everyone knew of it, which was why Josephine had so much time to linger over coffee with one person. She ought to be speaking to twenty allies in an afternoon, given her ambitions.

In a few days she would be free to do just that. Josephine's cousin would be able to return from his planetary prison. Josephine would be less likely to be caught up and destroyed by his anti-social nature. A cousin serving time in Hades 'at the Lady Governor's pleasure' was something to be avoided for those with political aspirations. Livia would no longer owe Josephine for her actions of the afternoon: Josephine would owe her. The world was back in equilibrium.

Let Alphonse have the small things, she decided, and left him at large to play what he thought of as sophisticated politics. She rather suspected that Constance would be his next target, judging from the mirror that young lady had received in the cave.

Parle du diable, she then said to herself, as she walked past Constance in the street. Constance was completely unaware of Livia's floating green presence. Her own attention was focussed on impressing the gallant who escorted her. The gallant in question appeared to be fixated on adjusting his eyepiece to properly survey Constance's overflowing bosom. Constance's dress style had certainly undergone a change since Livia had last seen her.

Livia assessed their interaction and decided "Husband-hunting." Not a bad move, at that. It might yet save her from Alphonse's dreams of hellfire. Idly, Livia wondered why Constance had incurred such wrath. Perhaps by sleeping with him and not idolising him? She had seen that before. Alphonse had an ego bigger than Io.

6

THE EATING PLACES OF PROSPERINE #3,

T rig's coffee house serves a limited range of snacks, but they are all palatable to most off-world humans, especially those familiar with the cuisines of European Old Earth. It's a quaint place.

In the bustle of the market square near the spaceport, it sits a little apart. Customers can admire the comings and goings of ships through the high windows, but while they do so, they sit in the eighteenth century of New Ceres, served coffee by indentured servants.

Most visitors consider it the first and the best of the New Ceres coffee houses, mainly because it's the friendliest towards outsiders. The staff and customers both leave the strictures and rules of Prosperine behind once they open the big wooden doors. It's neither galaxy nor planetary: Trig's sits alone and everyone meets there.

The pace never slows at Trig's because – for many of its regulars – it's both a place of business and a place to meet friends. It's crowded and bustling, but never frantic. Travellers meet at Trig's. They find their hosts there, or bargain for a cut-price place on a slow ship. They seek out the latest newssheets, both from the licensed distributors ... or not. A visit to the spaceport is never complete without a visit to Trig's.

There is, however, another side to this bustling coffee house. For a few, it's a place of hope.

There are two tables where the newest inhabitants of Prosperine always sit. These strays are refugees, war debris, lost souls who drifted down to New Ceres on the ships you can see through Trig's high windows.

There are many refugees on New Ceres: if you find a patron you are permitted to stay, no need for advance permissions or odd visas. Indenture is another path to residency. Almost everyone else who wants to stay long term on New Ceres lingers in Trig's in the hopes of finding a new path to a future. Some end up as servants. The rest end up on a ship out when their temporary visa expires.

Most refugees avoid the spaceport once they've been in Prosperine a while. Trig's and the processing centre are the only places you'll be certain of finding any. That group of regulars at Trig's is obvious the moment you walk in that big oaken door. Two tables of misery.

The drinkers sit there for hours at a stretch, watching the ships descend, dreaming that these vast globes contain relatives or friends. Some watch the globes drift upwards into infinity and wish they could travel away from their perilous new lives.

There is a special place at the end table. If someone tries to sit there, the regulars and the serving staff will combine to shoo them away. Buzz says that that chair's regular occupant is the very last human to escape Lost Earth. No ship can carry her home.

I asked the regulars what this famous refugee from

Mother Earth eats at Trig's. Fritters filled with fruit preserves, they told me, or a cheese pastry after the style of Old Vienna. The owner of Trig's has kindly given me recipes for both these snacks, in memory of this sad spirit.

FRITTERS FILLED **with fruit preserves**
    ½ cup boiling milk or water
    ¼ cup butter
    ½ cup double-processed refined flour
    2 tablespoons pulverised sugar
    2 hens' eggs (NOT new hens)
    a pinch salt
    fruit preserves

PLACE YOUR BUTTER in a small pan. Add your milk or water and quickly bring to boil. Add all the flour. Stir until the mixture defies the pan and chooses the spoon. Take pan off heat and gradually add eggs, beating constantly. Fry in deep fat, in large spoonfuls, until puffed as a politician and brown as a farmer. Drain. Fill with preserves. Sprinkle with sugar.

CHEESE PASTRY **after the style of Old Vienna**
    ½ cup fresh soft farmers' cheese
    (double-processed)
    ½ cup butter
    1 cup double-refined flour
    peach preserve

·   ·   ·

Mix all ingredients together until smooth. Cut into small pieces and set aside until firm. Roll each piece into a square. Place a spoon of peach preserve into the centre of each square. Take the four corners, bring them together and press until they hold like new lovers. Bake in a hot oven.

7

POLITE COLLISIONS

I f you want to run into someone, anyone, even nobodies, you go to a coffee house. If you want to discover the latest on-dits recounted by the best gossips, you go to a coffee house. If you want to make an assignation or buy illegal technology, you go to a coffee house. If you don't want to run into notorious and dangerous women, then you do not go to a coffee house.

Grania discovered this one day when she and Dal walked right into Livia.

They were on their way out. Livia was on her way in. The collision was literal and highly uncomfortable, despite the efforts of both Livia and Dal, who managed to exchange many sets of apologies.

What most annoyed Grania was that Livia had stepped on the hem of her skirt. She was almost positive it was intentional. There was the mark of a small hard heel deep in the fine fabric. It had been pressed and turned, as if something sharp and triangular had been twisted a few times. And yet Livia seemed to step back, as if the two had not touched. Grania did a quick inspection of the rest of the dress at once and found that some of the exquisite lace Dal had bought her a week ago had been half ripped off. Why would anyone do such a thing? Then again, why would anyone be Livia?

Grania felt dirty. She tried to stop wiping her hands on her dress to rub all of Livia from it.

Livia was amused by this, and by Grania muttering her excuses while looking at the floor. She was amused at playing childish tricks in a public place. Obviously, she thought, it's a day of rare entertainment.

When Grania went almost straight outside, Livia was even more amused: Earth manners were so abominable. She remembered the fate of Earth and felt almost guilty for thinking this, then recalled how many of her plans Grania had scuttled by marrying Dal. Livia shrugged. After all, the manners of Earthers were abominable.

Dal stayed a moment longer to make amends, demonstrating that his sensuous lower lip hid a slightly feral set of teeth and that he smelled of expensive tobacco.

Livia surveyed the coffee house and – to her great annoyance – found there were no free tables. She couldn't simply turn and leave. That would be undignified.

A man stood up, politely, to indicate she could join him. With relief, she saw it was Mr F. He really does understand the social niceties, she marvelled, and wove her way to his table. It was a pleasant change for someone she had nothing on to help her out of a dilemma. Why did she have nothing on him? Her face sported a very faint frown as she sat down.

"It seems we are always destined to meet at coffee houses," Mr F joked, standing up again to allow Livia to sit down with proper decorum.

Mr F's manner appealed to Livia. His apology was so perfectly respectful (just shy of obeisant) yet it held not even a touch of servility. Livia let the thought pass through her mind that there was the possibility of friendship with this man. He understood the social nuances so very nicely and played politics so very conservatively. She gave him all her attention.

The moment they were comfortably settled at their small table, Mr F opened his satchel and brought out some papers. Livia's eyes lit up. The reason she had ventured out this morning was because she lacked information. She currently had many small tidbits and no understanding whatsoever of how they fitted together or what they meant. It was extremely frustrating. It was also a barometer for her feelings: today was a bad day. She ought to be at home, thinking and planning. She wiped her hands on her skirt. Then she took a deep breath and found her composure.

While she was sorting herself, Mr F found the papers he was after. She hoped he had not noticed her momentary lapse.

"My new releases," he said, eyes modestly concerning themselves with the documents. "I had meant to begin the series next week, but the first is suddenly topical."

"Never waste an opportunity?"

"Never," Mr F sounded fervent. The man worshipped the printed word.

How Livia hated the joke 'New Series from New Ceres' – why couldn't people say 'The new serial'? Yet it was so ingrained in popular culture that she doubted any paper with more than one issue would be called a serial again. This new series was literature, of sorts. Even poetry, of sorts.

"The broadsheets of Old Earth contain many remarkable tales," Mr F explained, helpfully. "Each and every one of them reinforces the New Enlightenment because they are drawn from the Old Enlightenment."

"You know that every man and his dog will copy you," Livia pointed out.

"That is my devout hope," said Mr F.

Livia took a moment to study the sheet in front of her. It contained poems about highwaymen, comfortably crowded to fit on the page and give the buyer value for money. She read a stanza aloud:

Let us take the Road.

Hark! I hear the Sound of Coaches!

The Hour of Attack approaches,

To your Arms, brave Boys, and load.

See the Ball I hold!

Let the Chymists toil like Asses,

Our Fire their Fire surpasses,

And turns all our Lead to Gold.

"It's from The Beggar's Opera," commented Mr F. "From the original eighteenth century."

"It could easily be about New Ceres, and current."

"That's why I thought it was useful to bring these poems back into popular parlance."

"Very clever," Livia liked Mr F's style. "It demonstrates that even the ills of our society are simply a part of our New Enlightenment."

"I'm not condoning those ills, you understand."

Livia nodded, and turned the talk very slightly to highwaymen in general.

"The New Stilton Road is becoming increasingly dangerous," she said.

"Not many lives lost, at least," noted Mr F.

"All the lives lost belong to aristocratic families," Livia noted, tartly.

Mr F looked up in great surprise.

"I hadn't realised that," he said slowly. "I hope someone finds these highwaymen out and they come to trial. We cannot afford to lose the great and the good."

Livia reminded Mr F of her well-known ability to remember people from their body language, even masked.

"I have no doubt you would be more of a danger to a highwayman than a highwayman would be to you," Mr F replied. Livia examined him for insincerity and found none. This was the closest they had come to discussing the attack on her, last time they had met. Livia soon realised that Mr F was thinking of it. This might not be a long conversation.

"I almost find it within myself to pity the highwayman who robs you of your goods."

"Only almost?" Livia was 'only' almost arch. Mr F hurriedly changed the topic and asked about Esther.

Livia explained that her daughter was safe at Hightown already.

"Protected and ensconced and learning to be a useful member of society."

"Ah," said Mr F. "Swords and horses. Very practical."

"No, that isn't her style. She is a quiet, good child and is learning housekeeping. She will make someone an obedient wife. "

"Interesting," said Mr F, "That no-one ever talks about a boy making someone an obedient husband."

"A relic of colonial days," Livia was dismissive.

"I can't see it," said Mr F. "It seems more to belong to the New Enlightenment."

"Certain elements we have improved upon," Livia said, a dangerous glint in her eyes, "Women being integral to the wider needs of society is one of them."

"Yet your daughter?"

"My daughter is a throwback. I wish she weren't, but since she is, she will do society proud and will make a gracious hostess at someone's country estate." Not necessarily married, she didn't add. The way she sipped her coffee said it all.

After a few more minutes of safe but less interesting chatter, Mr F stood up and made an elegant half-bow. "I trust you will excuse me," he said. "Time and printing presses are not allies."

Livia smiled, but not outwardly. She had come seeking manna from the heavens: it was time to accept the gift. It was time, in fact, to investigate the very source of that manna. Her knowledge of printing was sadly lacking compared with, say, her understanding of food treatment and its politics.

As she herself slowly stood up, forcing Mr F's very courtesy to delay his departure, she wondered how long the urbanity he displayed in such abundance would endure. He was so carefully proper and so blatantly class conscious. He could read cues almost as well as she herself did.

"Let me come with you," she said. "I've always wanted to see the inside of Prosperine's greatest printery," she claimed.

Mr F looked a bit bedraggled and Livia enjoyed the small power play. He needs reminding that he's merely an adjunct of the Great and Good, she thought. As an adjunct, though, he did an excellent job. A small show of support would not go astray. Nor would the threat of her future presence. She particularly liked that Mr F was subtle enough to understand all of this and soft-hearted enough to be scared.

She kindly took the edge off his fear by engaging in a very gentle flirtation.

Mr F was above reproach. I must find out his proper name, Livia thought, as he escorted her to his printing shop, two blocks away. He stood on the street side, she noticed, and kept her sheltered from the passing traffic. He really was a good specimen of the best of the working classes.

They came in through an old-fashioned door of reinforced artificial glass.

"This is the back way," Mr F apologised. "The main entrance is two streets away."

"So big," Livia marvelled.

"Not really," Mr F was almost apologetic as he led her through a small reception area generously supplied with comfortable chairs and lined with shelves. "Printing is a complicated business. Those shelves hold small but select publications, for collection by clients. Take a look," he encouraged. Livia did just that and found nothing more exciting than fancy calling cards and dinner menus. "We keep this office so that the elite aren't forced to mingle with the hoi polloi."

Livia was almost disappointed with his honesty.

They walked out the other end of the room and Mr F indicated the censor's office on the left and his own office beyond it. Neither office was protected against the bustle of the big room they now surveyed. Livia counted four printing presses. Smaller and more archaic than the food processors she knew so well, they were compact and very wooden. Taller than she had expected, but narrow and with no extra flourishes.

"Where does the wood come from for your presses?" Livia asked. "Is it a native species?"

"Of course not," Mr F sounded mildly horrified. "It's Earth hardwood, from that strange township in the hills. The one that's all wood and wool and leather goods. Tenterfield? The building is old and has some pre-Enlightenment features." The right hand gestured upwards to the permanent lighting, "But we're phasing them out, as finances permit."

"The lighting, the door, the heating, they're all covered by the Third Amnesty?"

"The Second. This building and its companion were owned by the Lord-Governor at the time of the First Amnesty and were exempt."

"I didn't realise it was so old."

Mr F nodded. "As I said, we've been replacing what we can. We're very proud that it doesn't appear terribly techno."

He ushered her past the shelves and the whispering apprentices and through a door at the far side of the big room. "This is our water supply and kitchenette. The water supply is one of the main reasons my grandfather bought these buildings when he decided to expand."

"To expand?"

"He began near the spaceport, printing for the interstellar tourist trade. He also produced instructional manuals for people arriving on New Ceres. I took the business a step further. There was so much that even the people on New Ceres didn't know: we needed a direct connection from our leaders," and he gave her a miniscule bow, "to the people. I moved close to the Old Town and devised a new range of printed materials. You may not remember," Mr F came close to being too charming, too insinuating a young man, "but before I moved here no establishment produced fine engraved documents as well as the bread and butter broadsheets and books and plain printed cards, and none was willing to allow a censor free access."

"And so you became printer to the nobility."

"My profession and my need to serve New Ceres are a perfect fit." There was a moment's silence as they navigated the delivery area. "Do you wish to see the workshop where we do the binding? Or our third typesetting area?"

"Third?"

"There were two sets of typesetting equipment near the main presses."

"I don't want to take up more of your time," Livia said. It was obvious that Mr F's cleverness included a very well-guarded tongue. "Perhaps you could assign me your laziest apprentice?" She ventured a joke. "I could smile gently at him and he will never be lazy again."

Mr F simply nodded.

Livia wondered how she would get past his guard. This might be worth exploring, purely for entertainment.

"Give me a moment to find a suitable victim." He went back to the main room and in short order returned with a young girl. "I fear I really must return to work," he said. " Katie will answer all your questions and give you tea and biscuits. If you can wait another half hour, the censor will be here, and he will be able to answer anything that Katie cannot."

"You have times for his arrival?" Curious, Livia thought.

"Not generally. This is a special visit. He requested certain edits for tomorrow's paper."

Her second walk-through was much slower and more enlightening. Her third – with the censor - gave her a useful contact. More knowledge would help in her bid to move to the Lumoscenti. From there, she would serve the Lady Governor directly. Power through the Families was – after all – neither the only type of power nor the most appropriate one for her particular talents.

The most important thing she discovered was that Mr F could not possibly be the source of any of the anti-establishment broadsheets that had arisen recently. From the censor's voluminous explanations, she now knew about watermarks and how each press was distinctive. She knew that the censor hated and detested rogue pamphlets and unauthorised spreadsheets. He treated every single one of them as a personal insult.

It amused her that Katie held her ground but that every other employee either left rooms when she entered, or hid behind equipment and worked extremely hard. Her reputation had obviously grown until it was greater than her actual influence.

This piece of news was itself worth visiting to find out. If she were to become associated with the cloaked and guarded elements of the Lumoscenti, perhaps one day she could aspire to that, too. One day soon. Too few of the Six Families did the work they ought to preserve the beauty of New Ceres and its civilisation.

She absorbed knowledge of Printing and of Mr F in her usual spongelike fashion. The censor walked her back out 'the respectable door' as he called it, next to his own office.

In the reception area they walked past Lizzie, proudly flaunting her new business card. "Discreet," she was telling the receptionist. "That's my new business name. These cards are perfectly discreet – why, on one side they could even be calling cards."

The censor looked up at Livia, suddenly embarrassed. Livia was amused. She said to him, just loudly enough so that Lizzie could overhear, "She really is a floozy." Lizzie didn't trouble to look over.

At that moment Constance walked in. Everyone, it seemed, patronised Mr F's establishment. Livia graciously inclined her head in the precise greeting that would indicate that she was not referring to Constance, but to Lizzie, and the two passed each other in silence.

The censor returned to his office and the receptionist saw Lizzie out and then disappeared to find Mr F. Livia would have been fascinated to know that Constance had an appointment with the man himself. She would have been even more fascinated to see Constance and Mr F walk out the front door and immediately seek a very scungy coffee house.

"DON'T BUY THE FOOD HERE," Constance warned.

"How do you know such things?" Mr F was amused.

Constance just shrugged.

"Livia was there," she said.

"She tagged along with me, I'm afraid. She's growing her networks, and her knowledge. Moving beyond her social circles."

"We all know where she wants to be. If she joined them..." Constance muttered.

"Don't even think such a thing," said Mr F. "Instead, let us deal with this special order of yours."

"Here's the text."

"I'll make sure it reaches my friends." Mr F tucked it into his waistcoat pocket as if it were unimportant.

"That simple?" Constance laughed.

"Never that simple. But you wanted to ask me about something else?"

"Alphonse," Constance said. "This meeting is really about Alphonse."

"No wonder seeing Livia worried you." Mr F leaned forward on one elbow.

"I hear she might not love him so much right now."

"That's something, at least."

"Not for me," Constance's voice took on a bitter tinge.

Mr F looked up, surprised.

"He wants to kill me. He gave me clear warning at his eclipse party. So far he's been stupid about it."

"How stupid?"

"The usual. Untreated food in pretty wrappings."

"Clumsy." Mr F nodded as if clumsy were worthy of approval.

"It makes me wonder how much of what he has done has been Livia hiding behind him."

"If that's the case, then Livia's more dangerous than any of us thought."

"Any of you, Leander. I've always said she was evil." Her bitterness was now clear as a cracked bell. In fact, she sounded rather prosaic.

"I was looking at the games she played."

"She plays games. She also murders. And she has a Cause."

"Can we talk about something else?" Mr F looked discomfited.

"Certainly. Like how I'm to escape imminent death."

"That's easy," Mr F gave Constance a rare and sweet smile.

"Tell me what I can do." Constance sounded as if it was all business, but her eyes betrayed her need to be active.

"Not a thing. When I send this little beauty off, I shall send another."

"And what will it say? That Alphonse is a murdering bastard?" The bitterness was back, in spades.

"Not at all. We'll say that Alphonse is plotting against the Lady Governor. We might even say that our little group of loyal defenders of New Ceres see him as a threat."

"Will that be enough?"

"No," said Mr F. "If Livia is interested in our product then things are getting a little too close there, as well. We shall find a scapegoat."

"Who?"

"There is a certain know-it-all I should like to see diminished."

"You really do hate everyone with a title, don't you?" She smiled, but it was not the smile it should have been. This was not what she had expected.

"Constance, you know precisely why."

"He's a refugee."

"One with money and a loyal following who still says 'His Grace' this and 'His Grace' that. People like him nearly brought us into the war. New Ceres could have been destroyed."

"He refuses to use his title."

"He still acts as if he owns the ground he walks on."

"Those township years really changed you."

"I still support the New Enlightenment, you know."

"How is that?"

"Study your history. There were countries that threw off their nobility and royalty." Mr F said knowingly.

Constance laughed. "I'll look it up when I get home."

"I must go," said Mr F, regretfully.

"So must I," said Constance. "Too long here and we'll cease to look innocent." Both she and Mr F knew that they didn't look at all innocent. They looked, in fact, as if they were flirting. The gentle way Mr F raised and kissed Constance's hand just outside the coffee shop didn't do anything to lessen that impression in the eyes of any passers-by who might remark on such a thing. On New Ceres there always were passers-by to remark upon things.

A few days later Alphonse himself paid a visit to Mr F's printing establishment. It was a personal visit, because Alphonse always made personal visits. He thought he was the first to find out gossip. It was one of his trademarks at social events "When I paid a visit to Mr F's today." Everyone said how daring he was to mix comfortably with someone not of his class and how clever he was to have Mr F as a source of information. As 'everyone' would that night, in a small and select party attending the theatre.

Everyone would complain about aliens and about human visitors who were on New Ceres merely to grab trade routes to richer planets. Everyone would be thankful for the food issues that protected New Ceres from being one of those rich planets. Everyone would wonder when the fallout from the war would finally end, or if, indeed the war itself was simply continuing in another guise. And then everyone would listen avidly to Alphonse's gossip. It was invariable and inevitable, just as it was invariable and inevitable that Alphonse made one of his personal visits to Mr F the day of any such gathering.

Mr F found this visit of Alphonse's particularly useful. He was able to slip Alphonse a portfolio of the latest sheets and to let Alphonse know that he had heard of illegal sheets circulating near the horse markets.

"You understand I haven't been able to check them out myself."

"I will investigate them this very morning," Alphonse declared. "If there's anything untoward, I shall bring my men into it."

"Your men?"

"Livia interceded with the Lady Governor's Lieutenant and I have been assigned a special team to follow up infractions."

"That's very unusual. The Lady Governor must respect your work."

"Naturally."

"And Livia herself? Does she not want any such power?"

"Until her daughter is under control she can't do much. I work with her and we achieve mutual aims, however."

"Very laudable."

"Indeed. I can't see my cousin doing nothing, however. Wouldn't be surprised if she took another protégée."

A shadow moved in at the door and stood behind it, quietly. Mr F lost some of the polite neutrality of his speech, and successfully diverted Alphonse from that door and its shadow.

"Hope the new protégée doesn't meet the fate of the last one," he commented.

"A sad accident," said Alphonse, leaning forward a little threateningly.

"Another accident would be much harder to keep out of the street literature than the previous three," Mr F suggested, indelicately.

Alphonse shuffled in annoyance, "I thought you had control of these things."

"I am the lead printer and the government sanctioned printer, not the only printer. More and more moonlighting presses are appearing. No-one knows where they are and no-one knows how their broadsheets reach the streets. I can't touch them."

"Why should I believe you?"

"Do you want a complete explanation of how my business operates? I have already given one to your cousin." They eyed each other across the table, as antagonistically as courtesy permitted.

"Yes, I do," Alphonse stared belligerently down at Mr F's thinning pate.

Mr F responded at once, challenging Alphonse with detail and a direct gaze. "We have our own typefaces, so that all work from our press is instantly recognizable. The censor checks then to ensure this. My personal favourite is one I like to call 'Eloquent': it sings the original eighteenth century. Its letterforms are very Roman, with just a hint of Renaissance humanist. Although I admit I have put in an application for a new typeface that is quite superb. It's very English and I derived it from John Baskerville's original: it exactly reflects the society of New Ceres."

"All of you printers use these particular typefaces?"

"Oh, not at all. In fact, because my business is successful enough to support applications for typefaces, mine are quite distinct, which is one reason my work is so sought after. Clients can be certain of the reception of their work, when it is left in my hands. There are more common typefaces. The best of them are the ones based on classical models – that hint of Ancient Rome reflects our New Enlightenment so very profoundly, you see."

"And how much can you print in these magnificent fonts?" Alphonse sounded sarcastic, but Mr F was unperturbed.

"I print up to four hundred impressions an hour on each of my presses. That's two hundred one-sided pages."

"And others?" Mr F gave a slight sigh to indicate he was going to state the obvious. He put his dish of coffee on the table and tilted his head upwards to look Alphonse straight in the eye. Alphonse was still angry that Livia had stolen a march on him and Mr F's attitude was not helping. His cheeks were mottled red and his eyes began to protrude a little.

"Less, of course. Four hundred is the most a wooden press can achieve, and it takes two impressions for a proper imprint."

"What if they were willing to go with a paler imprint? What if they had a metal press?"

"It's not the shade of black that's the issue – it's printing that evenly covers the whole page. For a standard page, four hundred is the highest that is achievable without using illegal technology, such as an iron press. Perhaps you would appreciate a tour such as the one we gave Madame Livia?" That lady would have been astonished at how acerbic Mr F was at this point.

"I don't need it," Alphonse was dismissively certain of his

knowledge. "I understand you're loyal. I'll have a word with someone who might just be able to find out who isn't."

"You do that."

"You don't mind losing the competition."

"Of course I don't," said Mr F. "I also don't want the government to fall. We all have too much at stake."

Alphonse grunted. His hand moved over the handle of the press. "Any way someone could come in here and use your machine?"

"At night, perhaps. There are a few hours, very late, when there is no-one here. But there are no supplies missing."

"So they bring their supplies and use them."

"If you're not going to say it directly then I shall. The big advantage of our technology is that it leaves distinctive trails. Every single page of paper legally produced on New Ceres has a watermark and every single piece printed here has the characteristic marks of my press. Mine are the only typefaces, for instance, that have a true ligature between the 's' and the 't' as was done in the Great Enlightenment. It ought to be a matter of minutes to find out where the paper came from and where it was printed."

"And yet we don't know," Alphonse's purr sounded ugly and threatening.

"The paper bears no watermark and the printing press has slightly different flaws to my own. Or any others on New Ceres."

"Off-planet," Alphonse looked up, suddenly concerned.

"That's always a possibility."

"Don't even think it. Leave it with me." And Alphonse was out the door.

"What was that all about?" Constance moved out from behind the door.

"Just Alphonse. He's still after everything."

"What kind of everything?" Constance pressed.

Mr F looked across at her, wearily. "I wish you would stay out of this," he said.

"I need to know."

"Off-planet," Mr F said, slowly. "I think he's set his sights on managing star trade and planet trade."

"Everything that comes through the space port, then."

"That's big politics," Mr F offered.

"Dangerous," said Constance. "He could run into his own cousin. She may have a million pretensions, but I still contend she's the most dangerous woman on the planet."

Mr F nodded. "She's already killed four of Alphonse's stepping stones. He'll snap soon, mark my words."

"Battle between them? Curious."

"Bad for all of us," Mr F snapped. "Don't take warfare in that family lightly."

"Oh, I'm not," Constance smiled reassuringly. "And I know something you don't know."

"What?"

"Something I saw on the night of the eclipse. I think Alphonse has already declared battle with Livia."

"Damn."

"Indeed."

"You want knowledge in return, don't you?"

"Of course."

Mr F sighed. "Alphonse is still cultivating that Earther artist. She avoids him. I suspect she still thinks he wants her to be his mistress. She doesn't understand us at all."

"So why does he cultivate her, then?"

"Her salon has become a very good place to get politics done. I hear she doesn't even realise it."

"She is atrociously naïve."

"Dangerously so."

"Why does she assume he still wants her in his bed?"

"I hear she can be found at Trig's, regularly. She knows the refugee arrivals better than anyone. And pickings are becoming slim for the Alphonses of this world."

"Does her husband accompany her to Trig's, I wonder?"

"My sources suggest only occasionally and that when he does he only talks to people from his own planet."

"Thank you." Constance gave a slight bow.

"My pleasure. Now would you mind leaving? Next time, go through the usual channels."

"You know I shall." She blew him a cheeky kiss on the way out.

Mr F gave a sigh and settled down to writing an entirely innocuous editorial that would please the Lady Governor and all her people.

Mr F's observations about Grania and Dal were entirely correct, and also entirely incorrect.

Dal and Grania had finally determined on a balance between Dal's work and Grania's art. Dal had given Grania the capacity to hire masters to teach her and Grania had learned more about salons and their uses. At least, that's how it looked.

In reality, they had gone from a state of calmness and determination to trust, to another state that was more turgid. In short, they were arguing.

After Grania slammed a door for the third time in a day, she took a deep breath and looked at herself in a mirror. She was still Grania and the mirror might have simply been an Earth antique. Except it wasn't. She was Grania on New Ceres.

She looked at her round brown eyes and wondered where she had left herself until now. She suddenly realised that her feelings had returned, and she was astonished by them. There had been such a long time when her mind and soul had been veiled by a brainfog. If this was Earth she could get counselling, not just a mirror, but New Ceres had no experts on emotional trauma. The society that lives by the sword gets emotionally scarred by it, she thought.

So I'm emerging. I don't want to emerge. It was so much easier to be in that dull land with no nerves and no pain.

Dal noticed the white face and the temper and interpreted the slammed doors quite differently. One day, while she was out being fitted for what she called "More bloody new clothes", he called all the staff together. The whole household (except Grania, of course) was set onto suicide watch.

Dal worried about Grania. He felt that if she died his life would lose something ineffably important. He found himself waking up next to her, his nightmares expressed in a clenched jaw and stiff neck. Every morning he would tumble out of bed in a frantic hurry to prevent Grania noticing and he would set himself to exercise. By the time she joined him over breakfast, he was calm and relaxed.

For Grania, early morning became the loneliest time of day.

It was impossible for her not to notice the constant surveillance. It didn't help her frame of mind. It kept her physically safe, but it meant that some of the old symptoms of shock re-emerged.

Grania wasn't used to a servanted society, she explained to herself, to justify Dal. That's all it is. Just because it reminds me of the camps and their watchers, doesn't make it so. I can control this.

She went through everything that helped her previously.

Lists in the mind. List after list after list. Obsessive but not useful.

Some things helped a little. Deep breathing. A great deal of gentle exercise. Not bringing the nightmares into clear daylight. What helped most, however, was giving herself space. Finding ways of keeping the prying eyes at bay.

She began to sketch in secret and locking her studio so that no-one except her could get in. If anyone so much as glanced at her work without permission, she screamed at them. The screaming was unsatisfying, but it gave her back some space. She noticed that everyone, including the servants, averted their gaze from her work. Everyone, even the servants, respected the locked door.

When Dal commented "Good idea, that locked door. I hadn't realised how important privacy was to you," something inside her loosened in relief. It didn't even tauten when she discovered that Dal used her locked door to hide some very illegal publications from the servants. He thought she wouldn't see them, Grania realised, but he hadn't realised that every mote of dust was known to her. It was her private space.

She never read his papers. She simply noted their comings and goings in an abstracted way. She had ceased to care about Dal's politicking, perhaps. One more step away from those emotional ties that bound her to this house.

One day maybe I can leave New Ceres forever. When I sell my art again, she decided, I will keep a secret fund. An escape fund. I will start all over again, on a less fragile world. On a world where I can eat the food. On a world where 'sheep' really are sheep and where spiders scuttle more gracefully. On a world where I can breathe.

With that hope, she went downstairs. No-one noticed her. Grania checked the breakfast parlour, but lunch was not forthcoming. She asked one of the maids and got a shrug for her troubles. She realised there had been a shift in the attitude of the staff when she had started to lock her studio.

It was cleaning day, but that shouldn't stop her getting lunch. She told the maid she was going to the studio to work and would appreciate having lunch brought to her. "Yes, ma'am," said the maid.

Two hours later she was ragingly hungry and wondered where her lunch was. She pulled the bellrope. Eventually someone came. Eventually. Her own home felt like a bad hotel.

"I would like some lunch," Grania said, "If it won't cause too much trouble."

The manservant simply nodded. "I'll talk to the cook," he said.

A little while later someone came up from the kitchens. "I'm terribly sorry," he said, "But we served lunch in the dining parlour at the usual time."

"And why does that prevent me being served any food now?"

"That's what I want to know," and behind the servant was Dal's own man, Qan, waiting patiently.

"Especially since I said this morning that I would not be eating in the parlour today."

"You should have said something," the kitchen hand complained.

"I did. I asked that my lunch be brought here. Two hours ago."

The kitchen hand looked nervous, but his body language was obdurate. Yet when Dal's manservant touched him on the shoulder, he jumped.

"Take this money," Qan said. "Go straight to the first place you can buy Grania food and bring it directly back. After that,

I want you to go to the kitchens and tell the cook that if she can't get off her lazy butt to make lunch for her mistress then she can look for a new job."

"Sir," said the servant, and bobbed a little nervous bow.

This was his first bow. The staff were sending her a message.

Grania knew this wasn't good enough. She knew she needed to be in charge. She didn't want to be. She didn't want a staff of twenty-three and if she had to have that staff, she didn't want them to be so bloody invisible. Except when they were watching here. Invisible or always there – the staff terrified her.

Dal had dreams of changing New Ceres so that everyone had safe food to eat, but he took for granted that his every whim was more important than someone's free time or love life. She kept forgetting he was from an aristocracy. She should have realised it at that coffee house, the first night they met. She should have realised it and gone straight to the spaceport and somehow talked her way onto a ship off the planet. Except there were still almost no planets that would take Earthers.

It's as if we're infectious, she thought. What happened to us might happen to you. Or maybe you'll realise you were complicit in our murder. Except I escaped murder. I'm very much alive and it damned well hurts. And she found herself crying again. Crying started everything off. No wonder her orders weren't respected.

Grania found yet another temporary solution. She hid quantities of clean food and drink in her studio. Then she took to spending more and more of her day with various art teachers, learning approved techniques. She took up charcoal and pencil and watercolour and oil.

While the techniques came easily, she found they were

lacking. There was something in them that didn't light the flame inside. And without the flame, her work was dead.

One day Dal entered her studio without warning. He looked around at her various pieces. He didn't stop her working, but when she finally put her brushes down and shrouded her painting, he said "I can see you're making progress. I would like to see you try your hand at sculpture, you know."

Grania snapped, "This is what I think of sculpture on New Ceres."

Dal found a small ceramic head hurtling towards his head. He sidestepped neatly. They both looked down at the shattered pieces.

"I need to invest in some carpet, perhaps," Dal said, and made his escape before Grania could throw anything else.

8

THE SERVICES OF PROSPERINE

A sample of the business cards from the collection of Fred Xian, journalist and writer, contributor to the Galaxy Guide and to the Encyclopaedia of the Settled Planets, who is currently researching and writing from New Ceres. You will remember that he recently wrote us a set of pieces on the daytime activities of the aristocracy of New Ceres. He discussed how the need to play the part of eighteenth-century Europeans increases the appearance of leisure tenfold in these classes, with everything from salons to balloon ascensions occupying their days. A new set of articles from this outstanding writer will appear starting with our next issue. It will focus on the arcane nightlife of New Ceres. Xian will examine how a planet's addiction to the past of Mother Earth leads to strange darktime activities.

For all your safety and hygiene needs contact Mark Brown at Green Lane.

Pest control. Hat cleaning. Identification and disposal of untreated food.

Discreet.
Elizabeth Dalton.
For all your 'special' needs.
Inquire at the coffee-house on Arras Street
in the Old Town, or at the garment-hire
booth at the spaceport. Messages will be
sent promptly and your needs will be
attended to as a matter of priority.

Mr F, publisher and printer to the Nobility.
Purveyor of published and printed goods to five Great Estates.
Under the gentle patronage of several Noble Houses. Service to the
autonomous zones and to major townships of the Prosperine region.

9

SALON FOR OUTCASTS

Some things are just not what they are supposed to be. Grand romance. Psychic insights of everlasting love. Money.

No, Grania reflected, money was fine. Being able to paint and create made the rest tolerable. Learning old techniques to apply to new art almost made nights like tonight tolerable. Almost. Maybe.

"We are going to create a social and cultural existence for the dispossessed," Dal had celebrated. Grania loved that exuberance. She loved his flash-quick moods and his grandiose ideas.

The salon idea had been such a grand idea. Once a month a part of the huge house Dal insisted was theirs would open to others. An atmosphere, a buzz, a crowd intelligence of a superior kind would be created. The notion had swept her up with its fervour and excitement and sense of creating new realities.

What she didn't love was that Dal was alien to practicality. When it came to dramatic rescues and wondrous escapes, Dal was the man. When it came to daily life, her husband was more annoying than most.

"You need a keeper!" Grania commented to the top of his head. If he could give her a houseful of watchers, he deserved at least one keeper himself.

"I'm reading the paper," he said. "I hardly need a keeper for that."

"I bet that paper isn't published by Mr F, Printer to the Nobility."

He looked up at her, finally, and smiled. His eyes were warm and dark. "I would not like to bet against you."

"If you keep flirting with danger we could lose all this."

"My love, we have both lost so much, we can build again."

Grania didn't like to point out the obvious: Dal had lost a great deal, but he had kept his family, his friends, his money and even some of his possessions. She was so impressed with him at first, because he had been tortured in a way she hadn't. But he had a soul that bounced back from trauma. She wished she knew how he did it.

Grania had lost Earth. Every night her dreams reminded her. Every noise she heard made her jump as if she were still in that camp, where any moment could be her last. "Nervy," Dal said.

Her loss didn't fade over time. The numbness wore off, but the loss remained. She put up barriers to protect herself, making sure she never lost sight of the fact that she was from Earth, born on Earth, even though Earth was now a desolate waste.

"I can't bear to lose everything again," she said. She said it as contemptuously as she dared.

Dal's warmth was replaced by tightened lips. "Are you nearly ready to go down and greet our guests?"

"Just as long as I have this damn outfit sorted."

Dal moved to check her dress, twitching here, straightening there. "You need a maid," he commented, and went for the powder. "I don't understand why you refuse one."

"No powder," Grania commanded. "I am told it is not de rigueur these days."

"And you speaking as if you had never left Earth is not de rigueur either, but it is flouting fashion."

"Damned if I care," said Grania. "Don't push me."

Dal shrugged his shoulders. When Grania was like this, there was no arguing with her. He watched her as she grouched her way out of their private quarters. Once he was sure she was out of earshot, he called his manservant. "Take this," he said. "Check with Vlasha – find out what she knows about it."

"I have already done that, sir."

"And?"

"It's none of ours."

"Find out more. We need to know. This newspaper is a strange piece of work."

Livia's entrance put an end to Dal's investigation, and he motioned Qan and the paper to the door.

Livia had come to gloat. Dal wasn't surprised. There was no way Livia would visit without at least three reasons.

She had brought her new protégée. Between them they quietly asserted their superiority. They had also come to let Dal know that they could help a person from his world who was in trouble. Dal was torn. He didn't want Livia's help, not under any circumstances. But he hadn't heard that there was a problem. Something wrong with my sources, he thought and wondered what he could do.

Livia didn't even say "from your world." She called it "one of your set," intentionally ignoring social norms from off-Ceres.

Before he could commit himself to indebtedness and evil politics, Grania entered. He thanked all his deities for his canny manservant

Grania was remarkably even-tempered. In fact, she waltzed into the drawing room with some of her old style, the one he had fallen in love with on newscasts before she ever appeared on New Ceres. There was a life about her and a glow that no-one else in the universe possessed. Even injured, she was more than anyone else could ever be.

He looked across at Livia, nervously. He didn't want Grania to suffer by Livia seeing her as competition. There was no apparent problem, however.

Livia wasn't going to talk to Grania about Dal's people, either, which was a good thing. Time, he thought, gratefully, this gives me time. Time to find out. Time to stay out of debt. Time to help his person, whoever it was and whatever trap they had crawled into.

Livia's diversion was itself a baited trap, but a minor one. The new protégée, Maria, sat quietly while Livia talked politics, but the moment Grania was in the room her butterfly-gentleness was brought to the fore, as if Grania were a patron and Maria needed her support. Maria's hands sat elegantly on her lap, only emerging briefly and shyly. Her eyes fluttered trustingly at Grania. Her voice softened and every word she spoke was tinged with gratitude for favours not yet given.

Dal subsided into the background, moving to the safety of an occasional table and Mr F's most recent newspaper. He pretended to read, but he watched covertly and listened carefully. He wanted to know how and why Livia was doing this. Maria's eyes and soft face might look like a butterfly's, but any protégée of Livia's was certain to sting like a wasp.

"She's going to Hightown," said Livia, "to be finished."

"Like your daughter?" Grania asked, in all innocence.

"Different subjects, I think, and a different school, but she'll keep an eye on Esther for me. Won't you, my dear?"

"Yes, ma'am," Maria responded obediently. A little lamb.

Grania asked her about Hightown. Maria explained (after a small but not subtle nod from Livia) that it was a town full of schools, where the nobility learned what the nobility must learn, protected from the dangers of politics and plots.

Poor little soul, thought Grania. Hightown sounded like all the worst elements of a school or university city with absolutely none of the redeeming features. After talking to Maria for a little Grania's thoughts became Poor Hightown. Maria knew exactly what her impact would be on the place and on its people.

After a little, other guests arrived. Livia moved her protégée on to chat with the newcomers, Maria looking smug. Grania flirted with the idea of politics for just a second.

"Care to go to Hightown for a few days?" she asked her husband, quietly.

Dal looked at her intensely. He wanted to know what Grania thought. He needed to know how much danger she would put herself into, through her innocent interest in this new society. He pretended he hadn't listened to the conversation. "What's at Hightown?"

"It's where Livia's new charge will be studying."

"All the children of the nobility go there."

"Don't be so dismissive," Grania scoffed. "The young lady over there told me she intends to become a great poisoner."

"She hasn't been with Livia long," said Dal.

"Just a few days. How did you guess?"

"Poison is not something to be proud of in her circles, it's something one does as if by nature."

"You're joking," Grania was horrified.

"No, I'm not. If you want a holiday we can go to the spas

on New Switzerland, but if your only contact in Hightown is one of Livia's, then we shall avoid Hightown entirely."

"I only wanted to see what happened when young Ms Hopeful hits other kids her age."

"I don't want to see what happens to innocents when surrounded by Family politics," Dal said grimly.

"We should put in a word and save her."

"I don't mean Livia's young monster, my love. I mean you."

Dal chucked her under the chin and Grania reacted by saying "Don't do that. I'm not your pet." She picked up a small ornament and tossed it gently from hand to hand, all the time watching Dal's face.

She was pleased to see that he was wary. She walked her whole life with caution – it was about time Dal started sharing it. She felt both guilty and defiant for thinking this, but some of her responses were strange to her. Had been strange ever since the beginning of the end, when the aliens and their allied humans landed on Earth to 'free' it. Grania shook off the mood. Things were better; her reactions weren't showing it yet. That was all. She put the ornament on the nearest flat surface and focussed again on her guests.

Grania spent the next half-hour watching Livia and Livia's new child out of the corner of her eye. She slowly realised how very naïve she had been. Not for the first time, she wished her life would take back some of its melodrama and let her quietly work in her studio. Tomorrow, she promised herself, fiercely. Tomorrow I shall spend the whole day in the studio. I shall create that changing light using watercolours. I shall. I will. I must.

That changing light had become critical. Grania was certain that if she could create the effect using the old media, she would repossess part of her soul. Turner. She thought of

Turner and wondered if this archaic society had any books on his techniques.

While she was watching Livia and dreaming of light, she half-noticed a man of medium build watching her. His movement was smooth and silent, like a cat, and, like a cat he was focussed on her to the exclusion of all else.

A little later, Grania was wondering why she let herself get distracted. Everyone knew that her salons were not salons for politics, and yet her friends and supporters exchanged pieces of paper surreptitiously, smiling or frowning over them. If they wanted politics, she thought raggedly, they could have gone to a coffee house.

Today was becoming one of those days that never ever should have happened. She wondered, blasphemously, if she could go to bed now, and pretend this salon had never opened its doors.

An instant later she was called to the entrance to the room. Lady C had arrived.

Even Grania knew this meant her salon was 'made' and that it was now a particular stop on the social circuit. Lady C's opinion on any matter of etiquette was law. Her innovations quickly became custom. This was why Livia had turned up with the new lamb.

Grania, however, refused to kowtow to anyone. She welcomed Lady C in her typical way, warmly, but without gush. She couldn't help noticing that everyone watched Lady C and that Lady C was watching her. The universe was full of eyes.

Lady C was gracious about the welcome. She made Grania think that ordinary politeness was quite sufficient between two people destined to see more of each other. They talked for a few minutes then Lady C moved on, leaving Grania dazed. She didn't know how she was dazed or what she had done, but somehow she had passed a test. And everyone knew it.

Dal, in fact, came up to her when the crowd was less and whispered a "Very well done, my dear," in her ear.

"I didn't do anything." Grania was frustrated. How could she win a battle without even entering the war.

"That's the point, I think," her husband answered. "You were the hostess and you behaved perfectly towards a new acquaintance."

"Everyone was expecting me to instantly become a fawning fangrrl, weren't they?" Grania felt accusatory and then felt a twinge of guilt for feeling so.

"'Fangrrl' is something I do not know, but yes, most of your guests expected you to fawn. As a newcomer of uncertain status..."

"I was expected to suck up bigtime." And now Grania was angry. "Except I'm not of uncertain status. My background is perfectly respectably–"

"Middle class," her husband finished. "Your art only goes a certain distance to excuse you from that. Your manners will have to take you the rest of the way. And just now, my love, your manners were perfect."

"I hate you, you know," Grania informed her husband, her voice carefully emotionless. He kissed her hand, whispered a promise for the night, and returned to his perfect social behaviour.

Grania knew the art of keeping an eye on key concerns while holding intelligible conversations. It was a skill she'd learned at her exhibitions. She wanted to know real reactions to her creations and was always trapped by people who wanted to know where she got her ideas from. She used this skill to keep an eye on Lady C. With the same corner of attention, she noticed that the man who had watched her earlier was watching her again. She'd seen him at her previous salon, too. I wish he would just get himself introduced. Then I could tell him I don't like being stared at, even by someone wearing beautiful clothes.

Lizzie was there, as usual. Lizzie dabbled in watercolour and had a certain talent, so Grania made her welcome despite other new friends suggesting that Lizzie was not a useful addition to her social dignity. What Grania found interesting, was that Lizzie and Lady C avoided each other's eyes. It was noticeable.

Grania was certain Lady C would be scrupulously polite should there chance to be an introduction. She did wonder, however, about the correct procedure should Lady C and the woman rapidly becoming the city's most notorious high-level prostitute be forced together. She also wondered what the correct way of getting rid of Lizzie was, should she need it.

So much for her sophisticated grasp of New Ceres' manners. She could see Lizzie and Lady C being pushed closer together by her very curious other guests. There was about to be a scene and Grania could do nothing.

Grania nearly giggled as she wondered if she should ask Lady C what to do. Lady C, after all, was expert at advising on how to avoid social solecism. She had a regular column in Mr F's most respectable paper.

Such a small woman, though, to hold so much dignity. Those eyes saw everything and accounted for everything.

Grania swallowed her laugh and moved towards Lizzie, hoping to change the direction of her motion away from Lady C. If they did actually meet, then the likelihood was quite high that Grania's salons would be the talk of the town and even higher that the wrong crowd would descend on her. This was probably why Lizzie should not be there. She was damned, though, if she had to give Livia time and space and not give the same to Lizzie.

Besides, she thought as she edged closer, there but for the grace of God and Dal, go I. Although I doubt I would do it nearly as well as Lizzie. The thought brought her three steps away from her target.

In an instant, her problem was solved. I didn't even have to take those last steps, she wondered. Lizzie was escorted out the front door by Dal's manservant who was surely overstepping his role (yet again).

Grania turned back to Lady C. Lady C was deeply involved in a conversation with Constance. It was not a good conversation, but it was so strange a subject that Grania found herself listening rather than politely interfering.

Constance was prodding (unsubtly) for news of eligible bachelors. Lady C was scrupulously polite and entirely non-committal.

Again, the problem was solved before Grania could motivate herself to intervene. This time it was Lady C who sorted things out herself. Grania reluctantly found herself admiring the duchess of decorum.

"My dear, if you continue this conversation, I might be in danger of disbelieving you genuinely wish to marry." Constance gave her a sharp look and Lady C smiled sweetly.

"I hope that one of your status doesn't speak of these things," Constance said.

"My dear, a lady does not. A lady also does not mention dates, as you seem to do all too frequently."

"Dates?" Constance looked genuinely bewildered.

"2324 has no meaning. Nothing happened. Yet I have heard you mention it to three people today."

Constance looked puzzled. "I'm sorry, I can't recall having said 2324 at all."

Lady C smiled brilliantly. "I suggest you keep it that way."

"Especially in such mixed places as an artistic salon?"

"We understand each other, I think," and Lady C's air of kindliness was replaced by a sharp look for the barest moment.

Grania found the whole thing bewildering. From men to a nonsense about a date? That date stuck in her mind, though, and so did the conversation.

Later, much later, Grania found out about 2324. That was later, however. Within the hour, however, she reported the conversation to Dal who frustratingly refused to enlighten her. He merely looked intrigued and commented blandly "Is that so?"

"Is what so?"

"Nothing, my love."

"If it's nothing, why do you look so very happy to hear it?"

"You mistake, I think."

"You love saying that. I think you've read too much Georgette Heyer. Or maybe it's this society. Instead of reviving the real eighteenth century, they've revived Georgette Heyer's version of it."

"This conversation is no longer making sense."

"Yes, and do you know why?" Grania was suddenly angry. "Because you won't answer a simple question. Tonight, you sleep alone. My role model is Lysistrata."

"Who?"

"Oh, learn some bloody history! Not everything important to humans happened since your totally bloody colonisation."

Before she could lose her temper satisfactorily, a hullaballoo intervened. Dal and she exchanged a glance and threw themselves into the noisy group from different directions.

Instantly the room quietened and within a few short minutes, Dal had elicited the order of events and Grania had obtained the offending papers. Grania felt like a high school teacher. She wanted to tell Dal that he did 'bossy' particularly well. It would annoy him to be told so, which tempted her beyond reason. He loved being quietly commanding but never 'bossy'. She stored the thought for next time.

What they uncovered was a small scandal. Three different leaflets. The doctor, Benjamin (who Grania couldn't stand, though she was supposed to enjoy his company, since they were both Earthers) had stupidly brought one and given it to Josephine. It had been bad enough that Josephine and Livia had turned up, since the last thing either Grania or Dal wanted was a salon of high politics. Art was the order of the day, and culture.

She and Dal would have to have a talk.

Dr Benjamin had been sucking up to Josephine and Josephine had used the leaflet as a chance to make a bit of a show. She had explained to Dal how iniquitous it all was. Dal tore up all the leaflets unexamined, listened to Josephine very closely while he walked her to the door. He convinced her to leave.

"You need peace and quiet," he said "All these awful papers are evil and wrong and I can promise you I will never let them in here, knowingly." After a few minutes, she left and the drama fled the room with her.

Grania heaved a sigh of relief. Her impossible husband knew just what he was doing, as he usually did. Mostly usually. Just not with her. She turned to other guests and spent the rest of the afternoon redirecting conversation into safe channels.

In the meantime, Vlasha had found Dal and taken him quietly aside.

"Your man sent for me. I don't know a thing about that newspaper article." She sounded as if it were a personal offence that something could happen in Prosperine and she not know.

"Good," he said. "There is something else. Another paper has just appeared. If you don't know about this one, then I rather suspect we have a problem on our hands."

"That was what Josephine was fussing about?" she asked. Dal nodded, and Vlasha frowned at the torn paper. "Highwaymen," she said.

"Yes. Very romantic."

"Not us."

"Then take all our people off the roads, as soon as you can. If these fools want to play at highwaymen games then they may."

"Yes, sir. And if we need distractions?"

"Then find something else. A balloon ascension, perhaps? Something that has no air of illegality. We cannot afford to play that game if other people have entered it. And this is a hell of a place to have this conversation."

Vlasha looked around the room with an air of superiority. "The only people these society folk pay attention to is themselves."

Dal sighed. "These are my friends, Vlasha."

"Sorry, sir." But she wasn't, and they both knew it.

Dal's lips twitched in a fraction of a smile. "Just for that you can mingle for the next little while. Minimise the impact of the highwaymen, if you can."

"Yes, sir."

"And tell me why you keep calling me 'sir.'"

"Because you've forbidden me to call you 'Your Grace,' sir."

"I'm not either. Not here and now. Never again. That's one thing we have left behind us. See me in the library before you leave."

"Yes... sir." With that last taunt, Vlasha lost her pretty self in the crowd of artists and writers.

Grania, in the meantime, took a few minutes for herself. She took her stolen time in her study. This afternoon there was too much happening at once and she wanted a moment to think it through. She also wanted a separation from the incessant head-banging grumble of sound that the salon had turned into. I want to be less flavour-of-the-second soon, she told herself. Then she hid her head in the leaflet someone had handed her.

Someone walked up behind her and gently rubbed her neck.

"Are you ill?" asked her husband.

"If I'd known what a torment a salon could be, I never would have hosted one," Grania said.

"It will ease off soon. Something else will seize society's interest."

"Then I'll stop getting everyone and anyone here?"

"In a few months."

"Well, I wish society would decide on a new fascination before then." Grania threw the sheet of paper on her desk. "We're being used as a place to pass information, disseminate gossip, and propel rumours into reality."

Dal looked down at her, a smile in his eyes. "Why do you say that?"

"Read it." Before he had time to do more than scan the first paragraph she interjected, "The salons would be less of a trial to me if you stopped putting us in so much potential danger."

Dal was amused. "None of mine," he whispered to Grania.

"I don't care. I've had enough of being scared."

Dal looked down at her in sudden consternation. "Oh God, I forgot."

"Carried away by the heat of the moment?" said Grania.

"I hope you meant that sarcastically."

"I didn't. It's like when you married me. The moment is all. And you never care about consequences."

"Oh, I care," said Dal. "And marrying you was the wisest thing I ever did."

Grania turned away quickly, so that Dal couldn't see her tears.

She didn't want him to know just how much regret she felt for the romance of that first day. She would make this marriage work the way all the wealthy on New Ceres made marriages work: through charm and determination. Love was obviously only on one side - no matter what reassurances her husband gave - and she would have to learn to live with it. Her husband was in love with his politics and his secrets. Everything else was words to him.

"I can provide a distraction," Dal said, as if it would solve everything. "I will arrange some friends to hold a hot air balloon display. A series of them. The chattering classes will be drawn there, I'm sure."

"And that will solve all?" Grania didn't feel conciliatory.

Before Dal could say anything to resolve things or make matters worse, the next complication descended on them.

Vlasha and Qan were waiting for Dal in the library.

Just as Vlasha commented to Qan, "That Grania certainly believes in owning books," Dal entered. Both of them stood up, and bowed their heads respectfully. Dal looked irritated.

Vlasha said, "There's no-one here to see. You can't expect us to give up everything!"

"I thought that was the whole point of secrets and plots," Dal said, wearily, "That we gave up appearances so that we could push this idiot society in a saner direction."

Qan smiled serenely, "This means we should stop goading you? I shall miss your teacherly reactions, then."

Dal tilted his head towards Vlasha. "She was serious."

He sat down and the other two waited a miniscule period of time before they followed. Dal sighed again. This time he rather thought both of them were serious. "Tell me the situation."

"We rather think we've found a group trying to change New Ceres."

"How much like us?"

"We don't know yet. Certainly, some of their targets are ours, but it's an aristo group, we think, so it must entail some self-preservation."

"We think they're more interested in safe food than a better-governed society," added Vlasha.

Dal looked thoughtful. "The way the Six work, they might be linked. Do you know that the Six is not entirely hereditary?"

"How can a set of families not be hereditary?"

"When the Lady or Lord Governor can appoint a new head to any of them. When every single one of the Six believes devoutly in assassination."

"Not every single one," Qan's face was quiet, despite the big statement.

"Lady C?"

"She's not one of the Six. She's one of the old families. An aristo. They have a great deal of social status, but don't control the paid officials."

"I knew that," Dal was irritated. "The Six don't have titles. The Six use first names or use Madame and Monsieur. But Lady C is given so much respect..."

"You forgot," prompted Vlasha.

"Lady C is your equivalent, in a way."

"How do you mean?"

"If this planet is destroyed, she and hers will survive. She has everyone's respect."

"But she's a rebel? Who else?"

"That's what we were trying to say," Vlasha sounded annoyed. But then Vlasha always sounded annoyed. "We think that Livia's daughter might be involved."

"Holy Gods!"

"That's what we thought," said Qan.

"Constance, too."

"So two of the Six and one of the pre-Enlightenment aristos. Interesting."

"What worries me is that the rebels, and Livia, use your wife's salon."

"That was one of my hopes in setting it up: there aren't many truly neutral places on New Ceres. There are the coffee houses, which are unpredictable and public, and now there is Grania's salon. I expect they will continue to appear."

"We can listen for that code of theirs."

"Yes, Vlasha, we can. In fact, I thought we were. Have we made any progress on what 2324 means?"

"None. We can ask them."

"You are a naïve, Vlasha."

"What? What did I say?"

"We will contact them when we know more. I'm not convinced they're safe to work with. Their operations are surprisingly transparent."

"To us, sir," reminded Qan. "I don't believe their own people have so much as noticed them."

There was a small silence while Dal thought. "We shan't contact them yet. Vlasha, make sure there are enough of our people watching so we can extend our list and find out more."

"At least we know their code."

"Thanks to Grania."

"At least she's good for something besides warming your bed," muttered Vlasha.

Both men turned to Vlasha with very cold looks.

"I don't like her," Vlasha sounded a little defensive.

"And she doesn't like you, but she doesn't tell the whole world."

"So who's behind it all?" Qan was an expert at providing just enough distraction to calm the waters.

One by one they went through everyone they knew, from the improbable (Lady C and her ilk) through the unlikely (the Constances of this world) to the uncomfortable (the Alphonses). They stuck at Alphonse for a moment. In the end they decided that he was obvious, but too interested in self-aggrandisement to be the real threat.

"We're skating around it," Dal said. "If we say her name it won't make her appear."

"Did you know," Qan said, almost conversationally, "That there is a group of food workers who use her name as a curse? I discovered this just the other day."

"Why do they use her name as a curse?" Dal humoured his man's thread of thought.

"She was a senior representative for the Six Families in the food industry until recently. She's 'moving on' as they say here, but until recently she was responsible for food safety."

"How many people died?"

"None, by violence or intentional poisoning. Many indirectly. They lost their jobs and she made sure they didn't get another one. They couldn't afford treated food."

"This system is evil!" Vlasha's passions ignited again. This time Dal thought she had reason.

"Let us watch Livia then, above all others. She may be the hardest to watch, but she's certainly the most likely." Dal suddenly remembered a number. "Don't take your gaze off Lady C, either."

"I still think that's a false lead," said Vlasha.

"Maybe," Qan shook his head in thought, "And maybe not. She appears kindly enough."

"Although she's not beyond affectation," Dal noted. "Does anyone know her real name?" One by one he checked his colleagues' face: they were all blank.

"Does it matter?" asked Qan.

"That's the question. We're having this conversation because of something she said in my wife's salon. We can't dismiss her without checking. She may be an enemy, but it's also possible that she's a potential ally. We need more information."

From there they made a list of other potential allies, starting with establishment people who were linked to the number 2324.

"No-one approach them. We need to know more," concluded Dal.

"What do we need to know most?"

"What that date means. If it's symbolic, it will help us decide if they're useful to us or a subset of the establishment. Vlasha, you do it. Compile reports from the others and do your own investigations. Whatever you do, don't give even a hint we exist. I want to know about that date, but not at the price of revealing ourselves too early. Now, Qan, report."

"We're doing well, particularly in the west. Two of the proto-colonies are almost self-sufficient."

"That's excellent," said Dal. "How long?"

"Very soon. Their structures look old enough and their 'history' is complete, so that when the government discovers them, they ought to fully qualify for autonomous status. We only want one of them to be found, however, because of the other's spaceport."

"Spaceport?" Vlasha looked surprised.

"Every group of our settlements has one, you should know that, Vlasha."

"I knew it on paper. I had no idea we had advanced that far."

"How do you think we set-up an 'ancient' colony that would pass the Lady Governor's scrutiny?"

"I hadn't thought about that. That's all. No big deal." Dal looked intently at Vlasha for a moment, as if he were gauging her soul with his deep searching eyes, and then he allowed things to move on.

"If you truly want us to stop thinking of you as our lord, you really should stop doing that... sir," said Qan, not at all deferentially.

Vlasha ignored them both and fretted. "How do we get spaceports on this cloistered planet?"

Dal took a deep breath and Qan leaped in. "Read some local history, woman. New Ceres closed our region to settlement very, very early. There were issues. Food issues, for one. The government here has developed a fear of even monitoring the wilds. It wouldn't know what colour the sky was in wild zones without extrapolation."

Vlasha looked ready to explode: Dal spoke up before she could blast words at Qan. He really could have done without bickering today. "So we can get people to and from the planet without the Lady Governor knowing."

"Yes, sir. We're using the refugees' skills."

"When will they be prosperous enough to accept more people?"

"It's a matter of months, sir."

"Then the loss of the diversions on the highways isn't the end of everything."

"It won't even dent our activities," said Dal's manservant.

"Pity we couldn't reach this stage before Earth fell," Dal was sarcastic.

"We couldn't do a thing until we found a way to process the damned food, sir."

"He's right, sir," Vlasha looked as if it gave her indigestion to have to agree with someone. "We needed the new technology."

"I know. It doesn't make the loss of billions of humans easier to bear."

"You take too much responsibility on your shoulders."

"Do I? I've come to believe I scarcely take enough. Have our scouts look for other habitable places that are out of satellite and freighter sight paths."

"Why, sir?" asked Vlasha. "These towns can take hundreds of thousands each."

"They may have to, long term. Right now I'm more worried about not creating technological hotspots. We can hide only a certain amount."

The door opened and Grania came in, carrying a tray with drinks.

"Can't you get a maidservant to do that?" asked Vlasha, slightly irritably.

"I could," Grania said, calmly, "But I'm not you."

"These arcane Earth customs only go so far before they entirely annoy me," Vlasha said.

"It's just as well I observe them," Grania said to Dal, rather than to Vlasha. "Otherwise we might be catfighting or duelling, since almost everything you say to me suggests I am an inferior being."

"If there's a duel, I'll fight for you," offered Dal's manservant.

"If there's a duel I'll know it's Vlasha's fault and she will cease to have entrance to this house." Dal sounded very firm.

Grania gave her husband a timid smile and he gently put his arm around her waist.

Vlasha gave the two a small, tight bow and left.

"I think you've upset her," suggested the manservant.

"I think she upset Grania," said Dal.

"And his high graciousness is not amused."

"If you want secret meetings, then you could lock the door," observed Grania. "Then I'll know if Vlasha is wearing her polite face or if she's going to pick on me."

Grania couldn't work out which of the several possibilities implied by her statement had caused the looks of astonishment on their faces, but she rather hoped it was the sound of a mouse roaring.

10

'THE DEVIL RAT MY SOUL IF THE LADY POWEL BE NOT DEAD WITHIN THESE 3 WEEKS'

ote on file copy: Key extracts only. These have been authenticated as seventeenth and eighteenth century English texts. This has been verified by several researchers. It is possible that they are being used as commentary on current events as the dissidents see them. We cannot find the authors or printing press. Hold on file. Withhold action until more known.

The tryall and examination of Mrs. Joan Peterson, before the Honorable Bench, and the Sessions house in the Old-Bayley, yesterday; for her supposed witchcraft, and poysoning of the Lady Powel at Chelsey: together with her confession at the bar

The witch of Wapping, Or An exact and perfect relation, of the life and devilish practises of Joan Peterson, that dwelt in Spruce Island, near Wapping; who was condemned for practising witch-craft, and sentenced to be hanged at Tyburn, on Munday the 11th. of April, 1652. Shewing, how she bewitch'd a child, and rock'd the cradle in the likenesse of a cat; how she frighted a baker; and how the devil often came to suck her, sometimes in the likeness of a dog, and other times like a squirrel. London :
Printed for Th. Spring, 1652.

'the woman was condemned for Witchcraft, and seemed to be very much dejected, having a melancholy aspect: she seemed to be not much above 40 years of age, and was not in the least outwardly deformed, as those kind of creatures usually are'

11

"THE DEVIL RAT ALPHONSE'S SOUL"

Vlasha's great strength was her ability to keep an idea in the back of her mind and to poke at it when she could. Thus it was that she kept 2324 in the back of her mind. When she saw a client, she would talk about New Ceres' history almost casually, soliciting information for various dates at random and using as a cover the explanation that "I've missed so much by not being brought up here, you see. I want to catch up."

One patient bought her a book. Another took to bringing her articles from the paper and copies of the more historical broadsheets. Not a soul reacted to 2324 in any interesting manner. They did, however, react to the woman herself. The queries and conversations opened them to talking about her medical status and to finding out more about her techniques.

Now, Vlasha's medical status was something she was supposed to keep quiet. Dal had advised her of this over and over again. "New Ceres likes everything to be from Earth," he would say.

"Most of what I do is from Earth," Vlasha was always impatient. Always.

"Not from Europe and most definitely not from the eighteenth century."

"Older, in fact." They had this conversation so many times, and always Vlasha managed to inject some gloating.

"Vlasha," Dal would say. "These people don't care about older. They care about England, and they care about France, and they care about the eighteenth century."

"I don't use techno stuff: I'll be fine."

"Promise me that you'll at least keep up a pretence of having your patients over to visit rather than for treatment?"

"Living the lie," Vlasha was scornful. Ever and always. Scornful.

"The operative word there is 'living'."

Dal remembered that conversation when he paid a visit one day.

Vlasha opened the door herself and promptly started to complain. "Today isn't a good day, sir. Things are busy. Sorry about the mess."

She didn't wait for Dal to explain his business (which could have been done at the door) but ushered him into a very crowded living room. There was a gentleman sitting uncomfortably on a chair too small for him, and a half-undressed lady occupying the settee. Scattered in some mysterious order were jars and rocks and various strange implements.

Dal stood and looked at it, relishing the scene. He only wished Grania could see it with him. He memorised it to describe it to her, later on. The lady had pulled her dress into a near-semblance of respectability, and she was flushed from doing it. Neither she nor the gentleman would look at him.

"The trouble with a divided house," Vlasha complained, "Is there is no privacy. I need two extra rooms, one for treatment and a waiting room for a client's spouse." She glared significantly across at the man. This is when Dal realised that it was not his own presence that was troubling Vlasha – it was the fact that the husband was present for the treatment. He carefully hid his smile.

"If my wife was in a state of undress, you could work behind the drawn curtains," the spouse of the ill said, brusquely. "I see no other need."

"Where I come from we work in offices, and alone. We respect the privacy of our patients."

"Where you come from is not here. If my wife didn't want to see you, I would find a New Ceres' practitioner, but she claims that you help her megrims and so I must tolerate you. Tolerate, you understand, does not mean give in to your whims and fancies. Whims and fancies from a far planet, might I add, and of no relevance to New Ceres."

Vlasha didn't ask Dal what he wanted or, in fact, give him an opening to volunteer the information. Not that he could have explained a thing with strangers present. He decided the best approach was to wait quietly and be polite until Vlasha's patient and the husband of the patient left.

It was a strange hour. Vlasha used the array of materials near the settee to treat first one patient and then a series of others. At no stage was he left alone with Vlasha and at no stage did anyone say a word to him. Dal soon became used to the drift of folks and the quiet murmur and the fact that strangers treated him as part of the furniture. It rather reminded him of his childhood at court, in fact. This was a reminder he could have managed without.

Eventually, to Dal's surprise, Alphonse drifted in with a friend. Dal noticed that he alone saw Dal sitting quietly in a corner. He greeted him with a curt nod, and Dal leaned forward as if to rise from his chair then sat again. The greeting of people who knew each other, but who did not want to extend the acquaintance.

Dal distrusted Alphonse deeply, and was not pleased to see him at Vlasha's. He wondered how much politics Vlasha really understood. The fact that she had independently escaped to New Ceres, he realised, might not make her as sophisticated as she acted.

Dal began to watch Alphonse's body language very closely.

It was worrying. When she worked, the patient took all her attention. Vlasha was entirely unconscious of Alphonse, the same way she was still entirely unconscious of Dal. Dal noticed that Alphonse reacted to some aspects of Vlasha's treatment, and not others. When he reacted, it was with eagerness. Noting it. His eyes looked greedy when Vlasha did some simple manipulation and when she clicked on a small gadget to help adjust the spine, he looked like the cat that had swallowed the cream.

"How modern is that technique?" he asked.

"Oh, old," said Vlasha absently.

Alphonse looked disappointed. When Vlasha placed the gadget on an occasional table, he picked it up and played with it and admired the metal in the light and for a moment looked quite smug.

Finally, Alphonse and his friend left. Dal obtained Vlasha's notes on recent conversations and he left, very concerned. He would have been even more concerned if he had known that Alphonse came back the next day, alone.

Alphonse was very courteous and instigated a lively conversation with Vlasha. After he left, Vlasha got to think-ing. She decided it was best to write it up and make sure it reached Dal. She would rather have reported it herself, but there was no time for an appointment and he only visited each of them once a month himself. Mind you, this was more than any other ex-noble did. He would never understand that they respected his station because he had never left his duties and responsibilities behind.

That night, Qan checked the incoming information, making notes in cipher and burning the original, page by page.

"Aren't there better ways of doing this?" teased Dal, regularly.

"Quite possibly," Qan answered, "But none of them are as much fun."

This note was not much fun. It informed him that Alphonse was interested in Dal and in Vlasha. Or maybe it simply meant Alphonse was still besotted with Grania. When Dal came into his study to get a book, Qan told him as much.

"Can you summarise the note for me? Quickly. Grania is waiting and she is a little tetchy. I believe someone cleaned a palette or tidied a desk."

"I know exactly who it is. She pays even less attention to Grania's instructions than the rest of the staff. I might send her to the country."

"Do that. While you're at it, remind the rest of the staff that Grania is their mistress, even if she doesn't manage matters directly. In the meantime, what does Vlasha say?"

"Not enough," grunted Qan. "She told Alphonse that both of you come from Holotor. He said that you were a minor noble and she told him you were the King's close relative. Damn fool. She claimed she wasn't paying attention. She says that this is the only bit of the whole conversation that wasn't public knowledge and that she has no concerns on the matter."

The next day Vlasha wasn't so sanguine. She was, in fact,

in court, answering a summons. Qan and Dal only heard about the summons after the day's proceedings had begun.

"This is very quick action by Alphonse," said Dal on the way to the courtrooms.

"Too quick. It's to stop her getting help."

They hurried, but still arrived after the preliminaries.

Expert testimony was brought early in the New Ceres' legal system and by the time Dal and Qan had found a seat at the back of the wood-panelled room, Dr Benjamin was seated before the judge, answering questions.

"Yes, I know something of these techniques," he said, just as the two sat down.

"Do you use them?"

"No, I was trained in traditional medicine."

"Traditional medicine?"

"As practised on Earth in the mid twenty-first century. Holistic varieties of medicine are only brought in when scientific approaches fail to achieve their goals."

"Holistic?"

"What this lady does. On a base that is theoretically traditional, she uses a combination of faith healing and manipulation of the musculo-skeletal system to encourage the body to heal."

"And that's all?" The questioner sounded disappointed.

"No, the rest of her system fuses diagnosis and treatment from Ayurvedic and Chinese traditional systems."

"How does that differ from your traditional system?"

"Mine is Western, like the culture of New Ceres, for one thing. And it relies on the late modern scientific method."

"Which means?"

"My medicine is better tested than hers, with proper method and checks."

"Does her method work?"

"I have no idea. We did a unit on something similar when I was at university, but only on the Earth variant."

"Let me ask you something more important, then," and the judge leaned forward to emphasise that this question was a crucial one. "What are the dates of Dr Vlasha's system?"

"I don't know that you can call her 'Doctor'" argued Benjamin. "She has no Earth-equivalent qualifications."

"I understand she was trained by apprenticeship. We accept that, within limitations. Her training is not currently the issue."

"Not? Then what is?"

"When were her treatments brought into modern or near-modern form?"

"How the hell should I know?"

"If you do not even know why you should know, then why are you seeking citizenship?" All eyes turned to Benjamin.

"My citizenship application is at the earliest of stages."

"It is on my desk, in fact," said Justice Harber, ironically. "Since I had to approve you to give testimony today. Believe me, I would not have done so if I had known how very ignorant you were of the fundaments of our New Enlightenment. Let me explain it at a level that perhaps suits your advanced inter-galactic intellect." He paused for effect.

"You were not asked to testify about the effectiveness of the medical techniques. You were asked when they were in common use on Earth. That is all – absolutely all – I am interested in at this time. So tell me, young doctor, when were these techniques you describe in popular use on Mother Earth?"

Benjamin started confidently and well. "Some of them go back to Ancient China and India. We were taught that they might be traceable back over two thousand years." Within moments, however, he became very, very muddled. He had slept through his history lectures and had not taken up options that dealt with variants on other planets. He was so used to measuring medicine for its effectiveness and its relationship to the health system he was trained in that he was totally unable to make the switch to historical explanation that Justice Harber demanded.

Alphonse leaned forward at first, and it was almost inevitable that the leaning would take him further and further forward and until he found himself standing. From there it was a mere five steps to the front of the court, where he pushed Benjamin aside and said, "I have something important to say."

Benjamin remained standing, Alphonse's humiliated shadow.

"This is all irrelevant," Alphonse said, with passion. "It is perfectly obvious to all intelligent beings that the woman, Vlasha is at the heart of an evil conspiracy of witches. We need to use her to flush out the others and to clear our society from this contamination. Justice Harber, I leave this task in your hands."

Alphonse returned to his seat, radiating certainty.

Harber's face was stony as he instructed Benjamin. "You will cease work as a doctor until you can convince me that you understand enough of our society to practise without yourself flouting our laws. You will not appear as an expert witness until that time. Your citizenship application will also be held until you can convince me you understand New Ceres and genuinely want to join our endeavour."

"If you don't know the dates for work of the woman on trial, it is to be presumed you don't know your own medical history. You, sir, are a disgrace to your profession."

He then addressed the crowd. "I find that this matter must come to trial due to the gravity of the accusations and due to the lack of suitable expert testimony. For her own protection, the accused will be placed in confinement until the trial itself. I will consult with the Esteemed Company of Judges whether I myself shall preside over the trial or whether another judge will be more suitable."

During the pause that followed this instruction, he called Alphonse over. "Next time, find a local as an expert witness. These strangers are unreliable at their best – they make useless toys and even worse tools." The justice was looking across at Alphonse's latest flirt.

Harber's comment hurt. Alphonse shook off the arm of his temporary woman. He tried to explain that the woman he was with was from an Outer Planet, as if it would make a difference, but he didn't get it out clearly and he knew it and he became increasingly fractious. Harber looked down at his friend and repeated "Don't use off-worlders. They're unreliable and stupid." He then walked away.

Alphonse took out his anger on his new woman. He became louder and more public in informing her over and over that she was only a sex object. "You're an off-worlder – you don't understand society well enough to give it dignity."

Harber hadn't gone far. He had taken himself to the nearest officer of the law and had informed her that Vlasha needed to be put in prison for her own safety.

"I fear the mob," he said with a nervousness that almost looked real. "The crowds deal with witches in a very evil way." The constable nodded. The crowds would deal with any number of things in a very evil way, and Justice Harber had just given her enough money to make sure it happened. Vlasha would be safe in prison and the streets would ferment against her. It was all the off-worlder's fault anyhow. It always was.

Normally the general public would have agreed with

Harber's internal sentiment and would blame off-worlders. Especially the more squidlike, who were blamed for losing Mother Earth. More and more the people of New Ceres saw their planet as the only one that had resisted all the blandishments of modernity and thus was the true inheritor of Earth. It was the human planet.

Perhaps, Grania thought, as she read about the riots and worried about Vlasha, it was the great power and idiocy of humans that they could do something as stupid as worry about witchcraft on a planet that claimed it was following a New Enlightenment. Food that poisoned and obviously witches were to blame, because, if it wasn't witches, it would have to be the government and the Lady Governor is the closest thing they have to God on this soulless lump of rock.

Why am I worried about Vlasha when we hate each other so very much? Why do we hate each other? I hate her because she hates me and she hates me because I'm not noble enough for Dal. How odd. I can't talk about Vlasha and myself, but I can ask about the witchcraft. And so she did.

It led to a gloriously pointless three part argument at first. Dal and she and Qan could find no understanding in this irrationality that had suddenly appeared in the middle of a contrived Age of Reason.

Dal maintained that superstition appeared because the whole society was contrived. Qan argued that this might have been true as recent as a hundred years ago, but that after two hundred years everyone was brainwashed and believed in the Age of Reason.

"Actually," said Grania, "They don't. They believe they're in the eighteenth century and they call it the New Enlightenment. If you look at the books, though, they're not all Voltaire. They're also Walpole."

"You always describe concepts using names of dead

people," complained Dal.

"What's wrong with that? They're interesting writers."

"Who but you reads them?"

"That's what I'm trying to say," Grania slowed down her impatience and looked her husband straight in the eye. "Some of those books play with notions of horror. Vampires were really and properly invented in the eighteenth century. Gothic everything. And there were witch trials."

"On Earth?" asked Qan, "In the eighteenth century?"

"Yep," and Grania felt strangely triumphant. Her particularly obscure taste in books was finally vindicated, as was the undergraduate literature she had studied before transferring to Art. "I can make you a reading list, if you like."

"Grania," said Dal, gently, "We do not read."

"You're perfectly literate. You read all those newspapers and broadsheets."

"We don't read books."

"We?"

"Anyone from Holotor. Our society is quite different to yours."

"Well, if you don't read then I can see how you'd miss the obvious. Also, you could be in trouble with the New Enlightenment. Everyone reads on New Ceres."

"You say this as if it's a good thing," said Dal, his mouth scrunched against a bad taste.

"Reading books is no solution to irrationality," added Dal's manservant.

Grania looked up at both of them and felt a familiar tightness in her stomach. These tall men and women were more foreign than they looked. She dealt with the feeling the way she always dealt, she talked. She rattled words out so quickly that the others were unable to break into her tirade.

"Not reading is hardly a solution to irrationality in an Age of Reason. And just because your people don't traditionally read, doesn't mean you should remain ignorant. It just adds to the problem, in fact. Look at what's happening, with Vlasha, with the witchcraft accusation, with everything. Humans are always destructive when they play this kind of politics. And if you read, you would know that once something like this gets started then it's infectious. Do you know how Earth was destroyed? How all the colonised worlds just sat back and watched while billions of people were slaughtered like so many sheep? It was because of attitudes like yours. 'We don't need to know how other people think. We're fine the way we are'. And once everyone started to hate and distrust and the Alliance started to fall apart, we started to die. All my family. Every one of my friends. Everyone I have ever met in my whole life. Dead."

Grania stopped suddenly, then stumbled on.

"Like an infection. Dead. When things fall apart a little, everything falls. Foreigners are all in danger." She stopped again. Dal and Qan watched her as if she were a killer rabbit. Monty Python, Grania thought. Why would these people know a thing about twentieth century literature when they didn't even read from the eighteenth?

"Do you know the irony?" A sudden thought hit her. "You're closer in culture to New Ceres, despite the book thing. You're hierarchical and political and self-absorbed. I'll lay you odds that panic about witches hits me before it ever hits you. Infection, you see. If I'm not careful they'll tell me I killed one planet and will kill me before I kill another. And it wasn't us at all. It was you lot who killed Earth, with neglect. Damn allies." And Grania swept herself up and out of the room before she could say anything more that she would regret.

"I didn't realise that she was so distressed."

"No, sir, she keeps quiet about it."

"Most of what she said was – of course - emotional tripe, but I fear she might be right about public accusations and anger. She hasn't done anything to deserve it, but she is visibly unique."

"I can set up watchers for her outside the house for the next month, sir. She will walk in safety and would be entirely unaware of what I have done."

"You're right, of course. If we tell her she will object. And maybe it will help her stop worrying." There was a trace of wistfulness in his tone.

"Genuine safety would be better for that," the manservant said, tartly. "We need to bring her into our plans. She was a freedom fighter back on Mother Earth, you know."

Dal shook his head and gave no commitment. "She's been through so much," was all he said.

Livia was puzzled too, though in an entirely different conversation.

Every single one of her informants and gossips told her about Alphonse's meeting with Vlasha. She wondered to herself what he was really up to. Something unsubtle, since it was Alphonse.

She couldn't see how it could concern herself, but, given he had made two obvious attempts at her life recently and might be behind the coffee house incident, she would watch events a bit more closely. The moment he took an official mistress or married, Alphonse would die, Livia decided. Alphonse had almost outlived his usefulness.

Time to let him know. Because it was Alphonse, she wouldn't even try subtlety. That's the way it had always been, after all.

She sent for him.

It was a simple meeting, in Livia's most formal room. From the moment he was ushered in, Livia could see his eyes roaming the pale blue and gold chamber, trying to discover a reason for his summons, trying to puzzle out why he was being treated so formally and coolly. Livia called for tea and the maid came in almost immediately.

This made Alphonse more nervous: Livia had obviously planned this. Yet, out of politeness, he had to wait until she broached the subject.

Damn, but he hated modern manners. If it were even twenty years ago he would have been able to ask directly what she wanted, but these days even close kin had to wait on the host's pleasure.

Livia's pleasure was not of the nicest kind. There was that particular smile she wore to discomfit people. A very small smile that suggested much evil. At least she wasn't wearing that in this damn frigid room.

She finally poured him a dish of tea. As she looked up to give it to him, she smiled, a small, still, insane smile. He nearly dropped his tea. You'd think I'd be immune to it. I've seen it often enough.

Alphonse shuddered and Livia noted that shudder. She remained silent, giving Alphonse the opportunity to recall every single event he associated with that smile. She had not thrown tantrums as a child or torn the wings off butterflies. She simply asked for things and if she did not receive them, she made sure that she would receive them the next time she asked. What, he wondered, would she ask of him?

Finally she said "My dear Alphonse." His flood of memories stopped short and he looked at her rather than at the fireplace behind her. "I thought you should be the first to know some thoughts I have been having about my relatives."

"Indeed?" Alphonse wondered why he had ever taken this woman for granted. Why he had ever thought of murdering her. It would have been better to set up a luxury life on New Switzerland than to have her look at him in that faintly inquisitive manner, carrying that particular smile.

"I fear that your dinner parties have become too déclassé for me. I fear I shall have to drop you."

Livia never dropped people. When they ceased to be of use they simply... his cup clattered to the floor and shattered.

"Excuse me," said Alphonse. "I forgot... I must leave... a meeting."

He ran out of the room and slammed the door.

"Pity," Livia said to herself, "that the set is now incomplete. I rather liked it." She rang the bell for the maid to clear up. "Don't eat from the tray," she suggested, kindly. "I suspect the food was not properly treated, and I would hate to see you ill." The maid, tight-lipped, merely nodded and started mopping the floor.

Livia could have told anyone who asked, that when Alphonse was scared he found a victim and yelled at them. If the yelling didn't work, he would use his fists. He had done this since his childhood. As an adult, he had become very proficient with those fists. No-one, however, asked.

Vlasha had enough in common with Alphonse to not be surprised when he visited her.

"This is for your own good," he said. "My advice may save your life, if you will take it."

"Your advice?" Vlasha was at her scornful best. "You're the one who had me arrested. The only thing your advice will do for me is get me killed in a more ugly way. I don't want you and I don't want your advice."

The next thing she knew, she was nursing her cheek and leaning against the wall. Alphonse was more scared than he had ever been in his life. Vlasha, however, was merely a little dazed.

"I've seen bullies like you before," she said. "During the war." Alphonse hit her twice, with his palms open. First the right hand connected with her right cheek, then the left. "Aren't you afraid there might be bruising?" she mocked.

Alphonse grinned in a friendly manner. "Aren't you afraid no-one will care?" he asked.

Vlasha squinted up at him, then screamed, carefully and calculatingly. The guards were there in an instant.

"Is there anything wrong, sir?" one asked.

"Not a thing," said Alphonse, full of bonhomie. "She needs a little discipline."

One of the guards left straight away, the other looked Vlasha up and down and bit his cheek, then looked across at Alphonse. He left.

"It helps to be one of the Six Families. We enjoy certain... freedoms in exchange for our work," Alphonse explained, and then proceeded to beat her up very methodically and rationally. He wasn't worried that Vlasha might scream. The mere feeling of flesh and bone relieved his tension. He left her battered, on the floor.

After a while the guard who almost stepped in came back and cleaned her up. He bandaged what could be bandaged and salved what could be salved. Then Vlasha was alone with her bruises.

She dozed on her hard pallet for a little, very aware of her body and very aware of how much she hated Alphonse. When the door opened, however, Vlasha was on her feet instantly, ready to face whatever came next. What came next was Alphonse again. This time he accompanied Justice Harber.

Harber explained himself as a witness. "For the trial, you

see. I need to be able to verify that your answers are not coerced." Vlasha snuck an almost-triumphant look at Alphonse, who appeared unworried. It was then that she realised that the violence had nothing to do with the trial. It was not torture. It was Alphonse letting off steam.

I hate New Ceres, she thought. Dal was right. It needs to develop compassion.

Over and over again Alphonse asked the same questions. What do you do? How do you do it? Is there magic involved in your rituals? Do you use medicines that were unknown in the eighteenth century? Do you use metals that were not used in the eighteenth century? Do you use off-planet drugs? Are your drugs derived from Earth originals? How far have they been adapted for other planetary conditions? Have you cultivated them on New Ceres?

Over and over again Vlasha admitted to exactly the same things.

"Yes, I used off planet cures and more recent alloys when I first came here."

"No, I do not know their history."

"I brought in seeds when I arrived on the planet and I grew the plants myself. No-one else was involved."

"When I found there were limitations on use of off-world substances, I torched the garden myself and I replaced new metal with old. I didn't find about the plants for a year because plants are low tech, but when I realised that it was possible that they had deviated from the Earth originals I realised I could not use them in my treatments."

"Of course, I do not use any witchcraft. Anything that looks like ritual is merely a part of my treatment methods."

Over and over again.

"I do not use any witchcraft, white or black."

"I have never used witchcraft of any variety."

"Witchcraft is hardly known where I come from."

"I was trained as a medical doctor under the apprenticeship system common to the three planets of Holotor."

No matter what she said, Alphonse cheerfully contradicted her. He explained to her over and over again that she was a witch. He had seen it, he claimed. He invented incidents that had happened, magic cures that had resulted from her medicine. Vlasha reiterated what she had said before.

Eventually, it became very dull. Vlasha simply lay down on her bed and faced the wall and refused to listen. Both Alphonse and the justice left. This time, Alphonse did not return.

The wait for the public trial was surprisingly short. Vlasha's bruises were livid and it still hurt to move, but she stood there as custom demanded, proud and upright before the three judges. Harber was the head judge, which did not surprise her. Vlasha was beyond surprise.

She was also beyond focus. Her mind drifted in a strange current. Testimony came and went. Arguments came and went. Vlasha would pick up a train of thought running from witness to witness and follow it, ignoring the main part of what the person said.

For instance, for a spell of time all she could hear were people implying or saying outright that folk from other planets were unreliable and that the ideas and the technologies of other planets were even more so. "Unsound" was a word that kept appearing.

"Use chiropracty along with an apprenticeship," a schoolteacher testified "And you might as well use crystal data storage. Where would we be with no printed books? How can we trust our doctors if they don't learn in a university, as the very best doctors did in the Golden Age?"

A little later she found her wayward mind listening to

stories of the use of her own magic. Alphonse had trained these witnesses very carefully. Vlasha resolutely turned her mouth down and listened disapprovingly to their testimony.

Alphonse and his stooges managed to insert strange detail into the testimony of two witnesses Vlasha had never met. An apparition, for instance, was apparently often seen in Vlasha's vicinity. It looked like a black cat and disappeared without warning. This was not the small, gentlemanly ginger feline that belonged to her neighbours, but a giant cat that stalked and glared with baleful gaze.

One witness claimed, more correctly, that Vlasha talked to animals. She apparently had a strange knowledge of off-planet politics (very strange, considering she herself was an off-worlder) and the doings of those better than herself.

Apparently, these expert witnesses knew for certain-sure of her pact with the Devil and of her intent to murder using medicines and help of the Devil. This latter caused a learned discourse between the three judges. They felt it important to determine whether it was possible to admit the Devil into the New Enlightenment.

Evidence concerning the prosecution of witches was brought forth by a rather antiquated gentleman, showing that this type of belief was sufficiently extant in the Old Enlighten-ment to be acceptable in court. Justice Harber professed himself not happy with this, as it countered the whole idea of Enlightenment, but conceded that historical reality must triumph over his personal feelings when determining what was acceptable to prosecute.

Livia came in to watch for a bit. Vlasha refused to look at her directly. She was reasonably certain that Livia and Alphonse were related to each other and if Alphonse was bad, Livia was worse and at that point, Vlasha just did not want to know. Since turning her head meant that her eyes were trapped seeing the bench of judges, she saw Harber's eyes go from Livia to Alphonse and back again, as if weighing them both on scales. Vlasha saw that Livia noticed this, also and thought I really need to let Dal know about this. Livia was merely giving orders to a maid.

Grania was there, too. At the back. Very quiet. Watching. Utterly horrified. She slipped out and asked the maid what Livia's orders were. She gave her very first bribe.

"Nothing much," said the maid, "I am to present a basket of pastries from her own household to the justice. The mistress says it's to sustain him during this difficult trial."

Grania couldn't face any more and so didn't go back in. There were people enough to take her seat.

Instead she took the long trek to the spaceport and found her usual chair at Trig's. Grania found a broadsheet at Trig's, too. It was not there at random. Someone knew her regular table and had placed a copy at her table, neatly. Grania looked at it and she wondered.

'The Devil rat my soul if the Lady Powel be not dead within these 3 weeks' Grania read.

Grania pondered in anger over the tale of The witch of Wapping, Or An exact and perfect relation, of the life and devilish practises of Joan Peterson, that dwelt in Spruce Island, near Wapping; who was condemned for practising witch-craft, and sentenced to be hanged at Tyburn, on Munday the 11th. of April, 1652.

It was interesting that Mrs Joan Peterson in once-upon-a-time England, had been on trial for witchcraft and poisoning. Vlasha's trial is so much like Joan Peterson's path, she thought. Was someone so very unimaginative that they couldn't think of how to persecute someone at all? Or was it a case of performance art? She guessed that Vlasha was on trial for witchcraft because poisoning and being poisoned was so commonplace on New Ceres.

She thought of the monks at Alphonse's eclipse dinner and the death inspired by them and realised that what was done reasonably subtly at the dinner party was being done very openly here. This pamphlet didn't change a thing.

With a start, she realised that she had almost come to accept the food-deaths amongst the poor and that half the worth of a job was safe food. She could never accept the social poisoning of high society. This was very wrong.

While the accusations didn't quite match the ones from court, the situation certainly did.

Alphonse had set Vlasha up for a fall. The object of the fall was to have Vlasha implicate someone. If she didn't, she would die. This leaflet was a warning to all who knew Vlasha that she was not being accused of witchcraft, she was being blackmailed by the State.

Alphonse was the link between the State and Vlasha, quite obviously.

How much do I know about Vlasha? wondered Grania. I know she's from the same planet as my husband and that she's involved in his schemes. That's the terrifying bit. Dal could be Alphonse's target. Or me.

Grania shuddered. She pocketed the leaflet and went home, where she could feel sick in private. Where the small society of this planet couldn't follow her to give her more hints and portents.

I need more information, she told herself. I've been on the edge too long. But how can I get information when my whole existence is managed by other people? There must be ways of gaining my independence even in this regressive society. And there must be ways into politics so that I can protect my own.

A small spark of Grania's previous self glimmered deep

inside. I wish I could do something for Vlasha and Alphonse's victim. I hope the target's not me or Dal. I hope. I hope. I'm too dependent. I need to change that, so that if ever this happens again, I have ways of helping and defending.

If it attacked her and hers, then at least she knew what the defenceless did. When she arrived home, she started packing an emergency kit.

"Qan, I want you to help me. I don't know if we'll need it, but I want all of us to be away in an instant if Dal is the target."

Qan silently nodded.

"Can you find a way to get as many of us off planet in a hurry if we need it?"

Qan nodded again, and they both went to work.

Grania had assessed the situation fairly. Dal would have agreed with the assessment, if she had shared it with him

Harber walked into the court with Alphonse, after a refreshment break. Dal nodded to himself: Alphonse and his pocket justice were behind everything. Alphonse walked Harber to his seat and, as they went along past the bench, he shook hands and exchanged pleasantries with almost everyone. The vast majority of them were his personal supporters.

When Harber brought up a new charge, the death of Lady Denman by unnatural causes, however, Vlasha was handed a paper from the floor. She gave it to the judge. It was signed by Lady Denman's regular physicians and it testified that she had died through natural causes.

Harber didn't even both calling in the physicians to testify. He dismissed the case for sorcery against Lady Denman out of hand. Dal noted this, too. The aristo connection was a strange one, never clear. Not even Harber would push too far along those lines.

And that was the day's proceedings.

Dal went home and was faced with Grania and the pamphlet. He wondered why the Lady Denman incident had even been raised in court. It was not one of the original charges and had no legs to stand on. Also, it seemed half the city knew about it before it appeared.

The next day was even less comfortable.

Since the Lady Denman assay, Harber changed his approach. He sent out word through the court officials that any witnesses for the defence would enjoy a stay in Hades if they appeared in court. Even the name of the prison was enough to deter all but the bravest.

Those who turned up faced jeering from the court officials. The comments could be heard right from the back of the courtroom.

"Are you a witch?"

"Is that all you can say for yourself?"

"Go back to your hovel."

Grania had felt queasy during the early testimony. It had kept her quiet at the back. As the days progressed, she felt worse. Twice she had to go outside and throw up. Dal commented on her sensitivity to the testimony and to her delicate nerves.

"Don't worry," he said. "If I had wanted nerves of steel, I would have married a fighter pilot."

Grania wanted to throttle him, but she felt too wretched to reach out and start strangling.

Constance used Grania's pallor as an excuse to suggest Grania go home and rest. Even as she said this, she was flirting with Dal. Grania noticed her eyes in particular, catching and holding and teasing. She flirts with everyone, Grania realised, does she even know she's flirting? She couldn't hold the thought before another wave of nausea struck.

"Do you want to go home?" asked Dal.

"No, but if I don't I could become a public embarrassment."

Dal went outside with her to call up a sedan chair. Constance, eyes fluttering, promised to save his seat. By the time Grania was immersed in the seasick-inducing clattering ride, Dal was back in the courtroom. He was probably absorbing every detail of the trial, just as Constance was probably absorbing every detail of Dal. This day was not the high point of Grania's year.

Dal found his seat again just in time to hear the verdict. The evidence had obviously been rattled through summarily.

Astonishingly, the bench of judges announced a unanimous verdict.

"Witchcraft," said Justice Harber. "Guilty beyond doubt."

Then came the twist.

Vlasha was promised a reprieve. In public. In front of the court and its enthusiastic audience. Justice Harber himself had turned to her and said "I can give you a reprieve."

"How?" asked Vlasha.

"Testify against your master. Show us all that his off-world habits are undermining the balance of our society and the civilisation of our planet. If you do that, you can go free."

Everyone in the room turned to look at Dal. His pose was nonchalant; his face showed nothing.

As the crowd settled again, Alphonse was called one more time. He explained what a peril people like Dal were, hiding their evil behind the work of others. He pointed to Dal directly. Everyone present turned and looked at him accusingly for a second time. Dal smiled at Alphonse.

He was unsurprised to see that Constance had moved to a less vulnerable seat. Several people stood up and quickly joined him. His people. Always.

"If there's violence," murmured one of them, "You won't be the one who gets hurt."

The moment passed. Dal's people remained clustered around him, however.

Vlasha was still considering the strange offer of clemency. She was adamant and strong. She was brave and she was stupid. It was her undoing.

"No," she said. "My lord saved many lives in the war. I won't take his in order to get reprieve from a crime I cannot possibly have done."

The trial was over and the farce complete.

One of the conspirators came to her, quietly and secretly, visiting her in her holding cell. Vlasha was again offered a deal. "Bring Dal down and we can free you," she was told. "We can train you in real medicine and license you. We can give you special permits for your medicinal herbs."

Vlasha responded quickly and promptly. First, she punched the man on the nose. Then she called him a rascal and punched him again. He did nothing. Presumably he thought he could still persuade her. Or maybe he was under orders. For whatever reason, the only way Vlasha could rid herself of him was by calling the guards and saying that he had attempted to bribe her.

The guards were amused, but they rid her of the injured inquisitor.

Next, Dal came to see her.

She told him about the attempt to corrupt her. "I'm going down," she said. "I'll not jeopardise our people on this rotten world."

Dal felt helpless. He offered to try bribery, "Since corruption seems to be the key to this game."

"No," Vlasha said. "We won't play their games."

"But your life is at stake."

"No," said Vlasha again. "We won't play their games. You said it yourself, we'll change their society, and we'll do it our way. You said it would take time and there might be sacrifices. I knew that. Just make sure you use what I'm giving you."

"I will," Dal promised, though he had no idea how.

He felt so helpless. He thought he had saved all his people with his cleverness. He thought the move to isolated New Ceres would be magical relief from interstellar warfare and local betrayal. He had been wrong, the whole way.

He wanted Vlasha to live.

When Dal reached the street, he let his tears show. When he arrived home, Grania met him and held him tightly. He held her as if she were his only succour.

Grania looked at his face and the vibrancy she loved had been replaced by a series of emptinesses. For the first time she realised just how pale his eyes were. Their intensity normally made them look dark, and now they were leached of all their force. Pale eyes in a dark visage made all his confidence look hollow.

After a little Grania said gently, "We need to find out how this happened. If we can piece that together, we can see if there are any weaknesses."

"Weaknesses?"

"Did I ever tell you how I escaped home?"

Dal looked at her, bewildered. "Escaped home?"

"Left Earth before I was herded with the rest of humanity and killed like cattle."

"Oh."

"One of the allied leaders liked to think he knew art. He ignored the fact that I had been in the Resistance. He let my pass come through."

"I thought a friend arranged it."

"Yes," said Grania, patiently, "But if that single person

hadn't pretended there was nothing to see, I wouldn't have got my pass, or been in touch with the freighter captain, or reached New Ceres. It all rested on one person pretending not to know anything. One person. A weakness."

"So we need to find out how Vlasha was framed. Then we need to find out if there are any weaknesses."

"That's right," said Grania.

Dal's face lost its vacancy. "We can do that," he said.

He searched for paper, pen and inkwell with his usual intensity. Grania ached for him and suddenly couldn't imagine that she had ever not known him.

Dal put his people to work, trying to find out how it had happened. It didn't take long at all to find out. Someone had bribed an acquaintance of Vlasha to make the accusation.

"I bet it was Alphonse," said Grania, bitterly.

"That much is entirely obvious," Dal said.

"I didn't know a society could be so corrupt."

"Shame we lost the paradise that was Mother Earth," a friend of Dal's spat the words in her face.

Grania stood up, looked him in the face and then walked straight out of the room.

She refused to come down to dinner. She refused to get up for breakfast. When Dal was distracted for an hour, he found her missing entirely. He went to her studio: it was locked.

"How is she going to eat and drink?" He worried at Qan.

"I believe she keeps supplies there now."

"When did this start," Dal felt haggard.

"Not long ago."

"Why did it start? Why didn't I know?"

Qan's gaze was more troubled than usual. "My wife says it's because your friends treat her as an idiot and the staff pay no attention to her. She says your wife has created a space for herself and that we should respect it."

"How could this have happened without my knowing?"

"That, sir, I cannot answer for you."

"And your wife?"

"She can, but won't."

At first Dal blamed himself, then he blamed Grania for her timing. Then his mind went back to the cruelty of throwing someone's suffering in their face.

Yet he could do nothing until she emerged from her retreat. Almost nothing. He issued strict orders: anyone who mocked Grania's past would be dismissed from his service, instantly. And his friendship. And his close circle. No matter how many generations of loyal service and no matter how perilous New Ceres was. He knew Grania would disapprove of this, but he also knew it had to be done. If he had set their little society up so that Grania was not given the respect she was due, then it was up to him to make it clear that there had been an error.

In the meantime, his little band of tactless volunteers had been busy. They found the missing link in Vlasha's case. It was a young woman named Trena.

Dal had her brought in and wooed her with food and flattery. She refused to testify in court.

"You don't understand. This isn't like home," she said miserably. "It's my family or her. They will throw me out of my job and take my husband away from his coach and we will be forced to live on the streets, eating untreated food."

Not even Dal's offer of new jobs would change her mind. Whoever was threatening had imposed such great fear that her testimony was going to hold. Whether it was fear of those half-invisible agents who were loyal only to the Lady Governor; of food; of dying unexpectedly of a knife wound: it didn't matter. There was no weakness to exploit.

She was hardly out a side door when the next crisis

presented itself at the front entrance: Alphonse appeared with an investigation team and a warrant.

"I have received word that you have a stock of illegal papers. We're going to find them and I'm going to eliminate you and your games from my world. Where is your wife?"

"Grania is indisposed and resting in her studio," Dal said, stiffly.

To Alphonse's gaze, he looked as unworried as ever. The taut voice was perfectly polite and the tone one any unwanted visitor would receive.

Under his calm demeanour, however, Dal was distressed. He was a tiny animal trapped in a bright light. If he could not think his way past the light, he would fall and all his people and all his plans would shatter.

Alphonse ignored Dal's stiffness. He marched right in and knocked on the studio door.

"Go away," said Grania.

"It's me, Alphonse. I have a warrant to search."

"Search my studio? Why would anyone want to do that? Not even you could be that stupid."

"Impudent bitch. I intend to search the whole house," said Alphonse, impatiently. "Now let me in."

"Come back when you've checked everywhere else, then. I'm not going anywhere."

"I'll set a guard outside your door. I won't allow any food or drink in."

"You do that. Come back when you've messed up the rest of the house. Do a good job, please. The place could do with a spring clean."

"You can't leave until we're finished," he said. "The search may take a day or two."

Petty revenge, Grania thought, is stupid. In another universe I'd be flattered that he desired me enough to want to exact humiliations. In this universe I still think he's a puffed up toad. All she said was "I assume that you will leave me in peace until then?"

"Certainly," Alphonse said.

Dal said nothing. There was a great deal he wanted to say, but his hands were tied. Alphonse was watching and listening. Dal couldn't give the least warning to his naïve wife. The rest of the house was safe, but the cache of papers hidden in her room was very large. There were too many that had not quite reached their destinations. And the thing was... the thing was that he had put them there, but it was Grania who had put Alphonse off. Alphonse would remember Grania, not him.

Dal could save himself and his people and his plans. Or he could save the woman he loved. The woman who was suffering so much that sometimes it hurt him to breathe as he watched her. He was helpless.

He hated being helpless.

Alphonse took Dal with him into every room in the house and left a guard to watch while Dal slept. Dal was prevented from talking to anyone. Even his orders were relayed through the guard.

Dal was worried about Grania. He was worried about every person he was responsible for. And Grania had warned him. Stupid, he was stupid. Triply stupid to hide his cache of broadsheets in Grania's studio and to not tell her. She would be caught with them and would hang with him. Or she would hang alone. He would lose her.

His mind revolved gloomily through scenario after scenario and found no way out. Dal's psychic abilities had failed him and his common sense had failed him and everyone he cared for would suffer from his failures.

There was nothing he could do, not with Alphonse riding his tail. Nothing except wait.

Nearly two days later, Alphonse knocked on that studio door.

"You left me until last?" Grania said as she opened the door.

"I hope your stay in your little cell was comfortable," mocked Alphonse.

"I didn't notice," Grania lied. "I was taken with an artistic vision. Let me show you."

Alphonse and his cohorts took over the room and one of them reached over to the objects on the table.

"Careful," Grania said, "The paint takes a long time to dry. They're still sticky."

"Are they for a ball?" asked Alphonse.

"No, they're for a display. Someone suggested that work such as this would be an interesting development for me."

"They're sad," one of the henchmen spoke up, very surprised. "I mean, I can feel those faces."

"If you leave your details with my major domo," Grania said, "I'll invite you to the party I'll hold to celebrate the installation when it's complete."

"Enough," said Alphonse, and turned to his people. "Search the room."

And they did. And they found nothing. This was because every single incriminating paper had been transformed into the papier-mâché masks that were sitting, sticky, on the table.

DAL SMILED TENTATIVELY AT VLASHA. She frowned back.

"Let me," he said.

"Go away," she answered. "I don't want you to put in an

appeal to the Lady Governor. I don't want you to, because it's not going to help."

"At least tell me why you think that. Bribery is such a common currency here. It has to help."

"Go away and don't come back."

"Tell me."

"Why should I tell you?"

Dal held his impatience tightly in check and his temper was even more closely reined. "You won't accept that I can help you?"

"Because you can't. I know this absolutely."

"Then accept that the information might help those of us who remain."

"How?" asked Vlasha.

"If we can't go down a route, we need to find others to explore. If we don't know we can't go down a route, we may spend months vainly trying to find the feeder road."

Vlasha diminished before his eyes, crumpling into herself. He gave her as much time as he could, but the gaolers were waiting and would show him the door, very shortly. After a little, he pointed this out.

Vlasha sagged. "They came to me. Alphonse and Harber. They tried to bribe me. Gods, it was a bigger bribe that I thought existed. And they offered me a permit for my plants as the icing on the cake. I could do everything, be who I wanted to be ... and betray all of you."

"What kind of betrayal were they after?"

The burden on Vlasha's shoulders looked heavier than before. It was crushing her and turning her into an old lady, even as they spoke.

"You," she said, softly. "They want to kill you with justice. If I testify that you're a witch and a traitor, then I'm free. They promised me I would be safe if I testified. They promised me everything. Everything except the one thing I want."

Dal looked at her lost eyes and saw in them the truth. She had not joined their cause to change an unjust universe. She had joined it to be near him.

"So there's nothing we can do?" His voice was the merest whisper.

Even if Grania never spoke to him again, his heart would be always hers. He couldn't even pretend to give Vlasha a heart that was entirely held by Grania.

Vlasha tried to hide behind something else that was deep in her. It was the reason she had been accepted into their band of rebels and it still shone in her eyes, one pain shining through another.

"I've seen all this before," Vlasha said, her voice harsh with despite. "Our planet fell because of trumped-up charges. I'll not use them against anyone."

"Then you'll die."

"And you'll carry the guilt for my death for the rest of your life. And for that I'm sorry."

So it ended.

Vlasha was sentenced to hanging, drawing and quartering, then burning in the public square. Just like the woman in the broadsheet.

Dal insisted on going to support her.

"I brought my people into this corrupt society," said Dal. "And I am responsible when it kills them."

Grania wanted to remind him that Vlasha was only a new arrival in Dal's circles and that she had brought herself to New Ceres, but she couldn't. She knew the hurt. She couldn't make it worse with petty pedantry.

That night, when Grania was asleep, Dal walked around the house like a ghost.

His manservant found him.

"Don't you dare," he said to Dal. "Don't even think it."

Dal's gaze didn't even rest on Qan. It flitted as if Dal could find no rest.

"You wanted to kill yourself when you realised we had to run. Now you want to kill yourself because someone is being murdered on your watch. And it's boring. It's also lazy."

"It will all be over. I need it finished."

"Finished for you," said Qan, tartly. "What about us?" He took a deep breath. "If you're gone then everyone who comes from Holotor, from any of the three planets, is tainted. These people on this planet believe just as much in reputation as someone from Boced. If you commit suicide, you will shame us all in their eyes. We'll be tainted. Do not kill yourself."

Both Dal and Qan knew this was an overstatement, but it was one that Dal needed to hear. His eyes started focussing again. He was almost convinced. Almost, but not yet. Qan sighed. It might take till dawn to convince him fully. It had last time.

Grania had woken up and found her bed empty. She came to find him and caught this conversation. Quietly she disappeared and came back with something in a hessian bag.

"Listen to Qan," Grania urged, stepping out from the dark shadow into the pale moonlight. "You need to be here for the rest of us. Self-immolation is selfish and will bring all of us to disaster."

Dal's pale eyes were empty as they turned to her. "I can't bear it."

"You have to. There are ways. Take this, for instance." She handed over the bag and he reached in and pulled out a sketch she had made.

"What do I do with it?" he asked, then looked at what he had just unrolled. It was a charcoal sketch of Vlasha's face.

"You give me permission to make it into one of my masks." There was a hesitance in the pause. Grania's request was unexpected.

"It's tribute to Vlasha," Grania explained. "It'll remind you why you need to live. What you're fighting for. Every one of your people who is lost needs their own face. It's important to keep them alive in memory. Every single one of them. It's even more important that you don't follow them into the darkness. They need to be remembered, but we need you to help us live. I'll draw you sketches, one for every person they take down. I'll make faces. We won't forget them."

"That's futile," Dal's voice lost a little of its iron control.

"Why?"

"If you had done a wall of art for yourself, then this would make more sense."

"I'd need enough to reflect all the peoples of Earth, I know, but this is a new planet and we can start afresh. There's a chance here that we can live free. It's only a chance, and we need to get involved in the politics. The display will remind you who we're doing it for."

"Vlasha."

"No. Us. She sacrificed herself so that we could play their games and maybe get free of them. The mask is a reminder that we need to play their games to get free of them, but that we're only donning masks – we're never, ever going to become what they are. Never Alphonse. Never Livia."

"I'll remember that," said Dal, and he held the sketch for a mask in one hand and held Grania close to him with every other fibre of his being. For a fleeting moment he thought of telling Grania what was going on and why Alphonse wanted to take them down, then he realised just how much peril she would be in if he did.

He was torn. The only safety was in holding her to himself.

THE CROWD and its boisterousness troubled Grania. How could they think it a fine entertainment? Someone was being killed.

Dal found them places near the front, but Grania could only see parts of the proceedings. I ought to be grateful, she thought. If they were any more modern, then the grounds would be sloped and everyone would have a glorious view of this insanity.

The yard, however, was flat, and the platform just high enough for the hanging. The executioner was in black and his face was hidden.

Grania couldn't help comparing the messiness of the crowd and the number of times the executioner had to tell blindfolded Vlasha what was happening with the tidiness of adventure reality games. You could feel everything in the games, but it was all neater, and, of course, there was always a last-minute save. Not in this world. This world didn't have the technology for adventure reality games. Everything here was real.

Finally, Vlasha stopped under the noose. It was put around her head. The executioner sprung the door below her and she was strangled by the rope until she was nearly dead. Then came the drawing and quartering. Her intestines were spilled out onto the wooden platform.

She's still alive, Grania realised. She's feeling her body being cut open. She sees her guts on the ground. I can't take any more.

She couldn't leave, however. Dal and his company were all

in shock. Their eyes watched that evil platform in fascinated horror. Dal's hand held her own so tightly that it hurt.

Grania resolutely looked towards her feet, hidden under her brown skirt. She didn't need to see this. She didn't need to add this to her stock of memories.

Grania saw Constance through the crowd. She was watching the judicial murder and then turned her head to talk to someone. Grania caught a direct glimpse of her face and thought, She's no happier about this than we are.

The crowd shifted for an instant. Grania turned to her artist-gaze to distance herself from what was happening. She saw scenes and those scenes were like drawings by Hogarth, telling snippets of story. Full of the colour of the eighteenth century and full of individuals whose faces showed that there were stories behind the snippets she saw.

In one scene Grania caught a glimpse of the person talking to Constance: it was Livia's daughter. The crowd shifted and formed and shifted and reformed, as some moved forward to get a better look and others moved back. Livia's daughter was replaced by Livia herself, who looked a bit pale. This surprised Grania, who thought a nice bit of murder would be right up Livia's alley.

When she looked to Constance again, Constance stood alone.

If Grania had been able to read the cause of the emotions rather than seeing merely the scenes, she would have discovered that in Livia's purse was an anonymous note, accusing the late Frederick of importing illegal tech in order to view pornography. Private pornography. No public gain.

Such a small thing and yet it could bring her down.

Livia didn't notice the outside world. If she had looked at

herself she would have said that her body language separated her from both the living and the dead. In her mind, she was rehearsing every single place she could recall in every single household Frederick had been in contact with. All her plans would go on hold until she could check them all and find that pornography. When she had destroyed it and all records relating to it, she could progress.

Livia didn't doubt the tech's existence – it was so much the sort of thing Frederick did. He would have enjoyed the illegality and especially enjoyed leaving it as a booby trap, to suck her in when he was no longer around to protect it from public gaze.

Livia saw a broadsheet drifting in the summer breeze. She bent to the ground and picked it up. On one side was the Old Earth story of Joan Petersen. On the other half of the fold was the story of Vlasha. The title asked, 'Who will save us from our own corruption?'

She read the words 'The devil rat my soul'. Livia thought I'd rather the devil ratted Alphonse's soul. Someone had to pay, after all. Always. Someone.

Once she had eliminated any possibility of Frederick's flirt with pornography and tech and once she had ensured that the illegality of it all would not bite her, then Livia would see to Alphonse. Or maybe sooner than that. Wherever she turned there were reports of his activities and each and every time they were more about his personal plays for power than about the good of New Ceres. Time after time he hurt the society she so much loved.

Livia had reached the stage where she wanted to watch her cousin die. Maybe, she thought, at his own table with her as hostess. Livia's tongue snaked out as she tasted poisons in her mind, working through until she found the best one for her purpose. Her serpent tongue stilled, and she smiled.

INTERLUDE: MR F PRESENTS

I have remarked upon occasion that the various gentlemen's magazines proffered by lesser printers present little of the gentlemanly, and much of the scurrilous. I give you a verified and actual magazine from that period of Enlightenment on which we model so much that is of importance. I present to you entertainment and education in a fair and elegant typescript. I add to my catalogue, in short, The Gentleman's Magazine.

It was originally published in England from 1731 by "Sylvanus Urban" also known as Edward Cave. I have taken the liberty of replacing traditional orthography with the twenty-first century spelling standard on many planets, that this interesting work may reach a wider audience.

Interlude with Arms:
  The Three Worthy Butchers

It is a sad fact of life that the roads to the Great Estates and between our cities are plagued with the curse of armed robbers. It is a small reassurance that the Grand Period also knew of these criminals. This English broadside is evidence that they were so inflicted.

Mr F., Printer

A story I will tell to you,
  It is of butchers three:
  Gibson, Wilson and Johnson,
  Mark well what I do say;
  Now as they had five hundred pounds,
  All on a market day,
  Now as they had five hundred pounds
  To pay upon their way.
  With my hey, ding, ding, with my ho, ding, ding,
  With my high, ding, ding, high dey!

May God keep all good people from such bad company!

Now as they rode along the road
    As fast as they could ride
    Spur on your horses says Johnson,
    For I hear a woman cry;
    And, as they rode into the wood,
    The scene they spied around,
    And there they found a woman lay
    A-swooning on the ground.
    With my hey, ding, ding, with my ho, ding, ding,
    With my high, ding, ding, high dey!
    May God keep all good people from such bad company!

O woman, woman! Johnson cries,
    Oh pray, come tell to me,
    O woman, woman, Johnson cries,
    Have you got any company?
    Oh, no! no! no! the woman cries,
    Alas! how can that be?
    When here has been by ten swaggering blades
    Who've robbed and beaten me!
    With my hey, ding, ding, with my ho, ding, ding,
    With my high, ding, ding, high dey!
    May God keep all good people from such bad company!

Now Johnson, being a valiant man,
    He bore a valiant mind,
    He wrapped her up in his great coat,
    And placed her up behind.
    And as they rode along the road,
    As fast as they could ride,
    She put her fingers to her ear

And gave a screekful cry.
With my hey, ding, ding, with my ho, ding, ding,
With my high, ding, ding, high dey!
May God keep all good people from such bad company!

With that, came out ten swaggering blades,
    With their rapiers in their hand.
    They rode up to bold Johnson,
    And boldly bid him stand.
    Oh, I cannot fight; says Gibson,
    I am sure that I shall die!
    No more won't I, cries Wilson,
    For I will sooner fly!
    With my hey, ding, ding, with my ho, ding, ding,
    With my high, ding, ding, high dey!
    May God keep all good people from such bad company!

Come on, come on! cries bold Johnson,
    I'll fight you all so free!
    And, woman, stand you here behind;
    We'll gain the victory!
    The very first pistol Johnson fires
    Was loaded with powder and ball,
    And, out of these ten swaggering blades
    Five of them did fall.
    With my hey, ding, ding, with my ho, ding, ding,
    With my high, ding, ding, high dey!
    May God keep all good people from such bad company!

Come on! come on! cries bold Johnson,
    There are but five for me,
    And, woman, stand you there behind;
    We'll gain the victory!

The very next pistol Johnson fired
Was loaded with powder and ball,
And out of these five swaggering blades
There's three of them did fall.
With my hey, ding, ding, with my ho, ding, ding,
With my high, ding, ding, high dey!
May God keep all good people from such bad company!

Come on! come on! cries bold Johnson
There are but two to me,
And, woman, stand you there behind;
We'll gain the victory!
As Johnson fought these rogues in front,
The woman he did not mind
She took his knife all from his side
And stabbed him from behind.
With my hey, ding, ding, with my ho, ding, ding,
With my high, ding, ding, high dey!
May God keep all good people from such bad company!

Now I must fall says Johnson
I must fall to the ground!
For relieving this wicked woman
She gave me my death wound!
Oh! woman, woman, woman,
What have you been and done?
You have killed the finest butcher
That ever the sun shone on!
With my hey, ding, ding, with my ho, ding, ding,
With my high, ding, ding, high dey!
May God keep all good people from such bad company!

Now, just as she had done the deed

Some men came riding by,
And, seeing what this woman had done,
They raised a dreadful cry.
Then she was condemned to die in links,
And iron chains so strong,
For killing of bold Johnson,
That great and valiant man.
With my hey, ding, ding, with my ho, ding, ding,
With my high, ding, ding, high dey!
May God keep all good people from such bad company!

From the Private Collection of Dal.

Handwritten annotation:

    Collected at the space port on arrival at New Ceres.

12

LIVIA MEETS A HIGHWAYMAN AND PLEASANTRIES ARE EXCHANGED

It was the dullest of dull days. Equestrian events and swordfights were boring when she herself suffered from education and she found them even less of interest now.

Instead of watching, she drifted among the crowd. Livia renewed acquaintances with some. Others she reminded of old friendship. They were quick to agree, and just as quick to deny when put to trial – this was a problem with fear as politics, Livia realised. She needed to consolidate a few deeper alliances to make up for those which would surely shatter.

Her chief purpose for this journey was to check up on certain officials. There had been some talk in certain circles that those responsible for overseeing the Hilltown schools might not be toeing the line. Livia's protective coloration made it possible to find out if the talk had any basis or if it was simply mischief-making. It looked like the latter around late morning, but Maria's report should make the situation entirely clear.

All in all, it was turning into an excursion well spent.

Lunch with her protégée was the best time of the day.

Maria was shaping up nicely. She had lost the tendency to boast and pretend naivety and had started collecting serious information. Livia would leave Hilltown much better informed about certain members of Society who were otherwise outside her reach.

Still not sufficiently informed. It was troublesomely difficult to collect material about the inner workings of the social elite. They sealed themselves off from the Six, which was foolish, because many of them had married into earlier governing families. Doubly foolish: they lacked real power and could gain it with careful interaction. Yet people like Lady C took on the mantle of old nobility and protected their privilege.

Once Livia had queried this. It was explained to her that the people involved were acting entirely properly in protecting their privilege and that, in Old Earth terms, she herself was only noblesse de robe and they were of the blood. There was eighteenth century precedent. That precedent protected them. Their ancestors kept them alive, and out of administration.

These people had little civil authority and she was not envious of them. She fretted, however, about their impregnability. If they were responsible for social disarray and the current porousness of authority, it would be very hard to bring either of them under control.

To appease her frustration, Livia asked Maria if she would like to buy a meal for her particular friends. Maria had obviously expected this and within the hour they were at a very select eatery indeed.

At first the gaggle of girls was cowed by Livia, but as she didn't give them her special smile and was content to play Lady Bountiful and provide for their needs, they soon reverted to natural behaviour. She listened a great deal and ate very little.

Livia discovered that Mr F sponsored apprenticeships throughout the industries allied to printing. The apprentices were from families who needed help. Where one of Maria's new friends saw beautiful deeds, Livia saw a little empire. A potentially dangerous empire unless she could control it, which at this moment, given her relations with Mr F, looked perfectly feasible.

It was interesting that most of Maria's own protégées came from the same needy background as Mr F. She would do well long term; her client group would owe her their lives before very long. Every single child was needy, greedy and Maria had obviously played her cards well and made them entirely reliant on her.

Maria had earned the gifts and funds Livia had brought. She might survive longer than Livia's other girls. By choosing her personal clients from such a needy greedy group, Maria ensured her own safety.

Maria had been brought up by a nursemaid and was a hoyden when Livia found her. Now she was entirely different. Comfortable in herself, supportive of her friends, modest, and always watching for Livia's interests.

When lunch was over Livia emptied her purse of the jewellery she had brought in case Maria proved herself and then filled it with three stacks of paper, neatly folded over into wads and tied with pink ribbon. The young student had explained them as poetry, but Livia knew they were her latest sets of reports.

Maria had an innate good sense, Livia noted. The jewellery was duly admired, then carefully stowed out of sight. Livia didn't object to escape plans: she needed a protégée, not a successor.

The early afternoon was devoted to meeting with her own child. This meeting was not so satisfactory.

Esther was angry with her mother and with the world, and she was tasteless enough to let her anger show. She explained – far too loudly – that she wanted to move from most of her current classes and maybe even the school.

"Mother, I've done all of these subjects before. I know them. They were boring the first time round and now they're enervating. All I do in class is sleep and I still get better marks than the little ones who study with me."

"You're there to meet those little ones and develop contacts."

"We have so much in common."

"Don't be sarcastic, dear. You lack the skill."

"I will not develop a coterie to support you."

"It will secure your life."

"And how is that?"

"If you have friends who are useful to me, I will continue to support you."

"If you let me learn a trade I can keep myself. In fact, I can move out of your life forever."

Livia forgot herself enough to hiss. "I need a child and you are the only one I have. You will behave or your brain will die a death and I will carry your soulless body around and cry on the streets for sympathy."

"I hate you."

"That my dear, is entirely irrelevant."

The conversation was cut short by the arrival of Livia's carriage.

"You're going to drive through the night?" her daughter was astonished.

"No, dear, I shall stay in New Stilton. I have some work to do there."

"Well, enjoy the cheese. And don't feel obliged to visit me again any time soon."

"Continue to follow the program I have devised for you and I won't have to," Livia promised. She brought out a small purse and gave it to her daughter. "There's enough here for small extras, should you require them," she said. "You may take that look off your face. There is not enough to fund a change of schools or subjects. You will find this is merely pin-money."

They kissed each other politely and Livia climbed into the coach and was about to signal the coachman she was ready to depart. A deep voice cried "Hail the coach!"

That fat doctor, Benjamin looked in the window.

"I thought it was you!" he said, triumphant. "I was visiting here and my possessions were stolen. I wonder if I could impose upon you for a ride back to Prosperine."

"I will be staying in New Stilton overnight," said Livia, coldly.

"I can sleep in the coach," promised Benjamin. "I have a few coins for food, but that is all."

Livia sniffed. Did he know what an insult he had just given her? Obviously not. She was tempted to permit him to pay for his food and to pass an uncomfortable night in the coach and continue to insult his superiors. He was turning into a deadweight on society, however, and amusement wasn't sufficient.

She opened the door and let him in, then signalled the driver that they were ready.

The doctor almost fell over as the coach started up but settled quickly enough. Once he was settled, he talked, and talked, and talked. There was no end to his babble. Livia was silent, thinking just how troublesome Benjamin was, how strange his movement were, and that Maria had informed her that he was playing politics and that he'd applied for teaching positions at several schools.

Eventually she decided that Benjamin would never be a feature of her circle. His incessant chatter reinforced this – the man never stopped, never learned, and never knew anything worth knowing. Embarrassing Alphonse in public was one thing. Undermining society by teaching and by denying the tenets of New Ceres was, however, a far more serious matter.

It was time he was out of her sight and out of her business. If he talked to her at a public place from this day on, she would give him the cut direct. No, better, she would have Josephine give him the cut direct. If he wished for a patron, he would have to learn to cease bumbling.

ONE STOPPED off to buy produce, always. A quick visit to the supervisor's office had that appearance, anyhow. Benjamin could stroll around the small milk-endowed town of New Stilton and show off the company he was in, while she had her quiet meeting. Reporting directly and openly would reveal too much to those who watched.

Livia knew that New Ceres was as liable to shatter as a strained friendship. Her planet was on the brink of falling apart and she'd be damned if she'd let it. She would be ruined, but ruin was something she played with as a cat played with a mouse: it didn't concern her.

While she was on the rise and New Ceres kept its New Enlightenment, nothing else mattered. Not friendship, not love. Not wealth. Not family. The Six was a product of New Ceres: New Ceres could always produce a new Six.

This meeting was crucial to helping resolve certain problems faced by certain officials at the New Stilton food processing plant, and it was equally important that it be kept private.

What had alerted Livia to the need to consult quietly was the rebellion at Tenterfield. So far no-one knew about it, but once word spread then rebellion might. This was the time to nip it in the bud.

The supervisor of the cheese plant agreed. He also had some useful information.

"It's the Saddler family," he said. "Never met them. No-one does. They control things round Tenterfield."

"It's never quite been within the Lady Governor's domain," Livia said slowly.

"Never. Settled by a bunch of rowdy Australians early on. Only accepted New Enlightenment in exchange for self-rule. Very culturally retentive. Not at all respectful. Had a daughter who married there. Used to get news. Then they all got angry with new regulations. Still get some news, but not enough." Livia nodded. This was one reason why she was here. "Enough to know the Saddlers are arguing for culture from Australia. Claims they're in danger of losing it. Claims that the Six is working against their autonomy."

"They're right about that last," said Livia. "I don't know this planet 'Australia.' How does its culture fit into ours?"

"It's not a planet. Old Earth country."

"It had an eighteenth century, then. I can't see the problem."

"Settled by Europeans at the tail end. No Enlightenment, really. And they have a focal point, which is funny."

"Funny?"

"They've never met her. Their hero hasn't been outside Prosperine since she arrived. Wouldn't know a Tenterfield Saddler if one walked right past her."

"Who is it?"

"That artist, Grania."

"How did she become their hero?"

"Last Australian to leave Old Earth. Resistance fighter. Big reputation."

Resistance fighter? This didn't fit the Grania she knew. This was something she had needed to hear, but not something she wanted to know at all.

"This complicates matters," Livia said. The supervisor nodded. "We do need to take care of Tenterfield."

"The wood they produce is particularly important," warned the official.

"I know that," Livia moved impatiently in her chair. "If it weren't so very important, a much more junior family member would be here."

The supervisor looked across her desk, unmoved. She knew she was safe from machinations and family politics. Not just her. All the senior officials. It was the price of their complete support. Along with the possibility of entering the Six, should a Family lose its next generation of trained children. Along with saving daughters from rebellious loggers, Livia suspected.

"It's a balancing act," she said, suddenly. "I can't see that we can avoid deaths entirely, but we can minimise them and give limited warning. Supporters of the Lady Governor will be able to avoid damage."

"I would appreciate that," the supervisor said.

"A balancing act," reiterated Livia. "You're our link into the chain of command. You're our link in the chain of food processing governance. "

The supervisor nodded again. She was thinking it through, quite obviously and she knew that she was already treading a very thin line.

They talked about possible approaches for a little. How could they silence this Tenterfield process? There was no question about it being stopped and about it being very thoroughly swept under the carpet. This was why Livia was in New Stilton. They simply had to decide how to regain control over the whole town. It came down to how many deaths were feasible.

The superintendent was obviously distraught by having to take even partial responsibility for murders. Even though she would not be carrying it out directly, it was patently difficult for her. Livia became increasingly bored as the other woman rehearsed all the options verbally, over and over again, trying to come to terms with it.

"If we kill the whole Saddler family and blame highwaymen, that would be simplest," she said, trying to control the litany.

"I would not like to see a complete family die in such a way," the superintendent said cautiously.

"It would be a tragedy," said a deep voice from the back of the room. The superintendent jumped out of her chair, but Livia merely looked across, curiously.

It was Benjamin. He had not knocked. He had simply walked in the door and stood there, listening. For how long, Livia didn't know.

"It reminds me of another tragedy, not too long ago." Benjamin sat in a chair, without an invitation.

"Your second husband," and he nodded to Livia, whose tongue immediately darted from her mouth as she tasted the air. Nothing. There was no indication of mood or even where Benjamin was headed. No way of knowing who he was working for unless she heard him out. She sat up straight, closed her mouth tightly, and listened.

"Please correct me if I have not heard correctly," and he

graciously nodded to Livia again. Livia was finding him entirely obnoxious. "I hear that your late husband was negligent with maintenance of a food processing machine in a hamlet near Tenterfield. The breakdown resulted in thirty-three deaths."

"It was not a matter of negligence," the supervisor was hot in her defence of the establishment. "Our off-planet supplier sent us poor quality components."

"I visited Tenterfield a few weeks ago and they say the old machine has been brought back to the region and is going to be used for a wider range of processing. That they've asked for tests to be carried out to ensure that it's safe and that no-one has carried out the tests."

"I've heard some of this," said Livia.

"I've also heard that they're seeking autonomy to run the machines themselves."

The room went silent.

"Where did you hear this?" asked the superintendent.

"At Trig's."

If it was known at Trig's then it was known everywhere. The government's hands were tied.

"I had heard it differently," said Livia. "I heard that the Lady Governor was considering giving the people of Tenterfield the opportunity to become a fully autonomous zone. They have the cultural continuity and integrity. They would have to buy treatment machinery outright, of course, which would indebt them to us for a little, but it's a small price to pay for independence."

Benjamin nodded. The superintendent nodded.

Livia gave the tiniest sigh of annoyance. A twenty-eighth autonomous zone was the last thing the planet needed. There hadn't been a new one for almost two centuries and it would have been far better if there weren't ever any more. Right now, however, it was more important to keep timber and wool flowing through the highlands to civilisation and more important still to completely dampen any rumour about violent solutions.

This was wrong on so many levels. Yet another zone with insignificant control by the Lady Governor – bad, bad news. Bad news for Benjamin, too. She had already been considering shifting him out of her life. Perhaps a more permanent shift was in order.

She wondered briefly if one could become addicted to death the way one was addicted to a fine meal. Unlikely. Death was an expedient. Fine food was always a delight.

In the interim, she bought cheese. Purchasing cheese was logical and rational and contained a smidgeon of joy.

The carriage was uncomfortable after they left New Stilton. Benjamin had decided that the accommodation and food Livia had provided did not reflect his worth. This was a little strange, for someone who had declared himself ready to sleep in the carriage. Unless... unless he had planned something else. Yet if he had, how could she have missed signals?

She watched him covertly for a little and then realised that he was watching her watch him. She gave her little smile and Benjamin did not react in the least. His information about her and possibly about their society was lacking. How... interesting. That explained why he bumbled and assumed he was a treasure to be snapped up. He thought he was privileged.

Eventually it was Benjamin who broke the silence.

"What was so special about Cheesetown, anyhow?"

"I had business there," answered Livia, stiffly. She didn't see why she should gift him with comfort in conversation. He had barely earned basic courtesy.

"Sleeping with the lower classes, heh?" He leered. He most definitely leered.

"That is very rude and entirely inappropriate to a private conversation." This time the stiffness was real. In a moment, Livia would become angry and they would both regret it.

"Everyone does it," he said, and shrugged. "Even your friend Josephine."

"You will kindly excuse me for choosing not to participate in this conversation." Livia turned just a little of her anger outwards and then closed her eyes to indicate that she was not going to join Benjamin's games.

Beneath the shelter of her eyelids, she fumed. Josephine's future was planned. It included her remaining above reproach in public. It most certainly included Livia being the only one who had any holds on her. Josephine could not survive affairs at this stage. Yes, they were common enough, but one had to be established. One had to be above reproach before venturing into the land of the demi-monde as a person of consequence. Otherwise the future was social and fascinating, but politics were impossible. Who could trust someone who indulged in pillow-talk?

It was also deeply troubling that Josephine had broken class, even for one night. And with this white lump of lard!

She looked across the carriage and decided that she must dispose of Benjamin. No doubt of it. Sooner rather than later. How amusing, she thought, that he had gone from being shuffled to one of those boring autonomous boroughs to being given a gentle death to meeting the most uncomfortable quick death she could think of that would leave her reputation spotless. All she needed now was opportunity.

They reached the rough point in the road, a product of a local squabble a decade before and Livia clenched her teeth.

A half-hour of bumping and jolting and the road would be clear to New Ceres.

After a few minutes, the carriage halted entirely.

"If you would be so kind as to find out which particular pothole has caught which particular wheel and perhaps assist in getting us clear." It was not a question.

Benjamin chose to treat it as one, however, by replying "Certainly."

Pushing the door open, he peered out, his body ready to follow. He pulled his head right back in, and sat down, pale as whale blubber.

"Highwaymen," he said.

"Oh dear," said Livia, as if she were troubled.

'You in there," a confident voice said. "Come out."

"Do it," Livia advised, wholly entertained.

Benjamin did so, and she herself stayed inside.

"Madame Livia, we know this is your coach. If you would kindly come forth, you will save yourself much trouble." This was a voice that was comfortable in its ability to hide a Family accent. It was not Alphonse. How curious. Livia decided to step outside to see a bit more.

"I'm coming," she said. "I do hope the ground is not muddy."

"The ground is dry, ma'am," said the coachdriver.

"Shut up, you," said a second voice. This one was not aristocratic. Even more curious. She could also swear she had heard it before. She could not place it. Maybe a face would help, or, failing a face, the size, shape or body movement.

Despite her curiosity, she moved slowly, savouring each second. After all, there was some possibility of her dying and it appeared these rogues were seeking her. She kept her movements gentle and soft. It was far too rarely that she could hold full centre-stage these days.

She stepped out of the coach and pretended to a faint unsteadiness. No-one rushed forward to help her down the steps. Good.

She looked up very quickly and saw only two highwaymen, with pistols. One pistol was trained upon the coachman (who had obviously been forced to step down from the coach) and one upon herself. The good doctor was standing next to the coach door. Both highwaymen were thoroughly masked and rugged up in heavy coasts. The masks limited their peripheral vision.

She smiled a very little and made sure they saw. Then she started to step down.

Livia stumbled, catching her arm on the door and pushing it back against the coach. It gave a sharp retort. Covered by the sound, the coachman tackled one of the highwaymen. He fell onto the other. One of the guns went off. Her coachman grabbed at the other gun.

The highwaymen moved very quickly. Back to their horses. Onto their horses and gone.

"Over so quickly," Livia mourned.

"Yes, ma'am," said her driver, struggling with his own horses. "I think your guest might be in trouble."

And so he was. The shot intended for Livia had gone wild, thanks to her coachman, and Benjamin was wounded. She applied pressure to the wound, calmly and competently, and as soon as the coach was sufficiently stable, she helped him into it. A moment later they were on their way.

Livia smiled, but only to herself. She joked "Physician, heal thyself."

Benjamin looked across at her, his hand trying to staunch the blood.

"Don't you know that quote? It's from Old Earth. Religion. And very apt at this moment, if I may say."

She mocked him the whole way home, even after he had died from the second wound. The second wound? The wound that had mysteriously appeared in his side when it became obvious he was going to live. That was from her own small pistol.

While she mocked, she rehearsed in her mind the things she needed to remember and decided on a strategy for maximising the usefulness of Benjamin's death. She wouldn't have to do more than this - the highwaymen had been extraordinarily useful. Maybe, Livia thought, she would put on hold considering just how familiar the first highwayman was.

'Maybe' didn't stop her collecting data. Livia memorised their voices and movement and how they worked together with the flavour of the cheeses. Three cheeses; three people memorised. Her tastebuds had processed what her eyes hadn't. There were three highwaymen. One was much slighter than the other two and had only been visible on the edge of her vision, after she had processed everything. From two to three, thanks to the power of cheese. Two of her own class, Livia thought. And one rather common ruffian. A very odd mix.

When it came to reporting the incident, she was prepared. Everything was straightforward.

"He died before my eyes, in the carriage," and her voice was a shocked murmur. No-one asked her about details because it was obvious how much she had suffered. No-one thought to ask if she carried arms, or to look at Benjamin's wounds, or to do any kind of autopsy.

Still, it was all very slow. Livia didn't reach home until late, and she had business to finish before she could let the incident go. She knew her reputation. She knew that everyone believed that her little smile meant someone was going to die that day.

Popular rumour was useful and she had encouraged it, in her own way. She had practised that smile that so matched her reputation. It wasn't how she worked, though. Livia believed devoutly in her senses and her memory and trusted them implicitly. She did not, however, believe in instinct. Senses and memory needed fuel.

When she reached her home, she extracted two cheeses from the New Stilton packages. The first was small and soft and expensive enough so that it came in its own basket.

She took it out of the woven jonquette, with love and with care. She sniffed it gently, remembering the voices and the movement of the three who tried to kill her. Then she stood over her washbasin and squeezed the cheese until it was drained dry: this was her promise of revenge.

Her next step was to close a chapter. Without completion, memories tangled. She took her second cheese, a Roquefort style she had bought for her cellarer to sample and perhaps match with a wine. Livia sliced it small and ate it, dry, one sliver at a time. She relished every single flavour in the complex cheese. When it was finished, Livia cleaned her gun, ready for the next unfortunate accident she would encounter.

While Livia polished off her adventure, Grania was entertaining Constance. They were getting on surprisingly well.

13

WARNING TO TRAVELLERS

This pamphlet is provided to you – a new arrival – to help you understand some of the dangers you may face while visiting New Ceres. It has been loosely adapted from an article by Fred Xian recently published in The Intergalactic Traveller. In issuing this leaflet we in no way condone or support the Code Duello and it should not be considered an expression of opinion on any secret society that monitors 'correct' behaviour and activity.

WHILE THE INHABITANTS of New Ceres consider their duelling codified according to ancient practice, matters of honour are touchy and the codes are inconstant. In theory, only the aristocracy will engage in duels, and studies of New Ceres society will back that theory. In reality, however the situation is more precarious. If you unintentionally offer insult, accepting personal humiliation is almost always preferable to engaging in a duel.

Mr F is a printer notorious for upholding the New Ceres regime.

We recommend his Code Duello (stolen unashamedly from an eighteenth century original - Mr F is far more concerned with upholding the New Enlightenment than in publishing new writers), not because he has any particular skill at arms or knowledge of the high graces of armed duels, but because any code printed by him has in all likelihood been informally approved by the office of the Lady Governor.

Duelling codes are technically aimed at affairs of honour. Honour is very important to the ruling classes. They are considered to be civilised especially if the preferred lower grade (pre-modern) weaponry is used. Since a potential outcome of each engagement is death, however, the Code Duello merely ritualises a violent and barbaric activity. Its chief redeeming feature is that modern weapons are illegal and eighteenth-century weapons are primitive, so death is relatively rare. Disfiguration is a high risk due to the archaic medical systems practised on the planet.

The Code Duello reflects the ruling classes, and the lower classes are generally free of its constraints. Many seek to be included in the Code, however, as the right to wear a sword and to challenge generally runs alongside the right to patronage and the right to accept senior civil appointments. Once in those elevated circles, a system of honour prevails and challenges may be made when honour is besmirched, even in such minor matters as seating at table.

Not all matters of honour must be addressed by a duel. Nor do all challenges result in a duel. For those who cannot fight - due to infirmity or poor education - a full public withdrawal relating to the cause of the challenge and a full apology will normally suffice. When a full public withdrawal and apology is not possible (for whatever reason) participants feel that they have 'no choice but to accept' the duel.

To outsiders, the causes of duels often seem trivial. Each 'trivial' cause, however, has a firm rooting in social behaviour and underpins the retention of customs necessary to the survival of the New Enlightenment.

The authorities condone research into the Code Duello as long as those studies do not threaten its existence. Specialist studies have been written about the causes of duels, about the odd fact that honour can be satisfied even if the challenger loses, that outcomes do not affect social standing, and that death by duelling is rare but not unknown. Punishment for noble duellers mainly occurs when the duel fails to follow one of the codes or if a dueller is proved to have cheated (especially by using forbidden technologies). For those who refuse to duel, punishment is invariable: it leads to a loss of status and opportunity within the ruling class. The only exceptions to this are those within the Lady Governor's inner circle and its spy-system, who are considered above insult and injury of this sort.

In theory, the lower classes do not duel. Exceptions are made for those with extraordinary arms skills, who may advance their social situation by duelling and strategic marriage. Children do not duel, although the classic study by Gick (2341) demonstrates that the games of children from the upper class and upwardly mobile upper middle class and wealthy trades persons will mimic duelling.

The chief weapons for duelling are the sabre or pistols. The chief reasons given for calling someone out are insults, physical slaps (generally to the face), accusations of lying, accusations of using new technology etc.

Duels are also called over slights of various kinds, to character, to family, to virtue. Impoliteness and overly familiar touching can lead to duels, although many women in polite society will feign weakness and call in a constable to avoid confrontation. These women are not necessarily regarded with favour by other women, who see their unwillingness to duel as leading to a diminution in women's social standing.

A well-fought duel, advocates claim, does more than establish the honour of both parties; it establishes their suitability to be fully active members of the ruling elite. The Code Duello was drafted to mediate between these two groups - to make it clear when any adult of the appropriate class might engage in a duel or have a substitute engage in one.

Duels with pistols have their own rules. Accurate pistols are not preferred, as they lead too frequently to death. This preference highlights the underlying ambiguity of the role of the Code Duello on the planet New Ceres.

Duelling with high technology weaponry or even pistols that postdate the late eighteenth century in design - if caught - is considered cause for publicly shaming. Under certain conditions the level of shame may be considered sufficient to warrant suicide by the cheat. If the guilty party does not suicide voluntarily then the likelihood is high that he or she will suicide involuntarily, with the assistance of the 'monks'.

For visitors, our chief recommendation is that they plead lack of honour rather than engage.

If you do not fight a duel, however, there will be a stain on your reputation which will lessen your acceptance in the best circles. This has inevitable consequences for career success. We strongly recommend that you obtain Mr F's unofficial guide to the Code Duello. Mr F's guide - while tendentious and sycophantic - will ensure that you have an even chance on this unfair field.

Your best hope in any duel is to have the support of one of the Lady Governor's circle and the best way to ensure their presence is to send a formal notice requesting an attendant to ensure that the code is adhered to. Despite the scholarly claims that lives are not lost, those lives that are lost tend to be those of migrants and others who live on the borders of society.

14

GRANIA AND DAL EXPERIENCE A FALLING OUT

Grania woke up very early and very out of sorts.

She worried as she always did. It happened too often and there was no real solution. Aches and miseries and the welling of tears were simply part of her life. It was one thing to feel this in a dark cargo hold in interstellar space, it was another thing to act like a wounded animal when her life had reshaped itself. The fact that she didn't recognise herself in her new life was no excuse.

Mostly she hid her concerns under bustle or early morning quiet. When she could, she drowned them in a cacophony of learning. Her art progressed, and so did her knowledge of New Ceres.

More rarely, she subsumed sorrow by losing her temper. When she lost her temper she immediately felt relieved, as if all the tension had drained from her. She made up for it by carrying guilt round all day and bathing in a miasma of self-dislike.

Today she felt her temper building. It was one early morning and one sore neck too many. She focused on pounding coffee. Grania could have used the little hand grinder, but she wanted to get rid of her hurt in an outpouring of physical energy, and pulverising coffee with mortar and pestle was a socially safe route to this. If she pounded with enough vigour, maybe she could face the world later.

As she pounded, she distracted herself with the rich fragrance from the coffee. It was from the highlands near Numos, so aromatic that it was almost sweet. Coffee was one of the few aspects of New Ceres that had improved upon home, she reflected. She treasured the chocolate-tinged aroma.

It had taken a full-scale quarrel with the cook before they had come to an agreement that – for her personal coffee only – the kitchen would roast and she would grind and brew it herself. It had become her path to morning sanity. Also, it had become a way of documenting where she was at in this strange new world (and why this strange new world that had such people in it didn't quote more Shakespeare, Grania wondered – she missed those silly Shakespeare quotes that liberally peppered Australian English). Grania ground away with her heavy stone and felt her anger flowing through. She could measure her life by how she ground coffee, if she could pay enough attention every day.

Today was bad, but not impossible. The coffee was – for once - roasted to the right crackling stage. If she had this mood and the coffee was over-cooked (dark upon dark was New Ceres' favourite roast) then her past would swell up in her throat and would spill out of her in anger. Grania would march down to the kitchen and explain exactly the degree of roast. Then she would hold the hurt within her and feel ashamed at having to rely on servants. Machines were so much harder to hurt.

Today it wasn't over-roasted, but it was over-pounded. All Grania's fury had pulverised out of her.

This didn't stop Grania from becoming rather morose while she sipped her hot drink. It's pregnancy, she realised, and her thoughts kept returning and returning to the possibility of an abortion. She didn't know what the people of New Ceres thought about abortions. She also didn't know what relics the war had left inside her body, to trap an unborn child.

Grania wanted to consult with Benjamin, who at least had been a new migrant like herself and whose grandparents had been from Earth. She had left the consultation too late, however, since he had died. Killed by highwaymen. An angry laugh bubbled up in her throat. Nothing was easy. Nothing was ever easy.

By the time the coffee in her cup was merely mud at the bottom, she had made her decision. Maybe some decisions were less hard than they looked. She remembered that her husband came from a different society to her own.

"Counts and countesses and dukes and duchesses. Not the fake titles of New Ceres, where everyone invented themselves into Europeans, but the real thing. Hierarchy and lordship and succession." Qan had finally explained this to her. Far too late, but at least she knew.

She decided to have the baby. Dal needed an heir. She could say that she owed him one, since he saved her life, but that wasn't the real reason for her decision.

She decided to have the baby, really. For Dal. To make him happy. To heal that lost look that hid his soul when he thought no-one was looking.

I do love him, though I can't think why.

She didn't want to sit in a coffee shop and be squizzed by passers-by. It was the socially acceptable place to be, but she didn't want anyone to see with those peering New Ceres' eyes, just how strong and public her emotions could be.

Home was no comfort. Coffee was no comfort. Grania left the coffee shop, not looking further than the next step. She headed for somewhere to buy haberdashery. Ribbons would do for now, but she needed to know what materials New Ceres had for baby clothes.

She hid her thoughts behind the errand, but continued pacing in her mind, thinking things through.

She berated herself for sounding so very G&S when she was confronting herself in the coffee shop. Gilbert and Sullivan aren't, after all, New Enlightenment in any way, shape or form. Just think, a whole society that refuses to sing The Mikado because it was written a bit too recently. The Mikado is such a perfect piece of literature, she thought. It dawned on her that, "If sometime it may happen that a victim must be found" fitted Livia precisely.

She made a mental list of potential victims and started to think about Livia's motivations. She hummed as she thought and as she played with the colours on the shelves before her. Then she pulled herself up. To hum was to trivialise the evils of this new society. Except... except... this was a part of her that had been missing since the invasions of Earth. She began humming again, louder and more determinedly. Behind the humming, Grania's brain was working furiously.

She wondered if Dal really understood how vicious the society was. Sure, he wanted to protect her, but that was because he saw her as one of life's innocents. He didn't know that her personality was split in half. Art and abstraction and ignoring life gave her a cosy feeling of safety.

She was not always in that safe inner land. Grania had played politics and had meant it, too. There was toughness inside and a streak of ruthlessness. It was how she had fought the invasion and how she had made the contacts that allowed her to escape. None of her family and none of her friends had that streak nor that political awareness. None of them had listened to her. Every single one of the people she loved had died in those terrible holding centres. Or elsewhere. She had closed her heart and shut down her emotions.

Now her heart was open again.

Admitting she loved Dal and that he might need saving was a big step. The baby complicated things, but at the same time, it simplified. It crystallised a truth: the most important element in her new life was Dal. Not her memories; not her losses; not her terrible aches. Dal.

LIVIA ALSO HAD a revelation that day. She saw Grania looking at ribbons and laces with her face hiding some very deep emotions. Livia found her step changing from the famous floating glide to a distressed, tight walk. As if she were protecting herself.

Grania was not an irritant in an oyster, despite the beauty she created. Grania was an imperfection in the world.

Livia looked at herself the way she normally looked at other people. If Grania was such an annoyance, then she was possibly obscuring Livia's judgement. Perhaps New Ceres would be better off without the artist. Certainly, much had fallen into disarray since she had set up her salons. Grania was the sort of person who provided a focal point even if she herself was unnoticing. This could be dangerous.

Livia passed down a side alley, in the next shop to the milliner where Grania had now turned to a close examination of straw bonnets. The owner saw her come in and raced to serve.

"I've found something for you," he said, under the cover of showing her a rather mediocre oil. "If you would come over here." Livia sat down and the shopkeeper brought a portfolio out from the drawer under the counter. "It's not from Earth, but it has a sense of it. The lines are perfect. I was tempted to keep it, but I knew it was for you."

And it was. A simple charcoal sketch. A servant at work, scrubbing a tiled floor. Perfect in every respect. Livia knew exactly who had drawn it.

"How did you get this?" The man raised his forefinger to his lip, to indicate it was probably stolen. Livia nodded. "I'll take it. I will also take that watercolour from the window. The one that lampoons the activities of the upper classes."

"There are three of them, madame."

"I want the one set in the caves at Pluto. My cousin has a rather nice series of caverns and I suspect he will appreciate it."

"Ah, that would be Alphonse. I believe I have heard of his dinners." So, they had descended from respectability to infamy. This picture would be her first farewell gift to him. One more step in that final dance.

The shopkeeper hid the charcoal sketch by Grania behind the cavern parody.

Livia was so busy contemplating the pure lines of the sketch that she quite forgot Grania was in the next shop. Grania herself might be a blight on existence, but her art made Livia dream.

That perfect artist was about to leave the milliner and haberdashery when she saw Livia pass. She came to a sudden stop and called on every ounce of quietness she possessed. Don't let her see me. Please God, don't let her see me.

It was as if their normal roles were reversed. Grania noticed Livia and saw all her mannerisms and took them in with her big eyes. She saw clearly how dangerous Livia was to Dal and even to herself. Much more dangerous than Alphonse, despite his obsession, despite his bribes and bluster. She started girding herself emotionally for the fight she needed to win – keeping both of them (and the unborn child) alive.

Livia was a murderer, Grania was certain. Even if it could be proven, she would go free because that was the nature of New Ceres. Grania was so distressed she went straight home and started to make coffee again. Grania's attack on the coffee beans took on a regular rhythm as she contemplated how to keep their family out of Livia's reach.

She noticed Dal leaning against the wall, watching her pulverise.

"What?"

He just laughed.

"Tell me!"

"You're making enough coffee for a week, yet we are promised to meet with Constance."

"I hardly know Constance. We spent an evening talking, that's all. I'll drink here. I feel a little queasy."

"Please come," his voice was coaxing. "It might lose you your melancholy."

"Does it ever occur to you that sometimes I like my bloody melancholy?" Dal just laughed and held out his hand. She relinquished her coffee and found her mood suddenly friendly. "I guess I can get to know Constance."

"You're out so seldom."

"Sorry, but I have projects that have been eating my brain for so long. I want to spend all my waking hours working on them."

"Sometimes I think you work on them while you're asleep, too."

"Of course I do!" She smiled, "But I'm allowed coffee breaks from time to time." She didn't want to tell him she had just returned from time out, because that might open the door to telling him what she had found out about herself.

They took a chair to a coffee house a little way away. Not too far to walk, but too far to walk on a day like this, so warm that the horses made the closed streets of the old district smell like the sad end of a stable. Grania wished the weather would break, or that the state would pay street sweepers rather than leaving their income to the random generosity of passing strangers. She knew what everyone would say, "No-one paid them in the eighteenth century. What's a little fragrance in midsummer compared with a completely enlightened society?"

When they finally reached their destination, Constance was examining a copy of the newest broadsheet. Grania commented as she sat down that the whole society was ruled by these stray bits of paper.

Dal laughed. "So it is."

Constance looked very smug. "It's about the Highwayman meeting Livia. Everyone's talking about the incident. Livia, of all people! This poem is better than anything else I've seen. It posits a secret romance. Here, let me read you a few lines."

"Everything seems to be interpreted as secret romance right now," Grania's annoyed mood had returned. It was Livia, creeping into her morning uninvited. She didn't wait to hear the lines, but suggested that Mr F's shop was just a street away. "You can find out if there's anything that's even newer," she suggested to Constance.

"What an excellent idea," Constance was bright as a button. "We can have coffee afterwards."

Just outside Mr F's establishment, Grania saw an alien. The tentacles and lumps and flickering skin were half-disguised by the black and white tidiness of late eighteenth-century male clothes. All cravat and starch. Shaped almost human.

"What's it doing here?" She was horrified.

"Presumably it's a tourist."

"Not 'it'," interpolated Dal, "He."

"Well, he'd better stay away from me," Grania muttered, in an angry voice.

"What's it – sorry, what's he done to you?" asked Constance.

"He or his cousins killed every single one of my relatives."

"Oh, not personally, surely. I've seen the intercasts."

"When did you see the intercasts?" Dal pounced as if he had just seen a snake. "How were they available here?"

"During Saturnalia, of course. Even the highest tech is available then, and we were all keen to see what was happening to Mother Earth."

"My family was taken when they found that Sydney harboured a seat of the Resistance," Dal looked down at his wife, suddenly, scared. She had never spoken of this, like this. "A few at a time they were taken, and tortured, and murdered. Not by humans."

"By–"

"Don't ever say that name," Grania interrupted. "Not ever, not within my hearing. Not one of them is innocent. Not one. They divided humanity. They emptied Earth. They murdered my family."

Just outside the printer's, the squid-like being approached Grania. It was obvious to the others from his demeanour that he was interested in flirtation. That he found Grania attractive.

"Excuse me," he said, in his burbling voice, and touched her cheek with the tip of a tentacle.

This was too much.

"No," she said, and backed off. The questing tentacle followed. "No," Grania blurted, her voice rising. A moment later, the tentacle still seeking, she started screaming and could not stop. Dal took her inside. Constance held the door against the alien.

Dal held Grania close until she quieted to sobbing. He sat Grania in one of the comfortable chairs, and quickly whispered an explanation to the boy on the desk.

"I'll get her some tea," the boy said. Before Dal could say 'thank you' he was out by a door behind the desk. Dal sat down and gently put his arms around his wife. He held her close and smoothed her hair and whispered loving nothings until her sobbing slowed and her breathing deepened.

A few minutes later Mr F came in from that office door. He carried tea in one hand and a copy of his newspaper in the other, open at a particular passage.

"It might help," he said without preamble, "if you read this."

Grania read Lady C's latest advice to the etiquette-challenged and she didn't know whether to laugh or cry. It explained to women of quality exactly how they should handle encroaching males, including those of squidlike tendency.

The aliens she associated with pure evil came to New Ceres for very particular reasons: New Ceres was so far from reality that tentacles indicated an alien libertine. She decided, finally, to laugh. It was time to remember that she had survived. That humanity had survived. That her challenges could be measured by the size of a single planet, rather than by the interplanetary war.

She echoed Lady C's question when she asked herself "How should I deal with those encroaching tentacles?" She looked at Lady C's answer. "I shall quietly remove myself from the scene in future," she promised her husband.

"Carry the hatpin and salt in case," he suggested. "The salt in their eyes really hurts. We used it during the war."

"Lady C says to treat alien lifeforms with dignity."

"And so you shall. It is far more dignified to walk away or flick salt in their eyes than to poison them as evil pests."

Grania managed a weak smile. "I bet Livia would poison them."

"True, but only if they challenged her."

Grania gave him another feeble smile and then bent her head to drink the tea. Her hands were still shaking. She was determined not to spill a drop. Her dignity demanded it.

Then she remembered, "Dammit. Dal, I forgot to tell you."

But Dal had wandered away and was engaged in a very intense conversation on the other side of the room. She saw the look in his eyes and realised he had forgotten the personal and was involved in politics again. She tugged his sleeve and whispered that she'd get herself home. He nodded absent-mindedly. He had the attention-span of a gnat.

Grania really wanted to take a chair, to keep her safe from terrifying tourists, but at this moment she knew it would bring a return of her queasiness. She walked and she looked firmly at the ground, so no-one could approach her. She felt she was walking a great distance, but she got by the dubious corners with ease and without so much as a lewd remark and by the time she was at home, Grania was calm.

She ordered coffee and cake from the kitchen. Her sweet tooth was going to be indulged today, just because. While she was waiting for it, she brought out the box that contained her early memorabilia from New Ceres. It was time to look back at it, she thought.

Suddenly her mood turned from bravely facing that transition time to pure nostalgia. She wanted to relive her first meeting with Dal. He had become such an important part of her life and of herself that she wanted to remember how it all started.

She rummaged in the box for the menu from Alphonse's dinner. She reminded herself of some of the people at the table. It was a strange exercise, because everyone looked so different now from the way they looked then, yet it wasn't that long ago.

She annotated it. "This was the closest I have ever come to Livia's friends, so these are the people who might bear watching."

A list of the dinner guests, with a note as to where they were now and what doing.

Frederick – dead

Benjamin – dead

Livia – Madam Ick

Grania – me, still alive, married, possibly rather pregnant

Josephine and husband – on the rise, thankfully nowhere near me

Alphonse – accepted my refusal, thank God. Avoids me. Possibly dangerous if we contact again. I wish the Families had been part of the briefing when I arrived.

Dal – amazing how everyone important was at that one dinner party. Amazing how important Dal is to me, despite everything. Or because of everything. Or whatever. I want to take him on a harbour ferry. Sydney Harbour still existed, she thought, in surprise. It was the people who were missing. No-one to captain that ferry. Dal would never see North Head or Government House.

Constance – looks frivolous, but avoids me at the oddest moments. I'm suspicious of people who avoid me. Or is it that New Ceres is getting to me?

"I forget the rest of the guests," Grania realised. "Everything was too new." She looked a while at her little list and then she ripped it up into shreds and used it to make more papier-mâché. This wasn't a society where notes to oneself remained unread by others, after all.

While she looked at the pile of paper a little helplessly, wondering what she should do with it, there was a knock on the door.

How extraordinary, someone polite, thought Grania. Unless it's Qan. Qan is always polite. I bet he was born polite and thanked everyone who came to his christening. If he was christened. "Come in," she called out.

"Ma'am, I'm so glad you're here."

"Something's wrong," Grania stated badly.

"You know, already?" Qan was surprised.

"All I know is that something is wrong, because you never call me 'ma'am' unless something's wrong."

"Oh," Qan took a moment to compose himself. This is when Grania realised just how wrong the something wrong might be.

"Start at the beginning," she advised. "I would rather know everything."

"Yes, ma'am."

In the silence, Grania wondered what could have so perturbed this man, who had stood so well with his master over the departure from Holotor. It must be bad.

It appeared that Dal had not left the printery quite as soon as Grania thought he would. An acquaintance had dropped by to collect the latest papers 'from the source,' as residents of Prosperine said when they wanted an excuse to gossip in Mr F's front office.

After a pleasant chat, Dal had stood up to leave. At that moment, someone who had been standing just outside the door had chosen to walk in and Dal had nearly bowled him over. There were apologies from Dal's side, of course, as was proper, but the gentleman had stood stiffly in the doorway, blocking everything.

Dal asked if he might leave, and the man said "Wait just a moment." He withdrew his glove from his right hand, and slapped Dal lightly three times, as was proper, right cheek and left cheek and right cheek again.

Dal had been challenged to a duel.

Qan was very excited.

"I know a man," he said. "Someone from back home. He has been writing articles about New Ceres and he knows about duels. I checked with him."

"You checked with him?" Grania asked slowly. This was all so unexpected and even out of character for Qan. He was acting as if it was serious, but also as if it was exciting. Something to admire. A good thing to happen.

"The man was from one of the Six Families. Or maybe a noble. Everyone was excited. He's someone who does not just challenge anyone."

"Dal is not just anyone." Grania said this slowly, puzzling it out.

"For so long we have been telling him he should be acknowledged as who he is here on New Ceres. To be challenged by a family member means that he can't escape that recognition. They know who he is. They have as good as admitted it."

"But?" Grania prompted.

"He was probably put up to it by Livia or Alphonse."

"They want Dal to die."

"Yes," and Qan was subdued again.

"Tell me more."

"There's not much more to tell. We don't know yet who

put the man up to it. We can't get him to back down, which means it's completely intentional. He's very well known as a hit man for the Six. He's exceptionally good and exceptionally fond of killing."

Grania nodded. "Get your journalist friend to advise Dal," she instructed. "And bring me a big bowl of water."

When she had her bowl of water and was alone, Grania took her paper strips a handful at a time. She dipped her fistful of paper into the bowl of water and squeezed and squeezed until the fistful was just a messy lump. Then she threw each sodden lump at the wall with all her strength. With each throw she screamed. It was a day for screaming.

Two screams in and a servant peeped in to see what was happening. His head disappeared very, very quickly and Grania was left alone until her temper was done.

15

MENU

G rania's menu:

The menu from that night at Alphonse's. Why are pivotal nights so hard to put up with? That Livia person sitting two people away from me designed the menu. She told me so three times. It's based on real food eaten at a royal court, because Alphonse, she says "Has a touch of royalty." I never know if she is serious. All I know is she reminds me of a serpent. Even her dress had scales.

Alphonse offers you, his honoured guest:

Potage aux marrons

Potage à la gouvernante

Chestnut soup and a soup the Lady Governor invented. Which makes it recent.

.   .   .

Entrées

Tourte à la viande (boeuf or veau, selon choix)

Such a fuss to make about meat pies

Terrine d'ailerons de poularde

This looked like something I would have sculpted. Interesting, but inedible. I said a polite 'no' - you never know what goes into terrines, anyhow. Especially here.

Saucisses

Just sausages. Gourmet sausages, but just sausages. How do you eat sausages with any grace, anyhow?

Mélange de fricassées

This platter reminded me of a casserole gone wrong. Too much gravy and everything was fatty. I didn't touch it.

Foie gras au philosophe

There were two patés. I don't know what was philosophical about this one, but it was made from goose liver and absurdly rich. I ate a knifetip of it and nearly gagged. The other was supposed to be "in the manner of Lost Earth" but they were lying.

Pâté de lièvre au façon de Terre Perdue

Grandes entrées

Five different sorts of meat. Lamb that was so old it was mutton (almost sickly and overpowering, despite all the spices), good old roast beef, and lots of marinated roast meats. I did well on the roasts. First time all night food looked like food, too.

Carré de mouton en fricandeau

Bouf rôti en façon antique

Other roast meats (chicken, pheasant, veal)

Artichauts braisés

Artichoke hearts made to taste funny.

Croûtes aux champignons

Mushroom pie. Rather nice.

Aubergines à l'Alliance

This was just plain weird. All sorts of crustings and growths in a way apparently really current on Alliance planets. I never want to see eggplants looking like that again, and I said a polite 'no' to tasting it.

Légumes et salade du jardin de la gouvernante

Your basic undressed salad. Stuff of kings on this planet. Says it all. Depressing, but I took a big serve and didn't let anyone see the tears. Mum used to grow all these.

ENTREMETS

Ragoût de truffes

Something to titillate the tastebuds, Livia said. Looked strange to me. Truffle stew? I'm guessing here. Their French isn't my French and their fungi aren't my fungi and for all I know it was barbecue chicken.

Fruit

A platter of seasonal Earth-origin fruit

Tarts of apricot and peach

Confits of Earth-origin fruit (cherries and apricots)

Assorted creams and jellies and compotes.

Glace aux macarons Rich chestnut icecream.

Shame they only served me a little.

Massepains de pistaches

Some sort of pistachio dessert. Was so busy looking for more of that icecream that the waiter thought I was saying 'no' and I didn't get to taste it.

Fromage glacés

The menu said frozen cheese. I am not going to eat frozen cheese. Ever.

.   .   .

To drink

Wine (after the style of old Champagne, Bordeaux, Chateauneuf-du-pape and Italia, with grape types pinot grigio, muscadelle and pinot noir)

Liqueurs and eau-de-vie aux fruits (de poire)

Chocolate frothed in the ancient manner

Port and brandy (for the men only, after the third remove, to be served with cigars)

Tea (for the ladies only, in the salon, while port is being served)

I DRANK THE PINOT GRIGIO. Nice drop. Didn't get to the rest of the drinks. That was when I fell out with Alphonse. Well, he had it coming

16

UNEXPECTED ENCOUNTERS

"So tell us," ordered Dal, walking up to the apparently-knowledgeable journalist, "What do I need to know for a duel on this planet that I don't already know? And don't tell me it follows duelling patterns of Earth in the eighteenth century. I don't want to hear it."

Fred Xian was nervous. His jumpiness was certainly not made any less by Qan, who followed Dal like a dour shadow.

"The Code Duello is all I know, my lord."

"Not 'my lord', and you know it."

Xian stepped back a little and then resumed from his new, less terrifying standpoint. "It appears that you gave offense to this person. He therefore insulted you in public. You have chosen to duel, rather than to withdraw. At least, that's how I interpret it."

"Close enough."

"You're remarkably cavalier with your life," Xian said.

"Perhaps, and perhaps not. I'm not unfamiliar with duels. I simply need this one to follow the very letter of the code, so it will all go away politely once the occasion is over."

"You've decided on weapons, I assume." Xian had no idea

how to handle Dal, and wavered between high courtesy, garnering information for potential articles and getting the occasion over with just as quickly as possible.

"What do you think?" Dal was as sarcastic as only he knew how to be. "Since we are in an unholy place at an unholy hour and carrying swords."

"With a growing crowd, no less," Qan pointed out. The crowd was a fringe of people hovering at the edge of the playing field. It was quietly getting bigger and Dal rather suspected they would all descend for the kill.

"In a moment," said Xian, "I'll cross the field and see if we can avert the duel. Failing that, I shall ensure that the weapons are fair."

"If he cheats?" Dal spoke far too disinterestedly, given the occasion. It was as if he were only going through the motions.

"Then I believe we may hit him, though I sincerely hope that it is not necessary."

"You would rather Dal was hit?" growled Qan

"I would rather this was not happening at all," Xian was honest and Dal laughed.

Dal had a sudden thought. "What does your code say about methods of cheating?"

"Not much, although it does warn against modern weapons hidden in duelling pistols and of swords charged with off-world power devices."

"You, too, will be defeated by crystalline energy and magnetic powers," Dal showed his toothiest grin.

"Sorry, sir, I don't understand," said Qan.

"Your master has been reading space opera," Xian informed him. "And not the best space opera, either."

"My wife says I should read it. Over and over again she says so. Read books, she says. Classics. I'll reach classics one day."

"Please, sir," Qan said, with careful patience, "Worry about the duel today and your wife's literary recommendations tomorrow."

The other party, in the meantime, had strolled close enough to be scrutinised.

"Your opponent appears very honourable," Xian commented.

"Your research informs you of this?" Dal was acerbic. He did not appreciate being associated with the less savoury members of his family again, even through someone as inoffensive as this journalist. There was too much close respect and even fear in Fred Xian's manner for comfort. "Or is it your role as a spy that gives you this knowledge?"

"I've already told you twice," Xian was becoming impatient and was fast losing his respect and his elevated language, "I'm not a spy. For the record, I wish you had never been denounced and that your damn brothers had been thrown out with the galaxy garbage."

Dal spared him a downwards glance. "Then tell me, why do you think this challenge is an honourable one."

"Gloves," noted Xian.

"Gloves?"

"He's not wearing them. It's a minor point of honour and shows that the challenger is a gentleman."

"This means I ought to take of my gloves too," Dal said, matching his actions to his words. "Pity. I had hoped to avoid getting my hands cut up."

"That's the thing, sire," Dal looked exasperated at the title and Xian briefly bowed his head in apology. "I think it means you're both avoiding cheap cuts. Sir."

"But you're not sure?"

"No, sir."

"Then at least avoid the bad jokes. Anything that wounds my hand is not a cheap cut."

"Yes, sir."

They waited a moment, watching the honourable opposition talk with his deputy.

"What does your Code Duello tell you now?"

"Exactly what I informed you in my note... sir."

Dal laughed again. "Go and have your consultations and mark your square. I'll be ready. And gloveless."

"Yes, sir," Xian bowed and went to the other party. Dal's shadow detached himself and followed. Dal looked suddenly alone and defenceless, standing there in his quiet garb.

The challenger, although gloveless, was not dressed soberly. He was a veritable peacock in full plume. His model was far too obviously the middle of the eighteenth century in France and the amount of gaud he displayed made Dal almost regret not choosing pistols. Such a bright target would be easy to hit.

As Dal watched, however, he stripped off his jacket and his waistcoat and beneath the plumes, his dress was sober black. Two shadows on a green field, with metal flickering between them. That's all the crowd would see. Dal was tired and wanted the whole thing over. It would not have made any difference if Dal was fired up and angry, however. The duel was going to happen slowly.

GRANIA WATCHED the leisurely movement on the field and felt fear build up in her until it distorted her vision. Dal was a stranger to New Ceres. He couldn't possibly win against an experienced opponent. And what would happen if he died?

She wanted to go and hide until it was over, but she had

been informed by one of her new society friends that this would be markedly improper. So here she was, waiting forever to watch her husband murdered according to an arcane ritual.

Two men detached themselves from her husband and met two others in the middle of the field. They talked and stood around and talked some more. Two of the figures walked slowly to the four corners of the duelling space and marked the boundaries with white handkerchiefs. The other two watched.

"Do something," Grania wanted to scream, but she stood protected by a cluster of her salon regulars and waited.

Eventually the second pair of men wandered towards the weapons and discussed them and examined them seemingly forever. Dal waited on the field, alone. Grania's eyes kept returning to him. Early dusk was casting long shadows from the crowd across the green field. Life was illuminated and turned into techno-art.

It wasn't just the sun shifting, Grania realised. Something had been resolved and the crowd was moving in. After a moment's resistance she found herself pulled with the throng, closer and closer, until she could see everything. Grania was not at all certain she wanted to see everything.

Both Dal and his opponent had been given swords while her attention was distracted. His opponent looked quiet and expert. Not as rangy as Dal, but compact and neat and dangerous. Dal looked nervous, Grania thought, although she couldn't be certain, given how expert her husband was at hiding his feelings.

There was a moment of complete silence.

There was a moment of flash and sparkle and movement. Everything was over. It happened so quickly, Grania had no idea of any of it, except that Dal was standing. Her heart turned over and she almost fainted with relief. Who would have thought I was so very emotional, Grania wondered at herself, as someone helped her up. She turned to thank the person and found that it was Constance.

"Who won?" she whispered.

"Why, your husband, of course," Constance sounded as amused as ever. "I didn't know he was such a fine swordsman."

"Nor did I," answered Grania, still in a whisper. "How did he win?"

"First blood."

"Oh. It's like something from a book."

"Except that idiot de Raimbert is wounded. Who would have thought that there was another planet that kept the tradition alive? And who would have thought that your husband would show such flair?"

"Alive," Grania whispered.

"It was a set-up that failed. I begin to like your husband. I also begin to understand why he and his chose New Ceres."

"I don't understand anything," said Grania.

"You're overwrought," Constance said, in a down-to-earth manner. They watched the surgeon clean de Raimbert's wound. Dal was surrounded by a small mob of new admirers and was handling them stiffly.

Grania realised, "He doesn't want to be there."

"De Raimbert will leave town for a while," Constance murmured in Grania's ear. "None of the swordsmen want to be humiliated by an off-worlder."

"I thought it was a fair fight."

"It was. Whoever put him up to this assumed his opponent was untrained."

"I didn't know that about Dal. I just didn't," Grania commented forlornly.

"That's your pregnancy speaking." Grania looked across at

Constance and noticed that her eyes were surprisingly wise. How does one identify friends when they hide their caring beneath so many layers?

"I should go home."

"Let me extract him for you. I doubt the constabulary will care about this little fracas, but it's always wise to disperse quickly, in case."

That night Grania and Dal were very quiet together and very tender. It was as if their arguments and happiness had faded into gentle. Very late at night, awake in bed, Grania realised again just how much of her life was dependent on him loving her and how much she loved him. Somehow, she had found what she needed. It was very far from the happy ever after she had dreamed of in the darkness of the cargo ship, but it was certainly a proper marriage.

She was silent in their shared bed. Happy, relieved, but disinclined to talk. She decided to treasure the news of the pregnancy for a bit longer. Maybe the morning would be the right time to have that talk.

They were still quiet and content together in bed the next morning. Grania loved the feel of him in the bed beside her, so she turned and leaned on her elbow and looked deeply at him. Dal woke up and smiled back. She forgot her news and grinned stupidly.

Over breakfast she dithered. She needed to tell him. She knew this. He had to know about his own child. His worry lines had returned, and his face looked sad and distant.

Not yet, she thought. Save the burdens for another day. Then she reconsidered, the way she had been reconsidering and reconsidering and reconsidering since she first realised that she might be pregnant.

Maybe if she gave him a hint? She had already done that with the nausea. He had been surprisingly obtuse. About not telling him, because he ought to know, but she looked at his worry lines and thought of the potential dangers for her and for the baby. This time, she took a slightly more direct route.

"Dal," she asked, "can you find me the details of a good doctor?"

"Qan will know," Dal said, absently.

Tomorrow, Grania thought. Tomorrow she would tell him.

Dal's thoughts, that had roamed so far from his wife, were entirely taken up with the matter of the duel. Someone was targeting him; he needed to find out who.

Probably Livia or Alphonse, Dal thought, since it was highly unlikely that any dissidents would be after someone with so much in common with them. But still, he needed to know, and quickly, in case any of his people became targets now that the duel had failed.

He sent messages into his various networks and he waited, with assumed patience.

Three days later, he was no more advanced. Time to check other sources.

"Do you still want to go to Hightown?" he asked Grania.

"Of course I do," she said. "You're the one who thought it would be dangerous."

"I still think you're impossibly innocent."

"Should I hate you for that?" Grania wondered out loud.

"Don't," suggested Dal, lazily. "I couldn't do a day trip with someone who hated me."

Grania felt like a teenager, with a treat being held out for good behaviour. The duel was so close in her mind, however, that she didn't want to challenge him. She just wanted to spend time with him. No games. She ignored the implied condescension. This once only, though, she told herself.

"What do I need for a day in Hightown?" she asked.

"It will be a very long day," Dal warned. "Most people drive for a few hours, stay over in New Stilton and make a holiday of it."

"You said a day trip?"

"You can do a long day?"

"If I know why. You never do things like this without reasons."

"New Stilton is dangerous for us. I want to spend no more time there than we need to."

"So we drive through it."

"Horses, Grania."

"I'm sorry?"

"We change horses twice each way. New Stilton is the only place that has decent meals."

"So a short stop, a long stop and then a few hours in Hightown then a long stop and a short stop and arrive back here with our own horses?"

"That's about it."

"How much stuff can I take?"

"Anything that fits into the carriage. If you want a picnic instead of a meal at an inn, pack enough for the outriders."

"Outriders?"

"It's dangerous. We will be taking four riders."

"Six of us, then."

"Horses, Grania."

"Six and hay," Grania was enjoying stringing him on.

"Coachman and assistant."

"You're a nob," Grania said.

Dal looked down, confused.

"Can't go anywhere without an entourage."

Dal gave a little smile. "Maybe I'm a schoolteacher?"

"How do you work that one out?"

"I'm going to tell you things until you learn them."

"You mean like horses?"

"Yes."

"One day I'll learn to ride," Grania said wistfully.

"You can't ride?" Dal sounded very surprised.

"Now you're laughing at me the way I was laughing at you."

"No," said Dal, slowly. "I forget that when we adopt something from Mother Earth it doesn't mean that people from Earth know it."

IT WAS A VERY, very early morning start.

Mist still clung around the streets and softened the limestone until Grania could half-shut her eyes and think she was in Adelaide on a winter's morning. The sense of home faded, however, after the Old Town. They transferred to their travelling carriage once they'd passed over the river and she lost the sense of Australia entirely. The mist had lifted and the hills were green as emerald. Grass that green was unnatural, Grania felt. Even worse than the water.

She half-dozed through the jolts and rattles and her mind processed why it felt so unnatural. The water reminded her of where she was, so its alien nature had become reassuring. She could wake up every morning and wash and see the taint in the water and know where she was. When she looked out the carriage window, though, it was neither home nor not-Earth. It could be Ireland, with that colour grass, or maybe Normandy. Ireland or Normandy. Places she could travel home from.

Having settled things to her satisfaction, she dreamed of old travels until they reached New Stilton.

"Do we act fashionable and buy cheese here?" she asked, as she clambered out of the carriage. The small steps and her big skirts were a combination she never could quite sort out.

"This used to be the centre of Livia's sphere of operations," said Dal, in answer.

"How does that work? She lived here?"

"The Six farm out their talented young. They supervise the paid officials and help control the industry and keep it under the Lady Governor's gaze. That's how the whole of the Six started off nearly two hundred years ago, as unpaid officials. They get their wealth from cuts they take and they get their politics through taking care of crucial operations."

"That sounds inherently corrupt," said Grania. "They ought to be paid public servants and there ought to be a ton more accountability. Legislation and stuff."

"And regular payments and paperwork make people less corrupt?"

"Where I come from they did," Grania felt defensive.

"Not here," Dal sounded regretful. "While the government controls the food and while no-one has civil liberties everyone is either corrupt or becoming that way."

This was the closest Dal had ever come to explaining what he did with his friends. Grania felt as if she ought to be grateful for every crumb of information, then she felt angry that she was only allowed to know fragments about matters that obviously affected her. Why would they have needed all the outriders if Dal had not got on the wrong side of Alphonse and Livia and their ilk?

Grania allowed her irrationality to flow through her until her moment of privacy in the inn's amenities had passed and until she found herself sitting down in a very green public garden with Dal. Everyone else ate at a safe distance. Money and prestige, thought Grania can make a person solitary inside.

Hightown was much prettier than Grania had expected and much more boring. It was nothing more than a place pandering to the schooling needs of the upper classes and those who wished to emulate them. Exclusive schools were hidden in deep estates in the hills and behind great walls. Less exclusive schools boasted wrought-iron fences and silent gatekeepers. Big houses hid the children of the middle classes, in the middle of town. There were many, many playing fields and sporting arenas and places to buy food.

Dal didn't take Grania to see any of the schools. He gave her a quick tour and lunch and then they went shopping. Grania bought as many books as Dal was willing to carry home: she watched his eyes carefully to find those limits. All the other stuff, from fencing equipment to slates, passed her entirely by. She noticed that, at several shops, he had some words with the shopkeeper while she herself was left to browse, while at other shops he assisted and made suggestions.

"Now I know why you only wanted a half day here," she said to her husband, as the carriage started rolling towards home.

"When there's an open day or a festival it's more interesting," he replied, "But I thought you would rather see everything on a typical day first."

"The sudden visit had nothing to do with the young man who slipped you a paper over lunch or with the broadsheets that have mysteriously disappeared from under the seat?"

Dal wore his most innocent look.

The trip to New Stilton was uneventful. In fact, the whole trip was uneventful, Grania realised, when they were about a half hour out of Prosperine. She heard a shout outside and the carriage jolted to a stop. Drabbit, I jinxed us.

The shout came again, more clearly.

"Stand and deliver!"

"Honestly," grumbled Grania, "Sometimes I think this planet is just a costume drama."

"Quiet," said Dal, listening intently.

There were no gunshots. Nothing except the faint creaking of the carriage and the sound of horses. A muffled groan. A shout.

"Out of there," a male voice said, and a big gloved hand opened the carriage door.

"A Gothic Romance," whispered Grania to her husband, as they slowly climbed out of their seats. Dal gave her an exasperated look.

Outside the carriage the world had rearranged. There were a dozen masked bandits, their shapes hidden by big coats. All four of the armed guard were huddled together with two pistols upon them. A smaller person, of gender unassignable, held a gun to the coachmen and two more held the horses. A semi-circle of big and dark masked men trapped Grania and Dal.

Grania looked up, curiously. She was scared but felt also strangely distant.

This was a costume drama, no more, and if it killed her where the invasion of Earth hadn't then, well, it was just too bad. Her fingers itched to capture it all in charcoal, but she doubted the marauders would allow her to make sketches of them. She would have to memorise. And so she did.

Dal stood defiantly, while little Grania looked up and examined. She realised that several of the men were actually women, just a moment before one of them laughed.

"What is it?" growled the tall man at the very end. Grania rather thought he would be slender but muscular if he took off that greatcoat and the heavy scarves.

"It's the way she's looking at us," explained the woman. "She's measuring us for shrouds."

"No, I'm not," defended Grania. "I was thinking how interesting you would all look in charcoal."

There was a silence.

"I doubt they expect you to make sketches of them," said Dal, mildly, his whole body screaming alertness.

"Then they ought," retorted Grania.

"Why is that?" asked the woman.

"Because we know you."

"Be careful what you say," the bass voice held a warning note.

"It's Zenobia, isn't it? You hold your head so distinctively. I've always wanted to paint it. You're Constance's friend."

Zenobia laughed again and stripped her face bare. "I told you this was a bad idea," she commented to the world at large. Dal's stance was still one of high alert.

"Did you want to kill us, talk to us, or make us feel really, really bad?" Grania was on a roll and enjoying herself.

"We wanted to warn you."

"Consider us warned," Dal said, almost threateningly.

Grania looked from him to the group and back again.

"You know, I think you're all idiots." The dark semi-circle of people tilted forward like standing stones about to fall. "I honestly think you should all be talking to each other instead of plotting alone in your cellars or attics or wherever you do your skullduggery." The silence deepened. "Since we have identified Zenobia, why don't we meet with her and anyone else you don't mind us knowing about? Somewhere neutral. Without me, if you prefer. I don't mind. I never understand why one should use weapons where talk will achieve the same effect."

"This is not an alliance," said the deep voice.

"I never said it was."

"So what are you suggesting?" asked Zenobia.

"That all of you talk. Nothing more."

"And what do you suggest we talk about?" The words faded into the air around them.

"Oh, I don't know. Common interests? I would like to know what 2324 stands for, myself, but no-one wants to play with me, so I guess that's not terribly important."

"Zenobia, travel back with them," the leader tipped his head towards the carriage and then to the road. "Talk about 2324. Nothing else. If you feel comfortable and you and Dal can find common ground, then organise that meeting Grania suggested."

"Thank you," said Dal.

"Don't thank me," he said. "Thank your wife. And you," this time his black eyes looked straight into Grania's, "May I suggest you don't try a stunt like this again. If we had been real highwaymen or if we had been your genuine enemies, you would already be dead, the moment you said Zenobia's name."

"They think I'm stupid," whispered Grania to Dal, as they climbed back into the carriage.

"Either that or very naïve. You give both impressions," Dal said, "Even when you know exactly what you're doing."

Zenobia asked to be dropped off near Leather Lane, just outside the Old Town, so they took the Old Prosperine Road, sealed before the New Enlightenment. Grania listened to Zenobia and Dal with half her attention and admired the beautiful road surface with the other. She couldn't understand this city, where people preferred to clatter on cobbles rather than to enjoy a smooth ride on a good surface.

"What do you want to know?" Zenobia had asked.

"Everything, of course," Dal had said, promptly.

"What does 2324 refer to?" asked Grania, more practically.

"In 2324 the then Lord Governor was presented with a new food processor," Zenobia wasted no time. "It was compact, portable, reliable, cheap and durable. Best of all, it was near enough in kind to the approved processors to not need new approvals for hi-tech."

"What happened?" Dal asked.

"Bloody murder," said Zenobia, grimly.

Grania was shocked, but not about the murder. "New Ceres doesn't have to rely on this government for safe food, then." She thought a bit further. "All processors are hi-tech?"

"Of course," said Zenobia. "There were no terraforming issues with Old Earth. Food was safe. Just because we like our particular society, doesn't make us inflexible. If food was safe on Mother Earth, it ought to be safe here: even the highest stickler for tradition can allow hi-tech for that purpose."

"Mostly safe," Grania amended, thinking of the miserable stuff from those last few months. "Food was mostly safe at home."

"Safe food wasn't a government monopoly," snapped Dal.

"No, it wasn't that," and Grania moved back to her question. "What happened to the processor?"

"Nothing," Dal said, "Otherwise we would not be in this particular pickle now."

Zenobia assessed him. "Not quite nothing," she said, "But as good as."

"What, then?"

"One of the townships was causing problems. It agitated for independence and it thought possession of the new processor would make it so. The Lord-Governor tested the machine on the township."

"And made sure it failed?"

"And made sure it failed. After all, a falsified failure meant that no-one could hope. The government control would remain."

"Why haven't I heard of this?" demanded Dal.

"It was covered up just enough so that it looked as if it were being covered up for the people's benefit. It was very cleverly done."

"How did you find out that the processor actually worked?"

"We have a contact deep in the Families," was all Zenobia would say.

Just before they dropped her off, she pulled a folded paper out from somewhere in her many layers of clothes.

"This will be out tomorrow," she said. "Enjoy it. This is a busy week for us."

The broadsheet contained a fuller reveal than the one Zenobia had grudgingly given. It went into vast detail about the existence of cheap food processing since the year 2324 and listed all the officials who had been responsible for the original cover up and those who had helped sustain the lies ever since. It pointed out that this government monopoly was killing people, as if such an idea was inconceivable, rather than a daily occurrence. It also detailed tests of the cheap food processing and gave blow by blow descriptions of the tests and of the farms on which they were now installed.

"Stupid," commented Dal.

"Brave," answered Grania.

"Maybe brave," conceded Dal, "But very stupid."

"Why?"

"Because they pretend to be highwaymen. Protecting something. The only bit of road they're protecting is the road we just travelled. Our people have known about the highwaymen on this road for a while and if we know, then other people must also know. Too many people know that the criminals are actually rebels. Not a very hard one and one to add."

"And?"

"And this paper." He flourished the paper so close to Grania's face that she snatched at it in annoyance. He saved it from her clutches and sat on it. Sometimes he was such a child.

She eyed him and repeated, "And this paper?"

"Makes it obvious precisely to whom they provide protection. Those farms they talk about..."

"New Stilton."

"It's their style, I think, to mock the establishment and New Stilton is so very much part of that."

"How did New Stilton farmers withdraw their product from the main processing plant without anyone knowing?"

"Maybe they haven't. Or maybe they've only done so partially."

"Send just enough stuff to the plant to convince everyone they have low milk production?"

"Not a good long term proposition, I should think," said Dal.

"Dangerous," said Grania.

"Dangerous and stupid," said Dal, "but every bit helps."

"I still think highwaymen make wonderful camouflage," Grania insisted.

"Oh, do you?" Dal asked, and kissed her.

"What was that for?"

"Later," he promised.

17

LIGHT READING

Before Dal got around to explaining the kiss, the revelations about the food processor hit the streets. They didn't hit it very far, because the authorities pounced on every single copy they could find. The Lady Governor's police made a very effective deterrent, but they couldn't stop the people of Prosperine wondering what was so important that so many enforcers should chase it and suppress it so very quickly.

Livia obtained a copy through one of her old contacts. Many others of the Six missed seeing it entirely.

The reason Livia obtained a copy was not one she would admit to anyone. This once, it was not her ability to taste the pulse of Prosperine politics, or her curious effects on those around her. It was simply that she was currently focussed on all the printed ephemera she could obtain.

Mr F asked if it was all his fault, when they met over coffee and she asked for his latest.

She said, "I'm afraid so. You have made me into a hopeless addict of the printed word. Maybe," she said, looking at him just a little coyly, "Maybe you could make amends."

She didn't mean this, though. Privately she carried out her own little war of destruction on papers she didn't want people to read. The two (in particular) that she would rather no-one looked at, concerned her supposedly-lamented husband, Frederick.

With every passing day Livia mourned that he was not still alive. If he had been, she would kill him herself this time round. His death would be slow. Slow and agonising.

She wanted to personally take a small knife to his guts and to twist it, watching his face all the while. Or a hot poker. Red-hot pokers were insufficiently esteemed, she thought, and needed more consideration as instruments of torture.

She wished the fashionable Gothic novels had an element of truth or a greater element of magic. She wished Frederick could be brought back to life again and again and again. She would find out all his secrets this time, and she would make him pay.

In the meantime, he was making her pay. Every month there was a new revelation. Every month she found herself derailed and having to make up lost time and status. Every month dead Frederick forced her personal goals further and further away. Every month, a new publication appeared, showing him to be the unadmirable gentleman she had always known.

Her late husband had not been nearly as tightly reined as Livia had thought.

The latest sheaf of papers she had been delivered had started well enough.

The first was a series of advertisements.

"I have received 32 small-arms, which I would sell on reasonable terms," one announced, while another indicated that "The household furniture of the chief magistrate of the township of Lourdes, which were advertised for sale at the next meeting of merchants, will be sold the tenth day of this month, by Frederick Wilhelm Champion and Honorée d'Aix, surviving trustees." Small town papers. Small town concerns.

The next few papers were all political. Public political. Safe. Complaints about the level of larceny practised by customs officials, wishes that taxes were lower on the iron for horseshoe nails ('so essential to the vitals of our society'), requests that speeches to the Parlement be published within a reasonable timeframe so that all citizens could read them. All very cautious. She flicked through them desultorily to get a feel for them, then put them aside to look at properly in a moment.

She found a couple of ballads, and the highwayman document. The highwayman document she pondered for a long time and she took notes.

These people should not play on my turf, Livia thought.

Then she went back to the political papers and read them, every single page. Slipped into the folds, were two other documents, lurking quietly. These were the ones that had sent Livia into an orgy of imaginary husband-murder.

Both of them were printed. One was a newssheet, and the other, a commentary on it using identical headings. Oddly, neither came from the press she had identified as producing most anti-government literature. Nor had the highwayman article.

She compared the highwayman article with the ones she had just discovered. Not the same. Three different presses, none passed by a censor. Even if she had not been personally concerned with printing and presses, this would have to be taken to the Lumoscenti. Livia smiled a little smile. This was a good thing and just what she had been after. An excuse to consult the public office of the Lumoscenti and to make herself known as interested in taking one more step in the secret dance.

This was– of course – before she read the paper in question.

The first of the two new discoveries described how a scion of the Families sold details of the Allied defences to the Alien Alliance at a critical moment during the war. This information had been the crucial element that weakened Earth's chances of surviving. The news would have stunned Grania and shocked most of New Ceres.

The paper made Livia furious. It wasn't the loss of Earth. It wasn't even New Ceres' involvement in that catastrophe, despite its public neutrality during the war. It was because the very end of the document named the 'scion of the Families' and the name given was her husband's.

Frederick. Possibly the biggest traitor in human history.

Livia had played the identification card too well. Despite their mutual antipathy, not a soul thought of her as anything but a most loyal wife. The only way to change this was to allow the public to officially know more about her other activities. Once her private life was publicly acknowledged, it would be finished. Livia's form of politics only worked in the dark. Public image was so important, and she and Frederick had both spent a great deal of effort on their image as a happy couple.

On reflection, she realised that this was worse for her than it at first appeared.

No-one wanted to be allied to the destroyers of Earth. If this got out, then New Ceres would be assumed to be allied with a group of human-settled planets that were increasingly isolated and distrusted in the post-war negotiations. It could ruin New Ceres' interplanetary relations. If it did that due to her husband's actions, then all doors would be closed to her.

She probed and examined her feelings in fine detail until she knew why she was reacting the way she was. On consideration, New Ceres (with Frederick's kind intervention) had won the battle, but in allowing Earth to be emptied of humans, they had lost the war. She was furious at Frederick's ghost.

How could she put this in her past? How could she limit damage to a respectably small zone?

It was impossible to kill someone already dead, and any public excoriation of Frederick would affect her own reputation and render her future miserable. She decided to bring forward his first memorial. That would deal with her rather wild emotions. The rest could wait.

Or maybe... she put the half-thought on hold until she had completed Frederick's memorial altar.

The memorial took a few hours for her servants to prepare.

Livia created a nice little platter for the dead in his honour, consisting of all his favourite foods... untreated. "This is what I think of you," she said, as she gracefully placed them on the flat dish carved into the tombstone. And it was over.

On to the next thing. There was a way to limit the damage to both herself and to New Ceres. It was rather drastic, but she would prefer to cause a little stir than drown in Frederick's ordure.

Livia packed the first damaging paper into her purse and ordered a sedan-chair.

It was a slow ride. Livia found fault with every aspect of it, but eventually she walked up Grania's front steps and knocked on the door.

"I'm sorry," the servant said, his face entirely unreadable. "Madame is not home."

"I rather think she is," Livia replied. "Please show me in."

"I'm sorry," he repeated. "Madame is not home."

She should have expected this. "I will send her a note. Please find me a pen, ink and paper."

He had no choice but to usher her into the front hall. He should have shown her to a room, but either Grania's house was disorderly or someone had given strict orders concerning Livia. She pursed her lips and thought of the beautiful Dal. It was unconscionable that she was not given due respect, but understandable that Grania should be protected. Well, she would simply have to bypass that protection. Her note would have to be fascinating, and it would have to be true.

"Madame," Livia penned in an elegant copperplate, "I find myself driven to make a terrible apology. Would you permit me to make it in person?"

She signed it, folded the note neatly and sent it on its way. The servant reiterated the, "She is not at home," but Livia ignored him. She found a small chair in the foyer and she sat on it, folded her hands neatly in her lap, and waited.

After a few minutes, Grania came tumbling down the stairs. Her hair was wild and she was wearing a painting smock. Splashes of colour decorated her hands and her smock and even her hair.

She stopped when she saw Livia.

"Oh," she said. "I'm sorry. I was certain this was a practical joke."

"Is it so improbable?" Livia stood up.

Grania gazed at her frankly. "I believe it is. If you will excuse me a minute, I shall tidy myself. Qan will see you to the blue parlour and will bring you refreshments."

"Thank you. I would appreciate that."

That Qan would also keep an eye on her remained unsaid. Grania might have discovered some courtesy, but she was still under protection.

It was not too long before Grania appeared again, respectable this time. They drank tea and made polite chit-chat until the first cup was finished, as was proper. Someone had coached Grania, Livia realised. Not one of her menfolk, either. She was curious about who and why, but it could wait. The fact that Grania was pregnant was even more interesting. Something could be made of that, too, given time.

"I am not quite sure how to explain this," Livia began. Normally she would put someone like Grania on the back foot, but in this one instance it was essential that she be conciliatory. "I have been doing some research into the activities of my late husband. You understand, it was a marriage of convenience and there was a great deal we didn't know about each other."

Grania nodded, more to show that she was keeping up than because she could see any reason for Livia to pay her a private visit.

"Some strange and unsavoury incidents have emerged since he took his own life. The dishonour that caused him to suicide appears to be the least of them."

"I'm very sorry for you." There was a truth to Grania's manner that was quite disturbing.

"Today I discovered this," Livia took out the paper, but retained her hold on it. If Grania read it first, all her own advantage would be sacrificed. "It proves that Frederick betrayed New Ceres in a far more serious way. Not one battle, but a whole war. Not a local skirmish, but the recent galactic one."

"Yes?" Grania was pale but held her own.

"My dear, I believe it was he who provided key information that let those villains occupy Earth. I came here at once, because I wanted to offer you my support if it becomes public and to offer you right now, my deepest and most sincere apology. I knew nothing about it, but he was my husband and you and all the brave citizens of Earth suffered from his actions."

There, it was done. Whatever happened now, Grania would be forced to say to the public that Livia had come to her immediately she knew.

It didn't matter if no-one believed her apology. The important thing was that she had made it before anyone knew there was a need for it.

"I can leave you the paper?"

"No, thank you," said Grania. "I appreciate you coming."

Before she could say anything else, Dal entered the parlour. The look of relief on Grania's face was unmistakable. Livia smiled sorrowfully and stood up to take her leave. Everyone shook hands or bowed and then it was done.

"The viper left quickly," Dal said to his wife.

She turned a look of grief to him. "The viper thinks I don't understand when she uses me."

"How?"

"Evilly," and Grania burst into tears.

"This is becoming a habit," Dal said.

"Don't joke," Grania said. "Not now."

"I won't. Especially given I've had another narrow escape. Perhaps Livia came to gloat about my demise."

"It's possible. I didn't read that in her, though. And why should she tell me that awful news if there was other awful news in the offing. Excuse me for sitting down. I feel sick."

"What awful news?" Dal was instantly all seriousness.

"She says she came to apologise. She said her husband betrayed Earth."

"Gods."

"I bet it's true."

"I expect it is, at that." Dal looked very tired. "Is there never an end to the wickedness?"

"It's past, Dal. Everyone who is gone has truly gone. I have no idea why what the hell game Livia was playing at, but we can be sure it's a game."

"Sometimes I feel haunted," Dal admitted. "I feel as if it will never be past and that there is no future."

"Oh. Then it's time you knew something. Maybe even past time."

"Livia again?"

"No, you. Creating the future. In here." Grania patted her stomach.

"You want a baby," Dal looked hopeful.

"We're having a baby. A little earthchild to help civilise New Ceres."

Dal let out a shout. Large and joyous and full of life.

Later, Grania got to thinking. She suspected that Livia might still have been responsible for the attempt on Dal's life. He was being taught a lesson, Grania realised. If that one failed, then maybe she would teach him another, more serious lesson. The duel first, then an accident and then escalation. That was Livia's style.

I don't like Livia, she told herself. But by God, I'm going to cultivate her until I find out just what she's up to. And whatever she's up to with that apology, I'm going to milk it. We will survive this, Dal and our earthchild and me.

18

———

COFFEE HOUSES

FROM *TOURING THE GALAXY THE FUN WAY: A GUIDE*

Volume 34, New Ceres

Coffee houses are one of the most delightful aspects of social life on the planet New Ceres. The proper and formal description of them is that they are establishments dedicated to the drinking of coffee and to fine conversation. The lowest class of them may also serve as outlets for servicing brothels. Everything about them is as close to eighteenth century Earth custom as possible. In many ways, they are the centre of the New Enlightenment.

Customers buy coffee by the dish. A waitress will bring the pot from behind the counter and pour the coffee from a pot into the bowl or cup that everyone calls a 'dish'. The coffee is poured from a significant height into this rather small piece of china. Locals explain with grand seriousness that the longer the coffee flow from pot to dish, the higher the froth on the coffee. Sit well back, because inexperienced or uncongenial staff may cause spillage and the coffee is extremely hot.

Because of the great heat, it is customary to hold the dish elegantly by its top edges and to inhale the rich aroma for a few moments before attempting the beverage itself. The drink is extremely rich and dark, laced with sugar and spices. The more expensive the coffee house, the thicker and richer the coffee and the more likely you are to have a choice of spices. You might be asked what flavour coffee you want. 'Orange' for instance, will give you a delightful citrus aroma, obtained by the addition of small amounts of orange peel during the brewing process.

The polite drinker will take occasional sips, letting the dish rest on the table or trestle between each sip, to allow the sludge at the bottom to settle. When you reach the sludge, do not attempt to drink it, instead, signal for a refill.

In most coffee houses, you can sit for as long as you like over a dish of coffee. Do not commit the faux pas of trying to sit alone, or that of ordering a beverage other than coffee. Asking for coffee substitutes is particularly uncouth.

Getting as far as the coffee is somewhat more complicated than it looks. A useful rule of thumb is not to join a table on which there is any object but coffee dishes unless you are actively solicited. Safer still is to ask the staff to indicate a public table. Regular groups at a coffee house will have their own table (elite coffee houses) or trestle (lesser establishments) where they will expect strangers to respect their possessions. You'll see everything from newspapers, board games and personal effects strewn across those tables.

Coffee may be charged for in sous or in shillings. There is no real difference between a sous and a shilling and why the two coinages are maintained is an oddity of government. Houses that charge in sous are more likely to have a gentle clientele and to have a food license. This license will be displayed above the main coffee counter and is your assurance that the food bought there is safe for human consumption. It is also a guarantee that the coffee house does not serve as an outlet for an illicit brothel. The existence of a food menu, therefore, means that the coffee house is safe for both men and women. If there is no food menu, be careful, for you might find yourself solicited. Many off-worlders have found themselves in prison through accidental prostitution.

There are other dangers in choosing a menu-free coffee house. The most concerning is the quaint food trays carried by vendors. Vendors walk between the tables, offering snacks. Except near the spaceport, those vendors who demand immediate payment in pennies are less likely to serve safe food. Always demand to see the license (as with street vendors) and scrutinise it carefully. While the holder of a forged license is liable by law, this will be of no avail to you if you have ingested untreated food. While in most cases a single serve of untreated food will not kill, off-planet visitors are more prone to extreme reactions than locals and, while medical attention can ameliorate the symptoms of many reactions it cannot return you the months of your life that each ingestion will demand.

Since 2546 the Lady Governor has recommended to tourists that they do not buy from vendors without licenses even if they apparently sell to locals. This is due to a series of deaths resulting from intentionally contaminated food sold to tourists through conspiracy between an unlicensed vendor and three other people. Since then, occasional groups of young bucks have tried to persuade many tourists to try untreated food, as a prank. It is safer to entirely avoid the trays of food vendors.

Always be prepared to cede on points of honour. A small amount of discomfort to your ego is infinitely preferable to an argument over the finer points of duello at rapier tip or the sight of a loaded gun at sunrise. The swordsmanship of the middle and upper classes is notoriously good.

While the Lady Governor officially disapproves of affront being offered to tourists and your Embassy staff may intercede for you if there is time, we are talking serious risk to life and limb. The authors of the Guide appreciate that the arcane codes of New Ceres are one of its attractions for visitors, however, the fact that gentle men and women receive formal training in duelling from their early teens and that coffee houses are known as places where young bucks actively seek fights, suggest that courtesy and polite demurral to others is a useful policy.

19

A POCKET OF STRANGERS

Livia and Grania were sitting across the table from each other at a very elegant coffee house in the Old Town. Neither of them quite understood how they had got there. Neither of them was quite at their ease.

Earlier in the day there had been an incident. Later in the day there would be reconsideration, but at this moment in time Livia and Grania were sitting across from each other, sipping from dishes that had just a little too much of the chinoiserie and wondering how they got there. Both of them were still surprised.

It started with Grania.

Grania had been playing with her new toy. It was the cutest tidiest painting package she had ever seen. An easel, a palette, a set of brushes, all the colours she could want for mixing, bottles with clear water, containers for every conceivable purpose (including lunch) and all in a neat carry case of very fine leather. She could carry it under one arm, which left the other free for whatever she used the splendid set to create.

Dal had apologised when he had given it to her. "It should have been a fire jewel."

"Why?"

"For first pregnancies, a fire jewel. We say it keeps mother and child safe."

"What do they look like?" Grania was curious, even if the superstition was not her own. "I've never seen a fire jewel."

"Translucent, like a moonstone. Blue-green like the oceans of Earth. In the centre, a burning flame that lasts forever."

"It sounds beautiful," said Grania, wistfully.

"It is. Beautiful and rare. Like you. Alas, however, unlike you, they cannot be found on New Ceres."

"I can wait, if it means so much to you."

"I've sent for one," Dal admitted, "But my sources say it will take a while to locate. Far too long. In the meantime, I had someone make you this." And he gave her the gift.

The moment the weather was fair enough, Grania took her toy to the Old City, to play with contrasts. One more step in turning the light she saw into light that other people could see. This time she would use sad remnants of hi-tech over-matched by limestone sculptures and monumental marble statues of heroes and gods and goddesses. Ancient Greece revived in streets and parks that once echoed with interstellar dreams.

The old spaceport would have even more contrasts, Grania suspected, but it was all parks and business districts and she loved the little shops of the Old City. She adored the square grid and the arcades and the way the movement of crowds flowed over and through the grid and the arcades and made it come to life. She found in herself a craving to do a series of watercolours showing the goddesses who roamed the parks.

She needed to keep herself busy, because she might have

a new toy but Dal was meeting with Zenobia. She had thought that he had her measure now, but apparently not. He had looked very polite and very apologetic as he explained what he would be doing, but he would not include her.

"It's too dangerous," he said.

Why did I marry a patriarchal man? How did I marry one, on a world where women are so powerful? And how the hell do I change him so he realises that I may be his woman, but I'm not a little woman.

Her mood was philosophical rather than angry, if the truth were known. She had decided to get involved in politics in her own way, and Dal's moody passion might suit her in bed, but it wasn't the way she worked in daily life.

She realised with a rush that she had discovered daily life again. The terror of her past had subsided somewhat. Grania smiled.

What to do now? She needed to learn a great deal more about New Ceres before she took any kind of an active role. Learning. That was her immediate future. Discovery and education.

Constance is a help, she thought as she dabbed at the mottling of Minerva's arm. Her advice had helped enormously with the social complications she faced every single day and Constance's clear understanding of her own planet's politics was making everything a little less obscure each and every time they spoke. Despite Constance's best efforts, however, it would take time.

"Hey!" Grania heard a shout. "That woman painting. Over there, near the arrow-lady. She's the last Earther, Grania."

A couple drifted over to see what was happening. They excused themselves and asked if she minded them watching.

"I don't mind an audience," Grania admitted, "But I need silence to work."

"We'll be silent," they promised.

Others joined them, however, and those others weren't as silent. Soon there was a chain of casual conversation linking the watchers as they clustered around Grania. Grania found it harder and harder to work. She looked around at the crowd.

"I'm terribly sorry," she said. "I can't paint in this noise. If it's essential for any of you to talk, then I would appreciate it if you carried on your conversations elsewhere."

There was an instant silence and Grania picked up where she left off. It was difficult, for she felt flustered and a little angry. She had never been a public spectacle in this particular way. She disliked it. It took her back to a second-year art class at university, where everyone assumed they were the most important person in the room and as a result Grania was pushed to the side and talked about and neglected.

How could I have been neglected and talked about at once, she wondered. My memory must be playing tricks. I know that resources were not allocated fairly and that Ms The-teacher-says-I'm-going-to-be-famous always got the first and best of everything, but that's not quite the same thing as being the class Cinderella. And even if I was the class Cinderella, this mob can't beat me. After all, I won the handsome prince and I made it in the art world, and I'm alive. I need to remember that. I'm a survivor. Besides, if they start chatting again, all I have to do is pick up my toys and leave. I may never make friends, but I don't have to sacrifice just to get by. Not now. Not anymore.

This intention kept her painting for a good half hour. At the end of that time, however, the dynamics of the crowd had changed.

Someone had started humming a silly tune. It was annoying at first, but not in any big way, so she let it go on. After a bit, however, it developed words.

"Run, run, run Earther woman.

Run, run, run when the enemies come."

That was all it said. Over and over again. Hateful and hurtful and so very wrong. Grania started packing up her things. I can leave, she told herself. All I have to do is walk past these people.

The crowd had created a tight circle around her. She clutched her portfolio under one arm and carried her painting gingerly in the other and the painting was smudging, and she couldn't move. She didn't know whether it was her legs or the watchers, but she was trapped in the middle.

"Shame on you!" A woman's voice cut through the crowd. A moment later a path cleared, and Livia stood there. She beckoned to Grania.

Grania walked towards her, a little stumbling at first, but soon the ground started to hold her steps and she could leave the circle. As she took the last step out, she felt a touch on her elbow.

"Wait," Livia said. She turned back to the crowd, which had reformed and was now Livia's audience. Her eyes met each and every person's eyes there.

"I trust you recognise the name 'Livia'," she said. "For it is mine." There was a ripple of disquiet in the crowd and Livia let it flow until they were all listening again, more intently than before. "I see you have heard the new broadsheet, with the Song of Lost Earth. To sing it to the woman named in it is shameful. To make her run from any of us is to echo our own crimes."

"We've done nothing but watch her work," a man's voice said from the back.

"Until I found out the truth, I might have agreed with you. You like that chorus – look at the verse. It tells the truth: New Ceres helped Earth die. If we had been genuinely neutral, no

Earther woman would have had to run. If you had genuinely done nothing but watch her paint, Grania would not have been forced to run now. I know all your faces. You know what people whisper about me. Do not let me see your faces or hear your voices singing again."

Grania and Livia walked away, together, Livia's hand still lightly tucked into the hook of Grania's arm. It was shaking. Grania was surprised. Surprised by the intervention – surprised that it had been so hard for this dark soul.

Livia was no less surprised. "I've never done anything like that before," she whispered.

"We need coffee," said Grania.

This is how they found themselves, speechless, at a small table in an elegant coffee house in the Old City.

LIVIA WAS IN A QUANDARY. What had started as a simple ruse to ensure that Grania would defend her against accusations concerning Frederick's actions had grown into something quite strange. She did not know what had possessed her to defend Grania in the park, to throw her reputation into the crowd as if it were a public possession, and she certainly didn't know why she was not able to coolly walk away afterwards.

Her actions were out of character. She knew this. With every fibre of her being, she knew this. And yet...

Livia stalked her house and gardens, sticking her nose in everywhere, upsetting routine, confusing staff. Her feet were wayward and her brain was not its normal functioning self. She could not plan Alphonse's fate or write the letters she needed to write, or compact stray bits of information into a web of understanding. How could she do any of this when she was capable of emotional outpourings to aid her enemies?

Perhaps Grania wasn't really an enemy?

Livia started to chronicle when she had seen Grania and where.

Soon it was far too obvious that Livia's own unruly legs had sought Grania out. She had gone to a different kind of function to those she normally visited and made appearances at far too many salons. Every time she had reasons for it. Information to be gained, people to be met. She knew herself very well, however, and was always honest when no-one could see. She could make any function work for her. The reasons were a gloss. Something about Grania fascinated her.

She knew what.

Livia wished she had not known anything. She never recalled her childhood. It served no purpose. Yet Grania had survived treatment as bad as that and had emerged radiant. Livia had survived and become twisted. She knew it and normally did not mind at all. It was who she was and she loved her life. Seeing Grania, though, made her think. She had defended Grania because no-one had defended her.

But what did it mean? How was she going to handle Grania in the future?

Friendship was not an option. Friendship led to complication on complication and friendship was never an option. For a moment, Livia felt regret.

What she needed to do was let Grania know that today's events were a temporary aberration, nothing more. A warning would do.

How to warn a person whose husband was already a target? How to make that warning very, very personal? Livia smiled. There was a traditional way of doing this, and Grania was already in a perfect situation. Chocolates, moreover, were always able to be presented elegantly.

Livia burned her papers, thoroughly returned to herself.

THE BEST PLACE for a secret meeting is in public.

The most public place on this particular Saturday morning was the park that once was the Old Spaceport. Society thought it was clever to appear en masse and watch balls of silk float away across Prosperine. Society dressed up rather well to see those balls of silk. Society thought that many things were clever that were in reality a trifle silly and this fad was less silly than most. The cleverness of it, according to Those Who Influenced, was that the park was where gravitic drive ships used to take off. Rather bigger round balls of stuff that was rather tougher than silk, floating away into infinity.

Everyone was there. Naturally. It was the place to be seen.

Some were thronging very capably. Others were patronising vendors of snacks and drinks. Young bucks were showing off their ballooning skills by issuing orders from their fancy baskets. One was inside the balloon as it inflated, experiencing the bellowing of air. Far too many people were hoping for an accident like the one last spring when three balloons collided in mid-air and one poor soul died.

Several groups had arranged secret meetings. Dal's people were there, of course, meeting with Zenobia's mystery man. They were also keeping an eye on Lady C, who wasn't nearly as closely affiliated with any group as everyone had thought. Lady C was an enigma.

Livia was there, finalising Alphonse's future. Alphonse

would not die that day, but threads of his life would be cut on that balloon field.

Mr F was present, of course, bearing advertising material for his new book on ballooning. He handed out cards with Great Enlightenment comments on ballooning. Grania took one and pinned it to her dress, and soon everyone did the same.

"Look," she said to her husband before he linked up with other conspirators, "I've started a craze."

He looked down at her fondly and ruffled her hair.

"Stop it," she grumbled. "I didn't get it cut short so that you could treat me like a toy."

"But it's so soft and fluffy," he teased.

"Like your brain."

Constance appeared and demanded Grania's attention and soon Dal was caught up in the crowd, lost to his intrigues. After a hearty gossip with her friend, Grania found herself wandering alone.

She enjoyed the sensation of watching. She watched as Livia spoke briefly to a young woman handling ropes, then drifted away into the crowd. She watched as Zenobia and Dal and a tall ebony man pretended light conversation. She watched as Alphonse bossed his way onto a balloon.

She listened to snatches of conversation and discovered strange facts. Her husband apparently owned the workshop that produced the balloons. The Lady Governor had no inspectors there, said the gossips. They talked about it as Grania was passing because Grania reminded them that such an important element in the silk industry was owned by an off-worlder. Some appeared happy that the Lady Governor's monopoly had been broken. Some felt it was a betrayal of New Ceres. Grania felt they were very talkative.

Grania wondered if she were imagining things. If she

wasn't, then more groups than Dal's and the 2324 had met this early morning.

One day I shall do a very private study, she promised herself. What is making this society fall to pieces? How long does it have? First, she decided, I shall have my baby. I need more people to love.

She wasn't the only one who needed more people to love. Maybe early morning was a bad thing. Maybe it brought out all the ill humours and everyone had left happiness behind in their beds. She noticed Zenobia arguing with her friend and Livia arguing with that protégée of hers. Alphonse would be arguing with everyone and she even glimpsed Dal in a quiet dispute with Qan.

Bad omens? Or bad temper?

As she floated across the edge of the balloon field, she kept an eye on the balloons. Incredibly slowly, they expanded from flat packages to lofty spheres of pure spirit. Grania gradually moved closer, until she was between the crowd and the balloon people.

"Come here. Yes, you in the maroon dress," called a voice from one of the groups manning a balloon. "We need someone to pull on a rope."

Grania obliged, and stood for a minute, pulling when she was told and letting loose when she was told. She wasn't paying much attention to it. The crowd behaviour was far more interesting.

A crack whiplashed through the air. Suddenly Grania found herself on the ground, a heavy body on top of her. She tried to get up.

"Wait a moment," the body said. "Wait until it's safe."

Grania waited. A moment later she heard a whistle. She found herself being helped up and brushed off.

"Sorry for knocking you over," said Constance, who

turned out to be the owner of the heavy body. "Someone was shooting at you."

"Who?"

"One of Alphonse's men," Constance said.

"Shit," said Grania. "Alphonse is here today, himself. I saw him. He doesn't believe in keeping away from the scene of the crime, does he?"

"Quick," Constance said to a girl standing next to her, "Find Grania's husband."

"Thank you. I really think I ought to go home."

"With your husband."

"He is in danger too?"

"Not this time. It was you he was after."

"But why?"

"Oh, lots of reasons. I'll tell you another time. Right now, we want to get you somewhere safe. Your home is best, but if you prefer elsewhere I can offer you a coffee."

"Home, please. And thank you for knocking me over."

Constance gave her a brilliant smile. "You're such a little thing. I felt as if I were crushing you. When you're old you'll be like Lady C – all eyes and personality."

Grania put herself back together and the group started to escort her to safety. One of them pointed over to the balloons.

"Look," he said.

A single balloon had broken away from its moorings. In the basket was a lone figure, waving his arms wildly and calling.

"Someone help me!"

It was Alphonse. One by one Constance's people turned to look up at the errant balloon. They looked and they pointed, and they laughed. Grania laughed along with them.

Dal didn't laugh when he eventually found her.

"When Alphonse comes down to earth," he promised, "that man will have something to worry about."

GRANIA FOUND A BEAUTIFULLY WRAPPED box waiting for her downstairs the next morning. It was accompanied by a small gilt tag saying "With respect, from Livia."

I need some advice on these, she thought. I also need my mind read. How on earth could I have got close enough to Livia for her to send me chocolates?

She put them in her dressing room to sit until she could discover what the right action was. Did she send something in return, for instance? Or a thank you note? Or ignore it entirely?

She opened the box and eyed them. They didn't appeal. One thing she was missing because of the pregnancy was chocolate. Maybe she would get the taste for them back in a few months. She closed the box and left it until she could get that advice. Constance would know.

20

PLACES BEYOND

It didn't matter what she did, Grania could not get the house staff to pay attention. She had told them a thousand times who was to be permitted entrance and yet here was Alphonse, a mere six days after attempting to murder her, and he had been admitted to her salon without a murmur.

Grania unclenched her jaw. She had to appear calm and a good hostess. Everyone knew about the gun and everyone knew about Constance saving Grania. It had been so very public. Grania would much rather that throwing Alphonse out of her house was not public at all, but she had no choice. She had to be calm and gracious and the perfect hostess all in perfect synchrony.

Grania had to do it without servants, as they had mysteriously disappeared. She would have to take it up with Qan, again. Whenever she did, she felt as if she were complaining about trivia. She felt selfish and greedy and a bad person, to demand personal attention. Even more selfish to complain when a servant being sacked could lead to them dying from untreated food. She tried very hard to keep her complaints to a level where no-one could be discharged from service.

Besides, while she could understand the servants' role in maintaining a large house in a low-tech society, she couldn't understand servants attending to her needs. She had refused a personal maid, just to make this clear to the household. Her underclothes were still the ones she was familiar with and all her dresses buttoned and tied in places she could reach. She was very unfashionable.

In this case, though, she had cause for complaint. Grania might be capable of doing a great deal for herself, but unless she had opened the front door herself at that particular moment, she could not have kept Alphonse away.

She was delaying. Grania was smiling at her guests and walking through as if she had a purpose, greeting one and nodding at another. The truth was, she was trying to work out how not to confront Alphonse.

A quiet voice in her ear made her jump.

"Is there anything wrong?" Lizzie asked.

Maybe she shouldn't have invited Lizzie, Grania thought, defensively, but she liked the woman. They saw each other little enough these days, and the salon was one of the few places where they could chat. Her friends on this world were so few, and she refused to let her own discomfort with Lizzie's profession get in the way.

"I have to work out what to do with Alphonse," she said. Be damned to New Ceres courtesies, for once she was going to be honest. "The staff slipped up and let him in and I can't find any of them to show him out."

"I don't blame you for not wanting to go near him your-self. What he did Saturday was abominable."

"I don't want him here. He's flaunting."

"That's despicable," Lizzie finished for her. "I have a great desire to embarrass him."

"I don't believe it's possible."

Lizzie laughed. "Watch and learn, my friend. Stand just behind the door over there."

Grania was curious and did as she was told.

Soon she heard Alphonse's distinctive tones. "Well, what did you want?"

She stiffened until Lizzie spoke. He wasn't speaking to her. He couldn't even see her.

"I wanted to thank you for coming here to find me. You have saved me a journey and I can give you my message directly." Lizzie's voice was very loud and very clear.

"What message?" Alphonse was querulous.

"From the Molly House on Steep Street. They can't visit socially themselves, of course, and you won't be able to do so once you've joined the particular group you have been negotiating with, but–"

"What the hell are you talking about?"

Lizzie sounded bewildered. "I was told that you were coming here today specifically to hear about your acceptance into a particular society. I'm sorry, did I get the message wrong?"

"I should think so," Alphonse was all anger and bluster. "Why would I do such a thing? Do you think I would enjoy the company of those...those..."

"Those what, Alphonse?" The man who spoke so quietly and gently moved within Grania's line of sight and she gasped.

She had seen this man before. He was the one who watched her in the salon. He was also the gentleman who had failed to kill Dal in that duel. Why hadn't she put those incidents together until now? And why was he helping her?

"You know who I mean." Alphonse's face was turning red.

"Men such as myself?" the man mocked. "I admit that I personally do not want your company. If you choose to accept that invitation, I will find a reason to challenge you. Also, I think, if you come here again."

"You would defend anyone in this household?"

"You know little of honour, Alphonse, less of the world, and nothing at all of virtue. The next thing you say – whatever it is – I shall take as a personal insult."

Alphonse turned and left in a great hurry. Lizzie laughed and said "Don't come out, Grania, we need to talk to you in private."

"It's one of those days, isn't it?" Grania asked of the air, and led Lizzie and her pet assassin to the studio. "Sorry about the mess," she said. "I'm more comfortable here."

"It's a wonderful room," said Lizzie. Her eyes roamed and she saw a pile of sketches. "May I look?" she asked. When Grania nodded, she bent to pick them up. Paper fell to the floor from a fold in Lizzie's dress.

Grania bent to pick it up. "This is yours," she said, and glanced at it as she handed it over. "Oh," she said.

"I work for your husband, I'm afraid," Lizzie admitted. "I should have told you earlier. I run the literary arm of his less public endeavours. This is Fabian, by the way. Fabian de Raimbert. We were talking yesterday at a place you probably don't want to know about, and we decided we ought both speak to you."

Grania looked at Fabian for a moment and then gave a sigh. "Forgive my manners," she said. "I don't think I'll ever get used to the way things chop and change here." She held out her hand. "Pleased to meet you."

"I'm sorry about the duel," he said.

"So am I. Thank goodness you spared Dal."

"I didn't spare him," Fabian was genuinely apologetic. "I was executing a commission. It was an error on the part of the one who commissioned it. The target should have been... someone else."

"He won't give names. He never does," counselled Lizzie.

"I can understand that. But why was it a mistake?"

"My employer thought that Dal was doing something other than what he was actually engaged in. My employer also thought that Dal was an agent for his cousin," Fabian gave an engaging grin. "There was also a certain amount of anger on my part and I failed to advise my employer that I was not neutral in this case."

"Not neutral?"

"He was treating you as a charming child. Every public gesture he made showed that. I found this intolerable."

"Why should that even concern you?"

"We'll explain in a minute," Lizzie advised. "It's why we're here, in fact. First you need to know something about Fabian's employment."

Grania gave them a questioning look.

"That was the last of my long-term contractual obligations," Fabian said.

"I'm pleased for you, as long as this doesn't mean you're suddenly without means."

Lizzie and Fabian exchanged a look.

"I'm missing something important, aren't I?" asked Grania.

"I no longer have to do the Lady Governor's dirty work. Nor dabble in off-planet politics."

"He's freelance and he's working for me," said Lizzie. "In a number of capacities." She winked.

"I am no longer obliged to take dishonourable jobs," Fabian explained. "Lizzie offered me the one condition I never expected to be permitted in any of my capacities."

"What was that?"

"The right to refuse any assignment."

"This means you keep your integrity."

"That's it exactly," Fabian looked at Grania assessingly. "I shall keep my club at the Molly House, however."

"I'm afraid I don't know what the Molly House is."

"It's a euphemism for a male club of a particular variety," said Fabian.

"Where the men can fill the roles they dream of and society will not permit."

"Such as?" Grania was tired of being bewildered.

"The most ordinary visitors often don dresses upon arrival. Does that give you an idea of the place?" Fabian asked.

"Oh, I would so like to see Alphonse in a dress!"

They all laughed.

"Lizzie thought you would understand," Fabian said.

"I don't know enough to understand," admitted Grania. "But I thoroughly approve of that clause of yours and I hope you will undertake not to try to kill my husband ever again."

"I have already so undertaken," said Fabian, giving a little formal bow. "Neither you nor yours, and he is one of yours."

It was a strange way of describing it. "Me or mine?"

Fabian and Lizzie looked at each other for help.

"It's a custom," said Fabian.

"New Enlightenment?" If it was just that, she could look up more history books. Grania was getting used to reading eighteenth century history.

"No, not New Enlightenment. Simply New Ceres. It's one of the reasons we have the New Enlightenment, however."

"I didn't know that," said Lizzie. "I always thought it emerged from the New Enlightenment. You know, those of us who can't fit into the hierarchy, making a place for ourselves."

"I believe it was the strength of the personal oaths that

cemented the attachment to the eighteenth-century ideals early on," said Fabian.

"Can you explain personal oaths?"

"Of course," said Lizzie. "It's like love. You fall in love with someone and you marry them, and you owe them obligations. Well, this is a bit like that. You discover someone you want to give your oath to, and you announce to them publicly or privately that you are in their service."

"So it's a declaration of loyalty?"

"Very much," Lizzie nodded. "It's like finding a lighthouse and swearing to maintain it so that it can continue to guide ships in from the sea."

"Dal as a guiding light – I like it."

"Not Dal. You."

This was something Grania had the greatest of difficulty with.

"Why me? What if I don't want it?"

"You have no choice. We take the oath together. We have already taken the oath. It's a courtesy to let you know."

"It can't be one way."

"It isn't. Remain true to yourself and the qualities that inspired us – help us remember why and who and how. Graciously permit us to help with the small difficulties of life from time to time."

"You're saying you're part of my life, even if it worries me. I know you a little, Lizzie, and I'm happy to be friends, but all I know about you, Fabian is what Constance told me."

"What was that?"

"You are a professional fighter."

"Also a professional whore," he said calmly. "And particularly good at both my chosen professions."

"But not happy with working for the Six. There are many

sides to a family, after all," added Lizzie. "We're going independent. Single contracts, right of refusal."

"Where do I come in?"

"You remain yourself. Through everything, you remain yourself. We took the oath precisely because of this. You're a very rare soul. You don't play with ethics or morality. You take them seriously. You don't seem to care if society approves of your art. You don't consult to check if the subject is fashionable or the theme is safe. You're independent."

"I haven't always been. And I've made mistakes. Terrible mistakes. I am the worst possible role model."

Lizzie nodded. "This is another reason why, when we talked yesterday, we decided to swear to you. In Prosperine mistakes are covered up or exploited. We ignore murder and hate and poison. You don't. You still care. We want to keep caring."

"You want to celebrate your humanity," Grania said, quietly.

"Yes," breathed Fabian, his eyes glowing.

"Would you mind taking a look round for a moment? I need to think."

Grania walked around her studio while she thought, touching a canvas lightly, or picking up a brush and putting it down again. A few minutes later, she came back to Lizzie and Fabian.

"I don't do hierarchy well," she said. "In fact, I really am uncomfortable with the whole idea of rank and perfect loyalty and stuff. The oath thing makes me feel odd – I'm sorry, but I just can't see why anyone would swear such a thing. I like your vision though." She paused for a moment, looking for the right words. "Can't we be friends instead?"

"As well, yes. Instead, no."

Grania laughed ruefully. "We're in a bit of a bind. If I say 'yes' I can probably tell you don't do this or that. But I'm saying I don't want to be a leader or have followers so I can't then turn around and claim the authority to tell you what to think."

"It's a quandary," Fabian's eyes sparkled. "Except for one slight error in your logic."

"Yes," said Lizzie. "It's simple. We can all work at friendship and what Fabian and I think about you and talk about is our decision. About the oath, not to get your approval of it. Approval is what Six Family sods do."

"If we lionise you, it flows from our free will."

"Thank you both so much for that." Grania was at her most sarcastic. "You're right, but I don't like it."

Lizzie was more hesitant this time. "You object to knowing us? Having us as friends?"

"Why should I do that?"

"I can't imagine you in my profession," said Fabian. "In fact, I suspect you might be too modest for comfort." He gave her an unsettling look.

"Nor can I," admitted Grania, ignoring the look. "I can't even imagine what a Molly House might be. But if you're in the business because you want to be then I can't see what I should have to object to. Don't sleep with Dal, though," Grania warned.

"You love him," said Lizzie softly. "I never get in the way of true love."

"And we're married. I believe in honouring contracts."

"I told you," Lizzie said to Fabian. "She would understand about you challenging Dal because of that damn contract."

"I do. I don't like it, but I understand," Grania admitted. "I'm relieved he turned out to be a better swordsman."

"We should leave," said Lizzie.

"I need to get back to the salon." She picked up that sheaf

of sketches. "Would you each accept one of these, as a token of friendship?"

Grania felt surprisingly warm over the whole incident. It was so strange and foreign that she really wasn't quite sure what it meant, but she liked it. This was New Ceres, so she couldn't be certain that either of the two were trustworthy. But she felt good about it all the same. She decided she would give Constance a sketch soon, too. Her three friends. It had been far too long since she had so many people to call 'friend'. That evening she quietly raised a glass to new beginnings.

TWO DAYS LATER, the reason Alphonse had been admitted into the house became a little clearer. Qan's warnings had been forgotten and something Grania had done had upset a maid and everyone was carefully being subservient and avoiding her and trying to pretend she didn't exist. Meals appeared on the table, however, so life was not as bad as it had been.

This changed the morning after Dal and Qan left on one of Dal's projects.

"Back in three days," he said, and kissed her forehead. Grania just grunted. Her mind was busy with a project.

That morning, however, she had woken up to the sound of loud chatting and the strong smell of floor wax. Two maids were polishing the floor in her room. She had to get out of bed by the end to avoid getting her feet all polished up.

Grania talked quietly to the housekeeper.

"If you're spring cleaning, you can send my meals to my studio for a day or two." Grania said. "I don't mind. And if you'll let me know what time you need access to my room, I'll make sure I'm clear of it. I'd rather not have anyone in there while I'm asleep or dressing, if you don't mind."

The housekeeper said "Yes ma'am," "No ma'am" "Three bags full ma'am."

Obviously there was going to be no attempt to meet her even half way this time round. Grania refused to get into a sordid fight. Qan had made it clear that he would deal with the staff when they decided last time that Grania was too middle-class for their elevated household. Let him deal with yes-ma'am-no-ma'am-three-bags-full-ma'am. If only she had a place to go when these hissy fits happened.

Anyhow, it was only three days. She could surely deal with three days of mild discomfort. There was her food stash, should the staff sulk reach mealtimes.

Three days later she felt less equable. She read the note from Dal that said he would be a few days longer. She suddenly wanted to scream and pull down the walls.

She went into her studio and surveyed her resources. No more food. The only drink left was coffee. She ransacked her coin purse, but Dal had encouraged her to open accounts at her favourite shops and not to carry cash, so it was empty. Normally there was enough for coffee and pastry, but she had stayed out of the house so much those first few days that even her coffee money had run out.

"So much for Happy Ever After," she said. "What I need is a big steak, some chips and a salad." Maybe the kitchen had sorted itself out and the next meal would be waiting for her. She asked and received a small courtesy and an "I'm sure I don't know."

She investigated and the table looked as if it had never carried food.

Grania was very hungry. She made herself coffee and dealt. She made herself more coffee in the afternoon. They can't deny me dinner, she said to herself.

The dinner table was also void. Grania went to the

kitchen to see if she could snag a couple of slices of bread. She was ushered out.

"When do I get dinner?" she asked.

"We're cleaning out the stoves," the head cook said. "No food until tomorrow afternoon."

Grania didn't know what to do. If this was home, she would zing a few names into her zipchip and she would visit a friend. She would download creds and go out to dinner. She would go home and demand food from her mother. At home, there had been options. Here the only option right now was to drink more coffee. She couldn't even visit her new friends, for she had no idea where they lived.

The staff problem had to be dealt with. It didn't matter how much Grania sympathised with the servant class and hated the fact that it existed, she could no longer avoid the fact that the servants hated her.

It wasn't a class thing anymore, it was judgement on their part. She had married their prince and they thought he had made a bad choice. And they were letting their opinion be felt. Very strongly.

It was about time Grania did some judging of her own. Grania was part of the household and her needs had to be factored into the daily routine, not treated as optional extras. And that was the charitable way of looking at it.

She sighed. Until then, eating was an issue. She was so hungry! She was also tired. She remembered this feeling and the memories were not good.

She hid herself from her stomach and her memories by sitting in her studio a few more hours and drawing caricatures of each and every staff member.

I should leave the pictures where they can all find them, she thought. Or I should go to sleep until it's all over. Maybe Dal will be back tomorrow.

She filled up on green water. Ham, she thought. Green water and ham, Sam-I-am. A slice of ham would be rather nice, on a thick piece of bread with some tomato. Even New Ceres ham, all stringy, would be fabulous.

Grania laughed at herself. She had been hungry before. She would get through it. It was, after all, only hunger. She went to bed and told stories to herself until she slept.

Halfway through the night she woke up and decided to sneak into the kitchens while everyone was asleep. Commando food. This wasn't dying Earth, after all. She wasn't waiting on a meagre ration. She was not in danger of death if she didn't behave. All she had to do was take a candle, tiptoe to the kitchen, and steal. Like an errant child.

There was a footman outside her door.

"Oh good," she said. "Could you please get me something to eat?"

"Ma'am," said the footman. "the head housekeeper has asked that you remain in your room."

"You're imprisoning me." Grania was angry.

"No ma'am. The floors are being done."

"And you can't get me anything?"

"There is no-one in the kitchen, ma'am, I can't get you anything."

"Let me say this very clearly, then." Grania felt a huge fatigue welling up. "I have let things slide because I was sympathetic to your dilemma. I know how important Dal is to you and I know that you all resent me. This is why I haven't tried to take over management of the household. But there's a big difference between annoying me and starving me. There's an even bigger difference between waxing floors and keeping your mistress imprisoned in her room."

"I'm writing everything down for Dal. If any of you try to take my notes from me then I will explain that not only have you imprisoned me, you have stolen my possessions. I'll tell him about those pictures that disappeared and about the times I haven't found my shoes. I will even tell him about his would-be murderer being allowed into the salon to spite me."

"Ma'am," ventured the footman.

"This is no longer negotiable," said Grania. "I don't see any logic in running way from certain death to suffer at the hands of bigots."

She paused.

"You can tell all your fellow staff members one more thing from me. Every other time you've been caught out by Qan I've said that no-one should lose their jobs. I know it's almost impossible for off-worlders to find jobs with clean food and I wasn't going to put any of my people through it. Well, you've all proven you're not my people. I hope you have other job skills than refusing to get me something to eat, because you may find you need them. And I hope watching me hurt has made you all very happy."

Before she could lose her temper any further, she slammed the door so hard the candle went out. Grania got back into bed. She pulled the covers right over her head and she cried.

When she had cried herself out, she tried to sleep. She was too angry and too empty inside and too tired. Sleep was impossible.

She crawled out of bed and lit her candle again and wrote the screed she had promised. Page after page after page. She hadn't realised quite how delinquent the staff had been, nor how much it had hurt her. Maybe the papers would have to be torn up, but writing it out was already making a difference.

There were tearstains on the pages and sniffles above them. Grania – fierce Resistance fighter – had turned into a Cinderella and she hated it.

When things were back to normal she would somehow find a resolution for this situation. There had to be one. It would have to be unorthodox. Grania couldn't see it yet, but that was because her mind was wandering. She was so furious and she was so hungry. She couldn't even go to the studio to make herself some coffee now that her door was being guarded.

She wrote all that down, too, and rested a bottle of perfume on the papers to hold them in place. The perfume was colourless. But water was green. Green water. The bathroom had plenty of that.

As she stood up, she knocked over the inkwell. It spilt all over the lovely floor. Grania laughed. Not happily. She should clean it up before it made a permanent mess. She didn't bloody care. She had worked herself up to such a state of fury that she didn't really care about anything.

To get to the bathroom she had to go through the dressing room. She dragged ink after her like a trail of dark rain. In her dressing room, she stopped. Chocolates. She had chocolates! She couldn't remember receiving them, but that was just brainfog. The important thing was that they were here, calling out 'Eat me!'

She carried the little box to her little chair, sat down and she ate all except three. She had to leave three, just in case she needed them later. She then had her green water to wash them down. She went back to bed.

It was very late the next day when Dal came home. He found the door to the bedroom locked. When he ordered the key, he found his wife in bed. Unconscious. Her bedclothes were bloody.

21

CONSEQUENCES

Two days later, Grania was conscious enough to be worried.

"Dal," she said. "There are some papers under the perfume bottle. Burn them. Please. Not good. Burn them."

"They are gone, my beloved," Dal reassured. Grania returned to her drugged sleep.

He mentioned her comment to Qan. "Maybe it has something to do with that locked door."

"And the fact that not a single servant checked in on her? I'll look into it." Qan was grim. Even in the days of hate, nothing had hurt one in his protection. It was pure good fortune that Grania was still alive. He would have betted it was more than mischance that caused Grania to miscarry in a locked room.

"The chocolates were poisoned," confirmed Qan a day later. "They were from Livia and Grania knew that. We still don't know why she ate them."

"And those papers?"

"I have a feeling about them. If no-one has destroyed them, then I'll have them to you by tonight."

"Grania will be allowed to sit up for a few minutes tomorrow."

"This is very good news."

"Not if we don't know what happened. If she poisoned herself then will she be safe alone?"

"And if one of the staff arranged things..."

"Exactly."

The clever footman who took the papers had not been clever enough to destroy them. Or maybe Grania's words had pricked his conscience.

Qan read Grania's notes grimly. He explained it to Dal.

"Grania wanted her notes destroyed to protect the staff."

"Against what?"

"Against us. What they did to her..."

Dal read it. His face was rinsed of light. "How can I not have known?"

"She protected them. I knew a little, but never how bad it was."

"She must have friends. Why didn't she go to her friends?"

"We've been guarding her so closely I can't see how she could have made the sort of friends who would take care of this sort of mess."

"No-one close."

"Our people shut her out." Dal's voice was uncomprehending. "How could our people have shut her out?"

"Our people nearly killed her."

"She ate those chocolates of her own volition."

"Did she know they were poisoned?"

"I don't know," Dal's voice was tight with grief. "I just don't know. She keeps telling me I treat her like a child, or a pet."

"So you do, sire, according to her culture. She comes from a different world. We don't know how to speak to people from that world. We think we do, because we all know Earth, but we don't, sire. She doesn't know how to speak to us."

"And we relied on our own people to see us through it."

"They thought so too, sire. They thought they were helping by getting rid of her."

"She wanted to save them from themselves."

"Yes, sire."

"She can't."

"I think, sire, that you should be the one to tell her."

"Stop saying 'sire' dammit. We've left it all behind."

"If we had left it all behind, sire, Grania would not have miscarried."

Before Grania was well enough to bear it, she and Dal fought. He had meant to tell her gently that the household staff was almost completely changed and discuss what would happen to the old staff. Instead, he remembered how she had tried to hide their actions.

Such terrible judgement his love possessed. Such tragically terrible judgement. Their earthchild was no longer. It was this thought he brought into his carefully planned conversation with her.

After all the most comforting and supportive beginnings, he blurted out, "Those chocolates. They were from Livia. You knew they were from Livia. You should never have touched them"

"I should just have lived on green water," said Grania, bitterly. "I know."

"You should have sent a servant to walk down the street and buy you something."

"With what money?"

"With household money."

"They won't. They don't. Not unless you or Qan order. And you and Qan weren't there. We've had this discussion before and you always say 'order things' as if ordering makes things happen. "

"Ordering does. I don't understand."

"For you. You have purple blood or polka dotted blood or hereditary rights to their soul or something. I am their equal and not from their planet and they know it and I know it and when I try to give instructions they only listen when it suits them. Or when it suits the household. Feeding me never suits the household on Tuesdays, for instance – there are too many other things they have to do."

Dal was stunned. "Every Tuesday?"

"We used to argue about it, the chief housekeeper and me. Now I go out and buy something, or spend the day in Trig's and fill up on pastry. But this time I was too sick and too tired and had no money and they had all taken the warfare up another notch and I had woken up in the middle of the night and just needed food and the chocolates were there. It's funny," she said. "I imagined I wrote everything down, but I must have been hallucinating."

"We found traces of ink on the floor."

"That's right, I spilled the ink. I was too tired to clean it. I went to get some water. I was so glad you broke with strict tradition and put in a bathroom. I've always liked it, but I like it so much more now. I could get some water, even when the footman wouldn't let me out." She looked guilty. "I wasn't going to talk about it."

"Why not?"

"Just how much trouble does someone get over something like this?"

"Just as much as they earned."

"I'm glad the papers have gone."

"We found them, Grania."

"And you asked me?"

"I needed to know when you wrote them. How you wrote them. I still need to know why you wanted to destroy your writing."

"Death is too easy on this planet. We're all alive. We all need to stay alive."

"None of the people involved will be punished with death. They have committed crimes, but nothing that severe."

"Even if you don't take them to court at all, they will be unemployable."

"Food. You're protecting them against food."

"Yes."

"Damn. I never even thought of that."

"Then you have to."

"They have already been dismissed. The whole household will be brought to trial."

"Make sure they can live?"

"How?" Dal genuinely didn't know. "They are criminals. You were haemorrhaging and unconscious and at least one of them knew about it."

"How could they have known? The door was locked."

"Someone came in to take the papers, my love."

"Oh. Damn."

"They will be punished."

"I can see that. I don't like it, but I can see it. I can also see you will have to dismiss someone. Just make it as few some-ones as possible – don't assume they're all guilty. And please..."

"I'll make sure that they are offered menial jobs, simply to ensure the food. I will not reward them for hurting you, but you are right, they should not die."

In the end the cook, the head housekeeper and two footmen were brought to trial. Eight other staff members were sacked. Five of the eight accepted the new jobs they were offered.

Then came the consultations.

Grania was still weak, so everything was brought to her. She helped interview the new senior staff. Each of them sat down with Grania to work out how the household should operate.

"I need to be a part of it," Grania explained. "How could a housekeeper have ignored me if I properly belonged?" Her needs were added to the schedules and she, in her turn, took on some responsibilities, including weekly talks with the senior staff.

Mrs Caselle, the new housekeeper, was very surprised that none of this had happened when she married. "It's normal procedure," she said.

"It's sensible," agreed Grania. "But Dal is too elevated to have run a household and I'm from Earth."

"Of course," said Mrs Caselle, "Big households here are like those of Old Earth, not your Earth."

"There may have been some homes like this on my Earth," Grania admitted. "But they were few and far between."

"We will all learn together," her new housekeeper promised, "I would like it if some of the customs of Earth were not forgotten."

"You would be prepared to reshape things?"

The new major-domo spoke up. He was taller than Dal and significantly more imposing. He carried his dignity with intent, however, whereas Dal's was casual. "Together," Franck said, firmly. "That is how we make a household into a home."

"You are very different from my previous major-domo."

"I should hope so." he said. "My family has served the old aristocracy for ten generations."

"It isn't a problem, working in a house like this?"

Franck smiled across at Mrs Caselle, who nodded back to him. "This is something the Holotor-trained staff does not yet understand. While there are many things that are similar between the Great Households of Holotor and of those here, there are real differences. The biggest is perhaps the respect accorded Earth. It should have been a source of pride to have you as mistress."

"I may not like this," Grania said.

"You won't even notice it after a very short time," Franck said, amused.

She wondered how she would not notice a private secretary and a personal maid. "Without servants who answer only to you there is no-one to look out for your needs above all else downstairs," Mrs Caselle explained.

"I thought you did that."

"After a kind, yes, but not in the same way. Your status downstairs is determined by the status of your people. With no-one there it is unknown and unknowable and few downstairs can handle that. Also, you need someone to help you dress."

Grania knew that Dal would entirely agree with this last. He and Mrs Caselle would deal well. She left the conversation wondering how Franck and Qan would work with each other. It could be interesting.

Dal then proposed that the two of them go away. "To let the household settle in and find its routine. To help you get some energy back. To see a really good doctor," he explained.

"I should have done that first."

"It's a few days from Prosperine. You needed to be well enough to travel, before I could arrange it."

"Fair enough. In that case, maybe I needed to know that the place I was going to go back to afterwards would be safe."

"Oh Gods," said Dal.

"We need to learn how to talk to each other," said Grania. "And I need more cash for emergencies."

"Where did you learn to be so practical about these things?"

"Where do you think?"

"Oh Gods," said Dal, again.

WHEN GRANIA WAS WELL ENOUGH to travel, Dal announced to the household they were going inland for a few weeks. Between the moment he checked with her and his announcement, Grania found herself wondering again why on earth Dal could even think about time out to somewhere unexcitingly inland when he refused to visit the spas of New Switzerland with their luxury and their safety. Maybe it was the hedonism of New Switzerland or its departure from regular social behaviour that made him refuse. Maybe it was his odd little public prurience and the association of the great spas with sexual shenanigans.

She guessed she would have to wait and see. After all, that's what Dal told her over and again, "Wait and see." Grania had completely forgotten Dal's comment about seeing a good doctor.

She kept telling him "I want to go to New Switzerland." And she did. Now her health was almost normal, she did. Want to go there. Want to go everywhere. Want to see everything. Want to touch see feel understand everything.

Now her senses were alive again she wanted to fill them with the sights and sounds of the new place so that it would get beneath her skin and become a part of her. Then she could be politically active. Then she could be content.

Because then, if her life were cut short, she would feel she had experienced something.

Travelling was a start. And Dal was with her. She could ask questions until he demonstrated his boredom by treating her as a pet kitten. Dal's people skills are sometimes rather strange, she reflected.

"Tell me about these folks we're visiting."

"I don't know a lot," Dal said. "I know they are interesting individuals with fascinating insights into life in the settlements. I know everything revolves around their religion.

"They settled as a block in the very early days of New Ceres. They produce a range of things that Prosperine needs, but were too strong and independent even then to be simply subsumed into the New Enlightenment. There was some sort of compromise. I do not know the details. I found them when they brought techno materials in through the spaceport. We get on well together."

"They have that much autonomy?"

"Oh, they have more."

"They still can't play off-planet by themselves, though?"

"It is part of an uneasy compromise, so, no."

"Why religious? What religion?"

"Who the hell knows? I am told that if I understood their history I would understand their independence and their isolation. They claim there is deep meaning in what they do. Personally, although I like the people, and their expert skills can be very handy, the history is unimportant."

"If it weren't for the isolation the Lady Governor would have snapped them up, wouldn't she?"

"In less than a twinkle of the mind's eye."

"So tell me again why we're going?"

"I have friends there."

"And?"

"They have real doctors. With real medicine. Low-tech, but no less real for that."

"They train in the autonomous zones?"

"Off-planet. I heard there was an Earther doctor. I thought you would like it."

"I would." Her voice was soft with wonderment and gratitude. She was not the only human from Earth in an unfriendly universe.

They ran into highwaymen on the way. This was even less interesting than running into Zenobia dressed as a highwayman. Dal had simply put his head out of the coach and shouted at them, "Go bother someone else," and they had fallen back, deeply embarrassed.

"My men," Dal explained.

"Your less-than-intelligent men," Grania said.

"They help me keep an eye on things out here," he said.

"Are there any real highwaymen on New Ceres?" Grania asked.

"Never run into one yet," and Dal grinned.

It took three days just to get there. This is why I had to see a local doctor first, thought Grania, very early on. Why Dal wouldn't take me to see a real doctor until I was almost well.

The first day of travel was on what Dal called a fast road. They had changes of horses and way stations and little luxuries where they stopped. That first day they covered nearly a hundred and twenty kilometres.

The morning of the second day was the same, though Grania was starting to ache deep inside. Then they turned off the major route. From there everything was uncomfortable. By the time they reached Rishon, Grania couldn't even stand. She sat there in her padded corner, hurting, until something made a small prick just below her left wrist. Within seconds she was gloriously unconscious. No pain at all.

When she woke up, it was to see a face looking down at her.

"How are you feeling?"

"I know you," she said.

"It was in another country,"

"And besides, the wench is dead."

"I still think you painted the best scenery of any of the English students."

"I never finished English," Grania said.

"I, on the other hand, most definitely did finish Med."

"You painted appallingly. And you're alive," Grania marvelled, "Unless I'm drugged up to the gills and just imagining you."

"You're drugged up to the gills, but I'm real. A blast from the past."

"Alive."

"It really gets you, doesn't it?"

"Why didn't you come and visit me in Prosperine?"

"How was I to know that Grania the Last Woman was actually Granny from Theatre Club?"

"You heard about me? You should have told me you were here. Alive."

"But it wasn't you. At least I didn't know it was. Last time I saw you, you were an undergraduate English student."

"It's like that with everything since uni, I think. Everything I've heard about isn't real."

"Tomorrow we'll sneak into the Footbridge Theatre a day early and discover that none of our props fit."

"And whose fault was it that they never fitted?"

"I mismeasured solely for the joy of your company at three in the morning. I lusted after you, you know."

"I'm listening," Dal's voice interrupted.

Both of them were brought back to reality and away from

Earth, with a shock. Suddenly they were living in a universe where everyone they knew was dead, all over again.

"He's your doctor," said Dal, into the silence. "He treated you while you were unconscious."

"The Earther doctor. It's you."

"It's me."

"How?"

"I'll tell you later. It's not a good story."

"Have you changed your name? Do people call you Harry?"

"I'm still Harry, but everyone calls me Doctor Levi. One of those things," he smiled apologetically.

"No more Levi jokes."

"I have a pair."

"Oh my God," said Grania, "The last levis in the universe." A tear rolled down her cheek. Then another. Then she was crying uncontrollably. A moment later there was another of those pinpricks and she found herself asleep, dreaming of the past.

When she woke again she wondered if she had hallucinated the whole thing. Running across Harry Levi in the wilds of New Ceres was the stuff of dreams. Running across him and finding he had a little bald patch just where his hair used to be thickest was a strange thing to dream about.

She raised her head and took a look around. The room was white, but not sterile. Flowers, nice fabrics... and Dal, dozing in an armchair.

"Dal?" she said. He woke with a start.

"How are you feeling?" he asked, as he crossed the room and took her hand.

"A bit tired," she admitted.

"They have finished the operations. Your insides are healing."

"That's good." She snuggled into his hand. "I didn't realise I was hurting until now, you know."

"What do you mean?"

"The pain's gone away."

Dal nodded. "Old hurts, repaired. The doctor said he would talk to you about it when you were ready."

"That's good." Grania smiled up at him, full of drowsy happiness. "You know, I had the funniest dream."

"About having met the doctor before?"

Grania sat upright so quickly it hurt.

"Don't do that," scolded Dal. "You've had surgery."

"But I didn't dream it?"

"No, the doctor is called Harry Levi. And you used to sleep together."

"You would think that. Actually, he had a lovely girlfriend. She always brought us coffee when we did late night fixes before a production."

"What were these productions?"

"Amateur theatre. Old, old plays."

"Oh."

"You got it all wrong, didn't you?"

"I did."

"I need to know how he got here. Last thing I heard he and his family were sick of having stones thrown at them because they were Jewish. They were moving to Israel."

"He married?"

"His girlfriend and he married before they were even out of university. It was the great romance in our theatre group."

"He said he lusted after you."

"He says that about every female. I think he thinks it makes us feel good."

"You smiled when he said it before."

"It brought back so many memories. And he's alive. Really, truly alive."

Grania wasn't sure she had convinced Dal she was still his wife and her past didn't affect that, but she didn't care. She smiled again and slowly lowered herself into the fluffy pillow and she slept.

When she was awake and had met her nurse and when her nurse had helped her get clean and she had eaten something light, Grania felt all washed out.

"I can get the doctor to come by after you've rested. He doesn't have to come right now," the nurse said.

"No, I want to see him," Grania was firm.

"It's exciting, isn't it?" asked the nurse.

"Yes," admitted Grania. "I also want to know what was wrong with me and how well I am now. I get the feeling there are things I need to know."

"Well, you just lie there and he'll be along in a minute."

"Thank you."

A few minutes later, a familiar voice with an Australian accent said, "Hello, stranger."

"If there is a cliché to be used, Harry Levi will use it."

He bent down and kissed her cheek.

"Watch it," said Grania. "I have a jealous husband."

"He's being entertained by my equally jealous wife."

"I would love to see her again."

Harry lost his smile.

"Fuck," he said. He sat down in the chair next to the bed. "Grania, it's not Leah."

"I'm sorry?"

"Leah and the children were murdered."

"In the war?"

"In possibly the greatest irony in the history of mankind, I left Earth before it all started."

"Tell me," Grania said.

"You remember the reason I left Australia?"

"You wanted to be safe."

"Yes. Too much anti-Semitism. It destroyed Leah to leave, but it just wasn't safe."

"It was the war before the war. We were all hurting each other."

For a moment they stopped and remembered. This was something that not a single galactic would ever understand, that it was possible to miss hate. Not to mourn it. Never to mourn it.

"How did it happen?" Grania's voice was soft.

"Your average fucking terrorist incident. A bomb on a hover. The sort of thing that has been going on for six hundred fucking years."

"And if they hadn't been murdered..."

"I wouldn't have come to Rishon."

"Why Rishon?"

"No-one has explained it to you?"

"Dal said something about a religious settlement... I thought some sect... " Realisation dawned. "Not some sect. Rishon is Jewish."

"Four Jewish settlements. They got as far as they could from Earth, hundreds of years ago. They wanted an end to the cycle of hate. And when that cycle hit me, I joined them. It was as far from Earth as I could get, too."

"How extraordinary."

"I remarried and I have children. I started again. I'm happy. I miss Leah and the kids more than I can say. Every day I miss them. Every day. And I miss home."

"I'm glad you weren't there for the end, though. It wasn't home, by then."

"There are things that went on," Harry said, "Weren't there?"

"Lots of things."

"I mean, they weren't above torture."

"We were kept pretty, for the intercasts. There was torture, but it was invisible."

Harry nodded. "I'm going to swear you to a secret," he said. "Not all the medicine we do here is low-tech."

"So you've scanned me properly?"

"We had a meeting to decide if we should. All the leaders and medicos from all four towns. And we thought that if anyone deserved proper medical treatment, it was you."

"I've always thought my body carried more legacies than I knew."

"Most of them are fixed. Or on their way to being fixed."

"How bad were they?"

"Let's just say that in a couple of years you would have found daily life rather painful."

"I always assumed I would get six kinds of cancer."

"Oh, that too. Inflammation immediately, and a range of problems from then. I saw you early enough, though. You'll be right. Though if I were you I would come visit Rishon every couple of years, just to check things out."

"Did the meeting agree that Dal should know?"

"Not about the level of technology. We've told him that we're fixing some of the war trauma."

Grania nodded.

Dal came in then and the publicly acceptable aspects of the conversation were rehashed. Grania's official reaction to the suggestion that she was being healed of old wounds was, "I escaped – why wasn't that enough?" Even though she knew it wasn't. Even though she was touched by what these people had done.

The baby might not have done well. "War leaves legacies."

"And now? You suggested it wasn't all finished?"

"Come back in a year. It takes times for the system to normalise. Take your medicine. Take care of yourself."

"Then come back in a year." Dal and Grania looked at each other and nodded.

"Eat properly," the doctor said. "Eating properly is terribly important. And don't have even a trace of untreated food. You were very lucky last time."

"That was lucky?"

"Oh, yes. There wasn't much untreated foodstuff in your system."

"Not enough to kill?"

"Enough to make you feel uncomfortable for a day or two. No more."

"So what happened?"

"The refuse of war. Not eating enough. The pregnancy. They all interacted."

"And you've fixed my hormones?"

"Such an Earth description. It's a long time since I've heard anyone say that. But yes, I've fixed your hormones. It's not as straightforward as it should be, because of the poisoning. I need your body to run one full cycle."

"Explain," Dal ordered.

Harry addressed himself to Grania, including Dal in by gesture. "The full hormone adjustment is on time delay. You'll experience the first part of the menstrual cycle normally. The pre-menstrual period might be rather bad, I'm afraid. It's when you'll experience depression and rage and so forth. Those hormonal showers will finish when the cycle is complete and then the contraception will kick in and your body will have a chance to heal properly. In a year you come back to me and I check you out properly. If all is well then, you can have children."

"How about my eyes?"

"I'm sorry?" said Harry.

"Were they affected by the treatment, by the war, by anything?"

"Why should they be?"

"Please, Harry, I need to know."

"I can do you another check, but your eyes ought to be fine. Why?"

"I thought something must be wrong with my vision. I can't see things and paint them the way I should."

"It might be the light of this planet," suggested Harry. "Or emotional trauma. You probably have post-traumatic stress disorder," he said it as if it were a perfectly natural thing to have. Grania drew in a deep breath and let something go. She had no idea that she was holding onto a worry so deep. Harry didn't seem to notice. "Give yourself time to adjust," he continued. "At least you have your vision. You can adjust and you can paint."

"You mean – at least I'm alive."

"I keep remembering that about myself," Harry apologised.

A few days later and Grania was well enough to go out to dinner. It was an extraordinarily strange dinner party in many ways.

Harry explained to Dal at the door that, "It won't be what you're used to." And it wasn't. For Grania, it was homelike, but for Dal it was hard work. Informal, with Grania called into the kitchen and Dal helping at the barbecue. There was even potato salad.

"Ancient Australian tradition," Harry explained.

"Not eighteenth century, though," called Grania through the door.

"God forbid," said Harry.

Eventually, Dal caught on, but by that time Grania and Harry had turned morose and the reminiscences over dessert were bitter rather than sweet. Long litanies of the lost. Grania tried to head the conversation in a safer direction.

"Two Aussies on New Ceres – is that enough to make a clique?" she wondered.

It worked for a short time, but there were too many memories for them to remain unsaid. It wasn't long before one of them mentioned the jacaranda tree at Sydney University.

"I always left my last exam study until it was flowering," Harry admitted.

"When it was too late," Grania laughed.

Dal and Harry's wife Rachel sat silent at the table, listening to the lost.

The next day Grania was given a special tour of Rishon while Dal was occupied with one of his many mysterious activities.

"Harry said you always liked making sense of things," her tour guide said, in her local accent. Those soft consonants reminded Grania that Rachel had been born on New Ceres. She had never known Earth. "We're a mixture of tech that fits in with the New Enlightenment and tech that keeps our lifestyles and health comfortable. We keep up with galactic news and research and we make sure that we don't appear too alien. We have a public image that fits Prosperine's notions of what eighteenth century Jews should look like, and we have a private reality. The costumes and the playacting are a small price to pay for the independence we enjoy." 'Costumes,' and 'playacting' – and yet she was born here. Grania was curious.

"So you like the New Enlightenment."

"Most of us hate it," Rachel admitted, candidly. "We won't jeopardise our families to change it, though."

"So you work with people like my husband when you can."

Rachel gave her a slanted look. "You see a lot. Dal assured us you knew nothing of his activities."

"I don't know details, but he knows I know some."

"Men," Rachel laughed.

"That's about the sum of it."

"One of the ways we keep our fingers in the pie with a fair amount of ease is through printing, of course."

"Everything seems to come back to printing. New Ceres is all about the printed word, isn't it?"

"I guess it is," said Rachel. "Would you like to see some illegal papers?" She sounded excited. Grania was curious enough to say yes, though she found walking around a trifle difficult. Soon she would have to confess and go back to bed, but in the meantime, illegal papers sounded fun.

"Actually, these papers aren't really illegal," Rachel admitted as she spread samples on a flat table. "These are rabble-rousing. The printer doesn't want the link back to himself and I don't blame him. If he loses his reputation then he's very vulnerable."

"I know that style of page," said Grania.

"Eye of an artist," nodded Rachel. "We get a lot of his work."

Suddenly some of the things she had heard and seen made sense. Constance's exceptional knowledge also made sense. Grania smiled. "Is this widely known?"

"Hardly at all."

"I'll keep mum about it," Grania promised.

"Harry said you would. He said you used to be the repository for everyone's secrets."

"That was a long time ago. But this is important. I can keep quiet about Mr F and Rishon."

"You won't see any of this tomorrow," Rachel counselled. "It's laxative time. It all goes out this afternoon."

"Laxative time?"

"Later," said Rachel. "You're pale and Harry left strict instructions."

The next day everything was a little different. The atmosphere moved from relaxed to the forever-tension that Grania had come to think of as normal for the planet.

The fault lay in the regular visit of the regular official. Everyone made the same series of jokes to Grania about the importance of regularity and every single Rishon person talked about the Deputy as if he was a form of laxative.

Grania was fascinated by the way the town changed. The public face of it became far more the focus of everyone's attention. Portable tech was moved out of view and bigger pieces of equipment were transformed into pillars and decorative art. Women wore dresses that looked as if they had been bought in Prosperine and they covered their hair. Men wore long coats and fancy fur hats. The whole town centre, in fact, looked like an Eastern European outpost of the capital.

"Would you like to meet the laxative?" Rachel asked, when she collected Grania.

"Should I?" Grania sounded doubtful.

"Doesn't matter one way or another," Rachel said. "You're here on holiday to spend time with friends. We always say that."

"You have a lot of friends."

"We're wonderful people," Rachel smiled.

"You all look theatrical."

"We love the laxative's visits," Rachel was genuine. Grania was astonished. They didn't even notice the tension in the air. Or maybe they enjoyed it, like going to a horror movie. How extraordinary, to feel so very safe that one could enjoy being scared. "It's playacting. We pretend to haskalah and historical correctness."

"When in fact, you're galactic."

"No, not galactic," Rachel turned serious. "We're ourselves."

"What's haskalah, anyhow?"

"It's the Jewish version of the eighteenth-century Enlightenment. Except we don't really know much about it. We never got into it. We make it up and look kind of antiquated and no-one checks us out too thoroughly because we're Jewish. I think someone wrote a book on it, if you want to know more."

"Maybe later. I'm fascinated by the inspection. It's so odd that they do it so lightly – they check everything else."

Rachel was very serious. "We get away with more than any other group, because we're Jewish. In the old eighteenth century Jews were considered a little alien and special. This means that the Lady Governor kind of has to leave us alone, otherwise she's breaking guidelines. We were here before the New Enlightenment: that was the grand good fortune. Luck, historical coincidence and a good lawyer were on our side.

"We walk a tightrope, and we know that. Sometimes we fall off. Sheni, in particular, does stupid things. It's lost more of its members to New Enlightenment enforcement than all of the other three settlements combined."

"Sheni?"

"There are four of the old Jewish settlements. We're all within a three days' ride of each other. Sheni was the second one settled. When we're behaving we call it Sheni but on laxative days and when they've done something incredibly stupid, we call it Chelm."

"Chelm?"

"In Jewish legend the people of Chelm were very stupid, and Sheni falls off the tightrope more often than anyone else. We tell stories of New Chelm. They always start, 'There was once an idiot from New Chelm...' We always mean someone from Sheni. They hate it."

"But you still enjoy walking that tightrope?"

"You bet."

The tightrope was going to be particularly interesting this visit. The regular inspector had been replaced by one of the Six. The warning came through just in time and Rishon was able to up its level of security, hide a variety of objects rather more securely, and send word to its companion towns.

Dal and Grania were with Rachel to welcome the inspector ("No use hiding you – better to show you off."). When she stepped out of her carriage it was to the surprise of all.

"Livia," said Grania, as she saw the pale face and angelic hair poke out of the carriage window.

"Livia," said Rachel, much more quietly. "I've heard of her."

"This is going to be interesting," said Dal.

LIVIA WAS courteous to all and was elegance personified. She wore a hunter-green travel dress and looked as if she had just stepped out for a ride.

"You need not be worried," she explained, in that tone of voice that implied since I was going to trap you and make you squirm and then swat you like a fly anyway. "I've been assigned this task in order to learn. You have a fine history, and I respect it. I shall inspect Rishon, of course, and only one of your other towns. I shall not transgress ancient agreements. I trust that my inspection won't interfere unduly with your regular activities."

Livia was thanked for her kindness by four different people, all dressed to demonstrate that they were dignitaries. Grania was particularly impressed by Harry's tall fur hat and the sudden growth of locks of hair that curled in front of his ears. She noticed that Dal noticed her looking at Harry. She made a face at her husband.

Livia noticed the byplay. How could she not notice? She had been instructed to watch but not to look too closely. She had been especially instructed not to damage relations. She had been instructed so carefully, in fact, that she ached to find out what Rishon was hiding.

It was impossible. She had been given permission to slow down or prevent those scurrilous materials she had identified as coming from this centre, but that was all. The only industry she could show any interest in and avoid discipline later was the printing. It would have to be enough. It was useful for her advancement and it would not do to jeopardise that advancement at this crucial point. In other words, Livia was on probation.

The people of Rishon didn't know this. They thought that it was they who were on probation. They watched Livia glide down the street. They noticed everything about her, from the sun brooch she wore to the way her mouth opened slightly as if she were tasting the street.

Livia memorised the taste of the air. It was fresh and clean. No taste of subterfuge, which was amusing under the circumstances. She cast her eyes quickly around those present to determine how she could remain within her limits, without either showing she had been so instructed or losing her reputation's edge.

"Grania," she said, as she came closer. "What a pleasure." She let the tone show that she had identified someone who needed to be watched. "I would be honoured if you would accompany me on my inspection. If you will allow me sufficient time to change my dress, we shall start with Rishon and then perhaps take a look at Sheni." A moment later Livia was gone with her minder, to take care of her personal needs. Grania stood there, her mouth agape.

"You know Livia?" Rachel turned on her like a whirlwind. "You didn't just know her face. You know Livia."

"If her sending me poisoned chocolates counts as knowing, then yes."

"Why would she want to walk with you?"

"She's always been fascinated by me. Wherever I go, she appears. I think I should just tell her that I'm here to see Harry and Dal should keep acting insanely jealous and she'll dump us all as a bad idea." Grania was only half joking.

Dal gave her his 'don't go there' look. "How do we minimise damage?" he asked, "Seriously."

"You're friends of Harry. Here for him. Your wife is right, we should use that."

"I should disguise my weakness then? Pretend I'm perfectly well and not out of the hospital on a ticket of leave?"

"You should not," Harry had come over. "You're here for your health. Staying with your old university friend. I'll move your things and your husband's to my place at once. I'll tell the family we're expecting you to lunch."

"Unless Livia decrees otherwise."

"Try to protest," suggested Rachel. "The less time you spend with her the better."

"And me?"

"Dal, come with me. Let Livia think we're best mates." Dal gave Harry his feral smile, and so the minuet began.

It was a difficult morning for Grania. It wasn't made easier by Livia saying to her – when they were out of earshot of the others - "It was only a warning, you know. How was I to know it would damn near kill you?"

Grania marvelled at the emotion in Livia's voice.

"My body had never recovered from the war," she explained, "And I was pregnant."

The silence was as high as mountains.

"We can't be friends," said Livia, defiantly.

"I'm beginning to see that," said Grania, tactfully.

She was unwilling to say that she'd never wanted to be friends. She wondered why Livia couldn't read it in her body language or taste it in the air.

Then she realised that Livia didn't want to see that in her body language or taste it. Part of Livia wanted to be friends. Part wanted to hate. Livia herself probably didn't even know she was divided against herself. The only place Livia's two halves would come together was in eliminating a complication from her own life, and the best way Livia knew to do that was through murder. Anything Grania said would only make things worse.

Grania took refuge in silence.

The Rishon side of the inspection went almost without hitch. There was a moment when Livia terrified a group of schoolchildren by telling them how pretty the song they were singing was, but Grania had defused it by saying, "It sounds like Waltzing Matilda."

"It's a psalm," the teacher explained. "Dr Levi gave us a different tune for it a few years ago and the children like that tune."

"It really does sound like Waltzing Matilda," Grania assured the children, who had moved closer to her.

"Can you sing it to us?" one little girl asked.

"You sing your psalm at the same time," Grania suggested "And we can find out if they're the same tune or not. One, two, three, Once a jolly swagman camped by a billabong..."

"Shir ha ma'alot b'shuv adonai," sang the little girl.

The tunes were identical. Everyone was laughing except Livia. Livia stood alone, watching Grania.

Rachel was even further out of the circle. She was laughing, but also watching Livia watch Grania. She reported back that evening, when Livia was safely locked away for the night. It was obvious, she said, that Grania was the cause of Livia's preoccupation. The inspection had been lighter than usual because of this.

While the people of Rishon were happy about Livia's preoccupation, Dal was scared. His mind whirled the whole time, trying to find out reasons and discover solutions. He knew that up until now Livia had been toying with him, cat with mouse, and leaving Grania surprisingly whole. For him, Livia's fixation on his wife was proof of an unwholesome sea change.

The second day, Livia and Grania went to Sheni. At the end of that visit, Grania decided that the leaders of Sheni were not only stupid, they were the ultimate in suckers-up.

"We know your husband," one of them explained to Livia, as if it was world-shatteringly important.

"He died recently."

"I'm very sorry to hear it. He liked our work."

"I wonder," Livia protracted the words and tasted them and relished them, "If you have copies of anything he ordered. I, alas, have very little and would like to do a little memorial."

"We'll hunt it out at once and send it to you by courier."

Grania passed this on to Rachel. Everyone worried. All Sheni could do is what they promised. The horse was out of the stable and it was too late to bolt the door.

"I hope it won't come back to bite us on the butt," said Harry. "But I can't do brain transplants for all our neighbours."

"Must be something in the water."

"Must be. Maybe the thing that turns it green."

"That's what I hate most about New Ceres," said Grania, "The green water."

"Me too," said Harry. "I feel as if I'm drinking plankton."

Dal looked at Harry and said, "I know what I hate most about New Ceres."

"Dal," Grania said, "All my friends are out of bounds. No duels. No hate. No more evil stares."

Dal smiled, reluctantly. "What will you do?"

"Remember Lysistrata."

"I don't even know who Lysistrata is. You never tell me."

"Look it up."

"Aristophanes," said Harry. "And I'm very glad Grania's your wife and not mine."

22

USEFUL INTERLUDES

One of the facts of life that Grania had to learn upon marriage was that her husband was impossibly restless. When he was at home and things were quiet, this manifested itself in any room that contained paper. If there was a way of disrupting a room through the use of paper, he would find it. If the paper were blank he might write on it, but he might also fold little working toys from the paper. Loose pages were put in order and only Dal understood the principles of that order. They might also be analysed, verbally and at great length.

This is what Dal was doing in Grania's studio. Grania only paid half-attention while Dal went through her working sketches, one by one, giving comments.

"I like this series," he said. "You should call it 'Dinner was late (again).'" It was one of Grania's vignettes, showing a table being laid under the old household management, where a job might have been done four times over, to different standards. For the sake of her visual narrative, Grania showed five different junior staff and three senior laying or re-laying or arguing over what was needed for the night's dinner.

A few pages later and, "What is this for?" he asked, almost disgustedly, over a series of charcoals of Livia's head.

"An idea for a bust. Don't worry, she won't like it."

"What are you going to do with a bust? Put it in the hallway?"

"I was thinking of an exhibition later in the year. Maybe selling some things. I don't know how to go about making arrangements, though."

"Livia won't like it?"

"Almost guaranteed."

"What else would you put in an exhibition?"

"Everyone wants to see light and line from me. I want to give them politics as well. I can't get the damned light right anyway. Just look at those sketches."

"They look good."

"They're clever enough. I don't mind people seeing them, but there's nothing special about them. My mind is full of a different light and I can't communicate it using eighteenth century technology. That's another reason to make the exhibition all about politics. I have things I need to say and things I need people to see and things I need to make people feel. At least I can do one of three."

"Could get into trouble for that."

"D'you think I don't know that?"

"We can't do it. It needs a sponsor."

"D'you think I don't know that, too? I have one, actually, but she says we have to do all the work. She'll lend her name to the proceedings and maybe protect us from prosecution."

"She thinks there might be prosecution?"

"She's seen all my sketches and she thinks it would be almost a given without her involvement."

"She is?"

"Lady C."

Dal was silent a moment. "Well, well, well."

"I was thinking of asking Lizzie for help with finding a hall and stuff."

"Mm. I can do that."

"Lizzie's one of yours."

Dal raised an eyebrow. "When did you find that out?"

"Not saying."

"Still, better have a higher class of organiser if Lady C is lending her name. I'll have Qan do it."

"Whatever you like. I just want to show. If Qan can find time, it might be an idea to test the waters, though."

"Maybe have a small showing or put a picture in another exhibition?"

"Yes. Of some sketches, for instance. Find out if I can really work using these media."

"There can't be any doubt of that," Dal said.

"In my mind, there is doubt," Grania waved her arms around. "None of this is new. None of it says anything special. It's all an exploration, trying to find that light and to see things differently."

"Livia is an exploration?"

"She's a part of it. My mother is another part."

"Your mother?"

"Wait and see."

Dal popped in on Grania a little later, when she was dressing.

"No art this afternoon?"

"A different kind of art. I'm attending Lady C's salon."

Dal was surprised. "That's very exclusive. Not even members of the Six are invited."

"Maybe. All I know is she invited me. She said I should bring you along if you cared to come. I rather suspect she murmured something about ornaments always being welcome."

"I don't believe she said that." Dal sat on the bed and admired his wife in the mirror.

"You can believe what you like. If you're going to come with me, though, you might want to tidy up a little."

"I cannot believe you just said that," said Dal, "When you yourself are so—"

"Say it and you're dead," Grania warned, brandishing her hairbrush in his direction.

"Let me tidy you," he coaxed. "Since your maid is unaccountably absent."

"Not unaccountably. She has two days off."

Dal raised an eyebrow, but didn't say anything.

"No funny business," Grania warned. "I want to be out that door in a half hour."

They were out that door within the half hour, barely. Dal took care of his own beauty before he left the room (since he eschewed the powder and wig and complex cravats of some sets), and the whole of the carriage ride was spent dealing with Grania's state of disarray.

"This salon makes my life much easier," he said to her, while they were sorting out her neckline.

"You were desperate for sex?"

"Always," he laughed. He wouldn't explain why Lady C's salon was the answer to his prayers, and he behaved almost perfectly throughout. His conversation was very quiet and very intense. He took someone aside from time to time, but he was perfectly polite with all of this, and never out of sight.

Grania was mystified. More of his secrets. She suspected that Dal lived on secrets the way other people lived on food, but it annoyed her.

She determined to ask him about it over dinner, but a

messenger was waiting for him at the door and he never came in to dinner.

Grania was descended upon by staff that needed to consult about a problem. It became clear that vacuum cleaners were a lot less trouble than junior cleaning maids who fell in love with footmen. This was the price of regular meals in the New Enlightenment.

It was a very small price, too. For the first time since she had moved into this oversized house, Grania felt she lived there. She might never understand why Franck refused to use his first name or why Mrs Caselle insisted on being called 'Mrs.' but she appreciated the way they ran her household. She still kept her stash in the studio, but that was more because she didn't trust life than because she didn't trust servants.

One other good thing about the newly-friendly staff was that she could work at night. Mrs Caselle made sure that there were always enough candles.

The lighting was bad for most projects. She wasn't going to let that stop her work, however. Grania understood ladies did fine embroidery before the fire, but it was too warm for a fire and besides, she had some thoughts that she needed to get down. Charcoal would do, and rough lines. Once she had it down, she could turn it into something finer by daylight.

What she wanted to draw was a strange sequence of events from Lady C's. She had been talking to Fabian de Raimbert, who was apparently Lady C's almost-legitimate nephew. He had been dressed in an entirely splendid waist-coat, embroidered with butterflies and flowers. She was admiring the waistcoat, asking what Fabian meant by 'almost-legitimate' and trying to avoid looking as if she was flirting (since Dal was watching and wore one of his more predatory looks) when Alphonse walked by, just a few feet away.

"How unexpected," said Grania.

Fabian looked around and tensed. "None of the Six Families are welcome here," he said.

"It's funny, I thought you were one of them. Something someone said. I guess I got it wrong."

"No," said Fabian. "My father was of the Six. A different family and not as notorious as that man's, but still one of the Families."

"Oh," and enlightenment dawned on Grania.

Fabian smiled his spectacular smile at her. An ordinary face was Fabian's, until he smiled. "Yes, that's what I mean by almost-legitimate. My father was from a bastard family."

"Bastard families," Grania's mind dwelled on the phrase while they both kept an eye on Alphonse. "That's very accurate, isn't it?"

Alphonse started chatting up a pretty young thing.

"I need an excuse," muttered Fabian.

"To do what?"

"Challenge him."

"Would insult to me do it?"

"Would insult to you do what?" Dal had moved close when they were unawares.

"Help Fabian challenge Alphonse," Grania was impatient.

"Fabian de Raimbert, at your service." Fabian bowed.

Grania looked on in remorse, "I forgot you didn't know each other."

"We fought," reminded Dal.

"That's only knowing in that idiot male bonding sense. And besides, Fabian was commissioned. Dal, don't look so bloody threatening. I'm not going to sleep with Fabian. He's going to challenge Alphonse to a duel, if we're lucky."

"Why?"

"Because he is scum," said Fabian.

"I can't argue with that assessment. I don't want my wife to be the subject, however."

"I agree with you, sir. How do we achieve this, then?"

"We don't," said Grania. "Duels suck. I've changed my mind. We allow Alphonse to die by breathing in his own noxiousness."

"You chose friendship with me. Friends handle the Alphonses of this world."

Dal's eyes turned feral. Grania thought he would snarl. Fabian looked back. This was getting tedious.

"Oh, for goodness sake, both of you. Be civilised."

Dal's mood swung. "Certainly," he said. "Monsieur de Raimbert, if you would kindly come with me."

The two walked up to Alphonse and Dal said something to him, very, very quietly.

"No!" answered Alphonse.

"But yes," insisted Fabian, all pose. "We insist."

Alphonse's eyes swung from one man to the other, all swagger gone. I never knew he could look so exactly like a frightened rabbit, Grania thought.

Alphonse's head went from side to side – Dal to Fabian to Dal to Fabian. "You," he said, finally, pointing at Fabian.

"Good choice," Dal said. "We will see you tomorrow, then."

Grania was not given any of the details of the duel. She was also very upset that they had gone ahead. There was a difference between slanging someone as a joke and challenging them.

Time to consult, Grania thought. She sent an urgent note to Constance.

I wish notes were as easy to send about household impossibilities as about duels, she thought. Although the whole experience had led to Harry, which was a good thing. Or it would be a good thing if Dal would stop looking at all my male friends as if they were about to rape me. Don't people have friends of the opposite sex on Holotor?

Constance was very practical.

"You're certain the duel is today?"

"Reasonably certain. It all happened out of earshot."

"Very irregular, too. No proper procedure. That means it must be by the Lachrymose. There's a place everyone uses."

Down by the riverside, it figured. It also figured that they had a special location for improper duels. Maybe the bodies were thrown into the river if it all went badly?

Constance packed a little bag. "Men never remember to bring dressings to an improper duel," she explained, as she put it on the carriage seat. Grania took a full five minutes to process this statement – this meant women were also involved in improper duels and the children at Hightown were learning swordcraft. It became too much and Grania laid her head on the side of the carriage and tried to put the images out of her head.

"I didn't realise off-worlders were so delicate," Constance was amused.

"Only about duels. They've never been part of my life."

"They're useful," said Constance.

"Have you... fought?"

"Of course. More in my twenties than now, naturally. I do prefer to avoid it, but there are moments when it's the perfect solution."

By the time they reached the banks of the Lachrymose, the duel was over. Alphonse was wounded. Fabian was cleaning his sword. Dal was sitting on a big stone, swinging his right leg. Livia was watching Alphonse try to staunch his bleeding.

"Livia?" Grania whispered.

"She's always Alphonse's second. Since they were children. And she never helps him with wounds, either. She stands there and watches him hurt."

"I didn't know she liked watching people hurt. I thought she murdered."

"She doesn't watch, as a rule. Just Alphonse."

How strange. Then all four were looking at them and Grania found herself turning red.

Dal lifted himself off his rock. "Here is our ride home," he said to Fabian. "I told you she would find us."

"Hi everyone," Grania said with very false brightness. How does one greet people like Livia and Alphonse anyhow? "I hope none of you were seriously hurt."

"A pinprick," said bloodstained Alphonse.

"Let me at least bandage the pinprick," Constance sounded oddly gentle.

"If it would please you," said Alphonse and sat down upon Dal's rock.

"When you are finished with him, I shall take him to a hospital."

"I didn't know you cared," said Alphonse.

"I don't," shrugged Livia. "I was your second, however, and you are still alive."

"And your promise?"

"Oh, don't worry," Livia gave her special smile. "I shall redeem my promise. Perhaps I shall add Grania to it. You would be happy together."

"What do you mean?" Dal moved forward in a flash and loomed over the small smile.

"She intends to kill me," said Alphonse.

"You're very cool about it," said Constance. "Don't move, Alphonse, I'm almost finished."

"Not cool. Accepting."

"Well, I'm not accepting. Livia, should you cause any damage to my wife, then you will pay for it."

Livia laughed. "Come on, Alphonse. And don't bleed all over my carriage."

~

GRANIA READ a note and it puzzled her. It was from Harry and had been sent express, at great expense.

"Dal? Are you there?"

"What is it, my love?" He appeared from his dressing room, half naked. Grania admired him a moment then handed him the note.

"Where did you get this from?" Dal was worried.

"Harry sent it. It came just now."

"If ever I thought anything bad about your old friend I cast it off."

"Damn. I was hoping it was a joke."

"I knew someone other than us had brought in something dangerous from off planet. This confirms it."

"What I don't understand is how Livia got permission."

"My people say that she is being tested in a number of areas. Her visit to Rishon was apparently to show that she could restrain herself and follow the dullest of orders."

"And this?"

"To show she is willing to use bio-weapons, I assume."

"She said that thing the other day."

"She did indeed. Alphonse would not be missed by the powers and your death might even be considered favourably, if it looked natural."

"As it would with a bio-weapon."

"As it would with a bio-weapon."

"I just wish I knew what to do." Dal sounded defeated.

"They never got out your way, then?"

"Gods, no."

"The trouble is that Harry says that there's one of each variety. I wish I knew how he knew about it, but I guess that's irrelevant. I know the preventatives for one, but not for the other."

"Preventatives?"

"We change our diet and give the weapon an inhospitable environment. It's easy enough."

"How do you know this?"

"Dal, all the bio-weapons were tested on Earth. In the holding camps, once the Rule of War broke down. During the Occupation."

"Gods. People you know."

"And me. I was in one of the groups that survived Bio-Az during testing. My test group survived quite unexpectedly. We may need to ask Harry to visit and check us all out once we know this is all over, but we can avoid being killed. The other isn't one I've encountered directly, but I've heard of it. It's chancier. Maybe Livia won't use it. She doesn't have the knowledge to check that it meets specifications, for one thing."

"This is Bio-Az?"

"No, that's the fatal one. The one we can prepare against. The one that's a problem is Spec-Bio. The thing is, though, it doesn't kill. It was developed to target specific personnel on ships and to incapacitate them."

"It doesn't kill?"

"The worst it can do is incapacitate."

"I'll send for one of my old experts. She won't be able to reach here for a week: I never expected to need anything like this on New Ceres."

"I'll speak to Franck and Mrs Caselle immediately. We'll

protect the whole household from Bio-Az starting today."

"If the diet doesn't work? If you're wrong?"

"Then we die painlessly. It could be worse."

"You are my little ray of sunshine." And he tussled her curls. Grania knew the mood he was in. She used to call it 'one more time,' treasuring everything. She sighed, held him close, then went to talk to her household.

It was a unifying time. We're all tense together, thought Grania, as she ate her very citric dinner.

"Our group was assembled because we were being treated against scurvy," she explained, "And some idiot decided to do it with diet instead of with proper treatment. We were eating a great deal of citrus – very acidic."

"Oranges and lemons," notes Mrs Caselle. Grania wanted to add 'said the bells of St Clemens,' but the household was too tense.

Mrs Caselle, fortunately, stepped in and turned everything into sense. Especially fortunately in this instance. If the food treatment failed, they were all dead.

Everyone knew it. From time to time, the tension snapped and someone became very drunk or a housemaid was found in tears or the footmen were found throwing a party outside, near the fountain. Everything became just a little unpredictable.

One evening, very late, Grania found herself having a drink with her dresser and secretary and Mrs Caselle. Together they became maudlin drunk. The next morning they were far too polite around each other. Grania couldn't remember what they had said. She hoped it was endearing.

Grania wished the waiting were over, but every day she woke up and thought "I'm still alive." She was surprised at her own astonishment but couldn't help it.

After two weeks of high nerves, Dal's expert arrived.

Canti went through every corner of the house and found traces of Bio-Az. Grania shuddered to think what would have happened if the old staff had still been around, blithely ignoring her. Thank God for Mrs Caselle.

Grania wondered what Livia was thinking of her experiment, given that every single member of the household was still alive. Grania kept on wondering while Canti checked every single person and found that the immunity offered by a high acid diet had worked. She neutralised the remaining Bio-Az, then she sat down with Grania and Dal to talk it through.

"How did you get your equipment through Customs?" Grania wanted to know.

"His Grace doesn't share this information with you?"

His Grace. Holotor. Half-memories of news intercasts of years ago floated through her mind. How could she have not realised? The King's brother accused of treason by his younger siblings in the dying days of the war. The sheer amount of money and power Dal carried with him and took for granted. His first staff must have thought he was marrying a commoner. Which she was. She had to find an answer for this very tall old lady.

"We share a little of our work, but no, I don't know a great deal. I come from a very ordinary background."

"You knew about Bio-Az. This whole household owes you its life. That's not ordinary."

"Dal didn't tell you how I knew?"

"He did. I feel he chose his wife very well."

"Only a few of his people feel that way."

Canti nodded. "They will come around."

"My biggest worry right now is the Bio-Spec."

Canti nodded again. "Justifiably. Although things may not be as bad with Bio-Spec as they were when it was first developed. With your permission, I will be a visitor for a while. I have the equipment to identify if a wound is caused by Bio-Spec and if we need off-planet help."

"New Ceres is very strict about getting off-planet medical assistance. It wants its new migrants to assume its eighteenth century."

"Then it shouldn't let its political underworld experiment with bio-weapons," Canti snapped.

"You're welcome to stay. In fact, I would be honoured to have you."

"That's that then."

~

THE OFF-PLANET WEAPON FAILED. Livia reported back to her superiors and a decision was made against using such things in the immediate future. 'More research' was the official verdict.

In the meantime, Dal danced around her in a way that no-one else had ever managed. Grania was still alive. The first was an insult and the second hurt. Or did it? She found herself relieved that Grania hadn't died. She found herself surprised that she had no wish for Grania to die.

So what did she want? She wanted Grania changed. She wanted Grania to hurt the way her very existence had hurt Livia.

This bore thinking about.

~

FABIAN WAS DISTRAUGHT. He tried not to show just how very upset he was, but Grania could tell. Particularly noticeable was the nervous tic in his left cheek. Fascinating. Right next to a dimple. She told herself she needed to find out what was wrong, and not notice the dimple. She especially needed to not notice men's dimples because Dal was possibly the most jealous man she had ever met.

Grania was at that troublesome moment after a big problem has been resolved where everything seemed funny. It's why she noticed the tic and why she herself was perfectly relaxed. If everyone was going to die due to the pettiest politics she had ever come across then all she could do was laugh. It was like escaping the Bubonic Plague only to slip on a banana peel and break your neck.

Except that Fabian had not been there for the Bubonic Plague. He also felt that it was his bounden duty to protect Grania from banana peels. She did her best to look composed and calming.

"Tell me before you explode," she said to him, handing him a cup of tea.

"Is it that obvious?" He smiled and Grania found that she hadn't quite sorted out how to be immune to dimples.

"Your cheek is ticking like a metronome." Fabian put his hand up to stop the tic. "Wrong cheek."

"Oh." He put the cup down carefully. "Grania, Alphonse is dead."

"Not unexpected," Grania said. "Who and how?" She could not find it in herself to regret him. She regretted that she felt nothing, but that was all.

"That's the problem," confessed Fabian. "No-one knows."

"Which means that if it was Livia we don't know enough to stop her using the technique on me."

"Yes."

"And the trouble is, we don't know if she still wants to kill me."

"I'm sorry."

"She tried, and failed. The thing is, I don't know if her heart was in it. I guess the first question is how Alphonse died. Whether it was the same stunt she tried on us last week."

"His body was found bloated and floating in a stream in the weaving district. No-one can work out how he died. The coroner said it was drowning, but I asked him privately later and he said that he had to write something."

"Could it have been one of those bio agents?"

"What?"

"Off-planet stuff. Developed for the intergalactic war."

Fabian shuddered. "I don't know anything about them. They're unholy."

"How many people have you killed?"

"Private question," Fabian gave a rueful smile, "Every single one of them was killed in a fair fight, however."

"How fair is it when you're the best swordsman on New Ceres?"

"Second best. Possibly third."

"But you kill." He nodded. "And you like your job, you said so."

Fabian was restless. "I can't see the point of what you're saying. We don't know if Alphonse had a good death."

"And you can only really protect your friends from good deaths. Sorry, I lost it."

"You're from off-planet. You don't understand."

"I understand that you're worried. I understand why you're worried. I'm doing everything I can to prevent Livia getting me or getting Dal. My fear is that if she gives up on murder, she might try something else."

"Like what?" Fabian leaned forward.

"I don't know."

"I can keep my eyes open. If there is something that affects you and yours..."

"You can help, yes. I would like that very much. And it's a lot better to deal with real problems than to fret about Alphonse's death."

Fabian's posture softened at last. "I would be far less concerned about Alphonse's death if I had caused it."

"I know that," Grania spoke sharply, then regretted it. "Just as I'm relieved that no-one I care for is guilty of murder."

Fabian nodded again. "There is much that is strange about your ways, Grania. I shall watch and protect, and should the protection fail, I shall act."

"You're happier?"

"Less unsettled, shall we say. It was distressing me that I should be so concerned about the death of someone who was only an ornament to society when he was not present."

Settling Fabian's concerns didn't make Grania's any lighter.

The biggest question was whether Livia had used the rest of the Bio-Az on Alphonse. It was such an odd killing technique for someone so terrifyingly loyalty to the New Enlightenment that it was quite possible she hadn't. But then, Livia or one of her agents had used it on Grania's household. Unless Canti could get the equipment to Alphonse's body without the equipment being seen there was no chance of knowing one way or the other. Though they discussed it from all angles, it was obvious there was no way of checking.

Their deep uncertainty wasn't helped when a small package from Livia was delivered to the front door, early one morning. Canti checked it straightway and pronounced it clean.

It was a charming statue of a serving girl. Did it mean they were all safe? Or did it mean that Livia wanted to remind them that she was thinking of Grania?

23

ALL THE FACES, ALL THE FACES

The Recreations of Prosperine draft for Chapter Six of *A Most Foolish Planet, an alternate guide to New Ceres,* unpublished.

ONCE UPON A TIME, people blew up giant balloons with volatile gasses and went up in them. They didn't go very far, most of the time, or even very high. They thought they were very clever.

Centuries later, people made giant balloons in strange shapes and floated tourists above the cities of Earth. They thought they were very clever, too.

Today the merchants and large firms of Prosperine sponsor balloon flights every Saturday. The Good and Great attend and pretend to be hoi polloi. The hoi polloi dress up in their best finery and pretend to be good and great. The ballooners themselves respect no-one. Ballooning is a mechanism for every sector of society to demonstrate that they have time to waste, resources to squander and that all of the divisions that make New Ceres such an impossible place are in the minds of strangers such as myself.

Strangers, such as myself, also attend the early morning ballooning. We pay for rides so that we can see the fair waterways of Prosperine from a familiar angle.

Nostalgia for the bygone era meets simple homesickness as we float over a town that really doesn't care about how it looks from space. We comment on how odd a city looks with a mild haze of industrial waste and with no air traffic. We laugh at how primitive the planet is and yearn for ancient days when life was simpler, and everyone died young. We forget to bring gloves and we all come down with colds the next day.

When we arrive home we romanticise about how green the parks are in Prosperine and how beautiful the chestnut trees that line the great avenues and how the red tiled roofs look quaint from the air and we forget how very rude both the aristos and the hoi polloi were to us when we came back down to earth.

We also forget that we bought food that morning. Balloons rise more easily with the dawn than at any other time the ballooners say, and dawn on a spring morning is bitterly cold in Prosperine. Bitterly cold fingers require warming with mugs of hot chocolate that can be bought from vendors who carry their own portable braziers heated with smelly little lumps of sea coal. When the vendors are jostled by the disrespectful crowd, they catch alight, which brings great joy to some of the rougher elements.

For every visitor to New Ceres who checks that their preferred vendor is licensed, there are ten who forget. Thus another sweet memory of ballooning for most of us is bed for a week.

It could be worse. The current fad for vendor food at this

sort of event is a risky one. Not all of it is fully treated. This is quite intentional.

The vendors meet a public demand. A significant number of young bucks turn up at such events wanting to taste something new. They want there to be an element of risk in their sampling. To please these young men, many vendors will add a small amount of untreated flour or a sliver of untreated cheese to their food.

In theory, such food doesn't exist in New Ceres. In theory no-one starves, too, but the strict government control of treatment plants makes all kinds of food trickery possible. New Ceres is a planet where people stroll between the law as if it's a broad avenue lined with chestnut trees.

Fortunately for hungry ballooners and cold fingers, there are enough aristos at these events so that no vendor is willing to make the risk level dangerous. The price for selling a cheese roll to a tourist who then lies abed for a week is negligible. No-one likes tourists, anyhow. We're mostly tolerated.

The price for hurting an aristo is a lifetime of servitude, either in the infamy that is Hades or through being dumped with no supplies on the shores of Incognita, the dangerous third continent. While a few people return from prison, no-one returns from Incognita.

And so the vendors play with our health at these public events, but never with our lives.

GRANIA LOOKED down on Prosperine and thought how much nicer it was when the mud wasn't splashing the hem of one's new dress. Everything's prettier from a distance.

She had been invited by the team that asked her to haul

on a rope last time she came to see the ballooning. They had sent her a note.

"We would have taken you up then," they explained when she arrived for her airtime. "But when politics interferes, we all back down."

"I don't blame you. I'm impressed you found my address."

"After the shooting, it wasn't hard."

"Too much politics in this city," said Grania.

"Tell me about it," said the head of the ballooning team.

"I know all about it," Grania said, "Because until ballooning became so very big, everything was happening in my salon."

"At least we get away from it here."

"Drift among the stars," agreed Grania.

"You've been among the stars, haven't you?" asked a middle age woman.

"I come from them, technically."

"It's hard to think about all that being out there and here we are, clinging to the surface of New Ceres."

"You've never even seen this planet from space, have you?"

"We all have globes at home. The mark of a ballooner."

"Your imagination is shaped by spheres."

"Nice image," said the chief ballooner. "Well, time to go."

And they did, and Grania felt liberated. She looked across at the other balloons. There was a friendliness to them, with their gaudy colours and their baskets full of happy people. As a balloon drifted close, Grania and her guide would shout out incomprehensible greetings and as it drifted away again they waved madly, as if farewelling old friends.

After a while, a green balloon drifted past. As they came closer to it, Grania recognised Livia with two other people. She felt a shimmer of fear. All they had to do was shoot at the globe and Grania would be undone.

"Livia," she breathed.

"Is that Livia?" her guide asked. "How exciting. I've heard of Livia, of course," and he peered over the side and waved frantically. Livia's companions waved back and everyone was smiling. Even Grania and Livia smiled across at each other in a restrained way.

Grania looked across at Livia's face and found that she could read it.

How alike we are, under the surface, Grania wondered. How extraordinary that this society could turn intensity and passion into destruction. And how sad that we couldn't trust each other and become friends. She regretted that Livia had obviously felt impelled to send those chocolates and the regret caused her to raise her hand and give a small wave. Oops, was her next thought. Not a good idea.

Nor was it. It upset Livia more than she could say and Livia had very few mechanisms for dealing with such emotions.

Grania's balloon finally decided it was time to touch the ground. Gently and slowly it lost altitude until eventually it landed with a bump, in the middle of a strawberry patch.

"Let me pay damages," she said to the balloon man. "This has been such an amazing experience."

So while they waited for the cart to come and for Grania's note to reach the household and produce Qan, they sat in the market gardener's lounge, sipping tea and eating strawberries.

"It's normally not as nice as this," confessed the ballooner. "I should always take wealthy people as passengers."

"People normally shout and scream at you for ruining their livelihood?"

"Where I can," said the ballooner, "I bring her down in a

field and we get shouted and screamed at for scaring the cattle."

The cart arrived first, and the ballooner was out the door. His team caught up with him and the balloon about to be packed. Grania went back outside to watch them go. She looked into the sky and saw that Livia was still aloft. She wondered to what strange lands Livia's unhappiness would take her.

The next day she voyaged in a different way. She was watching a gentle upward drift of a more techno sort when her mind went to a very peculiar place.

She was at the spaceport and watching a gravitic drive ship. As she watched the ship rise, her mind wandered. Passing the time until her ship was ready to board. The ship was new and immaculate. She had a small cabin, well-appointed. And the ship was fast. In next to no time she was at Earthport Sydney, looking out at a familiar place and watching for familiar faces. There they were! Her family. She raced through the terminal, and they all held each other and wept with joy.

As they hugged and cried and hugged and cried her sister said, impatiently. "Your friends are at home for you. Waiting. We thought we'd have a bit of party. They've missed you."

She was jerked out of this dream by a man asking if he could sit at the table. Everyone nearby turned their heads to see who asked such a thing. It was someone from one of the inland settlements. Trig's fell silent.

Grania surveyed the room and realised that she had become a Character. That she always sat in the same chair. That it was always waiting for her. That the only people who ever joined her - until this poor rural sod who didn't know better - were fellow-refugees. She realised that every single person who normally sat with her was lost in the past.

"You can have the table," she said. "I was just about to leave. Look, take my chair. It has an excellent view of the ships rising."

The last time, Grania swore to herself as she left. This is the last time I'll sit at this damn table and watch those damn ships and dream of one of them returning home. Dreaming of it isn't going to make it happen.

I must move on.

She found it hard. Even as she left Trig's and walked around the spaceport, doing some shopping to justify having come all this way, she automatically scanned a crowd for Earth faces. I need more than a resolution to move on, thought Grania, as she picked up some silk from an Outer Planet. I need to change my habits.

She pondered this for a bit. How can I stop looking? How can I stop remembering? What can I do to move on?

"Grania?"

She stopped suddenly, causing the person behind her to lose their shopping. She could still remember the faststairs of civilisation, but other people never developed those habits. She must keep this in mind. She must. New Ceres was different. Surely she had been here long enough to know?

By the time she had sorted her ponderous thoughts and scolded herself for being so very slow on the uptake, she had lost the direction her name had come from.

"Grania?"

There it was again. This time she looked ahead and there, at the bottom of the faststairs, was Dal.

"What are you doing here?" he asked, as he took her elbow and steered her out of the crowd.

'I know crowds,' she wanted to say, but she remembered his need to direct and control and help and she let herself go along with it. Accepting who Dal was might be part of finding her new path.

"I was at Trig's," she explained. She looked up at her husband and saw the old shadow cross his face at the mention of the coffee house. "I don't think I should go back there," she added. "It's not good for me anymore." He looked at her intently, measuring what she had just said and a sudden spurt of irritation overtook her. "What were you doing here, anyhow?"

"Meeting," Dal said, vaguely.

"I bet," muttered his wife. The shadow changed to irritation which grew as the couple bickered during the long river-ride home.

The creaks and rolling and drift of the carriage, the noise of it and the driver and the horse, and, pushing the whole thing to headache level, the incessant bickering with Dal. Grania lost her temper.

"Stop the coach!" she ordered peremptorily. Dal rapped and the coach obligingly stopped. Dal was not too far gone in snark to refuse to stop the coach, but he didn't ask why Grania wanted the coach stopped. Or if she felt all right. I could be dying and he wouldn't ask, she thought, crossly.

She clambered out, her midnight-blue skirts suddenly a gross encumbrance and, when she was safely on the pavement, beckoned the driver to keep on going. For the last two miles she strode along, wearing off her aggression bit by bit. She entirely ignored Dal and his vehicle following her down the street. She entirely ignored his voice and face and anything except the street ahead. She watched that with all her attention, finding peace inside.

Just before she turned the last corner, she stopped.

Something puzzled her. The streetscape was wrong, but

she couldn't quite tell how. She waited for the horses to come alongside.

"Tell Dal there might be trouble," she quietly called up to the coach driver. He tipped his hat and relayed the message.

"He says to tell you that you have a very vivid imagination," the driver explained apologetically, a moment later.

Grania looked at the street again. What was wrong with it?

The houses and gardens were all correct and present. There were a lot of gardeners at work. Could that be what was wrong? Perhaps. She looked at their clothes and how they moved and she wondered if they were gardeners at all.

She ducked back to the coach, reached in, and grabbed at her reticule with its little gun. Dal's hand held her wrist.

"No need," he said.

"And when they attack us?"

Dal looked outside and saw that the gardeners were moving out onto the street. Heading in their direction.

He moved with lightning speed. In a second he was out of the coach, carrying a brace of swords.

"Hold the horse," he told his wife. As she moved to the horse's head, Dal gave a weapon to the coachman and they both stood in front of the vehicle, one on each side of Grania. By the time the attackers arrived, their swords were ready.

Within minutes it was over. One attacker killed. The rest fled. They had obviously not been expecting a challenge.

Finally, we meet real highwaymen, Grania thought. I wish we hadn't. She refused to climb back into the coach, so she and Dal walked alongside it, together and apart at the same time.

When they were within the safety of their own home, Grania drew a deep breath. It wasn't just about the attack. She knew they would happen – it was part of the price she paid for Dal. The other part of the price was one that she was only just realising existed.

The duel had not been a blip. He had dealt with the criminals just now summarily, also. Even the coachman was trained in things military. The two had acted as if they had always worked together. Her husband and his people were rather more than ordinarily skilled with weapons.

What other skills were taught to a ruler's brother on his planet?

Instead of seeking answers immediately, she tried to drown herself in the sketch for an oil painting. This would help her move on emotionally, she reasoned. Everything else could be handled when she was calm and when she could pretend to herself again that life was really quite normal.

Late at night, Dal crept into Grania's studio. He lifted the sheet over the giant sketch. What he saw was a study of one of the camps of Earth. Face after face after face, all individual, all filled with life and personality: all dead. All her family. All her friends. Everyone she knew. All the faces, all the faces looking out. He drew a deep breath.

Dal realised at that moment that the magnitude of what Grania had faced was something he might never comprehend. He wondered if he would ever fully understand.

24

HIGH SOCIETY

Livia was in a happy place. That kind man from Sheni, Samuel Eliezer, had ferreted out every single paper her husband had printed through their press. Either he was incredibly stupid or Sheni had some sort of arrangement with the Lady Governor that kept people like Livia out. Probably a bit of both. Right now it didn't matter, although of course she would have to investigate it.

These little printeries were beginning to develop their own pattern. It looked very interesting and as if there was plenty of political headway to be made. This could be one of the openings she had in mind when she started looking at the New Ceres press as her next stepping stone. It was good to deal with Frederick's issues now and it was even better to have the capacity to leverage it into future fortune.

The typeface in one of them was familiar. It had the same peculiar cross bar to the long 's' as one of the most notorious broadsheets in her little collection.

This is where the little happiness came from. Mr F's education gave her what knowledge she needed, when she needed it. Livia would rather that they were on first name terms, but that he was complete in his affectation (and an outstanding flirt – each step in their dance was a delightful one) was part of his charm. She could destroy that affectation at any moment, by looking at records. She had done that with Lady C. Lady C was Lady Clark-ffynche-Border, but Jane was a very uninteresting given name. The whole fad of avoiding full names had emerged from a plain Jane.

From Mr F and Lady C, Livia's thoughts moved to the printer at Rishon. She wondered who else used their services. It was impossible to find out from Prosperine sources, because the nature of the autonomous towns and settlements meant that they did not report. Occasionally they might volunteer information and they certainly worked alongside the Lady Governor's staff on matters of mutual importance, but they paid for their autonomy and the Lady Governor insisted that this autonomy was respected. Respect, of course, did not exclude spying, but Livia was not quite in the position yet to access the records of such activities. One day perhaps, in the not-too-far-distant future. She was in a mellow mood and allowed herself to dream.

There was something she could do which might not get her the information, but which would definitely advance her capacity to do so in the future: Livia sent a note to the Lady Governor's office. It would not reach the Lady Governor, but it would reach the Lumoscenti and they were her target. Besides, they needed to know who produced that series of lies and tarradiddles.

She returned to Frederick's papers. They were mostly fumbling ploys to advance one woman or another in the public favour. There was a half-hearted ode to Constance. Her husband's affections had been less stable than the jelly that comprised his brain.

One page was different. The happy place disintegrated.

Livia wished she could take back the messenger she had sent, but he had long gone. It was a business card, a bit larger than average and with more text. If it had been distributed, she would have known. She wondered if the idiot zonals had even looked at what they printed. Or maybe they had, and included this to prove they hadn't.

Innocence might save them from the Lady Governor, but it would not save them from her. Not today. Not tomorrow. One day. Cold revenge, the perfect temperature. Sweet revenge, the perfect flavour. Like a chunky apricot conserve, perhaps, served cold with a roast meat to give it savour.

Even if they had never distributed it, those semi-legal printers were guilty. No-one should accept a commission such as this one. Guilty and stupid, since they had sent it on to her.

It was a simple business card. One of those overlarge ones favoured by those who were desperate to tout for more trade. With a few lines and space for a total on one side, it could be one that doubled for an invoice.

Livia turned the cream card over. Indeed, there was a list on the back, with a line underneath and the words AMOUNTS OWED to the left of the card, under the line. No total was given: very clever.

Apart from this, the card was anything but normal.

It purported to be a card from herself. Instead of offering the range of services a normal trademan's card would offer (since it was hard to make a living at only chasing rats or making hats, she presumed) it listed only one trade. It offered deaths of choice: strangling, hanging, poisoning. Instead of recommendations and sentence-long descriptions of her marvellous service, there was a list of satisfied clients, including herself (twice). The list on the reverse of the card was of those who had died. She knew when it had been printed, because the list of deaths was very precise and amazingly accurate. If Frederick had not shot himself, he would now be facing slow agonies.

25

THE GUIDE TO THE SALONS AT NEW CERES

(YOU NEED THIS BEFORE YOU GO THERE)
by Fred Xian

Look, you know and I know there are some things that no tour book can help you with. The salons of Prosperine are very high on this list. I mean, I made it to five different salons in my research for this article and I'm surprised I'm still alive. My friends on New Ceres were astonished I got into even one salon and yes, they're a bit surprised I'm still alive, too.

Prosperine is the capital of New Ceres. The salons were put into the official Lonely Whatever Guide (name very tactfully suppressed so they don't sue my butt off) with a couple of gracious phrases. That's the power-brokers of New Ceres for you. They live in Prosperine. They die (often young and of unnatural causes) in Prosperine. And they run most of the salon system in Prosperine.

It's not ownership in the regular sense. Money doesn't

count nearly as much as prestige and who you know and how much dirt you have on them.

Scoring an invitation to a salon isn't nearly as easy as scoring one to a ball. Invitations to balls are embossed and demonstrate all the latest forgotten printing techniques. They're normally printed by Mr F, printer to the Nobility and their Hangers-On.

When I'm safely off this planet I could be bribed by an enthusiastic editor into writing a reveal-all article about the truth of printing in New Ceres. It's supposed to be lots of little presses, all doing their own thing. All very lovely. All very antiquated. The truth is, though, that it's all censored. The censorship doesn't affect the salons, however. No printed cards.

You hear about the salons by being in the right circles. There's a whiff of a comment and you realize that Lady C (expert on etiquette and the closest creature to an Old Earth Steel Magnolia you'll find in the whole universe) holds her salons at a certain place and time.

After this comes the tortuous task of getting recognised so you're not thrown out at the door.

Don't go to the borderline salons first, is my advice. They're crowded with needy artists and hungry writers and chock full with fabulous politics. The changes to the planet happen here, around you, led by the astonishing Grania and her exceedingly aristocratic husband from one of the very dead inner planets. Grania's from even deader Earth. If you can find your way into one of those salons, you should, but not first up. Never first up. You'll never get invited to the elite circles if you're seen first at an artistic or a political salon.

It sounds like I'm saying, "You get in by being in," and that's mostly the case. Being recognised is painfully slow. You need to subtly insinuate yourself until you receive invitations to the right dinner parties. You need to learn an encyclopedia's worth of etiquette and be seen in the proper (inoffensive, elegant, old-fashioned) garb at the right ball. You need to know the difference between pantaloons and trousers and kneebreeches or between a morning dress and the right dress for a stroll in the most elegant of the parks in Pluto. You need to be able to talk casually about your friends in Pluto (who live in charming mansions in this uber-prosperous area of the capital) and you need to know the calling card etiquette appropriate to advancing these friendships. You need to look as if you live in your New Ceres costume and haven't rented it at the spaceport on the way in.

Above everything, you need to avoid politics. I know, I know. Salons are where politics happen.

Salons and coffee houses are where New Ceres ferments and leavening happens. Anyone who has read even a smidgeon about the planet knows this. The thing is, though, that New Ceres is so bloody hierarchical and so impossibly inbred and so amazingly internal and self-absorbed that you need to be in an in-group before you get to see any of it.

I still can't believe I made it to five salons. Having been, I don't want to go again. Everything happens so elegantly in New Ceres. A leading citizen blew his brains out a few months ago and he did that with great elegance and aplomb.

The real trouble with such subtly is that it's beyond me. I listened to poetry at the salons and I made polite conversation and I paid great attention to opinions on all sorts of useless subjects. I didn't get even a glimpse of this amazing social ferment that's supposed to be happening.

The trick is, you don't just need to know the right people and be in the right place and have the right knowledge: you need to be the right person. I wasn't.

The only useful thing I got from the salon experience was

a rather strange description of Old Sydney from one of Grania's hangers-on. Oh, and I now possess nine outfits that aren't a damned bit of use off New Ceres. Maybe I'll hold a costume party one day.

Anyhow, my advice on salons? Spend your time in coffee shops and your money on old-fashioned watches. The time-pieces of New Ceres are far more useful as conversation pieces when you get back home than a bunch of uptight New Enlightenment geezers who think that anyone who's not from New Ceres isn't quite human.

FRED XIAN WAS – against his will – attending a sixth salon. Qan had sent a servant around to collect him and Xian was forced to dress while the servant waited. He had just returned from off-planet and had been very pleased to see his piece excoriating salons taken up by a significant publisher. Now he was attending one. He wondered if he could revise his piece and sell it again.

"Why did you want me here?" he eventually was able to ask.

"Don't you just simply adore the arts?" Qan replied.

"Gods, you're a cynic."

"Grania needs you."

"Grania doesn't know me. She saw me once."

"Twice. She was watching the duel."

"Twice, then. What of it?"

"She commented that you were comfortable to be with."

"And this is what I've been striving for all my life?"

"Did you ever visit Earth?"

"And that has what to do with how lovely I am?"

"It might explain."

"Of course I did. Everyone does."

"Not everyone."

Xian was suddenly serious. "Qan, you don't get what it was like before the war because you're attached to Dal."

"What do you mean, attached?" It was like being on a see-saw, Fred thought.

"Blood oath, if I don't mistake. I bet you were his whipping boy when you were both young."

"Sometimes you see too much."

"Too often I don't see nearly enough. Let me tell you how it was while you were mured up in the royal palace, learning royal bloody politics."

"Go on."

Qan took a pair of drinks from a tray and handed one to Xian. He took a ginger sip and shook his head.

"You know how you've been trained to always see what people need and want, so that you can make Dal's life perfect?"

"That's one way of describing it."

"Yes, well, bear with me. Because we were like that with Earth. We grumbled about Earthers and we hated their insularity and we wanted them to see us and publish our writing and tell us how much we had grown. Every writer wanted to be published on Earth, even though there was no money in it. Every galactic artist wanted to be Grania, and to have exhibitions in Paris and New York. I couldn't believe Grania was so young when I saw her here. She's done so much. So many of us did so much before the war and then did... stuff... during it, but only Grania did it on Earth and escaped. Earth is special and everyone connected to Earth is significant in a way that nothing else in the universe can be."

"And?"

"Earth was never the planet. It was the people and the civilisations. It was the codes for all our pasts and the hope for all our futures. We were all part of keeping it to that old-time feel. Every single one of us conspired, whether we knew it or not. Grania told me once about the ferry at Manly..."

"She tells everyone about that ferry," Qan sounded wry.

"It's an important symbol. That ferry should've been replaced by hover centuries ago, but all the dreaming galactic tourists wanted to see and feel and touch and live the Opera House and the Bridge and the Manly Ferry and the Harbour. We wanted to be Earthers, vicariously. We loved Old Earth and we kept it alive just as much as these people are forcing this eighteenth century into zombie-existence."

"And your point?"

"When Old Earth didn't play our game, we became sulky. When it wanted to change to meet its own needs, we destroyed it. We said that if Earthers didn't want to play base-ball and cricket and step out of our history books, then we would..."

"Kill it?"

"Not directly, but yes, that's what happened." He paused. "So I have visited Earth. All citizens of the galaxy did. It went alongside being educated and considering oneself civilised. Our finishing school. To go, to admire, to copy and to announce 'I am galactic, but I know my origins.'"

"I understand. But, nevertheless, Grania is at ease with you."

"She is familiar with galactics who know their origins, I guess."

"Possibly, but there are very few galactics on New Ceres. She feels comfortable around you. While you are on New Ceres you will move in her circles. That is an order."

"As far as you are concerned, the Holotor ranks still apply. You apply the obligations as if life has stood still," Xian observed, "But I do wonder what your master thinks."

"My master thinks he is – as you – a galactic."

"You're telling me not to disabuse him of his disbelief?"

"It would be in your best interests. It would also be in your best interests not to bring your acquaintances into Grania's circle without going through me."

"Then I shall go mingle and keep your mistress in the world you wish her to be."

"And for that I thank you," and Qan gave Xian a New Ceres half bow.

What an interesting day, Fred thought, sardonically. And how sad for Grania that all the undesirables were scared off.

Royal wives on Holotor were always lonely. It was a tradition. He wondered if she even knew she was a royal wife. Given her manner, he doubted it. There was a fairytale in that marriage, but until he knew how it would end, he would not be the one to write it down.

Fred moved through the groups as best he could, trying not to step on toes or cause offense. He found these manners stifling. Maybe there was something here he could use in an article. Eyes and ears open, young Fred.

Soon he found the perfect material. He would have to make sure it never made it back to New Ceres, but oh, what a juicy piece it would be.

He had joined a trio of inveterate gossipers. One of them was bringing out the latest. Quite Shocking, he said, in a comfortable way. Never Heard of Such a Thing. How could anyone of repute publish such a card? Not the sort of material one would expect to see. Shopping for murder.

They passed the card around, the reverent silence punctuated by 'I see,' and 'Indeed, shocking,' and, from Fred, 'Wow.' He wondered if Livia really did charge for her services to society. He wanted to take it home for later examination, but instead he handed it on quickly. It looked like very hot stuff.

The next woman in the growing circle handed it on quickly, too. A minute later, three sets of eyes were looking up at Fred; three pale faces made him think of vid melodramas. A microsecond later he realized they weren't actually looking at him. He turned around.

Livia.

Her angelic face was stone.

The silence deepened as Grania came over to see what the fuss was about. The man currently holding the card silently gave it to her. She quickly looked at it. She ripped it up.

"I'll have none of the garbage in my home," she declared.

The group agreed with her sycophantically. Livia remained silent, but the action did nothing to endear Grania to her. Especially coming after the disaster that was Livia's own warning.

Grania was not only a loose cannon, she was annoyingly incapable of subterfuge. Some people, Livia thought, with a shrug, one must simply dislike. Grania was the dish that everyone calls wholesome but that one cannot stomach on the dinner table. There was no taste that summed up Grania. That was the fascination and it was also the problem.

Livia's tongue flicked lightly on the nothingness and consigned Grania to a place outside her own life. The question was what action should be taken. It was too early to know that.

Before she could pursue the thought, Josephine caught her eye. It was unusual for Josephine to attend one of Grania's salons, but at this moment, she would be a useful support. Livia moved in to stand with her friend. Josephine smiled at her and they moved in harmony to diminish the effect of that damnable card. Inside, Livia was even less happy – she would rather not owe Josephine favours.

The two spent the next little while circulating, shoring up

Livia's reputation as best they could. If Grania had not inter-vened, Livia could have used the card to her benefit and created sympathy. As it was, all she could do was ensure that the public voice given to it was that it must be a joke because the card's intended target did not take it seriously. So her voice trilled in laughter and her smooth step was light and joyous, while all the while she hid the hatred she felt towards Grania for not letting her handle her own problems.

While Livia was keeping her scandal from being taken seriously, Constance and Dal were on the verge of causing a scandal of their own. They had quietly slipped into the garden and hidden themselves behind the giant oak. They were arguing.

What no-one saw – not even Grania – was Josephine lingering a little way away.

"You and your people," Constance was passionate, "Don't understand what you're doing. Change has to happen gradually."

"While your glacial change is happening, people are dying off world and on New Ceres. How many deaths?"

"How many deaths if our society implodes? If we have no means of support? No way of regulating to ensure that the food is wholesome? No government?"

"It sounds good. But it's just an excuse for murder. Your people stood by. Billions of people. If there were trials, you would be found guilty."

"You're playing galactic politics with our lives. You're inter-fering with our rights. You–"

Grania joined them. Her hands were on her hips.

"I suppose I should be glad that you're fighting," she said. "I suppose I should be glad that you're not in a love nest. Five different people told me you were. Well, I'm not glad. Dal, you're my husband. Constance, you're my friend. I expect you both to be discreet about your politics. And I expect you both to help me at my salons, not do your best to bring them down around my ears. Constance, you know society best – how do we cut the scandal?"

"We go back and we talk, to each other and to everyone else. After a while, people will forget."

"If I can find a way to sort it out better than that, I will," Grania said.

"And I'll accept your sorting," said Constance. "Even if it causes me a great deal of embarrassment."

"Thank you." The others started to move.

"Wait a moment," Grania ordered. Dal eyed her fire lustfully. Grania sighed. "Dal, your timing sucks. Both of you find two of your followers each while you do the mingling thing."

"Could you explain?" Constance was genuinely curious.

"It's time you all talked, properly. I believe in people talking. Dal, if you take your people to the library after the masses have gone and Constance, you to the green room, we can sort this out."

"What do we do in the library?" Dal asked.

"You talk. Each with his own. Work out what issues you need to discuss more widely and what you need to keep within your own circles. Work out how you're going to talk. Work out what you need to talk about. When dinner is ready, I'll send for both groups. I'll arrange for a light meal. By the end of that meal I expect both of your groups to be communicating amicably. I don't give a damn if you change New Ceres together or not. I do expect you to talk, and without shouting."

"No accusations," said Dal, thoughtfully.

"None," Grania said. "Since you're not teenagers."

"Fair enough," said Constance. "I knew there was a reason I liked you. You're almost as forceful as I am." She gave her lopsided smile, returned to the throng and set to work.

Grania's intervention came too late. Josephine had been standing quite close enough to that oak tree to hear what had been said. She reported the conversation to Livia.

Livia acted almost instantly. Manna from heaven should never be refused.

Dal was arrested first.

Grania sent word to Constance. Constance and her friends went into hiding until her Family connections could go into action.

The impossible had happened, however: Dal had been arrested. Despite all his love for subterfuge, despite all Grania's fears of emergencies, this was not something for which Grania had prepared. Dal had no contingency plans. Maybe he thought his polka dot blood would keep him safe, Grania thought, but the people of New Ceres didn't believe in polka dot blood.

Livia was flower arranging when the news of the arrest was confirmed.

My small revenge, she called it to herself.

There wasn't enough evidence to see Dal hung. She wondered idly if she should have fabricated some. It would have been an especially fine irony to rid herself of Dal using the charge of treason and truly, Livia was tempted. The charge of conspiring to hurt the New Enlightenment should get him out of the way for ten years, at least. It was enough.

She smiled her special smile. This looked big, but it was small. She knew exactly how to change Grania's life the way Grania had changed hers. There was time, however. In fact, now that Dal was out of the way she had all the time in the world.

～

Dal's trial was even more of a mockery than Vlasha's.

Justice Harber directed proceedings. He selected some witnesses and barred others according to some arcane set of rules that only he understood. Everything hung on the incident behind the oak tree, though Constance's name was left out and Josephine was not made to give testimony in public court.

'His unknown interlocutor' and 'our reliable informant' were the phrases used over and over and over again. They made Grania feel sick.

It didn't help that she knew that Dal was guilty. The fact that he was being set up didn't change that. Grania felt exceptionally helpless.

The trial was held too quickly for comfort. There was no time for Dal's money to work and no time at all to seek help or support. Justice Harber ran the whole thing with a smug satisfaction, his voice and demeanour indicating that this particular event was past due.

At the end of the first and only day of the trial, Dal was detained 'at the Governor's pleasure.' It was the phrase no-one wanted to hear. It was what happened when you played with new technology or rebelled too far against the system. Dal was sentenced to spend the next ten years of his life in Hades.

Dal was packed up and sent away almost without time to say farewell. He and Grania had to endure what the broadsheets called 'an affecting moment' in full public gaze, at the spaceport. Grania nearly didn't have even that, because normally prisoners were smuggled off planet quietly, where no-one could pay them attention.

Dal was too prominent for this to happen. Also, his departure time had been leaked. Grania and Dal had their agonising 'affecting moment' where each looked at the other helplessly, then they held each other tightly.

"I'll do something," Grania whispered. "I will."

Dal nodded and said "Of course you will," but it was obvious he was merely trying to reassure her. Grania hugged more tightly as if that would show just how much she was capable of.

26

MEDICINE SOMETIMES HAS SIDE EFFECTS

When Dal had been taken care of, Livia reflected a moment to taste the moment, as was her wont.

Everyone knew that Dal was set up. If they had not, there would not have been a single sympathetic broadsheet, much less the four she had so far discovered. Livia fondly hoped that some of those people made the connection to herself and that they would be more sensible in future and not follow interplanetary madmen. The clean air of her garden was the clean mouthfeel of her triumph.

She had hoped to capture Grania with the same action. Grania had turned out to be untouchable, to Livia's surprise. Perhaps the air was tinged with smoke today? Faintly bitter. Almost a seacoal taste.

A small but select group of old aristos, who normally kept their fingers out of all pies, had intervened and quietly prevented Grania from being added to the list of conspirators. Four of Livia's enemies had been hung by the neck until dead. Dal had been transported. Grania was free. Grania still led a charmed life.

Livia fondled Grania's art and said to herself, That woman cannot possibly have refrained from creating. I will find where she keeps her stash and she can join her husband and his cronies. She despised her feelings about Grania as weakness. Livia was normally so careful about her weaknesses.

In the meantime, her life would be a little easier for what she had recently accomplished. Dal was gone and so was some of the other off world dreck. It wasn't a bad week.

If it wasn't for Grania's sad eyes looking across at her and pleading for help, it would have been a perfect week. Ideally those eyes should have been gouged out and served on a platter. One could not partake, of course, but one could gently refuse them and feel the satisfaction of revenge served up.

27

'COURAGEOUS WAIF FROM BEYOND THE STARS'

Grania looked at a blank sheet of paper and tapped next to it with her finger. Tap-tap-tap. Tap-tap-tap. tap-tap-tap. It could almost be morse code. Except it wasn't. It was Grania's brain bringing Dal back from Hades. If concentration could do the trick, he would have walked through the heavy wooden door opposite her an hour ago.

If Dal had not been so secretive, Grania would have a place to start. She needed to lodge some kind of appeal, but without changing the basic politics behind Dal's imprisonment any appeal would fail. Everything had been done on hearsay and there was no real evidence, so at least in theory Dal's conviction could be overturned. It was a matter of changing the political reality.

Grania laughed. Such a small ambition. Simply change the political reality.

Lizzie. Lizzie would know stuff. Lizzie's name headed Grania's list. And Constance. If Dal could be cleared then she herself would be less under threat. She was a known trouble-maker now – her cover had entirely been blown – but it would force the watchers to pull back a little. So Constance was on Grania's little list, even if Grania had to use Constance's mother's cousin's aunt to reach the lady herself.

There was one person who could solve everything, and that was Livia. This was when Grania wondered why she hadn't cultivated the serpent lady. Water under the bridge.

Lady C? Wouldn't help but might be willing to advise. She knew so much.

Fabian, of course. He wasn't good at initiating things, but he had all sorts of contacts and was willing to help. Was there anyone he hadn't slept with?

Then she thought things through a little further and her list became simply the beginning.

"I can't create a giant reality shift," Grania explained to Qan. "All I can do is pile up little influences. I want you to set me up a series of meetings. Everyone on my list and anyone else you think might be able to help. I want to create an atmosphere where an appeal is possible and where Harber is not in control of the appeal. Then I'll find the person who'll lodge the appeal."

"I thought you would lodge it?"

"It has to be someone with local status. I have a certain amount of notoriety, but we need a person with behind-the-scene influence. I think I know how to get someone, too, but I'd rather not say."

Qan nodded. "Mr F should be on your list," he said.

"Maybe. He's potentially in danger himself. There's a great deal of exposure in it if he supports us in any way. Let me think about how I can make it possible for him to help."

"You've done this before," Qan observed.

"I'm going to achieve my results this time."

"Last time was... not a success?"

"We managed to save five transport ships worth of people who otherwise would have died. We lost everyone else. So no, not a success. Can I not think about that, please?" Grania composed herself then said, "What you need to tell everyone before they start lobbying for help is that no-one we're talking to owes us. No-one has any great personal desire to sacrifice themselves to get Dal back. People just aren't that nice. They're essentially good, but they need helping. Each and every one of them has to be convinced that their bit is important, that it won't be difficult, that it won't hurt them. If it's easy and safe and if their egos are stroked, then they'll help."

Qan looked at Grania a long time before he spoke.

"I don't like it," he said. "It's like being back at Court."

"Despite everything, I believe we choose our lives," Grania said.

"Dal chose to play with power in a place where he was vulnerable and we are back at Court. I know."

"It doesn't make you happy."

"I wanted to spend more time in my garden. I never had my own garden until we settled in Prosperine. Besides, I thought you didn't play these games."

"I hate them. I don't play them until I'm forced. Don't play them is not the same thing as can't play them, however. Also, I don't play New Ceres games, or Holotor games. I play Earth games."

Qan grinned. "I think we should all be scared," he said.

Two weeks later and the dominoes were lined up. Without knowing anyone, Grania had called everyone. Lizzie and Fabian were particularly useful, reaching into parts of society that Grania couldn't access.

Lizzie had bowed to her. "Working with you is an education," she said.

There remained one step. It was no use lining up dominoes without having someone capable of pushing them over. Grania needed a person who would understand the way the dominoes would fall and who had the power to make that initial push. She knew who she wanted. She also knew that the old nobility had given up so much of their power that persuading them to take back even this much would be difficult.

She had Fabian work through his family. He set up a buzz.

The buzz complained that New Ceres was on the brink of major disaster. It moaned that the Parlement was never heard. It lamented that no-one was safe from Family politics if someone as rarefied as Dal was imprisoned. It challenged that it was time for the real aristos to dip their toes in the water. That nobility should support nobility. That the system of justice had to be defended, otherwise no-one was safe. How a political conversation in a private salon was something anyone could have.

The buzz picked up. The gossips started to spread questions. What was happening in Hades? Why was it off-planet and out of sight? Why were so many people being sent there? What was the Lady Governor doing with all the prisoners?

Grania had started the buzz. Once Fabian had assured her it was echoing down the corridors of the once-powerful, Grania made her last appointment.

"Many voices are singing right now. You're a very clever young lady," Lady C said.

"Why do I suspect that you did not mean that as a compliment?"

"I don't want to move on this. None of us do. We have been safe until now." Grania waited and looked and forced her to say the next words. Lady C looked at her shrewdly. "I'll do it," she said. "But in return I want a private showing of the exhibition I'm sponsoring."

"You can have as many private showings as you like."

Grania promised. "I thought you'd also like this." She gave Lady C a portfolio.

"May I open it?" asked Lady C.

"Of course," said Grania. "It's yours."

Lady C drew a deep breath then gave a shaky laugh. "All of them?"

"Every single one. Whether you like them or not, mind."

Lady C took her time. She looked at every picture carefully and slowly. Finally she asked "Is there a title?"

"Not really," said Grania. "They're pictures of Prosperine. The people and their lives. The people you're helping save."

"But first, we clear your husband and bring him home."

"If you don't mind."

The dominoes were set.

Lady C gave the last push. Her etiquette column that week examined proper seating for those with foreign titles at a hypothetical dinner party. Near relatives of foreign kings, if human, were placed next to the host or the hostess, depending on gender. Spouses took on the dignity of the higher ranked member of the couple. It caused a small debate, but no-one could contradict Lady C on etiquette. Her word was law.

Such a small article. Such a large effect.

There was a flurry from foreign ambassadors who were concerned that the New Ceres' refugees would run back into the cosmos and onto their planets. There was an equal flurry from a group of old aristos who commented very publicly that Dal's trial infringed their ancient privileges. Dal, they pointed out, as foreign royalty, might not be superior to the old nobility, but he was certainly not inferior. Ancient privilege applied.

Major business people put a series of private pleas to the

Lady Governor's Office, concerned about the effect of Dal's punishment on his business interests and on the economy.

A series of broadsheets emerged claiming the charges were trumped up and an entirely different series ran the streets pointing out that if someone titled was sent off-planet on hearsay then no ordinary person had a chance of justice.

Livia knew that Grania was behind the papers. They had her stamp, somehow. Maria suggested that Grania got to the old aristos through Lady C, but on balance it was improbable. Grania was such a newcomer and such a naïve.

No-one in Livia's camp could trace the ambassadors or the old aristos or the very wealthy businessmen who had put in complaints and pleas and requests. Some were faces familiar from Grania's salons, but only a few. Not nearly enough. Livia's tongue tasted gall as she worked the problem.

The answer was simple, but she never discovered it. There was one set of people Livia had never touched. She had such a distaste for the act of sex and the vulnerabilities it brought, that sex-workers and their networks were almost entirely outside her ken. From Fabian down, prostitutes reached throughout Prosperine. They had their own society and their own dignity. They required a stable society for their business to be safe. And they talked to their customers.

Those customers were in many places and were vulnerable to Grania's tactics. These ordinary people were persuaded to see a better society with Dal than without him, and they were also persuaded to see injuries to themselves possible in a society where a galactic prince could be punished after a show trial. What Dal had been accused of was bordering on the illegal. He had not broken any law. Some of their own activities were far less borderline. Grania made hay out of the way so many citizens abused the legal system on the planet. The sun shone on her haymaking.

So there was unrest on the streets. It was the logical consequence of the unrest in parlours and at dinner tables.

When the crowds started to gather, the Lady Governor was concerned. It was announced that she would make a proclamation.

THAT AUTUMN, Livia had additional concerns.

She traced that business card back to Sheni, but it took her a little time to decide what to do. In fact, normally she would hang onto the knowledge for longer and used it very strategically when the precise occasion arose. In this case, however, she needed the matter settled because it was stopping her from moving on. She had passed her tests and Dal was gone: she didn't want this small but annoying axe hanging over her.

There had to be more she could do with it than simply lay it to rest, however. It would be useful, for instance, if she could use it to reduce the autonomy of some of the regions outside Prosperine. Consolidate the Lady Governor's power a bit more. Make the business card work for her, as business cards should.

She paid a visit to Justice Harber and brought him completely into her orbit. It had been past time for that, anyway. And he was raging for a way to make an impact. Dal's trial had made him hungry to exert his power. He was enthusiastic about challenging the settlements. It had always irked him that they had their own legal system and that he was a nobody there. He set up a test case.

The issue was whether the settlement of Sheni had opted into the affairs of Prosperine by accepting the printing. It was a very flash trial. Dal's had been small and swift, this took weeks. It had arrays of witnesses and the testimony would have filled two thick printed volumes.

Grania used it to generate more of her buzz. The crowded courtroom and the even more crowded coffee shops nearby were excellent breeding grounds for her particular kind of political fermentation. While Harber made one sort of ruling, she created the atmosphere for another.

The days merged into each other. Evidence repeated and twisted and turned itself around. The papers – which had almost entirely ignored Dal's trial – turned up in full force and every day contained summaries of the evidence from the day before. Nothing much was said most of the time, but it was said at great length.

The most important point made was by the three aristocratic witnesses. They argued that the proper place to discuss this was in the Parlement, as the distinguishing feature of the First Enlightenment was the growth in parliamentary power. Issues like this belonged in parliamentary discussion. When courts took too strong a role, they became legislators and rule of law itself was corruptible.

These claims were much argued over coffee.

Prosperine suddenly realised that the law didn't have to be made on the fly by the judiciary. A whole group of intellectuals had simultaneously realised that there was more than one way of interpreting the eighteenth century. Grania read the summary of these arguments in the licit and less licit papers and smiled.

Someone, somewhere was reading and researching. One day she would find this person and introduce him or her to Dal.

Grania's favourite witness to Sheni's trial was Livia's daughter, Esther. She was introduced as having spent some time in various settlements and towns of various sizes and currently resident in Hightown, (escaping her mother, one would assume, thought Grania) a town of minimal autonomy that might serve to show that it was not essential to the well-being of town dwellers that their government be independent.

Esther listened to her instruction very carefully. If she had followed the model of the earlier witnesses, she would have reiterated the court's introduction, almost word for word.

Then Esther said, "I know nothing. My mother said to come and I'm a dutiful daughter, but I know nothing." The audience broke into spontaneous applause and Esther smiled out at them and bowed. "May I be excused now?" she asked. She was let go with no further questions.

Harber was out for a show ruling and intended his name to go down in history. It was a long judgement. There was much language of significance. Finally, in summary, Harber claimed that the independence of autonomous settlements was an aberration and that each and every one of them should be integrated within the normal systems of government.

Harber had played the crowd during Vlasha's trial. This time the crowd played him. Grania's little exercise had primed it.

Prosperine erupted. For three days the capital simmered barely below riot point. The Lady Governor's people kept it under control. Both the secret and the public agents were out in full force. Arrests, violence by the law enforcers, and even the burning of houses were the rule for those three days.

The Lady Governor's strict forces cowed the populace enough so that Prosperine did not actually burst into flames. It was, however, a close thing.

The Lady Governor herself was forced to step in. She overturned Harber's judgement. She had no choice.

One person who immediately benefited from the unrest was Livia. It was she who took the matter to the Lady Governor before too much damage was done. It was she who quietly suggested that the best way to take down autonomy was one settlement at a time, quietly, privately and very carefully targeted.

The Lady Governor agreed. She said, "I will rescind Harber's judgement when I make my other proclamation, tomorrow at noon. This is damage control," she said. "I will not make a custom of it. You will tell the Six that tools like Harber are not welcome."

Livia left her first face-to-face meeting with the Lady Governor with rather mixed feelings. Her tongue flicked to the air and tasted... bewilderment.

The Lady Governor's other proclamation was simple. Dal was granted a full and free pardon. It was an easy way out, but it was effective.

The crowds appeared one last time to cheer Dal at the spaceport and to tussle on the streets round the main court-house, then Prosperine returned to normal. The buzz in parlours and salons and dinner tables lasted a bit longer, but soon it, too, faded.

On a frosty morning Dal walked through the front door, weary and thin and very, very cheerful.

28

VIEWING GRANIA

Winter brought in a whole new range of activities for the leisured classes. Music and theatre and opera and dance. Art of all kinds.

The first proper art exhibition of the season was always special. Every painter tried to get a painting selected, to advertise that they would be showing their work later in the season and to ensure the crowds. There was a different kind of buzz when the exhibition list went up in the Town Hall. On that final list was a watercolour by Grania entitled simply "Dal".

To while away the time between the posting of the List and the display of the art it described, and to add to the anticipation, many artists put together small displays of their work. Grania also had one of these, although her watercolour in the Winter Exhibition would be the one everyone remembered as her first. This was the etiquette of the art world in Prosperine.

Qan rented a small hall for the unofficial reveal of Grania's art on New Ceres. It comprised three series of her sketches. Anything more permanent than sketches was disal-

lowed for these events, the art establishment being as inflexible as any other.

Her sketches were elegant. The hall was well-lit. The
refreshments were outstanding. The pre-exhibition display
ought to have been a brilliant success.

Livia had employed three thugs to go to the display every
day and complain. "Influence everyone who can't judge for
themselves," was their instruction. They obeyed this very
nicely for the first four days. On the fifth day they became
bored and livened things up with food fights and threats and
rough and tumble.

"The trouble with thugs," sighed Livia, when she heard.
"They show their lack of class."

Fortunately one of Lizzie's friends was there when the
fighting began. She raced out and found Lizzie, who brought
some of her friends and broke it up. They hauled the chief
miscreant before a wire-thin and whip-angry Dal.

During the interrogation (which is what Lizzie insisted on
calling Dal's questions) it became obvious that the men were
caught just in time.

"We were told not to damage the pictures," the thug admitted, "But it made no sense, so we brought our knives. We were
having a fine time. I reckon we would have brought those
knives out."

Thanks to Lizzie's friends, only Grania's ego was hurt. The
good news was that the inevitable broadside about the event
was all in Grania's favour.

A few days later they read the broadside in a coffee shop.
Then...

"I don't like being called a 'courageous waif from beyond
the stars,'" she told her husband, in bed that night. "Not even
in a song."

At that very minute, Livia was sitting at her dressing table, twisting copy after copy of the song tightly, and burning it in the flame of her candle. The hour struck and she raised her head, her littlest smile warping her face. She went to her curio cabinet and took out Grania's light sculpture. She smiled again as she brought it crashing to the floor. It bounced a little, but it did not break. She put it back.

"Gone," Livia said. "Gone. Quite, quite gone."

One day, Grania was walking in a park, near home. She didn't know that she had escaped her minders, because she had no idea she was supposed to have minders..

It was a glorious day and she watched the sunlight intently, trying to fathom how to translate it and her internal vision of light into oils. It was bothering her a great deal. She had sorted out so many things about creating using old technologies, but the light defied her and remained in her mind's eye.

She noticed the shadows, but it took her a moment to process that they were men and not interesting variations on the light. Six big men. Surrounding her. By the time she had become properly aware, it was too late.

A minute later the men were gone, and Grania was lying on the ground, screaming, her hands over her eyes, blood everywhere.

One day very soon after, in a coffee house, Livia was looking for somewhere to sit. She saw Mr F. He cut her, very gently. He saw her – she knew he had seen her – but he walked right past without a nod, or a bow, or a tip of the hat.

A week later, in the same coffee house, Livia called Mr F to account. He was sitting at his usual table. Livia loomed over him.

"We are not of the same society," he said, looking up and meeting her eyes quite directly. His pose showed classic apology – his eyes showed he had no fear – his tone showed disdain. "I cannot countenance bridging such a gap."

Livia couldn't argue with Mr F's logic. She wondered why he had taken so long to say it.

Why were an artist's eyes so very important to him? She wondered a great deal about Mr F, and she saw many interesting interplays with him in her future. At this moment, however, she must dismiss him from her life. He had found the perfect excuse not to sleep with her, and she could never elevate him to her level. A pity. He had more to him than any of her husbands.

She wondered why he had chosen this juncture to announce his views and why he had used the cut direct. It mattered, but it was something she might never discover. It hurt. Her mouth was closed, but there was still bitterness on her tongue.

Mr F would have been pleased to know it hurt. He didn't understand why he had been able to flirt with Livia, knowing she murdered, yet was unable to take coffee with her, knowing this. He couldn't. And he didn't. But he didn't understand why.

Livia didn't dwell on Mr F long, but she did decide that it was not necessary to dispose of him. It was enough, just now, to damage Dal and to reduce Grania to a nothing.

Dal felt it was enough, too. He had sat with Grania through her initial treatment and through a thousand subsequent meetings with a thousand inconsequential physicians.

"No, we cannot restore your wife's eyesight."

They offered ways of helping her get around town, methods of dealing with pain, but no solution. No vision. Grania had turned silent as a stone and would not say a word. Dal himself felt less and less like saying a word as the physicians become more and more blunt.

Grania was silent. She knew that Harry Levi could help her see again. The equipment that could treat war wounds could do eye implants. She couldn't say this, however. It would betray a trust.

At the heart of the trust were all the people of Rishon. If the Lady Governor knew of the illegal technology they possessed, then it would be confiscated, despite the special status of the settlement. Grania would have her eyes, but it might be at the cost of the life of a child or the lungs of a chemical worker. Silence was her only resort. Silence and drugs.

The pain was hard to deal with. She spent much of her days in bed, almost asleep, surrounded by opium dreams. Without her eyes the medicine practised on New Ceres didn't trouble her. Without her eyes she didn't care about addiction. She lay there in her dark and tried to forget how to speak.

One morning she woke up to a buzzing and humming. It disturbed her darkness and tempted her to break her silence.

"What's happening?"

"We've smuggled ourselves aboard a ship," Dal explained. "In three days' time you will have new eyes."

"Isn't it illegal?"

"Not illegal the way we've done it, just heavily discouraged. I talked to your Lady C about it. She said to tell you that if you could use buzz, she could use it too. It will be difficult when we return, but it won't be impossible."

"How isn't it impossible? We're breaking the bloody law just by being off-planet. I signed a bloody piece of paper. I thought it was such a stupid thing, to print a piece of paper just for me to say if I left I'd never come back." She let out a sob, then choked it down. "Sorry. I can't ever seem to stay calm these days."

"I wrote to Harry Levi. Your friend Harry," he inserted such politeness into that phrase, "says that you are still suffering from post-traumatic stress disorder. When we arranged this little voyage, he said to tell you that Granny would return. It might take time, but she will return."

She held his hand tightly, but didn't speak.

Eventually, he continued. "Grania, that paper wasn't the whole of the law. The old nobility is allowed to go off planet and so are their essential companions. I have brought a token scion of the aristocracy with us. We're his essential companions. Everything except the operation itself is quite, quite legal."

"Grania, can you hear me?" another man's voice spoke.

"I'm not deaf," snapped Grania. "Who are you?"

"She's not good at voices, however," said Dal. "It's Fabian."

"Does this mean you two are talking?"

"You can listen to us over dinner," Dal said. And so she did. They were very guarded with each other and Fabian was silent when Dal helped her fumbling self with the strange shipware. Grania suspected the truce would not last.

The medical facility wasn't on a planet. The layout was sickeningly familiar. She knew where each corridor would go, even without vision to help. She knew it from the scent and from the feel. It was gut-wrenchingly familiar. Ships like this had been produced for the war. Now it was a mobile state-of-the-art hospital. No experiments and hiding the appearance of torture in this place.

In fact, the biggest problem in getting new eyes was

preventing the medical team from playing with the colour or adding extra features.

"An artist could use a few extra colours in the world," she was coaxed.

"No," she snapped to every suggestion. "I'm happy to have very good eyes, but I don't want any of the 'we-invented-this-for-fighting' stuff. Good plain eyes."

And good plain eyes is what she got. Some discomfort, no pain, and four days to learn how to use them.

A week later the three were back. Grania was blindfolded again, so that she could adjust them to New Ceres' light gradually. Dal wanted her to see immediately and all day and had said so twenty times since the operation. Grania pointed out that the whole business would be better if she spent a little more time in recovery and if whatever Dal was going to do to make her path easier was already done.

"If the legal idiots turn up and forbid me to paint because of the artificial eyes, then we must leave," she said.

"I don't think it will be that bad," said Dal, mildly.

For once, Dal's optimism was largely correct.

Dal had an important step to take before Grania could properly emerge into the world again. Grania wanted to do it herself, but she rather suspected she couldn't make it stick. She tried explaining to Dal, but he never seemed to listen. Grania called on Qan. He also didn't quite understand, so she sent a message to someone who she thought would see the problem. Not only did Lady C see the problem, she had explained it to Dal, in no uncertain detail. Once she had done so, Dal felt a surge of relief.

"Of course," he said. "That's the only path. Why didn't I think of that?"

"Because you're a man and would rather have jumped up and down and made a big fuss."

"The big fuss would not help Grania. In fact, it would be very damaging to her. I see that now. I need to brave the lion's den before my wife can do anything." And Dal went on his way, thoughtful.

It was strange. Dal had been there for her the moment she had been brought home. He had not left her side. He had made everything happen. Yet he still didn't understand anything about art and the art world. Or even very much about New Ceres and its resistance to modern medicine. I guess that's what marriage is all about. Shared not-under-standings.

When he was ready (and had found the courage) he paid a morning visit to Livia. Canti was with him.

Livia found herself reading a document that showed how she had smuggled in Bio-Az and had tried to use it to kill.

"No-one will believe it," she said.

"If it's so much as mentioned in public, however, your future is contaminated."

Livia was silent. The silence dragged. "What do you want from me?" she asked, finally.

"I want two things. First, you leave my wife alone. Second, you put word around that your thugs were instructed to merely damage Grania, not destroy her eyesight. As far as you are concerned, there was a lot of blood but no damage."

"You leave me no choice."

"You made your own bed."

"What a sad metaphor," Livia mocked, "And who would have thought that you would have had the courage to smuggle Grania off world? And who would have thought an aristo would crawl into bed with you? Or was he in bed with Grania? Hard to tell, with that one."

Dal's lips whitened, but he didn't answer her taunts.

Canti moved very slightly, very threateningly. Livia

ignored her. Her tongue slipped out as if she were tasting the air to determine her decision.

"Very well, then, I shall do it."

Once they were safely away from Livia's house, Canti said "She's a rattlesnake. She will be far more dangerous now she's been trapped."

"I know," said Dal, "But I do think she'll keep her word about Grania."

"I pity anyone close to her for the next few days."

Esther would have agreed. Her visit from school was exceptionally badly timed. Livia took out all her fury and all her frustration on her 'drab excuse for a daughter.'

Two days with her mother and Esther quietly packed a bag, stole her mother's jewellery, and disappeared. She had decided that being a good daughter was too short of rewards. Besides, she had plans for her life. Those plans did not include her mother.

THEY WERE all in the same room at the Great Exhibition. Grania saw Livia (who was with Josephine) and whisked herself out of sight. Livia had put herself past forgiveness.

Esther saw them both, but herself remained entirely invisible. She was serving refreshments and was attired very nattily.

Livia saw only Grania's watercolour. It forced her to ignore her companion, which amused Josephine. As Livia's eyes drank in the picture, she didn't know whether to celebrate or murder. Grania's art really was superb. She felt honoured every time she saw a new piece.

It made her feel kindly that day and she decided that the style was a suitable one for the planet, after all. She wondered how hard it would be to obtain that particular painting. This didn't mean that Grania was off the hook. She can have a respite, thought Livia, to create beauty.

Livia had a rather special appointment after her visit to the Great Exhibition. There was a house in White Street. It was a rather ordinary house and its main feature was a large observatory at the back. Josephine was there to walk her there and give her dignity. She would wait outside, however, as Livia herself had done once, three days before Alphonse's curious dinner party.

She knocked on the door and was shown into the observatory. It was lush and very well-tended. The greenery was so rich and puissant that it made observation from the outside impossible except from the air which of course was not possible on New Ceres. Nesting in the green were a dozen masked figures in black cloaks.

The ceremony was over rather quickly. Livia swore her five oaths and received her insignia. An hour later she walked back out the front door, a small parcel under her arm and a great deal more power in her hands. Livia had been inducted into the Lumoscenti. She was met by Josephine, who gave her the closest thing to a celebration one is allowed in those closet circles. In return, Livia handed on her old brooch.

During her swearing-in into that secret society she felt warm through and through. Her home would be safe. The New Enlightenment would outlast the techno societies. And she, Livia, would help keep it so.

29

FRED'S REVENGE

 *n extract from "The truth about New Ceres: what the Lady Governor would prefer you did not know before you visited."*

THIS WORK and all extracts therefrom are banned on New Ceres and all its possessions.

THIS IS a society that runs on secrets. The Lady Governor meets no-one except her trusted few and she keeps a very tight rein on a very complex administration. When I first came here, everyone told me that New Ceres was run by paid officials. Very open. Very public. Very efficient. Very European.

The paid officials, are, however, under the express charge of the Family of Six. Initially, the Family was recruited from the paid officials and apparently this still happens when the numbers of the Family are too few. There is a popular saying, "When an administrator loses his soul, he is adopted into a Family."

Members of the Family are not paid. They live on bribes and paybacks and cuts from profits. They own people rather than places and lives rather than land. They carefully place members in the judiciary and keep a stranglehold on the courts. The law is theirs and so is most of the business world.

Sometimes a member of the Six is sent to become a paid official. This is generally strategic rather than a demotion. There is always a judge in Prosperine who is of that number, for instance. The current justice from the Families is Harber. This man is a tool in all senses of the world, a corpulent cat who has the world seeking favours and extending bribes so that he will judge a case favourably.

The only thing that's admirable about the members of this series of artificially created Families is their violence. They kill each other even more readily than they murder those not of their number and many of the citizens of New Ceres pray that they will murder each other and leave everyone else alone.

In a recent incident one of their most notorious members, Livia (who on most planets would have her personality re-shaped because of the magnitude of her crimes) killed her favourite cousin, Alphonse, apparently because he was in her way. Alphonse, himself – this year alone – rigged trials, murdered, bribed and generally was a force for evil in the community.

The danger of the Six is not just that they are beyond prosecution for their crimes, but that they often appear as public benefactors. In addition to their work in running the planet, they welcome refugees and set up as their protectors.

Others lead reform groups to address problems such as food safety (the over-riding problem in New Ceres). This appearance enables them to mix with the almost powerless aristocracy and to bring the middle classes and the artisans under their thumb. They are the glue that sticks New Ceres together, but it's a glue that contains too much industrial poison.

It took me a long time to realise that – despite their prominence – the Lady Governor's own staff don't trust the Six. Very few of that extended family make it to her inner circles. To keep them under control and to watch the population at large, her office employs a secret society. Everyone knows about it. No-one talks about it. The members walk the streets openly, their identities disguised by big black gowns and beaklike masks. Everyone knows, but no-one talks. Everyone sees, but the wearers of those masks remain anonymous.

The first hint that someone is linked to the Lumoscenti (maybe as an informant or maybe as a supporter) is the jewellery they wear. There is a distinctive sun shape that can be worn as as a brooch, a pendant or even a ring. This jewellery doesn't indicate how important the person is to the Lumoscenti – only that the Lumoscenti is important to them.

In the general population the Lumoscenti is feared. The silence is so deep it feels conspiratorial. If you mention the Lumoscenti, then you will usually find that the people you were talking to will leave you alone thereafter.

And these are the politics of New Ceres: the elegant nothingness of the ancient aristocracy and their futile Parlement; the poisoned chalice of the ruling families, the repressed paid officials and the dark Lumoscenti. Every one of them links back to the Lady Governor's office and through them, the Lady Governor has absolute power on New Ceres.

If New Ceres is – as it claims – the New Enlightenment,

then I personally think that the French Revolution is overdue. On the surface the world has all the elegance and manners and beauty the tourist guides claim. Under the surface, this is one of the most corrupt societies I have ever seen. Its charm is the charm of a rotting fruit. Its sweetness is rank decay.

NOTICE OF EXPULSION

The government of New Ceres gives notice that any ship bringing a human of uncertain origin who calls himself "Fred Xian" will have cargo and ship confiscated. Fred Xian is not permitted on New Ceres proper, nor on New Ceres settlements within the system.

SHOULD HE ENTER THE SYSTEM, he will be immediately consigned to the Lady Governor's pleasure. There will be no appeal. Other visitors should note that this is the consequence of impugning the honour of New Ceres.

FRED XIAN'S FINAL ARTICLE

This is about a story I never wanted to write.

For the past three and a half Earth years, you've read my articles from New Ceres. They began the way they should have: a curious investigation of an even more curious society. I wrote about coffee houses and duels and printing houses and costumes and the strangeness of the New Enlightenment. I never really understood the New Enlightenment, but I accepted it. Everyone who visits New Ceres accepts it.

Then there came a moment. At that moment everything fell to pieces. I realised just how corrupt New Ceres is, was and always has been. Even its initial planetary settlement was not ethical. To settle New Ceres we replaced native species with Earth species and we changed the planet to fit ourselves.

It wasn't my quiet report to the Twelve Planets that led to my expulsion. Oh no. The Lady Governor of New Ceres couldn't give a damn that sentient aliens were killed in the early stages of settlement. Her little planet doesn't have any kind of proper history: it only has the New Enlightenment.

So why have I so sadly left the green and comfortable city

of Prosperine? Why will my handsome visage no longer darken the door of another of those bloody salons? Let me tell you, I hated the salons. I couldn't say so, because all my communications off planet were watched. And I knew it. New Ceres patrols its reputation.

I knew when I arrived, at least. I forgot, bit by bit. I became used to the watchers over my shoulder.

When I wrote my last little article, I received a very quiet visit from the one group I'd never been able to crack. I was given a choice between leaving or occupying a nice green garden plot in someone's private graveyard. They think they're all-powerful, these Lumoscenti. They forget just how far humans have spread. So here I am, on a civilised planet, about to tell you what the Lady Governor thinks no-one knows.

My article was on the food supply of New Ceres. She controls it, does the elegant Lady Governor. Every bit of homegrown vegetable has to be fixed so it's edible by humans. Not a big deal, I hear you say. We've seen it before, I hear you say.

Well, it's different on New Ceres. Every user of the processing machines is licensed and controlled by the Government. Improved and cheap technologies are destroyed before they can be implemented. And recently the Government has taken to dealing with riots by starving the poor. Not just starving the poor. Poisoning the poor. Get rid of unrest by using social pressure to shut everyone up.

There was a riot last week. For the next two weeks, the whole district only had access to untreated food. No-one of influence lived in that district, of course, or if they did they visited one of those rural enclaves the rich and powerful like to hide in, usually when what they do to other people weighs on them, or for festivals.

And this is why I now bask in the salubrious warmth of a resort colony.

When I get another job, you may be sure that you, my loyal readers, will be the first to know. I will continue to wend my way around the universe, reporting on the strange and the improbable and the unseemly. One place I'll never return to, and that's New Ceres.

It's not only the poisoning of the poor. The government is corrupt. The society is on the verge of completely imploding. It's a tragedy in the making and I don't want to be there when it collapses.

The tragedy is that New Ceres was a refuge for the humans from Old Earth. It holds Earth memories for the rest of us. I met some of these Earthers. They will fight.

They were herded once and have sworn, never again. Many locals are with them. New Ceres won't go quietly into that good night. I couldn't stand to watch the tragedy in the making and so I wrote my article. I don't regret it.

That original article was destroyed, but I have a commission to write the book of the end of New Ceres. From the corrupt food to the even more corrupt government, I shall reveal the excesses and the catastrophes, the cover-ups and the rebellions, in blocks of three thousand words a week.

Subscribe now, before New Ceres is lost completely.

32

SET PIECE WITH TOMBS

Livia finally finished her own work of art. She had sought out Alphonse's favourite sculptor and specified very precisely what she wanted. Alphonse's tomb would celebrate his life perfectly.

The day of Alphonse's memorial, she had her servants prepare the food for the dead. She dressed in elegant black, with a veil to hide her features. She knelt by Alphonse's tomb, which was covered by a black cloth. At the end of the ceremony, which was attended by a great number of Family members (but not Livia's daughter, who was unaccountably missing), the cloth was gently removed. Underneath was the statue, in all its glory, including a perfect replica of Alphonse's favourite nappy.

While this was happening, Dal and Grania attended another unveiling. There was a new brothel in Prosperine: Lizzie's. Dal was confounded that it existed, but as her patron he had to attend. Prostitution on his home world was far less flamboyant. It was also far less sanctioned. Lizzie's brothel was entirely legal.

The unveiling was not held at the brothel itself but was an

elegantly drunken gathering at a nearby inn. It was close enough to home to walk and so Grania and Dal had done so, though Dal was better armed than he let his wife know.

Grania loved the atmosphere. It was warm and rich and funny and no-one could quite work out how someone as respectable as she was could be there, in an inn, drinking to a brothel's opening. Grania bubbled with amusement the whole time.

"I've never visited a brothel before," she whispered to Dal.

"I hope you don't intend to do so now," her husband whispered back.

"Can't I pay social visits?"

Dal laughed and Grania laughed with him and they were perfectly in accord.

If this is happy ever after, Grania thought. I could get to like it.

"I like being married to you," Grania said, when they were walking home, hand in hand. Dal's other hand was near his sword, just in case.

"I've always liked being married to you," Dal twinkled down at her. "Shall we resolve to live happily ever after?"

"You were reading my mind," she accused.

"Is there anything we should do?" asked Dal.

They went up the steps and in the door, still talking.

"Do?"

"To celebrate our new resolution. Something together."

If he can't ask directly, Grania thought, then I shall take it as an excuse for mischief. "I wouldn't mind going for a walk."

"Grania"

"Well, I wouldn't. I need to see things. Feed my soul through my new eyes. My soul is very hungry today."

Dal laughed and they were out the door again within a very few minutes. As he took her hand to help her and her long skirts down the steps, he whispered, very close, "I'll get even, my love. Tonight."

Grania shivered pleasurably.

It was a long walk. The couple found they had much to say to each other. It stopped very suddenly when they came across a new establishment just three blocks away. Not too far from the inn they had just visited.

"This is an extraordinary place for a brothel," Dal said, astonished.

"Too close to wealth?" Grania was acerbic. "It might ruin the neighbourhood."

"True." Dal gave his wife his toothy grin, "Which is what your friend is hoping, I suspect."

"My friend?"

He pointed to a big window. Seating on the window seat, her eyes focussed firmly on a potential customer, was Lizzie, already home from the celebration.

"I bet it's hiding more political machinations."

"I wouldn't be surprised," her beloved remarked.

Grania refused to let New Ceres dictate her life, and dropped in on Lizzie the very next day. From then on, she paid regular visits. She was always directed to the private door, not to the brothel entrance.

"After all," said Lizzie, "You're a friend. If you ever let that husband of yours go, though, I can find you someone juicy."

"Not a chance," said Grania. "I'm a prude."

"Besides" said Lizzie, "You're never going to let that husband go, are you?"

"Why should I?"

"You're no fool," agreed Lizzie. "Now all I have to do is persuade you into my brand of politics."

"Wait," said Grania. "I have my own brand. I need to learn this planet before I let loose."

"I always wondered why you were so quiet, when you had such a reputation."

"Who do you know who knew my reputation?"

"Oh, someone," Lizzie waved her hand vaguely.

"I'm quiet until I know what to do. Freeing Dal was my warning to the world. Be careful with me." They smiled together conspiratorially.

"D'you know who comes here most often?" asked Lizzie.

"I doubt it," said Grania.

"Justice Harber."

"That man just keeps on going, no matter what happens round him."

"He does. He's fat from his bribes and he knows everything and he really only cares if it affects him."

"One day it will."

"One day might just be very soon."

"How do you figure that one?"

"I hear that at the theatre two nights ago, Lady C gave Harber the cut direct."

"You know," said Grania, slowly, "I could get to like Lady C. I really think I could."

IT WAS the exhibition of the decade. That section of Larsen Street was barricaded, partly for safety and partly to keep the swarms of the curious away from the entry. It took the presentation of an embossed invitation, printed by Mr F and some of his finest work, to pass the barricades and join the queue that snaked around the street and across the road.

Beyond the barricades coachmen shouted and swore as they tried to get close enough to let their passengers out. Everywhere there were people, jostling and thrusting and pushing. It was as if half the population of Prosperine wanted to see Grania's first full exhibition since Earth had gone.

"New Worlds and Old; New People and Old." The title was obvious. The theme was clear. She was going to celebrate them. The most famous refugee after the tatters of war, and she was going to show New Ceres how to see itself. If the streets had been ten times the size, they would still not have contained the people.

Not everyone was equally welcome at the exhibition. More than one person found themselves halted at the door and turned back, after queuing for hours. Livia – although she had obtained an invitation - found herself on the list of the unwanted. She was not surprised at this, given the circumstances, but was very surprised that Grania had made a list. It appeared that new courage had been injected into the Earthwoman along with her new eyes.

Mr F was also halted at the door, although not denied entrance.

"I was told to detain you until your companion arrives," the doorman explained apologetically.

"I did not bring a companion," Mr F said.

"No sir. When she arrives, I will direct her to you. If you would just wait in the chair over there." The doorman indicated several upholstered chairs to the left, just inside the entrance. "Someone will bring you refreshments shortly."

A half hour later, Mr F was joined by Constance, to the surprise of both of them.

Mr F stood up and bowed, then looked across at his tall friend quizzically. "It appears that your Grania is more than she seems," he said to his co-conspirator. Constance sighed. "Shall we," and he extended his arm courteously to the lady.

"I cannot believe she's done this." She took his arm and they introduced themselves to society as a couple.

"Better this than public discourse about matters we would rather not see discussed."

"She can't know anything. She was bluffing."

"I'm honestly not certain of that," said Mr F, as they pondered the first painting. "She never learned to play our games. We always say that, yet we never think that this means we may not have learned to play hers. Perhaps we can see what she sees by looking at her art?"

"I can be your guide," Constance changed the subject. "Grania and Dal gave me a special showing yesterday."

"I would appreciate that. I honestly am not sure what to expect."

"She's not quite what I thought she would be," admitted Constance. "It's as if she's bigger on the inside. It's pretty obvious how she became so famous on Earth."

"I always thought it was puffery."

"Not a scrap of it. She uses light like no-one I've seen. When we get to the big pictures you'll see what I mean. If you don't get distracted."

"Distracted?"

"You need to see it. Yesterday it was if every protective layer I had ever built up was stripped off and I was seeing the world through new skin."

"That's a terrible simile."

"Never fall in love with a printer," said Constance, and sighed dramatically.

GRANIA MINGLED in a proper and polite way, those first few hours. She had expected to feel triumph. Her feelings were, however, more relieved than triumphant. There were no trumpets declaring glory and there was a definite niggling feeling that a headache had just gone away.

She had reached that point where she could communicate what she needed to say again. It had been so damn lonely until then. She thought she would be resplendent, or roseate with inner certainty. Instead she was just relieved.

The thing was, she still had so much to say. Years of experience to crystallise. Years of sorrow and anger and guilt and isolation and rediscovery to express. This exhibition was just the beginning. And as beginnings go, it wasn't bad.

MOST VISITORS WALKED QUICKLY PAST the sketches of daily life in Prosperine. They promenaded along, and stopped at each of the major points. A bit like the Stations of the Cross, Grania thought, irreverently.

The first major pieces were two heads entitled 'Zenobia and Vlasha.' Stuff for a small stop. Those who were scared they wouldn't understand Earther art spent longer there, admiring the slight angle and the inquisitive sparrow-like air of Zenobia and carefully avoiding the anger of Vlasha.

"She knows secrets," someone commented of Zenobia and the comment spread to all the viewers that followed. It even entered the article on the exhibition in Mr F's monthly paper for the more learned on New Ceres. "Zenobia's bright eyes hide secrets," the critic claimed, as if he thought of it himself.

One common longer stop was the cast bronze head of Roman Virtue. It was Livia, showing her stern but understanding, noble and forgiving. Everyone admired this and said "How true to life. How much like Livia," as if they were friends of Livia and knew her every passing expression.

The bust was set on a little pedestal and around the

pedestal were faint carvings. The tools of Livia's trade were etched into that base. A bottle that said 'Drink me' on one side, while scrolling around from the far side were the letters 'ison.' A hangman's noose. A hammer. An axe. A stockinged foot sticking out from under a house. There was some puzzlement over the last one.

In that pre-viewing Constance asked Grania about the foot.

"You need to read the book," Grania said. "I want people to stop taking Livia so seriously. She's evil, but you should never let evil set the tone."

"What book is this?"

"The Wizard of Oz: I'm Dorothy and she's the Wicked Witch of the West. Green skin and a terrible laugh and everyone who works for her is a flying monkey."

"Livia won't like this."

"No, she won't." Grania smiled.

"I'll have some copies of the book printed properly, if you like," offered Dal.

"Yes, please," said Grania, immediately. She felt a little smug. Finally, the real Grania was back. Things were going to be different on New Ceres. About bloody time, too. Not Granny, not yet, but Grania was a damn good start.

Facing each other across the hall were the highlights of the exhibition. On one side was a work entitled 'Faces of New Ceres.' Grania had assembled the masks she had created.

"We all look so hollow," Constance had said, during her private showing the day before.

"Sad," added Dal.

"It's this planet," Grania explained. "It leaves so many people empty."

On the other side of the wall was a set of three giant oils. If 'Faces of New Ceres' was sad, then its opposite was tragic.

On the top of the triangle was the first painting. It was of Earth.

"It's like looking at Earth from space," Constance said. "I mean, the painting is so realistic that I could be looking at Earth from space. Except for that," she pointed. "When I see that I just want to cry." 'That' looked like a child messing with the white paint, crossing out things that hadn't gone quite right. The south east coast of Australia was slashed out, for instance, and so was a large chunk in the middle of North America. There was an echo of scribble in Western Europe which wasn't quite visible and a large paint blot over the Indonesian archipelago.

The painting to the left was an interior view of a coffee house. There was a large trestle table in the centre of the picture. On it were steaming cups of coffee and plates of pastries. A newspaper sat folded in the middle. Its headlines announced, "New Ceres proudly takes its place in galactic politics." No-one was sitting at the table. No-one was waiting on the table.

The final picture was in shades of grey. People, some lightly sketched in, some fading, some so real you could shake their hand. People, all the sorrow of their ends shown in their faces. One arm outstretched. Reaching to the viewer. It was called, 'My Lost Earth.'

Underneath the pictures was a long broad strip of paper. It ran the breadth of the wall. It was entirely covered with copperplate script. It named everyone shown in 'My Lost Earth' and with each name was a factoid about the person and how Grania knew them.

Kim - Grania's mother. Brought up in Woolloomooloo. A teacher. Loved travel and knitting. Always wanted a son.

Paul - photographed the art for Grania's first catalogue. The best photograph he ever took was of a dragonfly hovering over murky water. Dreamed of photographing the full interior of a spaceship and finding just one insect in a dark corner.

Lucy - Grania's niece, age seven. Tortured and raped before entering the final holding area. When she grew up she wanted to be a ballet dancer. Wore her fairy costume to school for a whole week one September.

Pam – drove Grania's local bus route late at night. Insisted on Grania sitting up front with her 'because two women can deal with louts when one woman can't.'

Constante – owner of the best bread and breakfast in northern France. Practised magic. Loved stories about local witches but always claimed, 'No-one is a witch here, you know. Berri is where the witches live.'

Phil – owned Grania's favourite art gallery. 'One day you will make everyone cry. I never want to live through the events that make you create that work.' Committed suicide the day of the invasion.

Ravi – friend from the Resistance. Hated curry. Before we knew that the targets would be people rather than places, he said 'If I'm going to save anything, it won't be the Sydney Opera House.'

Arianrhod - Grania's sister. Was going to change her name to Arianna by deed poll, "Just as soon as I get around to it." Loved taking Lucy to graveyards and having picnics. She always said, "Maybe we will see the ghosts dance." When they didn't, Lucy would say, "Let me help them," and dance like a mad child.

"Your friend Phil was right," Dal said, as he quietly took Grania away from the increasing number of people who crowded in front of that picture, reading every word, looking at all the faces, and weeping. "On both counts."

WHILE ALL OF Grania's friends and acquaintances saw Grania's soul, Livia found herself home alone. Not a servant was visible. Presumably because they had learned to read their mistress' moods. And today, today Livia was dangerous.

Livia took herself to her own little gallery. In it, on a shelf that took the sunlight and reflected it through the objects on display, was Grania's little statuette, the one that Alphonse had given her, not that long ago.

She carefully took the piece down and spent a long, long time exploring it and all its nuances. She loved the display of light in it and the joy of the colours as they sang in perfect visual harmony. She loved and explored the piece until the sunlight was dimmed and the shelf held only shadow.

There was a knock on the door.

"Enter," said Livia.

"Madam, dinner is served," the servant said.

"I will be there soon," she answered, never taking her eyes of the glorious piece of art cradled by her right hand.

When the door was closed again, she held it to her eyes one last time. She threw it at the wall and it made a resounding crash.

Livia rang for a maid to clean up the splinters of glass and strange materials.

"Leave the hole in the wall until next week, I think," she said. "It reminds me that I have unfinished business."

APPENDICES

A Pamphlet:

Mr F, purveyor of published and printed goods to seven Great Estates and under the gentle patronage of several Noble Houses, brings you a series of Thoughts from the Great Age, not seen in print since the early part of the Twenty-First Century.

INTRODUCTION

The form of the Great Thoughts of the Enlightenment is returned to you in our New Enlightenment. Pity the poor Starfarers and Technophiles, who are unable to rustle the paper as you do now and cannot smell the sharp scent of fresh ink. Pity their mass-produced texts, where every mote is identical and where all books waver in mid-air at the mercy of light. Allow the crisp paper and the black ink to take your back to a perfect age; an age where the great Mr. Samuel Johnson expressed his thoughts for the first time in The Idler.

This pamphlet comprises notions that were first brought to the attention of an admiring public in The Idler, in June 1759 (Issues Sixty and Sixty-one). I present these thoughts to you because the role of critic shapes our present society: Mr. Johnson's pearls of wisdom have new meaning on New Ceres. Scandal broth and foolish comment were not the province solely of the Great Age: they appear here, in the streets of New Ceres, every day. You may visit the theatre pits and after the play, over coffee, imbibe through the gossip sheets what critics say about the piece. You may read the idle tattle of the lazy classes. The words of the eternal Johnson are the words of our society. Mr Minim is one of us. We should take heed.

Note: as ever, in our editions, we use galactic standard twenty-first century spelling and avoid the long s and regulate the use of the apostrophe. This is to be regretted. One day our treaties will allow our readers to enjoy the texts of the Great Age as they were seen in the Eighteenth Century, without the plague of standardisation. Until this day comes, please excuse our deficiencies, and buy these poor pamphlets that we may bring more of the population to the joys of the Great Age. Pray that one day the regulation of orthography may ease and that we may re-issue these works as they should be seen.

In the interim, you may wish to note that our schedule of publication includes all authors mentioned in this essay whose work has survived (alas, that the oeuvre of Otway, Waller, Denham and Swift have not withstood the decay that history brings) and that you, gentle reader, may subscribe either to this pamphlet series on the Wisdom of the Great Age, or to the publications referred to therein. Information and subscriptions may be obtained at Jervais Street, across from the coffee house.

Mr F, publisher and printer to the Nobility.

AUTHOR'S NOTE

One day I woke up with the view of a particular moon in my mind's eye. My character had been looking at it through an old-fashioned telescope, yet the moon had nothing to do with Earth. I wrote a short story from this almost instantly, but it didn't quite work for me. At that stage, I didn't know why.

I showed my story to Alisa Krasnostein and she and I and a group of other intrepid souls launched into a shared world project based on it. Cary Lenehan did most of the astronomy, I did about two hundred hours of history and culture and geology of New Ceres. Tansy Rayner Roberts also worked on the culture (the name Prosperine is hers, for example, and the crystals for reading, and the Lumoscenti in all their dark glory), Peter Cobcroft and Peter Hollo did so many things, from website to personal cards. My world-building classes built Prosperine, New Stilton, Hillview and Tenterfield as class projects. Thank you, Max Laursen, Kirsty Loaves, Elizabeth Fitzgerald, Antony Clarke, Olwen van Dÿk, Stefan Horarik, Alison Russell-French and those who asked to not be named. Teaching a shared universe changed my ideas about what could be articulated in a novel set in one.

Alisa had the brilliant idea of making the New Ceres world creative commons. Artists and writers then added their corners of the world, and, after I'd left the project, the book New Ceres Nights was published.

My stories never appeared (although an earlier version of Fred Xian's coffee house article went online in the magazine) mainly because that image I had dreamed of didn't actually belong to a short story. You've already guessed this, I suspect.

I quietly wrote the novel that the story required. Then I quietly sat on my novel, because I thought the time for New Ceres was past. A well-known publisher asked to see it and then sat on it for eight years. I gave up on it for the second time.

When Satalyte expressed an interest, I re-read my story and realised that the time is not quite past. When Satalyte folded, Shooting Star Press stepped in and it's due to the kindness of Cath Brinkley that this novel is not confined to oblivion for encountering too many obstacles.

I DECIDED to thank the work of all those wonderful people, by writing this story in a way that will allow other people in. My story is copyrighted and mine and I will guard it with my life... but the New Ceres universe is still under a Creative Commons license. The story of Grania and Dal is entire, but if their first happy-ever-after is rocky, there is always the possibility of other things happening to them. There are the Tenterfield Saddlers, and the off-world prison of Hades, and the whole continent of Incognita. As I said a moment ago, I'd changed my ideas about what could be articulated in a novel set in a shared universe. All my worlds have this much complexity (and some of them have more) but this time I've made it clearer and given enough detail for other people to join in.

I owe huge thanks to Alisa, obviously, for wanting to do the original New Ceres magazine from my story, and for everything that followed.

I am also grateful to everyone who has worked on New Ceres and has pushed me into articulating how history can help shape science fiction. My vision of a moon with volcanic activity was a thought-experiment in the use of history in fiction, which will surprise no-one who knows me. I began it before I had returned to writing up my research, but I have my notes in case an opportunity presents itself. I hope that readers don't wait for opportunities, however, but use the shared world kindly and with joy.

One last note: all the eighteenth century snippets and quotes are from our eighteenth century. They're out of copyright, and (unless I've said otherwise in the novel) anonymous. One of the things I love about being an historian is being able to read pieces like this, and one of the reasons I created Mr F was to bring some of these old texts to modern readers. If you want to read more of them, contact me on social media and I'll show you where to find them.

GILLIAN, January 2020

ABOUT THE AUTHOR

Dr Gillian Polack is a writer, editor, scholar and teacher. Two of her novels (*Ms Cellophane/Life through Cellophane* and *The Wizardry of Jewish Women*) and her 2016 research monograph were shortlisted for awards. She has edited two anthologies (one of which, *Baggage*, was also shortlisted for an award). While seventeen of her short stories have bene published, this is her first collection. One of her stories won an award and four others were listed as recommended reading on international years' best lists. Gillian was awarded the Best Achievement Ditmar in 2010.

Gillian has taught writing, history and cultural awareness/understanding at the ANU, at various Writers' Centres and to members of other professional writers' organisations.

She has a PhD in Creative Writing, one in Medieval History and an array of academic publications. Until recently, she researched how writers think of history and how they use it in their fiction, and now she's working on how other aspects of culture are encoded into novels.

She has received two writing fellowships at Varuna, several arts grants, and is in demand at SF conventions because she brings chocolate and because of her food history passion. She is one of only two Australian members of Book View Café and is also a member of The History Girls. She currently lives in Canberra, Australia, which explains everything.

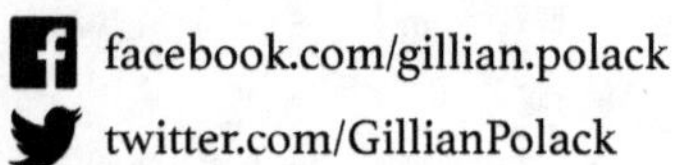
facebook.com/gillian.polack
twitter.com/GillianPolack

OTHER BOOKS BY THIS AUTHOR

Borderlanders, Odyssey, forthcoming 2020

The Year of the Fruitcake, IFWG Publishing, 2019

Mountains of the Mind, Shooting Star Press, 2018

The Wizardry of Jewish Women, Book View Cafe, 2017

History and Fiction, Peter Lang 2016

The Time of the Ghosts, Book View Cafe, 2017

The Middle Ages Unlocked (with Katrin Kania), Amberley Publishing, 2015

The Art of Effective Dreaming, Satalyte, 2015

(out of print)

Langue[dot]doc, 1305, Book View Cafe, 2018

Life through Cellophane/Ms Cellophane, Eneit Press/Momentum, 2009/2012

Illuminations, a novel, Trivium Publishing (USA), 2002

Five Historical Feasts, Eneit Press/Conflux, 2011 (out of print)